the vines we planted

the vines *we* planted

Joanell Serra

Enjoy!

Joanell Serra

E. L. Marker
Salt Lake City

Published by E. L. Marker, an imprint of WiDo Publishing

WiDo Publishing
Salt Lake City, Utah
widopublishing.com

Cover design by Steven Novak
Book design by Marny K. Parkin

ISBN 978-1-947-966-02-4

Printed in the United States of America

To Sonoma

That your vines may ripen, your wine be bountiful, your home be safe, the fires put out, and your loved ones be with you for another year's crush. The beauty and human warmth of this valley will always amaze me.

"I ride over my beautiful ranch. Between my legs is a beautiful horse. The air is wine. The grapes on a score of rolling hills are red with autumn flame.
Across Sonoma Mountain, wisps of sea fog are stealing.
The afternoon sun smolders in the drowsy sky.
I have everything to make me glad I am alive."

—Jack London

Chapter 1

"A bottle of wine contains more philosophy than all the books in the world."

—Louis Pasteur

URIEL MACON BEGAN RIDING HORSES BEFORE HE COULD READ, his hands grasping his uncle's waist as they rode the trails along the northern edge of the Sonoma Valley, inhaling the scent of ripe grapes. The easy rhythm of the old mare's back swaying side to side was Uriel's childhood lullaby.

By the age of seven, Uriel could saddle up the horses on his own. At fifteen, he taught riding lessons after school. Uriel understood how to coax an angry stallion back to his stall, when to let a horse run hard, and when to rein it in. He knew never to turn his back on a horse or put himself in the path of its temper.

But today was not his day. It was August eighth; the anniversary of his wife's death, and it had him on edge. He had been twenty-seven when Flavia died, the youngest widower ever in the Macon family. Today marked two years, and he found his mind pulled back into memories, like a spider returned to its own abandoned web.

The late afternoon sun beat down on Uriel's shoulders as he traversed the hundred yards from his uncle's winery to the family's stable. He brought a tall horse, Belle, out to her paddock. Uriel was the only one could manage this strong-willed mare. His hand ran over Belle's back, while his thoughts traced the details of his wife's death repeatedly, like he was sanding wood in his mind, trying to make the memory into something smoother. Something that wouldn't stab at him. To find a story that would make sense, not one full of the holes he'd never quite filled in.

Belle whinnied and brought him back to the present.

Saddling her up, he spoke to her in a low voice. "Okay, Belle, *vámonos.* Get me out of this mood, will you?"

He noticed other riders coming in—New York tourists that his cousin Jesse had taken on a guided trail ride. They were coming in fast, and Belle tensed.

One of the horses, a sixteen-hand tall paint horse, rushed in too close. Uriel barked at the New Yorker to grab the reins, but it was too late. The horse barged into Belle's territory, his eyes wide. Belle's head flew up, her teeth bared.

Uriel stepped between the horses, thinking even as he tried to shove Belle back, *This is so stupid of me.*

He saw Belle's teeth open a second too late, and yelled as she clamped onto his arm. Her enormous teeth bit down, crushing his muscle through the light T-shirt. The pain spread like fire up to his shoulder and down to his fingers. He bellowed, shocked. The bite made him too weak; he could not get her to release.

Jesse leapt over, smacking Belle on the backside. "Belle! Let go!" Jesse hit her again, her cheeks red with anger, and the horse released her grip.

Blood rolled down Uriel's arm. His lungs emptied, the pain leaving him breathless. Jesse dragged Belle to the far side of the paddock while the other horses whinnied nervously.

Uriel yelled for one of the stable hands to help as he stumbled toward the office, his steps unsteady. He called his uncle Freddie over the intercom, cursing as he knocked around the office looking for a clean rag. Blood soaked through his fingers, which shook with shock. Jesus Christ, his shoulder felt like it had a bullet in it. *Where did they stash the damn bandages?*

Outside, Jesse tried to calm the New Yorkers. "Uriel, you okay?" she called in.

"I'm good," he managed to get out. He leaned on the wall, trying to picture the first aid kit, his head pounding. Where had he left it when Jesse cut her hand the week before?

Freddie's truck pulled up fast, gravel spraying.

"Holy shit!" Freddie, pushing sixty-five, generally took his time moving from spot to spot. But surprise made him appear younger, even nimble, as he hopped out. "Get in the car, I'll take you to the ER."

"Seriously? I just need a bandage. And who did you leave in charge in the tasting room?"

"Just get in the truck, Uriel. Wait." Freddie jogged to the fence, panting, his belly falling over his jeans. He grabbed an old blanket. "So you don't bleed on my seats."

They flew down the gravel drive, every bump like a knife digging deeper into Uriel's shoulder.

Freddie shifted his gaze from the road. "This wasn't what you needed today."

Uriel bit his lip, musing on the irony that Belle would bite him today of all days.

Inside the crowded ER waiting room, Uriel adjusted from the hot sun to a blast of cool air. A mixture of scents and sensations hit him: antiseptic and coffee, fear and expectation. He stepped over a toddler stripped to a diaper and around the legs of a snoring old timer who reeked of the streets. He held up his arm to stem the flow of blood, but it dripped right through the T-shirt wrapped around it.

At the window, he caught an orderly's attention, a guy with a huge nose, wearing a Donald Duck name tag, *Danny*. "Take a number."

"Can I get some gauze so I don't bleed all over your floor?"

The man handed him a bandage, wrapped in plastic. "Sure. Keep it elevated. I'll try to get you in soon."

"Thanks."

His uncle helped him wrap the wound then filled out Uriel's paperwork. Known for his heartbreaking Cabernet's, his soul-healing cooking and his magic touch with horses, his uncle was the anchor of the family, as close to a real parent as Uriel had. Uriel scolded himself for causing the man more stress today.

"Freddie, you need to be at the winery to close up."

Freddie looked at the mayhem surrounding them. "Remember when we used to come down here to pick your mom up, like once a month?"

"Good times," Uriel answered. "Thanks for the memories." His mother, Lourdes, had made a few enemies on her drunken nights here.

Uriel's father had died when he was three, overdosing in a Reno hotel room. And Lourdes had never quite taken to parenting. "Freddie, this could be hours. You should go."

Freddie heaved himself out of the chair. "Okay, I'll get things buttoned up. Call me when you're finished."

"Send Jesse," Uriel said. "Or Chito." He rested his head on the back of the chair and tried to ignore the throbbing in his shoulder until his name was called.

The doctor, an older Indian woman, eyed him with interest. He wondered what she saw, the Macon family's high cheekbones, or the stubborn jaw? He had his father's broad shoulders, lanky frame, and heavy charcoal brows. From his mother, he'd inherited long hands and wide lips.

"That was one pissed off horse," the doctor said, sounding concerned but also amused.

"Apparently."

"I'm going to give you something to take the edge off. Then we'll clean and stitch it. You'll need a tetanus shot and some hefty antibiotics as well."

He squirmed as she cleaned the wound. Goddam Belle. He had let his guard down for a minute, not much more. But that was all it took, as if life demanded constant vigilance.

He had a theory about the magnitude of moments in life. Incremental choices that rippled. It was a moment, two years ago, when Flavia chose to hop in the car of a stranger from Texas, some guy she met while tending bar.

"You still with me?" the doctor asked, taping a bandage over the stitches. "You're very quiet."

"Yes." Uriel's voice sounded far away, like an echo. "I'm still here."

Jesse waited for him by the door, arms knit over her chest. Her thick hair was bound in a band, her hummingbird tattoo floating on the back of her neck. As usual, she stood ramrod straight, like she could put on a uniform and join a platoon anytime. She wore no makeup. Six years his junior, he'd only recently accepted that she was an adult, no longer the young girl that rode behind him on his horse, screaming to go faster. More like siblings than cousins, they fought over small things but laughed at the same jokes.

"We'll go upstairs to the pharmacy for your meds," Jesse said. "But I need to make a pee stop first."

Waiting for Jesse in the main lobby, Uriel stared at a middle-aged man seated near the coffee cart, sipping from a steaming cup. Was that Amanda Scanlon's father?

Amanda had been Uriel's only serious relationship before he met and married Flavia. Jim Scanlon, in pressed khakis and a pale yellow polo, appeared strangely out of place. He was an anachronism for Uriel, a figure from the past that gave him a sense of historical vertigo. Seeing Jim made the last five years temporarily dissipate. As if Uriel was twenty-four again. As if his life was still an unfurling ribbon, with the possibility of ascension. Not tattered twine, barely held together with scrappy knots.

Uriel had wanted to dislike Jim Scanlon. He was convinced Jim had undermined the young lovers' relationship. And yet, the few times they had met, Uriel could not help but admire the man's intense devotion to his daughter, his boyish enthusiasm about wine, travel and baseball, his brilliant eyes.

Although the Scanlons boarded their horse, Chestnut, at the Macon stables, he rarely saw them since Amanda left for graduate school. Had it been years? Grief made time slippery. Days crawled like weeks, but years could shrink to a single memory.

Scanlon tossed his cup in a receptacle and walked away.

Uriel wondered why he was here and worried, as he saw Jesse coming back, that maybe it was something serious. Perhaps he should have said hello. Curiosity about Amanda still brewed, buried under layers of other emotions.

Memories of Amanda rose up as he followed Jesse down the hall: the taste of her kisses, like sweet berries, the tiny scar carved deep into her chin, from being bucked off her horse as a girl. He was nostalgic, not only for Amanda, but for his younger self. He shook his head. The pain killers must be making him disoriented.

"The pharmacy is on the other side of the hospital," Jesse said over her shoulder. "Near the cafeteria. Mind if I grab something? I'm starving."

"Yes, I mind. This fucking hurts. I need to go home."

Jesse shook her head. "Dude, you are getting weak. I can't believe you let that mare-bitch bite you."

Uriel laughed despite himself.

As they went around the corner, Jim Scanlon stood directly in front of them, no longer possible to avoid. He looked lost, a slip of paper in his hand.

"Uriel?" Jim's eyes narrowed. His light gray hair was damp with sweat.

"Hello." Uriel tried to remember if he was supposed to call him Mr. Scanlon or Jim. He faltered, but reached out with his good arm to shake hands. "How are you?"

"Uh . . . " Scanlon looked perplexed, but took his hand. "Good. How are you?"

"I'm fine, thanks."

Scanlon eyed Uriel's other arm with a hint of skepticism. Uriel's pride kept him from explaining that he'd been bitten by a horse. He was supposed to be a horse-care professional.

After another glance at the signs on the wall, Scanlon accompanied them down the hall.

Uriel, in dirty jeans, broken-in boots, and a blood-stained shirt, felt self-conscious in the face of Amanda's father's tidiness. Aftershave wafted off Scanlon.

The many questions Uriel might ask the man bubbled inside him. *How is Amanda? Where is she? Is she still studying in the fancy university you paid for so she would leave here and step out of the noose of my attention? Does she still shake when she laughs hard, so her breasts rise under her T-shirt? Is her hair still deep red, and so long she can tie it in a knot? Does she still drive her old Audi? Read books about Indian rituals? Is she in love?*

More reasonable questions arose. *Why are you here today?*

Afraid to pry, Uriel took the safer conversational path. "Chestnut is doing well," he said. Uriel often paused to watch the Scanlons' horse trot gracefully to the fence.

Scanlon smiled. "Thanks. I know you all take good care of him. Well, I'm down here." He waved, as if they were friends who might meet up at the end of the day.

Uriel glanced at the clinic signs. All the offices had the word oncology in them. His heart raced a bit, surprised by the spasm of concern that welled inside him. Scanlon hadn't looked sick, but there was an out of character slowness in his step.

Uriel wished he could pick up the phone and call Amanda. To ask about her father. To tell her about being bit by the horse. To hear in her voice if she ever thought of him.

As if he still had her number. As if years ago, she hadn't slipped the key to his cabin under the front step and left a pine tree in a bucket to remember her by. As if he wasn't still wearing a wedding ring.

Chapter 2

"He makes grass grow for the cattle,
and plants for man to cultivate,
bringing forth food from the earth:
wine that gladdens the heart of man,
oil to make his face shine,
and bread that sustains his heart."

—Psalm 104:14–15

IN THE WEE HOURS OF THE MORNING, JIM SCANLON'S CATHOLIC
upbringing sent words to the surface of his mind, like bubbles rising
from an ancient sea bottom. *Our Father, who art in heaven, please.
Please.* What was he asking for, exactly?

He hadn't been to church in twenty years, but now he begged?

Since his visit with the oncologist, Scanlon had slept few hours, as
if his body sensed time shrinking, and he didn't want to spend it in
the dark. The doctor had said he had several options, but the one he
recommended was called brachytherapy. After an hour of reviewing
several articles from medical journals, Jim agreed with his doctor.

He stepped outside to drink his coffee on the back deck, absorbing the stunning view of the vineyards. Mid-August, and the scent
of ripe grapes sunk into every crevice of the valley. His own smallish
vineyard that he had planted twenty years earlier, had thrived. He had
chosen the rootstock carefully, testing his soil, talking with the local
winemakers. He made sure to pick local vines that would fare well in
the sun. He had examined the newly planted rows with young Amanda
traipsing behind him, explaining the process to her. Letting her touch
the roots, explaining how things went dormant and then bloomed
again. His grandfather had been a farmer in upstate New York, and

he'd missed the smell of new earth, the joy of picking fruit from one's own vine.

He brought his thoughts to the present, finished his coffee and laced his shoes for a morning run, determined not to drop his rituals, cancer or not. Both Labradors waited for him by the door. Their tails wagged in anticipation, bouncing off one another. Beaver, the younger of the two, leapt at Jim's knees, as if unable to contain herself. Out, out, out! The older dog, Lady, waited more patiently.

As he reached the foyer, Gloria, the maid, opened the door. She looked startled by him, her key still in the door. The dogs rushed out to the front porch, Gloria their arriving angel who had pried open the gates of heaven.

The housekeeper flushed. "I'm sorry, Mr. Scanlon! I didn't see your car. I didn't want to ring the bell because I don't like to wake Mrs. Scanlon."

"No problem, Gloria," he said, although in fact he found it odd, this casual entrance into his home. "No problemo." He tried to offer a reassuring smile. Gloria was the only housekeeper his wife Elena had ever been comfortable with.

He stretched on the front porch, half aware of Gloria inside, moving about in the kitchen. He thought of his own mother, always cleaning when he was a kid. He recalled her chasing her four sons around the house with her vacuum one afternoon, yelling at them.

"Pigs, pigs!"

They would laugh, passing a bag of potato chips like a football while leaping out of her way. "I'll beat the bunch of you!" she'd promised.

He wished he could see his mother, long gone, or his brothers, spread all over the world. He missed the feeling of being part of an irascible tribe, the swat of the morning paper on his backside for no reason as his mother passed by, the smell of sweat when all the boys piled into the station wagon.

Setting off, he willed his legs to carry him up the gentle hill, the path leading through the chaparral, giving off a musky smell in the sun. A thick band of fog hugged the lower meadows. The vines he'd planted there years ago clung to their stakes like a lace curtain in the shadows.

As he ran, his mind raced over whom he could, or should, share his news with. His best friend and business partner had left abruptly two years ago, after a falling out. He thought rashly of calling him, for support. Horrible idea. That relationship had already caused too much pain on both sides.

The trail meandered through an oak woodland, with an occasional manzanita tree, the bark a deep lustrous red. At the summit, both dogs frolicked in a clearing, waiting for him. Catching his breath before turning back, hands on his knees, he tried to assess: Was he out of breath because he was sixty-one or because of his diagnosis?

Jim's thoughts shifted to telling his daughter. His confidence faltered and his steps slowed. Amanda possessed the complicated amalgamation of the traits of both her parents: confident and hardworking like Jim, warm and kind like Elena. Secretive like her mother and headstrong like her father.

Amanda had pushed away from them as an adult, passionately seeking definition through her career in academia. Most important, she chose to be far away. Jim wondered how much a person could remember from infancy. Did the storm of emotions during her adoption plant a seed deep in her unconscious?

He wished he could visit his daughter without this news. He wanted to hike with her in the Andean hills and talk about life. Just a chance to see her laugh, her freckles multiplied from the South American sun, her eyes lit up as she chatted about her research. Telling Amanda could wait a bit.

When he returned home, Gloria had the dogs' bowls full and more coffee brewing.

"Ah, *mucho gracias*, Gloria."

She smiled. "You're welcome, Mr. Scanlon."

"How bad is my Spanish? Getting better?"

She shook her head, giggling as she took out the milk. "No, I'm sorry. I don't think so."

Ah well, he appreciated her candor.

In the shower he tried to prepare for the conversation with Elena. He couldn't fathom how to start. Elena was the logical partner in this cancer battle. She would be loyal, as always, and attend to his needs. If only he was worthy of her ministrations. Maybe he could keep it to himself for now?

His knees bent, and he slid slowly down to the shower floor as fear mounted in his chest. His head rested on the wet wall. The steam lifted around him, a murky curtain where he could hide his tears, briefly. Facing this alone was too hard even for the indomitable Jim Scanlon, and he knew it.

As he toweled off, he examined himself in the mirror, looking for evidence of his demise. He saw only the gentle swell of his belly that he'd fought for years, the uninspired cock, still hanging to the right, the frank blue eyes that had opened hearts with their intensity.

He dressed with care, as if choosing the right tie might soften his message. A pale blue shirt, deep purple tie. He crossed through the garden to Elena's art studio. Her late camellias bloomed, a palette of rust and amber. He made a note to compliment her on it, later.

Elena had moved upstairs to the studio years ago, a comfortable distance from his bedroom, far from any false intimacy. As he climbed the stairs, he gathered courage. They were still bound together. Despite the tough years, despite the ways they'd broken apart and drifted. They were committed, for better or worse, in sickness and health.

He took a breath and knocked on the door. "Elena?"

She opened the door, sleep still in her eyes, her hair pressed from the pillow. For a minute, he imagined taking her in his arms and begging for forgiveness.

"Jimmy?" She was the only one who called him Jimmy. He still liked it.

He took a deep breath. "Sorry to wake you, Elena. We need to talk."

Chapter 3

"They are not long, the days of wine and roses:
Out of a misty dream
Our path emerges for a while, then closes
Within a dream."

—Ernest Dowson, "Vitae Summa Brevis"

ELENA PACED IN THE PARKING LOT WHERE SHE AND HER SISTER met for their hikes. The women grew up in Columbia; Carmen took it as her Latina privilege to be at least ten minutes late, but Elena still came early. Elena brought a bottle of her sister's favorite "power juice" and a bag of trail mix so that Carmen would not get a sugar crash and cut the hike short. The park had once been the estate of writer Jack London and his wife, Charmian, and they would pass his crumbling cottage as they hiked. The aroma of eucalyptus trees and grapevines drifted in the air.

"I need to tell Carmen," Elena had told Jim that morning. "I know you want to keep it quiet, but I need someone to . . . to absorb this with me."

"Of course." Jim didn't look up. "You should tell Carmen."

Elena was eager to see her sister, to feel the solace of their shared history.

Carmen jumped out of her car, her buoyant hair in a high ponytail, yoga pants stretched across her bottom, beads of sweat already gathering on her upper lip. "Sorry I'm late!"

Although built differently, they shared certain physical traits—the shiny, dark hair, long necks, small feet, and a tendency to flush in the sun. Carmen leaned in for the usual quick hug, and Elena found herself holding onto her sister for too long, a lump in her throat, inhaling

Carmen: apple scented lotion, a tinge of wine in her skin from the night before, and L'Oréal shampoo.

"*Hermanita*, what is it?" Carmen's gaze searched Elena's face.

Hermanita. At fifty-three and fifty-four years old, Elena remained Carmen's little sister.

Elena blurted it out, the words feeling barbed in her mouth—cancer, prostate, treatments. "I'm so scared," she said. Relief flooded through her as she spoke. She hadn't been able to sleep or think clearly since Jim had told her.

"I'm sorry," Carmen said. "That sucks."

"I didn't know how you'd take it."

"What do you mean?" Carmen's eyes narrowed. "He's your husband. Amanda's father. I'm not a Jim Scanlon fan anymore, but I still care. And I think you still love him."

"I do. I mean, not like I did—but in some ways I do, very much."

"So, I care."

Elena nodded. The morning fog shifted up and away toward the hills, revealing rows of vines and woodsy hills.

"Let's walk." It would feel good to move her body. "I wish you and Jim hadn't fallen out," Elena said. She remembered years before, when her sister and husband would stay up all night debating politics, religion, everything.

"You know I adored Jim at first," Carmen said. "Or the guy we thought he was. I don't know—there's just so many sides to Jim I don't know how you keep them straight. He's like a chameleon. But if anyone can beat cancer, he can."

Elena's heart rate accelerated. "I honestly can't imagine him not beating it. I mean—can you imagine a world without Jim? Or my life without Jim?"

Carmen frowned. "Yes. You could go on, if it came to that. There is life beyond being Jim's wife."

Carmen had urged Elena to consider a divorce for several years. Elena found it frustrating—did Carmen think she could just leave? Her life would be empty without the family, the house, the holidays with all of them. Wouldn't it? The sisters had survived their parents' horrendous divorce as children in Columbia. Elena swore she would not repeat this.

Yet occasionally, when Jim secluded himself in his room and she went up to her studio, she wondered. As she lifted her brush to touch the canvas and something beautiful emerged. She would imagine, for a moment, starting a new life. She had refused to contemplate it for years, after they adopted Amanda. The adoption had felt like a contract, to keep the family whole. But now that Amanda was older, Elena wondered.

"I've been with Jim for so long . . . my whole life."

"No, sweetie. It just feels that way. You've been with *me* your whole life. Elena, I know now isn't the time, but don't put your needs away because Jim has cancer. You need more than this; a partner, someone who you can really share your life with."

Elena's hand lifted, as if she wanted to hold back Carmen's words. "Right now, I just need Jim to be okay. We have to be sure it hasn't spread."

They reached a fork in the path and Carmen chose the upper loop, striding ahead. Elena wondered if Carmen realized she attempted to lead the way at all times.

"You haven't started having sex or anything?" Carmen asked, glancing back.

"No, obviously. We haven't had sex in years, we aren't going to start when he gets prostate cancer."

"I don't know. It could be the thing that brings you back together. I would think he'd want to—test the equipment or something? Make sure it still works?"

"Oh God, Carmen. You are so crude."

"Hm. I dated a guy after he beat prostate cancer. He was fine—I mean, his shit worked."

Elena laughed despite herself. Their aunties, prudish Catholics, had raised the girls to never talk about sex. So, of course, Carmen enjoyed bringing it up.

"Elena, you *have* to have sex again eventually. You can't just give up that whole part of your life."

Actually, you can.

"I mean, since Jim hasn't been available, you could have gone elsewhere."

"Carmen, I'm not the cheating type. I don't miss it enough to go out and sneak around."

"I don't think it's cheating if your husband stops having sex with you. Think practically. I mean, if your hair cutter refused to cut your hair, you'd go to another salon. Or if the gas station stopped pumping gas, you don't just stand there forever waiting. You go to another gas station. Basically, you need a haircut."

"What?" Elena's eyes filled as she laughed. "You make no sense. Do I get my hair cut at a gas station? You're *loca*."

"Okay, well at least I made you laugh. But I do think you're too loyal."

Was it possible to be too loyal? Wasn't loyalty a virtue? Elena had always taken her daughter's side against the snobby girls at school. She had stood by Carmen through two divorces. She flew thousands of miles every year to visit her aunties. Loyalty was woven into her character, a thread that couldn't be yanked out without unraveling her very being.

They reached a level spot and Carmen stopped, catching her breath.

"You need to exercise more, Carmen. Heart disease runs in the family."

"Thanks a lot. Look, I don't have all day to hang around the tennis club. I work for a living."

Elena flushed, feeling chided. Carmen supported herself and one of the exes. She was one of the most successful real estate agents in the valley, selling many multi-million dollar houses a year. Elena, who hadn't had an actual job since being a restaurant hostess when she met Jim, was somewhat in awe of her sister's career. Carmen had not even gone to college. Elena had been the one with the good grades.

"Can you still come to Costa Rica in the spring?" Carmen asked.

"Costa Rica?" Elena tried to catch up.

"It's a week-long retreat thing, on the beach. We talked about it. Salsa lessons every night before dinner. Not that you need a lot of lessons, but seriously, it will be like old times."

"I haven't danced salsa in about twenty years."

"Exactly why you need to come. It's in May. Months and months from now—should be okay, right?" A trickle of sweat slipped down the side of her face.

Elena stopped. "I don't know—we haven't even talked to the oncologist yet. I have no idea what will happen."

Carmen strode ahead. Elena knew she was irritated in the way she held her elbow, the tightness of her shoulders. She knew her sister's body language better than her own.

"We'll see," Elena added.

"Okay." Carmen turned back. "I don't want to be a bitch. I mean, I get it, he has cancer. But, the problems are long term. Your house hasn't exactly been the House of Happy Walls."

"What?" It took Elena a moment to catch the reference. They were looking down at the visitor center, once the house of Jack London's wife. Mrs. London had called it the House of Happy Walls. Elena couldn't remember why.

"Anyway, didn't Charmian London build that house *after* Jack died?" Elena said.

Carmen shrugged. "Maybe. I just always thought it was a great name for a house. Anyway, just consider your choices carefully, afterwards. I want you to get a life."

A flame of frustration rose inside Elena. "I have a life!" Her voice echoed in the trees.

Carmen stepped back. "I'm sorry, too far. I meant, just let him know that after the treatments, things need to change. You deserve better than sleeping in the damn art studio like a guest. Amanda is raised, there's no more need to play house with him."

"Why are you pushing this?"

"Because I miss my sister!"

"I'm right here."

"I miss the one with a spine. Who didn't take shit from her boss or professors or anyone! The one who danced in the ashes."

Elena stopped, taken aback. It had been so long since either had referred to that day, that sometimes it seemed she had dreamt it. She took a deep breath, inhaling the morning sun, the hint of a breeze blowing the eucalyptus. "I'm still here," she said finally.

They walked on, quiet, the memory silencing them both.

Chapter 4

"Wine is earth's answer to the sun."

—Margaret Fuller

AMANDA SCANLON CLIMBED THE STAIRS TO THE INCAN MUSEUM in Cuzco, Peru, out of breath at 11,000 feet. Despite it being the winter season, today the high sun warmed her cheeks. She made a mental note that she should have applied sunscreen today. Being a fair-skinned redhead not only meant she stood out from the locals with whom she had hoped to integrate, but that she burned easily in the high-altitude sun.

From the top of the hill, she looked back over the winding streets of whitewashed houses, small children taking turns on a toy scooter at the base of the hill. Behind the city, the Andean mountain range rose. Llamas grazed peacefully on patches of grass juxtaposed against noisy busses grinding up the narrow streets.

She loved being here. Nothing made her happier than collecting information about the past—whether from the previous generation or a lost civilization. People, and the hints they left behind, were a bottomless treasure chest. The Incan heritage that wove like a tiny vein through the Peruvian families she interviewed—the rituals that persevered, the artifacts they unearthed—was intellectual candy.

As she caught her breath outside the museum, her cell phone rang, *Dad* flashing on her phone screen several times. Torn, as always, and immobilized, she let the call go to voicemail.

When she arrived back at her flat, her landlady, Patrizia, had pisco sours waiting and wanted to hear about her interview. The evening passed by in a blur, and Amanda forgot to return her father's call.

Her father left a second message which she heard in the morning. "Hey Amanda!" His voice sounded chipper, forced. "How are you, honey? Listen, I need you to give me a call today. If you can."

After another day of phone tag, Jim sent an email. She read it on her phone as she crossed the main square, late for a coffee date with another student. **Sorry we keep missing each other. I don't mean to worry you, but I need to let you know I have cancer. Meeting with doctor's today. But I'm okay. Let's talk soon.**

The stones in the street, placed there 600 years ago, liquefied and fell away underneath her. No, no, no. She dropped onto a bench; the word *cancer* seemed to suck the air from her chest.

When her father didn't answer his phone, Amanda ran, tripping on the edges of the cobblestones as she rushed to her apartment. She threw everything she could fit into her backpack and told Patrizia to keep the rest. She hugged her landlady goodbye, tears in her eyes. She could have shared this crowded third floor apartment forever, hot mate tea always steeping on the counter.

"But why do you need to rush home?" Patrizia questioned her. "Maybe it is not that bad?"

Amanda had briefly considered staying here and finishing her project while getting regular updates. But she couldn't let her mother be the only person there for her father; she couldn't be far away while he faced this. Most of all, she couldn't take the risk that he might die before she'd had a chance to heal the void that separated them. She cursed the lies between them as she dragged her bags down the steps into the taxi.

Amanda's father: the rock she perched on before she flew, the ballast in a storm, the encouraging voice in her mind as she meandered through her days. Despite the intricate dance they had done for the last few years, the secrets carefully tucked away like scribbled notes deep in a pocket, she needed him. To be home meant his scrambled eggs on the deck in the morning, late night gelato in front of *The Daily Show*, horseback riding together in the Sonoma hills.

She could not lose him.

Amanda left him a message that she would head home as soon as possible and would follow up with more details, then caught the next flight from Cuzco to Lima. She cried her way through a second flight from Lima to San Salvador. Before she boarded the third flight, she emailed her father that she was en route but didn't give him the flight information. He had enough to worry about without picking her up. She ate the airline sausages and drank too much Salvadoran coffee. By the time the plane descended onto the tarmac in San Francisco, she felt nauseous, wired, and distraught. The overhead speakers blaring in English sounded utterly foreign.

Amanda gave a taxi driver her father's office address in San Francisco then tried to reach him, annoyed at herself when he didn't answer. What if he hadn't gotten her messages? Or was in the hospital? He might be home in Sonoma, another hour away.

She ripped at the edges of a broken nail as the taxi merged onto the highway, hordes of cars flying by. She called her mother and left a message. "Hey Mom, I'm back! I'm trying to get to Dad's office now. See you soon, I think."

She knew she should have tried harder to reach them earlier. But they would have told her to stay in Cuzco, not to rush home. And she refused to stay away.

She had a thousand questions, but she feared the answers.

Jim Scanlon could talk to strangers in line at the grocery store and make any friend she brought home feel special. But he rarely talked about personal things. She had followed his lead, only sharing what he would want to hear. The family teetered on a relationship tightrope, never pushing each other too hard for fear of falling but always connected. She'd never mentioned her affair with her graduate school advisor, or her high school abortion, or that she still missed Uriel five years after their break up. She didn't push as hard as she wanted to on the details of her background. That was the most painful.

She had asked her parents again, on her last visit, to tell her everything they remembered about her adoption from the hospital in Ventura County. All they told her was that her birth mother did not record her real last name or list a contact. The father was listed as "unknown." It galled Amanda that her parents never looked any deeper into the situation.

Elena had been defensive. "When someone offers you a lovely, healthy, baby you don't say no—not when you long for a child. Of course we should have asked for more information. We see that now. But Amanda, we didn't want *contact*. We wanted you, and to be your parents. Your one-hundred percent parents. Not to share you. And does anything else really matter?"

Yes, it mattered. Amanda sometimes thought she had become an anthropologist because her own genealogy remained such a mystery.

The cab stopped in front of her father's building. The gold sign on the door, *Scanlon and Associates*, looked more regal than she remembered it. After Lima, San Francisco sparkled like a shiny new watch.

Her father flew out the door before she had a chance to pay the driver. His strong arms surrounded her in a bear hug and lifted her from the pavement. She stood back to examine him: graying short hair, bright blue eyes.

Cancer? Where?

He took her in from head to toe: messy hair, sausage grease on her T-shirt, and a dirty backpack at her feet.

"God, you're beautiful!" he exclaimed, as she knew he would. "I never meant for you to rush home, I just wanted you to know what was going on. You didn't need to leave Peru immediately."

She shook her head, trying not to cry. He took her back in his arms and they stood together in the street, wind whipping her hair. Her tears spilled out despite herself and seeped into his expensive suit.

"Will you be okay?" she finally managed to say.

"Yes," he answered. "I'll be okay."

They drove the hour north across the Golden Gate Bridge. The fog curled around the edges of the mountain like a scarf tucked around a woman's shoulders. They passed from suburbia to cow fields, crossing into Sonoma County. A flock of tiny birds skimmed the marshes, synchronized in flight, the last of the sun kissing their wings. She imagined them welcoming her home.

Their sprawling white Spanish villa perched on the slope of Sonoma Mountain, with miles of views and a well-tended, eclectic garden terraced around the sides. Pansies and violets burst from blue ceramic flower pots on the front porch. Her Columbian mother resembled an American 1950's housewife as she hurried out and waved, her hair in a tiny ponytail.

"I can't believe you're here!" Elena said. She kissed her daughter's head and squeezed her. She still had the hint of an accent from Columbia. "What a surprise!"

Elena wore her tennis clothes. "I didn't have time to change! I just ran to the store for dinner."

Amanda could smell her favorite dinner on the stove as she came through the front door, the dogs rushing to meet her. She inhaled deeply: the scent of fresh shrimp, basil, and cayenne. The dogs on her lap and the aroma from the kitchen grounded her; she was home.

They sat around the round stone table in the dining room, candles lit, and shared a bottle of Benziger Cabernet. The conversation bounced from Peru to local gossip, politics, and baseball. Everything except cancer. Her parents' eyes sparkled with the sheer relief of having their only child back in the house. Amanda tried to bask in their warmth instead of feeling smothered by it.

After dinner, the candles blown out, black smoke curling to the ceiling, Amanda followed her mother to the kitchen with empty plates.

"Sit down and have a cup of tea." Elena gestured to the breakfast nook. "Mint, okay? I'll finish up. God, you look tired."

Elena moved with fluidity from one task to another, as gracefully as she moved on the tennis court. Her mother never seemed like someone who hadn't finished college, who grew up poor, and who had come to this country with only her sister and a suitcase. She rarely spoke of her childhood, although the years of struggle hovered, stories never quite finished.

"Do you want to talk about anything? Your dad's cancer?"

"No, Mom." Amanda gave her a wry smile. "Not tonight. I'm fine."

Fine, but tired of circling the same secretive terrain. She wished she could tell her mother her troubles without consequences. Why she'd departed abruptly years before, why she hadn't been home often. She wished the two of them could step outside of themselves for a few minutes, meet like two spirits in a neutral zone, and be honest.

"Let's get you unpacked." Elena removed her apron from around her hips with a whisk of her hand.

"You're a matador, Mom."

Elena's eyes crinkled, but she looked like she didn't understand the joke.

Amanda picked up her mother's apron, placed it on her hips lightly, and then yanked it off. "*Ándale, ándale!*" she joked.

Elena laughed. "You know, I am always so happy to take that thing off. Apron comes off, and like magic—there's no more cooking or dishes."

Amanda smacked her own head, remembering something. "I need to show you what I brought from Peru." She had picked up a new apron for her mother at a market, months ago. Who knew her mother loved to take them off?

They slipped through the den. Jim dozed on the couch, the dogs at his feet. Ironically, asleep he appeared more tired, his jaw slack and hands open on the newspaper.

Amanda wished she could bless him with a magical healing energy, like an Andean Paqo shaman. She would send a spirit bird to the sky with the message that he was not available to travel to the next lifetime.

Please, not yet. There are too many secrets under the rug, too many conversations not finished. Give me more time, and I promise, this time I'll use it well.

Chapter 5

> "Give beer to those who are perishing,
> wine to those who are in anguish;
> let them drink and forget their poverty
> and remember their misery no more."
>
> —Proverbs 31:6–7

"I CAN'T AFFORD A LAWYER," GLORIA SAID TO HER COUSIN, Lourdes.

The two cousins were in the laundromat, the steam from the machines making the summer day feel unbearable to Gloria, even in a light sundress and her hair stuck up in a pony. She put a pile of her son Carlos' T-shirts in her basket and took a long pull from a large Diet Coke.

Lourdes sorted her bras and underwear, tiny little things. *Why is my cousin such a skinny one?* Gloria looked down at her own wide hips.

Lourdes also had a way of moving her small frame that made men's heads turn, despite her slightly rough edges. Lourdes' face was narrow, Gloria's wide. It was as if they weren't related. On the positive side, Gloria noted, Lourdes' teeth needed some work, and Gloria never missed a cleaning.

Lourdes put her hand on her hip. "Girl, you can't afford to *not* get a lawyer. What if someone you work for reports the income? You want to end up in jail?"

Gloria thought of Mrs. Scanlon with her soaps and lotions lined up on the sink counter, Mr. Scanlon's collection of soft brown leather loafers. Would they report her income some day? No, they wouldn't start now. She'd worked for them for ten years. Her mind raced over her other clients. The man who poured Champagne for a living, the elderly school teacher, the gay guys with a Chihuahua.

"Where did you hear of this lawyer?"

Lourdes counted out six more quarters from her stack. "One of my buddies at AA. You want to come to my meeting this week?"

"No, I'm good."

Lourdes went to AA meetings to meet men on Friday nights, before she hit the bars. Gloria had joined her a few times. She would like to find someone to fill the hole in her heart carved by her estranged husband, Diego. But flirting with alcoholics at their meetings seemed like a dubious method.

"And what's going to happen to Carlos if ICE shows up at your door?" Lourdes pointed out.

Gloria's heart leapt to her mouth. Her hand clutched a Giants shirt. "Okay, give me the card. I'll think about it."

Later that night, Gloria held a cold can of Sprite to her cheek and stood in front of the fan on the kitchen counter. *Dios mío*, almost ten at night and still boiling. It couldn't be much hotter in Mexico. She'd been woken by a commotion outside. Right across the street, five men stood in a line, their arms behind them in handcuffs. Through a crack in the curtain, Gloria watched an officer put a boy in the plastic cuffs, the young man's body twisting. She hadn't seen a raid like this in a few years, since she'd moved away from Diego's drug-infested apartment building to a safer area.

The idea of immigration officers snooping around made Gloria shudder. So did drug deals, which might be going on over there.

"What's up, Mom?" Carlos stood in the alcove between the door and the kitchen, his hair stuck to his head from sleep and sweat. "You all right?"

"Yes, *mijo*. Why are you up so late?"

"It's too hot to sleep. What's going on over there?"

"I don't know. Some cops, but the others . . . Maybe immigration?"

Carlos made a *tsk* sound, one he had picked up at school, a sound of angry dismissal. "Fuck immigration. This state was Mexican first."

Carlos had learned this in history class in fifth grade, and it had resonated. When an occasional rude person glared at him, or when he saw the anti-immigrant signs around, he'd remind her. It had all belonged to Mexico at one point.

"Well, it probably belonged to the Indians before that," she answered, thinking of the pictures she had seen of the Indians, enslaved at the missions.

"Huh. We got any more chicken?" He rummaged through the fridge for the third time that night. She knew he would leave a mess on the counter, and sleep too late in the morning instead of doing his chores.

Her fifteen-year-old used to be the cutest boy on earth, with a grin that made strangers smile back and wave. And someday his fifteen would turn into twenty. She hoped he would turn out like Gloria's boy, Uriel. A man she could admire. If she could just get through the Carlos of now. She headed to her bedroom, not wanting to scold Carlos before bed.

The blue and white police lights bounced off every surface in her crowded bedroom and set her heart spinning. As if they would come for you with sirens and lights, she chided herself, for working without papers. She took the attorney's wrinkled card from her pocket and put it on the dresser as a reminder to call in the morning for an appointment. *I'll just renew my papers. It can't be that hard.*

Two days later, Gloria examined her lawyer's desk with the trained eye of a professional house cleaner. The name plate, which announced that the desk belonged to Maria Salvatore, sat next to three cups of old coffee, one with mold growing at the edges. A sign on the wall said, *Se Habla Español*, and a poster listed the rights of immigrants.

That's a short list, Gloria thought.

Gloria had gotten a green card initially by being married to a citizen. But it had expired, and she doubted Diego would help her renew it. He came by the house only occasionally and rarely with support payments for their son Carlos. He existed "in between jobs." And money was always "tight."

Diego had the legal right to work in this country but didn't exercise it, while she busted herself cleaning houses so she could keep Carlos fed and in decent clothes. She lived in fear of being "caught" working. Gloria thought of the word Carlos learned for his English test: irony.

"Mrs. Flores! Nice to meet you." Maria Salvatore plunked herself down at the desk. She dropped a pile of papers on top of the stack and almost knocked over one of the cups of old coffee. The woman's presence struck Gloria. Her short hair, more gray than black, streaked back from a wide forehead. She had the broad shoulders and rough skin of a sailor, or a house painter. Her suit jacket strained across her back, contrasted with a thin gold cross at her neck.

"You can just call me Gloria. It's fine. I don't use the *Mrs.* My husband left a long time ago."

The attorney lowered her voice and gave her a small wink. "Well, let's not stress that to the immigration folks. You're still married on paper, and that will come in handy."

Gloria's hands clenched in her lap. She wanted to find a way to renew her card without involving Diego. She explained as much to the lawyer, pulling her pale blue sweater tighter around her shoulders as she talked. She'd worn a dress to the appointment, unsure how to dress for this. But the air conditioning made her regret the thin cotton.

"Tell me a bit about your background. How did you first enter the country?"

"I was five."

"Okay, so here for almost your whole life. Economic reasons?"

Gloria's thought of the deranged uncle they'd escaped from as a child. He had owned their house, their clothes, even their food, but his mind was twisted. One day, Gloria came home from kindergarten and interrupted his work in the garage, he'd slammed her hand in a car door with all his might. Her small finger had to be removed when infection set in. The day they left the hospital with Gloria's hand wrapped in heavy bandages, her mother announced they were leaving. They would find her father, who worked picking grapes in a place called Santa Rosa, California.

"Yes, economic reasons," Gloria said.

Ms. Salvatore ran her hands through her hair. "Right. Well, I think we need your husband in the picture. We'll explain to immigration that you let your card expire because you've been raising the boy—"

"Carlos."

"Yeah, Carlos. But we'll explain you're going back to work now. No need to drag your marital problems into the courtroom. This can be a simple process. I'll set up the initial request for renewal and call you when we get a date to meet. In and out. Hopefully."

Gloria took a breath. "But you'll need Diego? My ex?"

Salvatore nodded. "Right, right. He should be along. And for now, let's not call him that."

How could Gloria convince Diego to help? Probably a matter of money, again. "How much will this cost?"

"Well, if it's straightforward, we can do the whole thing for eighteen hundred."

Gloria wanted to make sure she had understood. "One thousand, eight hundred dollars?"

She nodded. "Unless it gets complicated. You'll need to pay half up front to get it going. There's fees and whatnot."

Gloria had $1,100 in savings. She had been trying for a year to save enough to move to a nicer apartment, maybe a safer neighborhood.

If she gave this woman $900, she would be down to $200 for emergencies, and back to zero for a bigger place. Her heart raced at the thought of going so low. And she'd still need another $900. "Do you think I can wait a while, maybe until I have Carlos out of the house?"

The lawyer's arm shot out of her shirtsleeve as she glanced at her watch. "God, no. You don't want to end up deported over this. Not worth it. You had a card—we can get another. But there's fees involved. Why don't you take the weekend to think about it, talk to your husband, and if it's a go, drop off the first payment next week? I hate to rush this, but I have two other clients here."

Gloria stood up, feeling like a date sent home early. She pushed a few tears away as she headed down the street to her aging Toyota, one of the few things she had gotten from the marriage. Her car and her boy. As surly and smelly as her teenager could be, she couldn't stand to be separated from him. Her thoughts leapt from problem to problem as she drove to the Scanlon's house where Elena was expecting her. Could she talk to Elena about this problem? Would she understand? Perhaps lend her the money?

As she drove from the busy downtown of Santa Rosa, past miles of vineyards and farms, she scolded herself. How had she gotten herself to be in this situation: alone, a single mother, without the papers to work? An immigrant in an often unfriendly place, but here for so long it was the only world she knew.

She clearly remembered the day the family arrived at her father's doorstep, a stranger to her. Her father had a mole on his cheek the size of a dime, with hair sprouting from it. He smelled like onions. Could this possibly be the man her mother had pined for? Her father took her in his arms while she squirmed.

"*Hija*," he said, "I don't bite. *Dame un besito.*" *Give me a little kiss.*

She gave him a tentative peck on his rough cheek. He took her hand and examined the bandage where her left index finger should have been.

"Does it still hurt?" he asked.

She shook her head to her father, embarrassed. "No."

"Good."

He gave her a doll with blue eyes that blinked and blonde hair, still wrapped in shiny plastic. Gloria forgave him for being ugly and spent the next twenty years trying to please him.

The day before Papa died, Gloria had woken early, slipped into her parents' room, and watched them sleep. She sensed something would go away but not what. Gloria had always had these *feelings*. Her mysterious Tía Hilda in Mexico called it *La Noticia de Dios. God's news.* Things slipped into her mind, like flashes of movies she'd never seen.

She had woken them.

"What is it?" her parents had asked, stirring from sleep. She didn't know.

Her father's heart gave out later that day, as he crossed the fields. His friends told Gloria that he had been in a good mood. He had joked over lunch and spoke of her brother's success in the army. Gloria and her mother were left alone, Gloria's mother's memory already slipping away.

Gloria met Diego a month later, when he came to deliver a new mattress to their home. Her mother's grief made it impossible to sleep in the bed she had shared with her husband. Diego took Gloria's number from the mattress invoice and called her that Saturday night. His teasing eyes offered a needed distraction.

I wouldn't have fallen for a snake like Diego, she mused, if I hadn't missed Papi so much. But she had fallen, hard. What's done is done, she reminded herself.

No hay mejor camino que el que ya has recorrido, her mother used to say. *There is no better path than the one you've travelled on.* So you go on.

For now, to move on, she needed to track down Diego. Which was like searching for a lost dog she didn't really want to feed.

Chapter 6

"We ought to do good to others as simply as a horse runs, or a bee makes honey, or a vine bears grapes season after season, without thinking of the grapes it has borne."

—Marcus Aurelius

THE WOUND DIDN'T HEAL EASILY. A WEEK LATER, PAIN FLARED every time Uriel shrugged. But he still rode Belle, just not as hard.

Belle had arrived at the stables two years earlier, a few days after his wife's accident. Uriel had come to the stables directly from the funeral home, where he'd picked out a casket for Flavia. He'd thought work might distract him from his crushing despair.

Jesse told Uriel to leave. "I've got things under control. You don't need to be here."

But Uriel couldn't be alone in his cabin, staring at Flavia's clothes that still clung to the furniture where she'd tossed them. He needed to work so hard that every muscle would hurt, to run the horses until he was exhausted, carry bales of hay, shovel shit. Anything.

Jesse had finally acquiesced. "We got a new gal." She nodded her head toward the back of the stable. "And she's a beauty. Name's Belle."

Uriel crossed the dirt lot and opened the barn, interested in seeing the horse. Belle lifted her head and stared. A chestnut mare with a white stripe like a splash of paint on her forehead, tall and smooth. Large amber eyes, pools of gold, looking straight into his heart.

"Holy Christ," he'd whispered. His heart started to beat again, for the first time since he'd gotten the phone call about the accident.

"Yeah," Jesse had agreed, coming up behind him. "She's something."

He gazed at Belle and tried to remember whether Flavia believed in reincarnation, or spirits.

Mi amor, Flavia. Is that you? Flavia's spirit stared back at him through the horse's soft eyes.

After Jesse left, Uriel stood next to the mare, one hand on her flank. Tears streamed down his cheeks as he wept with relief. He was not alone after all. Flavia was still with him. Uriel had cared for Belle since. Her stubborn nature and fiery temper continued to resemble his late wife, as did her eyes.

Tonight, he hurried to wipe the horse down, eager to get up the hill for dinner. Freddie was making his famous pozole, a thick red stew of corn and pork, with a kick from Mexican chiles.

As he made his way up the hill to the house, inhaling the scents of ripe grapes and blooming lavender, he mused that Freddie faced life like he faced cooking. He took all the ingredients, the loss and the gifts, the pain and the beauty, and turned it into a something good that fed them.

When Uriel's father had overdosed in a Reno hotel, vials left on the floor around him, Freddie buried his younger brother and helped raise his son. When Jesse 's mother moved to Mexico, Freddie had a bedroom ready. As Maya's MS grew more severe, he hired help and built a ramp.

His generosity of spirit led to his house being full, a gathering spot for delicious food, wine and friendship. There was always food on the stove, flowers on the mantle and jokes at the table.

Uriel took the front steps two at a time, pushing his aunt's dogs down as they nudged his crotch good naturedly. The rambling farm house, built in pieces over the years, had doors that squeaked, challenging plumbing, and needed a coat of paint. But it was a source of pride. The house first belonged to Freddie's father, Francisco Macon, who raised his children in the home; including Uriel's father, Jesse 's mother, and Freddie.

The family had emigrated from Mexico generations before with half a dozen horses and many ideas. From fixing tractors to peddling tacos, the Macon family worked hard. Francisco had dreamed of owning a winery. He planted his first vines on this land. Now the estate produced many cases a year, boarded a dozen horses, and employed much of the extended family.

The smell of the pozole wafted from the kitchen, where Uriel found Jesse and his aunt and uncle.

"Welcome," Maya said, as Uriel bent and kissed her cheek. She had been in a wheelchair the last few years but so far, her spirits persevered.

Uriel set the table, grabbing wine glasses, forks, and napkins with the smoothness of the frequent guest, while Jesse served.

"Red or white?" Freddie asked, as he went to the pantry.

"Red!" they yelled in unison, a family joke. They never drank white with dinner. Freddie popped open a bottle of their red blend. They could all recite the exact percentages of each varietal in the blend if they needed to. Always ready. Freddie's wine was easy to sell once someone tasted it. "Like heaven on my tongue," one reviewer had said. Freddie had cherished the compliment.

Fortunately, tonight there would be no selling, no work, only company.

"How are you doing?" Maya asked him halfway through dinner as he ripped a piece of bread. She eluded to the recent anniversary of Flavia's death, slipped between the talk of grapes, horses, and family gossip.

"I'm doing fine, Tía. *Y tu*?" *And you*? Uriel asked Maya.

She winked at him. "I'm fine as well. We brought in the last of the zucchini from the garden today. And Jesse planted the pumpkins."

Jesse raised her arms in a victory salute. "I rock."

Maya had taught all the cousins gardening: when to plant tomatoes, how to snap the beans off the vine, the importance of stakes. Growing up, Uriel spent weekends at the ranch, then gradually slept there on more weeknights. He liked going to school on a full stomach and having help with his homework after school. None of which happened at home. After Lourdes' second DUI, while Uriel was in high school, he stopped going back home to his mother's place and stayed full time with Maya and Freddie.

When Uriel turned eighteen, Freddie helped him move from the main house to an old cabin at the base of their vineyard. Uriel sank his roots into the ranch. It made him feel close to his father to live on the family's land, to tend their grapes and care for the horses.

After dinner, he offered to help clean up but Jesse waved him off. "I got it. Don't forget, you have that guy Noah coming this week."

Uriel had forgotten that Belle's owner, a doctor from the city, was coming to see the horse.

"You going tell him his horse bit you like a wild dog?" Jesse asked.

"Shit," Uriel ran his hand through his hair. He wished he'd been more careful. "I guess we have to, but it's going to freak him out. He's already afraid of her."

"He's one of my better customers," Freddie reminded him, "and I bet he's lonely now that his wife left him."

"I think he's better off," Jesse offered. "I never liked her."

Uriel said his goodnights and left, heading down to his cabin. The moonlight illuminated the stone drive. He breathed deep, enjoying the way it woke up his senses and chased off his wine buzz.

"Uriel, my mysterious missing friend."

In the darkness, Uriel made out Chito reclined on the deck, sounding mildly drunk. "Chito, my friend I never have to look for, he just appears."

"Fuck you," Chito said, although his voice held no rancor. He followed Uriel inside and grabbed the shot glasses from the counter. In the tiny living room, lit only by a Budweiser lamp, they claimed spots on the sunken couch. They clinked glasses and threw back tequila shots.

"To us," Chito said, afterwards, wiping his mouth with the back of his small hand. "And to my birthday."

"Shit." Uriel smacked his own head. He'd missed Chito's birthday. Again.

"It's okay," Chito said. "I found you. I wasn't going to let another birthday go by without a drink with my friend. My *compadre.*"

"I'm an idiot," Uriel said.

"Yes, but it can't be helped." Chito raised his brows in a resigned manner.

"I know. How old are we now?"

Chito poured another shot. "Like you don't know. We're old. Thirty. You have a month or so left of your twenties."

"Shit, man. That's it then. Our youth is gone."

"Yes. Well put. Now, have another drink and promise me this is the last time you blow off my birthday because your head is up your ass."

"I promise."

"It's time," Chito raised his shot in the air, "For Uriel Macon to get back to his fucking life."

Uriel drank to that, although not sure how he could do it.

In the morning, Uriel let Chito sleep it off on his couch. He drove over to his mother's place for her foul coffee and scrambled eggs, a frequent ritual. Lourdes lived in the corner of a trailer park, the trailer sinking into the ground on one end, everything off kilter. They sat out front at her splintery picnic table, as Lourdes poured him coffee in a mug from a casino.

"Don't put those canned chiles in the eggs." He swung his feet over the bench. "They're gross."

She hissed at him like a grumpy snake, then shook a crumpled paper bag. "I got fresh chiles, *mijo*. But beggars aren't choosy."

"This one is."

Lourdes preferred to cook and eat outside instead of in her tiny cramped kitchen. She set up the electric frying pan, connecting it by a long orange extension cord to a rusty outlet. A Guadalupe tattoo peeked up above the edge of a stretched Sonoma High T-shirt.

"Did you call that girl? I gave you her number, right?" Lourdes gathered her long hair back and made a quick, messy braid as she talked, securing it with a ragged hair band.

"Ma, I'm not gonna call some girl you picked up at a bar for me."

"It was at Bingo *mijo*, not a bar. What do you think I am?" She cracked eggs into the pan, tossing the shells into a paper bag. "I took one of the old guys from the nursing home. This girl was there with her grandmother. Nice girl, not like the trash around here." Lourdes nodded her head towards the neighbors.

He didn't point out that she lived in a trailer park, where trash might collect. She scraped the steaming eggs onto a paper plate in front of him. A whiff of the chiles made his stomach rumble.

From behind the trailer door, Lourdes took a bottle of vodka and topped off her coffee. "You want some?"

"No, Ma, it's eight in the morning."

For years, Uriel had achieved a blessed distance from his mother, only seeing her once a week. But after Flavia died, he'd gravitated to the trailer for these morning chats and breakfast. Ironically, Lourdes was finally feeding him. He remembered as a kid, when her drug use peaked, he had eaten the cheese packets from the macaroni and cheese boxes or picked oranges from a stranger's tree. Always hungry.

He arrived at the stables by eight-thirty. Belle waited for him and whinnied at his approach. He imagined the horse apologizing for the bite and noticing that Uriel ran a little late today. Or that he needed a haircut.

The horse didn't actually talk to him—he wasn't *crazy*. But they conversed in his mind, the horse his main companion over the last two years. He tightened the straps on the harness for a morning ride. Belle pulled at her bit and shook her head. Too tight.

"Sorry, Mama."

They rode north, his back swaying with the horse's steps. Hills stretched out on either side of the trail in both directions. The vineyards looked like a patchwork quilt, shades of purple, red and gold. They were well into the veraison, when the grapes turned.

A mile out, Belle broke into a gallop on a long wide stretch. They flew through the crisp air, one body, lifting and falling. This was the closest thing to sex he had at this point. Which was a problem.

Later that night he stretched his back in the cabin and pondered the dilemma. He needed to have sex again, someday. His body was ready, even if his heart resisted. He had kissed a curvy blonde a few months earlier, both of them drunk at a party at Chito's place. She'd stuck her tongue in his mouth and thrust her hips into him like a horny cat. His body ached for it. But images arose in his mind—Flavia, her ghost, even the horse. All of them jealous, with nostrils flaring.

A phone call from Chito brought him back from the memory.

His friend's voice sounded loud, maybe buzzed. "*Hombre*, where are you man? Everybody's at Reel Fish. There's a great band."

"I'm still recovering from your visit last night."

"I got something to show you. Come down and I'll buy you a drink."

Uriel was tired, but the world called. He forced himself up. He grabbed a clean, blue button-down he'd bought at Target, the cuffs now frayed, and combed water through his hair. He glanced at the mirror and winced at the length of his hair curling over his collar.

The restaurant buzzed, locals competing for a spot at the bar, a blues band hammering out a rendition of Sam Cooke's "I've Been Loving You Too Long." The side yard was filled with picnic tables and hanging lights. Folks huddled in their jackets, talking. Chito told a story to a circle of people, laughter erupting.

Uriel had no time to react when he recognized Amanda, to slow down a step or turn away before her gaze fell upon him. He knew in the way she smiled that she was expecting him.

Fuck, Chito. He'd set him up.

Should he kiss Amanda hello? Wave and leave? Old lovers confused him, so he avoided them whenever he could. She came forward, her arms open, red hair hanging over her shoulders, and he surrendered, returning her embrace. His arms circled her narrow waist, so much smaller than Flavia's used to be. Flavia had been solid, dark, grounded to the earth like the trunk of a tree; Amanda was more of a reed, slippery.

Amanda still smelled like warm pears and Dove soap, with a new smell mixed in. Maybe the wine on her breath. He'd forgotten how her hair shone, the way it fell around her angular face. She was a modern painting, angles and curves. Her eyes, outlined in gray, sparkled, and her fair skin glowed under the soft lights. He'd fallen for the whitest of white girls, back then. A stranger to him now.

Uriel and Amanda had met about six years ago, one summer day at the stables. She had reached out and tapped him like a goddess riding by, offering him entrance to her kingdom. He remembered her naked on his lap, small bud-like breasts and a sprinkle of freckles on her chest. He'd fallen hard, but she was from a different world. When she slipped the key to his cabin under a pine tree and left it at his door about a year later, he'd been devastated. But not shocked.

She had headed east to a university he'd never heard of for graduate school. He'd thought about following her for a minute. But he'd looked it up and found pictures of red brick buildings and men in blazers. Not California cowboys of Mexican descent.

Now he wondered if Amanda still slept in a 49ers T-shirt, still had those Labradors, still ate garbanzo beans right from the can late at night, and if she'd learned how to check the oil in her old Audi. He wondered if her father was ill, and whether his mother's cousin Gloria still cleaned her house.

"How are you?" she asked, her eyes filled with concern. She knew about Flavia, apparently.

"I'm good," he lied. "You?"

"I'm good, too." She turned to the bar and lifted two shots of tequila off a tray of otherwise empty shot glasses. "I saved these for us."

The first one always burned. They talked and drank. Amanda said she would be home for a while, working on her dissertation. He listened to her explain her interest in pre-Incan civilizations.

"There's this new tomb they discovered only a couple years ago. Wari. You wouldn't think we could keep digging up new things, but we do. It's incredible. I'm hoping to focus most of the dissertation on the impact the new site is having on current Peruvian thinking."

He tried to follow everything as she explained their architecture system. He had forgotten how smart she was, and that she could hold her tequila.

"So, how long does it take, this de-certification?" he said, later, the shots hitting him hard. He could hear the slur in his words but not fix it.

"What?" she asked, laughing. They swayed to the music from a blaring juke box. She leaned her head into his shoulder, and he placed his lips onto her hair. He inhaled deeply, holding onto the feeling. Nothing had changed. She hadn't left. He hadn't loved another woman. His wife hadn't died. His wife's spirit wasn't trapped in a horse that waited for him in the stable.

He stepped away from Amanda, sobering up as he took in her oval face, soft freckled cheeks, sharp little scar. He wanted to drop kisses over every inch of her, suck the hope right from her bones so he had it for himself, lock her away so she'd never leave again. Wanted to bellow in anger that she could slip back into his arms in just a few hours.

A feeling of certainty hit him. *She will hurt me again.*

"I need to go," he managed to say, before heading out the door. She didn't follow him. He heard Chito curse him as the door swung shut.

Chapter 7

"[Wine is] the nurse of old age."

—Galen

THE NURSE'S HANDS MOVED WITH A BRISK, EFFICIENT MANNER. She could have been sorting through a basket of lemons instead of moving his testicles out of her way. Jim felt like snapping at her but held back.

"This is just a marker, Mr. Scanlon, like a target, for the radiologist."

Did she not know using the word target anywhere near a man's groin was unnerving? They all used these words. Eradicate. Reduce. Eliminate. Destroy. He heard other words in his head, a voice-over from the Viagra commercials. Impotent. Erectile Dysfunction. Flaccid.

"Is my wife still here?" The blue paper gown crinkled as he moved.

"She's right in the waiting room. Lie back and try to relax. The medicine should start hitting soon, which will help."

Relax. In a cancer center.

The nurse, a dark-skinned, heavy-set woman with a mole next to her nose, pushed the bed down the hall smoothly, like a canoe in still water. Paintings hung on both sides of the hallway. Beaches, mountains.

"I'd like to be at that cabin instead of here. Wouldn't you?" He said to the nurse as they passed the photo of a cabin on a lake, the fog lifting off the water.

"Sure would," she said, sounding less brisk.

"I'll buy that place. Then you can come and visit."

She smiled as they continued down the hall. "I think the medicine is working now, Mr. Scanlon."

"No, really. New England is wonderful this time of year. You have to see it."

Her mouth turned up in a reluctant smile. "See you soon, Mr. Scanlon. Go ahead and shut your eyes."

He wanted to tell her he loved her, that she was the nicest woman he'd ever met, but he fell asleep.

On the way home later that day, he made Elena pull over. He stepped out of the car, standing at the edge of a vineyard that climbed up a gentle rise. A wagon and a stack of buckets rested in one corner of the field, as if ready for the next morning. The vines glowed bright yellow in late afternoon sun, the grape leaves incandescent. He wanted to walk through the vineyard and drink the light in, as if he had never seen it before.

"Are you all right?" Elena sounded concerned, her accent coming through. "Are you going to throw up?"

"No. I'm fine. I needed some air." If he told her he needed to get out and soak in the beauty, she'd worry.

They stopped to buy vegetables at the stand on the side of the road. He wandered through the wooden bins overflowing with late harvest tomatoes, squash, new apples, and mushrooms. He leaned over the mushrooms and breathed in, their scent taking him to childhood, to the Adirondacks.

His father used to go mushroom picking in the early mornings, returning with a bagful that he'd fry in a pan for breakfast, with fresh dill. They'd eat them with brown bread and ham. Now Jim filled a bag with mushrooms, stuffing it so it couldn't close. The mushrooms alone came to eleven dollars.

"That's a lot of mushrooms, Jim." Elena's eyes were skeptical.

He held the bag in his lap on the way home, relishing the anticipation of frying them up.

"I've never seen you buy mushrooms before. I didn't know you liked them. Are you okay?"

He examined his wife's profile. He imagined seeing her with a stranger's eyes. Attractive, with intense dark eyes, long lashes. She wore simple gold hoops that sparkled against her light brown skin. Her hair was up, accenting a graceful neck.

"Jim?"

He'd forgotten to answer her.

"Well, I have radioactive seeds planted up my ass, so not perfect."

"You have an excellent prognosis," she pointed out, taking the next turn sloppily. He grabbed the dashboard. Elena's driving always unnerved him.

He thought about her words. *You have an excellent prognosis.*

"Yes," he answered finally. "I know. The prognosis is good. I'm lucky they caught it early. I know I'm lucky. I'm only thinking. Maybe the seeds are shedding new light on things."

He was joking, but she looked confused.

"Did you buy mushrooms because they have so many phytochemicals?" she asked. They flew up the hill towards their home, hitting each hole and bump.

"What are phytochemicals?"

"Cancer-fighting vitamins. They're in mushrooms."

She surprised him with the things she knew from her voracious reading. "No, I just wanted mushrooms." He shifted in his seat. His ass started to hurt as the medicines wore off. Strangely, he hadn't really considered pain when he heard his diagnosis. Only fear.

He'd hoped to walk with the dogs that evening, maybe check his emails, but by the time he got home, his bed called to him.

In the morning, feeling vaguely hungover from the medicines but with no pain, he reviewed a guest list without much interest, while drinking black coffee on the back deck. His sixty-second birthday approached, and Elena wanted to throw a party.

As Amanda came out to the deck, he noticed two turkey vultures soar, hover, and circle above their property. He pointed to the vultures. "They're coming for me."

"Your morbid jokes don't scare me." Amanda stretched one arm and then the other high into the sky. She wore stretch pants and a T-shirt with a peace sign—her yoga clothes. Her long deep red hair fell loose over her shoulders, the color not unlike the leaves on the blooming Japanese maple.

He asked her about her dissertation and she gave him a tepid response.

"I don't remember. Are you researching yoga or horseback riding?"

"You're funny, Dad. I'm writing. I worked until midnight last night." She leaned on his Adirondack chair and looked over the guest list.

He could smell the soap she had used for years. Dove? It smelled like spring.

"Why don't you invite Victor to your party? It would be nice to have him there," she said.

His face flushed, hearing his name. "Because he lives in New York."

"I'm sure he'd come. I told you we had dinner when I was in New York last year, didn't I?"

"Yes." As if he could forget that. It had been an agonizing night, picturing the two of them sharing a meal, nervous and jealous that she had seen Victor recently when he had not. He prayed Victor would be discreet, felt sure he would be. Amanda considered him an old family friend. Victor would not ruin that.

"How did he seem?"

"He looked great. But he misses the Bay Area. I think he'd come back if he had the chance."

Jim didn't respond. She placed a kiss on the top of his head, as light as a flower petal, and left for her yoga class.

He couldn't finish his coffee, his stomach twisting with thwarted longing. Hearing Victor's name dropped so casually unsettled him.

He'd fallen for Victor at ten thousand feet, as if his attraction was a form of altitude sickness. They spent a week working on a deal in the stunning town of Aspen, Colorado. The snow reflected every color from the afternoon, and light poured through the windows of the conference room. The client, one of their toughest, crooned about Victor's work. Victor basked in the praise for a job well done, and Jim longed to reach over and take his hand, to kiss his warm, delicate lips, to arouse him. He had been attracted to men before, but he had never acted on it.

Jim made Victor a full partner after the trip. Elena thought it reckless, to give away shares of his company. But Jim knew Victor's smooth British accent and warm voice would open doors, and coffers. And he needed Victor in the office down the hall. Didn't he?

Years later, when the relationship faltered, he saw how foolish he'd been, how impulsive. Victor could have taken half his business when he pulled out. But he didn't.

Jim put the guest list down and switched to work emails, feeling flustered.

Later that night, he stood at the top of the hill, holding his phone, debating. Finally, he hit Victor's name, watching the call symbol, his chest tight.

"Jim?" Victor's voice from across the country sounded accusatory. Or upset? Jim was breaking the rules by calling him. Like shooting a rocket into a no-fly zone.

"Yes, it's me, Victor. How are you?" Jim tried to keep his voice steady as his heart sped.

"Jim? Is everything okay?"

Jim's vocal chords betrayed him, momentarily impotent. He opened his mouth and then started to cry. Embarrassing, gasping breaths escaped from him.

Victor didn't speak; there was a long pause while Jim tried again to talk and instead cried more.

"Jim, what is it?"

"The prognosis is good," Jim spit out. He wanted to start with that, didn't want to make it sound more dire than he needed to.

Victor's voice raised. "But you're calling me. And you're crying. That doesn't sound good."

Both dogs came closer, instinctively protective.

"I think . . . I just miss you so much." Jim spit the words out, feeling like they were pieces of glass on his tongue.

Victor said nothing for a minute. The high grasses, dry as old wheat, moved with the breeze. "What do you have?" Victor's voice sounded cautious.

Jim told him. Calming down, he explained the diagnosis, the treatment. No surgery, a decent prognosis. But he didn't want to talk about that. "Victor," Jim went on, trying to get away from the cancer. "I just . . . It's been two years. I never thought this would happen to us."

Victor's voice became irritated. "Never thought what, Jim? That'd I'd really go away? You expected I would live my life in the shadows indefinitely?"

The old arguments, appearing in their familiar way, like arthritis in a worn out joint, or a door that never closed quite right when it rained.

"I never thought that it could *hurt* this much. Victor, I'm scared. I have fucking radioactive implants in my prostate. My groin will probably be glowing like a bug light soon. But all I can think about is whether I'll ever see you again."

"You know this isn't fair, Jim. There's no room for me in your life. That's always been the problem."

Jim thought of Elena, back in the kitchen taking the chicken she'd marinated out of the oven. It had an orange inside it, with fresh rosemary placed over the top. It would be delicious, like always. Amanda would crow in happiness when she smelled it, and eat more than her share of the new potatoes on the side, but none of the green beans. He would open a bottle of the white wine. Where did Victor fit in that familial scene?

"I know, Victor. I know you're right." Jim sat down in the dry grass, next to the dogs. They sniffed his face and licked his drying tears. "I'm sorry I called. I know it's not fair."

He heard a sigh.

"It's all right. I can tell you're . . . not yourself. It was hard for me to move on, too. And a call like this sets me back. But Jim, I hope things go well. Really."

The call ended too soon.

Jim's therapist had warned him, years ago, when he'd contemplated this affair with Victor. She'd told him that affairs always lead to a heartbreaking choice. If you left, you broke up a family. If you chose to stay with your wife, you'd mourn the affair. It never ended well. She'd been right.

Time to go inside, to get ready for dinner; but Jim stood and absorbed the stunning sunset, layers of lavender and pink painted across the sky. A pair of deer moved with grace across a lower field. He had a sudden memory of his father, who used to take his rifle with him when he went on his mushroom hunts. It amused the rest of the family. Ostensibly, it was in case he encountered a deer, but he must have seen many over the years and never shot one. Now Jim thought his father just enjoyed the feel of his gun at his side.

I want to go shooting again someday. He'd like to do a lot of things again: shoot a gun, hold his new baby, ride a horse over the ridge with his wife, eat dim sum with Victor, take a run with his brothers on an early fall morning, dance at his own wedding, talk to his father, read a great novel, drink a perfect glass of cabernet right from the barrel. He'd done all of it, and he wished he could do it all again. It surprised him to realize that he might have had a perfect life. Messy, but rich.

Many moments of absolute joy, days he shared with the people he loved. He stopped on the door step to breathe the thought in. *Keep this moment.*

He went to the wine cellar and chose a Merry Edwards Sauvignon Blanc he had been saving. He glanced at his phone on the way and caught a text message from Victor, which made his heart pound. Christ, he was a sixty-one-year-old man getting hard-ons from a text message, like a kid. Well, not an actual hard-on.

Jim, I really am sorry to hear about your illness. Be brave.

Comforting, caring and discreet. Very Victor. He brought the wine in and drank a large glass by the window.

Elena sprinkled dressing on the salad. "Can you slice the bread, Jim?"

Jim took down the wooden cutting board they'd had for years. Had they bought it when they still lived in the city? He stared at it, as if seeing it for the first time, crisscrossed with so many cuts. "Where's Amanda?"

Elena shrugged. "I don't know, but not going to make it home for dinner. Maybe off with the cowboy she used to see."

Jim felt a shaft of disappointment that Amanda would not be there for dinner. "His name is Uriel," he said, knowing he sounded irritable. He never understood his wife's dislike of the men Amanda dated.

Elena lifted the chicken from the oven, the steam reddening her face. "Fine. Uriel. Don't be grumpy, Jim. It's not a good match for her. There's no future in it. It was bad enough the last time, but now she's twenty-seven."

He sensed a squabble coming and wanted to avoid it, to hold on to his momentary epiphany of the richness of his life. To forget about his call to Victor. Stupid, thoughtless, and selfish to call him. But maybe he should try again? If he could only *talk* to him.

Elena cut the cooked chicken into sections with sharp, well-practiced movements. The fragrance of the fresh meat and rosemary wafted across the room. He placed a hand on her bird-like shoulder blade, and it softened. She handed him the plated chicken, her lips curving into a small smile.

They carried their plates to the round stone table in the dining room and drank another glass of wine as they ate and talked. Elena didn't bring up Amanda's boyfriend again until after dinner, while they tidied up the kitchen, both of them tipsy.

"Amanda doesn't want a future with him. It's really unfair to him." She opened the dishwasher, steam billowing around her.

"He's a grown man. He can take care of himself."

"Jim, he grew up in the trailer park. The one right in town. Did you know that?"

The trailer park.

The things not said between them floated in the air with the steam from the dishwasher, the scent of chicken and lemon, the heat too high. He leaned on the counter, unable to meet her eye. *Now, Elena? We are going touch that topic now?*

Elena saw he would not take the bait and went on. "Anyway, he can't possibly provide her with the life she's accustomed to."

Jim didn't answer. They discovered the charred potatoes in the oven, forgotten. He threw them into the garbage, where they landed on raw giblets from the chicken. A surge of nausea hit him hard as he looked down at the red, raw parts. He leaned against the wall.

"Maybe Amanda doesn't want the life we are accustomed to," he said, his voice sounding foreign to him, like a stranger on a stage.

"What is that supposed to mean?" Elena sounded defensive. She stood barefoot, her shirt spotted from a spray of water. The untidiness made her look looser, more like the girl he met thirty years before.

He rinsed the dishes, running the warm water over his hands. He wanted more of it, to get into a deep, cleansing bath. "I don't know what I mean. I think I need to lie down."

He passed pictures of the three of them, hung on the walls—from beaches to mountain tops. Elena had made the frames herself. One of her many talents that emerged over time. Their wedding photo showed the two of them in front of the vineyard where they had their reception. Elena looked like a child in a wedding dress, so young.

When they met at a salsa club one night, they had danced so well together, he'd impulsively brought her home. He loved her laugh, like a soft bell, and her curiosity. He knew his family was shocked when six months later, he announced his Columbian girlfriend had agreed to be his wife. Knew his friends thought it was odd, being from such different worlds and without much in common. In retrospect, they had been right.

At one a.m. he woke from a deep sleep when he heard Amanda come in. Her boots dropped in the front hall and a cabinet door opened. *She's making herself mint tea.* She often did that at night, and sometimes toast as well.

When she leaves, I'll miss hearing this. The sounds of my daughter rustling in the dark.

Home for weeks now, and he enjoyed each day of it. He wished she would stay forever. But he would never tell her so, wouldn't suffocate her that way. He grabbed his robe from the hook, a warm gray flannel Elena had chosen for him years ago.

"Sorry if I woke you," Amanda said, as she poured the boiling water into a tall blue mug.

"It's okay. Not sleeping all that well." He squeezed her arm lightly then sat at the breakfast nook table.

"How are you feeling?" she asked.

He smiled. She sounded so formal. "I'm absolutely fine."

It hurts to piss a little, but I won't discuss my prostate with you.

She joined him at the breakfast nook while she had her tea and he peeled an orange, eating one slice at a time, trying to really taste it. His therapist called it mindfulness. He usually found it boring, but tonight he enjoyed the spray of juice on his tongue.

Amanda told him about her day: yoga, a meeting with someone at Sonoma State about her research, and dinner with friends.

"You mean your friend Uriel?"

Amanda ran her finger over the edge of the mug. "No. I saw him last night, though." Her voice held the hint of a dare, as if ready to defend the decision.

But he just wanted to know how she felt. She had been so dreamy the last week, detached. "Do you still love him—Uriel?"

Holding her tea tentatively, Amanda leaned back. A line grew between her eyes as she contemplated the question.

Jim thought of how uncomfortable he would have been if his father had asked him such a personal question. His family discussed baseball scores and politics, never love. "I'm sorry," he added. "I don't mean to pry."

"Why do you ask?"

He smelled wine on her breath. He gathered the orange peels into a tidy bundle. "Your mother brought it up. I guess she's concerned. Or confused. Not sure whether you're serious about him."

"Why does it matter?"

Because you are everything to us. Because we long for you to meet the right one now, not twenty years from now, to have the kind of love that has escaped us.

"It doesn't." After a minute, he added, "But you could talk to me about it, you know. You never do. And I wouldn't mind knowing what's going on with Uriel, or anything else."

She stood, placing the cup of tea in the sink, her back to him. "We don't talk about that kind of thing, do we, Dad? Who we love? Or what we want?" She gave him an ironic smile. Her scar looked like she had pressed a tiny sea shell into her chin, hard, and left an imprint. A fossil print from her childhood.

"I'm only saying I'm here—happy to listen. If you want." His voiced sounded forced to himself.

"Me too." Her eyes did not quite meet his. "I'm here for you."

Yes, she was buzzed. She leaned against the counter, one bare foot resting on the other leg's inner knee, like a ballet dancer at rest. She appeared ethereal in a long flowing sweater over her jeans. "You could talk to me, too, Dad."

"Okay." It sounded more like a dare than an invitation.

"So, your turn, Dad." She released a tiny burp. "Do you love him?"

The cold air of the evening crept under his robe. He wanted to go back to bed. She wasn't making sense. "I barely know Uriel."

"Not Uriel, Dad. I'm talking about Victor. Do you love Victor?"

He halted, dumbstruck. The silence stretched, a rubber band across the kitchen. He couldn't hear. The blood pounded in his ears. It was as if someone shook him upside down, his secrets falling out of his pockets, his carefully stitched lies unraveling. Everything, life as he knew it, broken open.

"Victor told you?" His throat tightened so much it hurt to talk.

"No." She shook her head. "I did ask him about it. But I've known for years. I told him he should stop pouting and come home."

Jim's eyes burned, and shame covered him like a wet mist. "Amanda, I'm so sorry. I never wanted . . . I meant for things to be safe for you, stable."

She stopped leaning on the counter and placed both her feet on the ground. "It worked, Dad. Things were very stable and safe and lovely. You succeeded. But now I'm an adult. You can let go of the sanitized world you created."

He did not speak for fear his voice would betray his misery.

"Don't you want to know what he said?" she asked, her eyebrows raised over her sharp green eyes.

No. Don't tell me what my lover said. Don't make this any worse.

"He told me not to tell you that I knew. That he didn't want to be the reason things fell apart with Mom. You needed to make the choice yourself. He doesn't want you to be with him as a default."

This sounded exactly like something Victor would say. "So why did you tell me?"

"Because you aren't going to make the choice on your own. And life isn't forever."

"Amanda, it's not that simple. You know that . . . your mother . . ."

"My mother sleeps in the art studio. And you two never talk. She deserves better."

He could not deny this. They both glanced out the back window and across the courtyard to the studio where Elena slept, the windows dark.

"She needs to move on, too. You're both so . . . stuck." Amanda said the word with a sort of revulsion.

The righteousness of youth.

The moments stretched on in a terrible, rib-crushing silence.

"I don't know what to say," he managed to get out. He didn't want to cry. It would make things so much worse.

Her hand was light on his shoulder, her touch muted by flannel. "You'll figure it out, Dad."

She disappeared down the hall.

He stood at the picture window, looking out at the vineyard in the moonlight, thinking about the girl who had followed him through the vines. About the lies he had told, the dreams he sacrificed, and the secrets he had planted, deep in the earth of his heart.

Chapter 8

"Wine prepares the heart for love unless you take too
much."

—Ovid

"HEY!"

Gloria called her ex-husband rarely, but when she did, she was
always taken aback by his confident, "Hey! How's it going?" As if they
were buddies. As if he was happy to hear from her, not guilty for going
so long without visiting his son or paying child support.

"Hi, Diego."

"What's going on, Gloria? Everything okay with Carlos?"

She paced, checking out the kitchen window. She didn't want Carlos
to come home in the middle of the conversation. She tried to picture
where her Diego might be, just past seven p.m. At a bar? In a strange
apartment? With someone?

She forced herself to speak. "So, I don't know if you're busy, or at
work or anything."

"No, no. It's fine. Not working right now. But I'm getting something
soon. Maybe at a hotel. My uncle's getting me an interview, so you
know, I'll have something soon. Sorry I'm behind on things. That why
you're calling? You short on rent or anything?"

"A little." She was always short on something. "But I wasn't calling
for—well, I was hoping we could talk. Can we meet up somewhere?"
Her stomach knotted. She didn't want to see him. Why was that damn
lawyer making her do this?

"Well—tonight? I mean, tonight's out. But what's going on? Carlos
okay?"

She sat at the kitchen table, rolled an apple around the hard surface of the table. "Carlos is okay. I mean, he's pretty good."

"Did he make the soccer team?"

"He didn't go out for it this year." *Tryouts finished a month ago!*

"Really? Why? I been meaning to call him. He never texts me anymore."

Gloria clenched the apple. She needed to avoid a fight, for now. "He's with his friends a lot. Skateboarding."

"Good, good. What did you want to talk about?"

"Can we get together tomorrow maybe? About four?"

She heard him calculating whether that would work. "Four . . . Yeah I think that would be all right." *As if he had conflicts. He didn't work!*

"So, you want me to come by your place?" Diego asked.

She pictured his body in the room, the scents that wafted off him lingering when he left. "No—I can meet you. Are you still living by the Target in Santa Rosa? I can meet you up there."

"I'm in that area, yeah. Just moved to a new apartment."

"How about La Ronda? Can we meet there?"

They used to go to La Ronda with baby Carlos. They'd have the nachos and Carlito would get a children's plate. She didn't know why she'd suggested that. It was too full of memories. "Or the coffee place by Costco?"

"No," Diego interrupted her. "I'll meet you at La Ronda at four. Sounds good. Bringing Carlos?"

She thought of the topics to cover—immigration, money. "No, not this time."

Gloria arrived at La Ronda ten minutes before four, leaving the crisp day as she entered the stuffy restaurant. The smell of grease, onions, and frijoles hit her like the scents of home. The place didn't appear to have changed at all, decorated with a combination of fake jungle animals and traditional Mexican crafts. When the waitress dropped the greasy menus on the table in front of her, Gloria half expected to see the same prices as ten years earlier. But no such luck.

A few old timers at the bar and guys in cable company uniforms knocked back beers. Gloria sat where she could keep an eye on the door. She ordered a Coke and placed the papers the lawyer had given her on the table, as well as their son's latest report card.

Quarter after four, and Diego had not arrived. Gloria was torn between leaving and having a drink when a text message popped up on her phone: **On my way.**

Christ. He probably sat around watching TV all day and still couldn't get here on time. She ordered a beer. Her chest was hot, and sweat trickled down her chest. She peeled off her sweater, checked to see that her bra didn't show through the T-shirt, and applied a new layer of lipstick just as her ex sauntered through the door. Damn, she didn't want him to think she was primping.

Diego nodded to one of the cable guys like he knew them. A jean jacket hung over a clean T-shirt, and his Nike sneakers looked brand new. He could have been twenty-five, not forty-three, with just a hint of gray in his hair. As he bent over to kiss Gloria's cheek, she reminded herself to focus—she had a purpose here. Getting laid was not it.

"Hey, G," he said. After he dropped the light kiss on her cheek and squeezed her shoulder, he tucked himself into his chair and leaned forward. His eyes met hers briefly and she remembered feeling like she could swim in them, like deep, dark pools.

Pools of bullshit, as it turned out. The waitress saved them from the awkwardness as she took his order. Diego ordered a margarita and some chips; Gloria asked for a glass of Pinot Grigio, which she'd recently discovered she liked. She willed her heart to be calm and her mind to be clear in dealing with him.

"Then my phone rang," Diego was explaining why he was late, some story about a possible job, and car problems. "It's tough out there, you know? Most jobs are gone before I even get there to apply."

"You should try working with expired papers." The words jumped from her mouth. She'd planned to warm up to the topic.

One eye brow lifted. "Yeah? Oh, that's what you called me about?"

She took a sip of her wine. "Not just that. I mean, I thought you'd want to hear how Carlos is doing."

"Of course, I do. He's my son. It's not like I never see him. It's just been a few weeks."

A few months.

"So, how is he?"

She slid the report card over to Diego. "Not bad," she said, feeling a bubble of pride well up inside. Keeping Carlos on track was a full-time job, and there was not one D or F on the report card. Diego perused the card, his finger inching from class to class, grade to grade.

"He got a C in Art? Why? Carlos is good at drawing and shit. And math. He shouldn't have a C in math. He's great with numbers."

Gloria yanked the card back across the table. "High school's hard now, Diego. He has too much work. But he's doing good." She flushed, annoyed at herself. What did she expect? *Good job, Gloria. You're doing a great job raising our son alone, since I'm a useless father.*

Diego held up both hands, like her glare was a gun. "No, it's okay. But he could do better. We both know how smart he is."

"Maybe you should spend some time with him, and you can tell him to do better."

Diego didn't take the bait. His lips curved in a half smile. "Fine with me. Kid just has to text me back. I'm not going to chase him."

Gloria shook her head. "That's what you do with teenagers. You chase them."

"Not me."

Because you are a teenager yourself.

Diego placed both elbows on the table, his eyes on hers. "So, what's up with the green card?"

Gloria played with her key chain. "It's expired. I need to apply for a new one."

Diego slurped his margarita. "Okay."

"But I need you to . . . " What had that lawyer said? "Participate."

He leaned back in his seat. "How?"

"Just state that we are still married. That we need my income. Things like that."

"In court? You want me to lie in the court?"

Her hands came down on the table too hard. "It's not lying. We do need the money—who is supposed to take care of Carlos? You haven't given us money in months. And we are married."

"I gave you money on the fourth."

"The fourth of July, Diego. It's October."

He sighed, as if exhausted by her presence, her demands. She remembered that sigh, every time he came home and she asked him to take out the garbage or play with the baby.

"It's not like you've never lied before."

He didn't meet her eyes. "Not in court. But also—I needed to tell you something, too."

A shiver went up her blouse, like cool air was blowing up from the floor. Or a premonition. What was it? It occurred to her that if he had a life threating illness or got into real trouble, she would be devastated. He wasn't her husband anymore, but he remained Carlito's father.

He cleared his throat. "I met someone, you know? Someone I'm serious about."

Gloria almost laughed. Diego "met someone" about every six months. It would blow over.

"And she wants me to get a divorce. To get the papers done and everything."

Gloria's throat tightened, a combination of anger and hurt rising like acid from her stomach. Diego was moving on. He wouldn't back her up with INS. She would never get her damn green card. Who was this bitch? "Why?"

"You know. She wants a clean slate. Tie up the loose ends. It's not like we're—you and me—ever getting back together." He gestured into the air. "Right?"

"Right." Her jaw snapped as she answered.

"So, she'd like me to be, like, single. For real."

Gloria wanted a tequila shot to dull the feeling of being cracked open like an oyster. "You going to marry her?"

He shrugged. "Maybe. Yeah, I think I might. Sheila's amazing. I mean, we get along really well. And she's got a great place—I stay there with her. She wants to meet Carlos soon."

Gloria's hands tingled as if her blood had rushed from her heart out to her fingertips. She stared at them for a minute. Nine fingers, not ten. All rough from cleaners and scrubbing floors. Parts of her that would never be smooth again, never look young.

"Gloria, I'm sorry, man. I didn't think you would care."

"I don't care, Diego."

"Babe, you're crying."

Hot tears slipped from her eyes and she tried to brush them away. God, it was unbearable to cry in front of Diego, after all this time.

"I mean—we aren't moving that fast or anything. I'll give Carlos a chance to get used to her."

"Carlos won't care, Diego. He barely sees you. He doesn't remember us together. I don't care either." She continued to push away the tears that defied her words. "But it's this green card problem. I can't work without it, not legally. And if we aren't married, I don't know what happens to me." Now the tears turned into a torrent. *What will happen to me?*

Why had she counted on this idiot of a man? To still be waiting for someone, anyone, to take care of her, made no sense. His announcement sliced through the rope that tied her to this place, and now she floated in a cloudy sea. There was no one to help her. She steered this boat alone.

She stood up, gathering the report card, her papers. "I'm going to go outside and calm down," she said. "Then maybe I'll call you later."

"No, no. Gloria, wait."

The chair scraped as she pushed it back, as if protesting the unfairness of the world. She moved towards her car, unsure whether to drive away or calm down and talk. Fallen leaves gathered around trees on the edge of the lot, shades of yellow and orange layering the ground like a soft quilt. She remembered when Carlos gathered armfuls for a project in first grade.

"I like dead things," Carlos had said, sounding earnest. "Dead leaves are more beautiful than alive ones."

She'd laughed. He was so sincere then, wide open to the world. Not so tough and distant.

"You okay?" Diego stood next to her, both hands shoved deep into the pockets of his jeans.

"Yes. I'm fine."

"I wasn't sure how to tell you."

"It doesn't matter, Diego. I'm just surprised. And I'm worried about my papers."

"Yeah." He didn't say he would help. He didn't say he wouldn't. He took three fifties from his wallet. "I know I owe you a lot more, but this is something. I just sold a couple things on eBay."

She took the crisp bills, having learned to take whatever he offered. Long lean times stretched between Diego's payments. He must owe her thousands by now.

"I'll talk to the lawyer," she said at last, "See what my options are."

He apologized again. Responses blared in her mind: *What are you sorry for, Diego? Leaving us? Not taking care of your son? Not paying your bills or planning for his future?*

She knew he was apologizing for falling in love again. He'd never brought up divorce papers in all these years, so Sheila must be different. She was probably young, ready to have a family. Diego would have more children. New children. Carlos would become an afterthought, baggage from Diego's previous life.

She did not accept the apology. She would not forgive him for abandoning Carlos. As she left the parking lot, the car wheels slipped on the wet leaves. She straightened them out, hearing them peel behind her. Dead things. She was driving over dead things.

Chapter 9

"Come with me while the wine shop is still open.
We are dizzy with meeting each other."

—Rumi

URIEL WAS PAINTING THE BARN DOOR WHEN HE NOTICED Amanda across the parking lot. That morning, Freddie had decided the brix, the sugar in the grapes, remained too low for harvest. Uriel was trying to get all the other chores done before crush time.

Amanda stood twenty feet away, unlocking her car. She turned, as if she sensed Uriel's gaze. She wore her hair in a low bun. He thought of taking it out and brushing it, like he brushed the mare's tail. She came over to him, but didn't quite look him in the eyes.

"Looks nice. Great color."

"Dressage Red," he said. He tried to keep the paint from dripping on his shoes as he stood up. "Maya chose it."

"Even the paint is equine."

"Could have been called Cabernet."

She gave him a small smile. "Do you think we could take a walk?"

He wondered if Belle sensed Amanda's presence. Did horses get jealous? "I'm working right now, pretty slammed."

Amanda held her riding helmet under her arm. Her jeans were dusty, and sweat beaded on her lip. Her eyes looked pink. Had she been crying? He thought of her father.

"I'll come see you tonight," he said. His hunger to be with her surprised him, the same way he would find himself ravenous around three o'clock when he skipped lunch.

Her emerald eyes shifted to a darker green as she thought. "I'll come to you. You're still at the cabin, right?" She tipped her head towards the cabin.

His gut tensed. It had been Flavia's house, too, briefly, and besides, such a mess. But Amanda had turned away.

"When?" he called out to her. The sun shined off the keys she swung in her hand, sending off glints of light.

"For dinner. About seven."

Had she just invited herself over for dinner? He thought of the state of his kitchen, the dust-balls gathered in every corner of the house. Crap.

Later, he gave Belle an extra rubdown.

"What am I going to do?" he whispered to the horse. "I need someone, you know? Someone who can talk to me. Someone real."

The horse leaned into him. The sun had shifted, the shadows longer and a chill in the air. Over the last two years, the mare's company had been such a comfort—her strength, and the ease with which she carried him when he felt too heavy to move. He could taste betrayal in the back of his throat, although he knew it was absurd, thinking Flavia's ghost hovered in this horse.

The horse shuffled her feet then pissed on the ground, splashing Uriel's boots. "Christ, Belle!" He jumped back, waking from his reverie. The mare nosed her empty trough. Uriel washed off his boots with the hose and dumped some feed in the trough.

At the Sonoma Market, where everything was organic, delicious, and expensive, he bought bread, steaks, artichokes, and corn. At the last minute, he threw in some fancy chocolate. All together, it cost a quarter of his weekly paycheck.

He stopped at his mother's, waiting for young boys on bikes to get out of his way before he swung the truck into her driveway. Had he ever been as carefree as those boys?

Lourdes was out, but he went around back to her tiny garden plot, picking fresh cilantro, tomatoes and basil. She drove up as he put the vegetables in the cab of his truck. She carried a brown bag and stopped to eye the food he'd picked.

Her thin eyebrows rose. "You could ask before you take shit from my garden."

He smelled the alcohol on her and knew what she had in the bag. "I pay the rent half the time, Ma."

"You got a girl?" she asked, looking amused. "That who you're cooking for?"

He didn't answer. He picked up her garden hose tossed in a pile; he wound it up and placed it on the brass post which he'd bought for this purpose.

"It's about time you got back out there." She put down her bag to find her key, her braid slipping forward over her shoulder. She wore an old leather jacket of Flavia's. "You know that horse isn't Flavia," she said.

Uriel winced. He'd confided his theory to her once, after too much tequila.

"I know that, Ma."

With that, he took off. He drove past several vineyards where workers were still picking grapes into the evening. He hoped Freddie was not having the grapes picked too early. His uncle relied largely on instinct when it came to the timing of their harvest, and it made Uriel nervous. But so far the caliber of Freddie's wines had proven him right.

At home, Uriel took his clean shirts off the dining room table and hid his dirty laundry in the closet. The cabin looked like hell. He lit a candle a student at the stables had given him for Christmas and wiped the hairs out the bathroom sink.

After he did the dishes, he trimmed the artichokes, snipping off the edges like Maya had taught him and wrapping the corn in foil, with fresh cilantro and butter. He opened the wine to let it breathe and wiped out the glasses. He placed the steaks on the counter with salt on one side, pepper on the other.

As Amanda's car came down the road, the lights glowing in the dusk, he poured the wine. He had planted the pine tree she'd left him at the side of the cabin, near the frayed hammock. Would she recognize it? It towered now. Five years is significant for a pine tree. The five years had been significant for him as well, only instead of taller he felt diminished, as if he'd eaten the wrong cookie in Wonderland and shrunk down in the face of life's tricks.

Amanda strolled to the door, a basket of strawberries in her hands, a long loose dress over her cowboy boots. "Hi," she said, her voice low and shy.

Uriel accepted the berries, purposely not touching her. *You left me. I'll be damned if I make this too easy.* He gave her a glass of wine, glancing sideways to examine her for subtle changes.

Amanda had a light sunburn on her fair shoulders, and her hands were perhaps less smooth than five years ago. But the flaming hair that made him notice her in the first place, the angular throat and the habit of running her finger on her lips all remained. He had wanted her from the first time he saw her, when she'd ridden past him, her back straight, ass sticking out a bit on the saddle, her legs firm.

"It's nice to be here again," she said, glancing around.

"Good," Uriel answered. He led her out to the deck; two wooden chairs waited by a splintery table.

"I forgot how killer your view is."

"It's mine," Uriel said, speaking of the view, "and I'm used to it. But you're right, it's beautiful."

"All of that," her arm spread wide, "is yours? Your family's?"

"Ha, no. I wish. We own to about that fence up there, and another plot on the other side. We get a lot of our grapes from elsewhere. But our vines are good, we've had an amazing few years."

Amanda raised her glass. "An Esperanza Zin? It's delicious."

"A Syrah, actually. Freddie is pretty excited about that one."

"It's cool to think of your family's legacy in a bottle."

He smiled. He had forgotten how her words sometimes sounded like poetry. "You could write wine descriptions." He motioned for her to take a seat, as he brought out cheese and crackers.

They talked about Chito, their only mutual friend, the stables, the horses. Was this how the evening would go, he wondered? A social call? Nothing that cut to the bones of their past? Maybe that was for the best.

"My dad's sick," she blurted out when he rose to get the steaks on. Uriel sat back down.

"I know," he answered.

"He has cancer." Her eyes filled as she said it, as if the word itself hurt to say.

"Yes."

"How did you know?" Her eyes drew together, suspicious.

"I didn't . . . " Uriel blew out a breath. "I ran into him at the hospital a few weeks ago. And he was heading to oncology. He looked pretty distracted."

"You didn't tell me."

"I wasn't in a position to call you and ask about it. We weren't in touch." Uriel heard the edge in his voice. Not angry, but not soft either. He stared at the wine in his glass. He could get emotional if he drank without eating. This night could go in directions he wasn't anticipating.

Amanda sat back, seeming to take stock. She crossed her arms. "He has prostate cancer. It's probably going to be fine. He's had good care. I just hate the word cancer."

Uriel let out a slow breath. He wondered if she would have called him again, ever, if her father hadn't gotten cancer? Was she just lonely? "I'm sorry to hear it."

Her sharp green eyes changed to sea glass under the tears. "I'm sorry about not calling you when . . . " She paused, wiped her eyes with her hand. "I can't believe we haven't talked in all this time. I knew what happened, Uriel. I heard from Chito. About your wife. And I wanted to call you, but I just couldn't . . . I didn't know what to say. What should I have said?"

His legs bumped the table as he jumped up, motioning towards the kitchen. "How about I make the steaks? I have artichokes boiling already. Probably close to done."

Not waiting for her response, he took long strides across the deck and yanked the screen door open because it always stuck. It sounded rougher than he meant it to. His thoughts raced. He hadn't wanted her to call after Flavia died. He didn't want her to call at all, or for her to be here tonight. What had he been thinking?

"Uriel, let's start this conversation over, okay?" She stood at his elbow, tall and present. It made him think of her manner with Chestnut. Her ability to calm him.

"Remember our first ride?" Uriel said, picturing the afternoon again. "When you got stung up?"

A smile broke across her face. "There had to be three bees in my hair alone. Five more in my shirt. God, that was awful. I still can't believe Chestnut didn't buck me off and run home without me."

"You screamed like a wild woman. And I had no idea what happened, so I just thought you saw a snake or something." He laughed. "Your face was like a basketball the next day."

"Yes, thanks for that memory."

The conversation flowed from there. They talked about movies, the taste of the wine, their enjoyment of the steaks and what people eat in Peru. They didn't discuss her father, Uriel's dead wife, or Amanda's departure years ago.

In certain moments, he slipped back through time like a feather falling to soft ground, as if he were twenty-four again, falling in love for the first time. She wrapped her long sienna hair around her finger as she talked, and he still found it mesmerizing. She knew a hundred things he'd never heard of—books, movies, places. Instead of finding it intimidating, her knowledge excited him, as if his proximity to her opened doors to worlds he didn't know he was missing.

She still ate like a guy, attacking the steak, pulling the artichoke leaves through her teeth with gusto, dipping them into the butter and licking her lips after each one. "God, I love artichokes."

"I know."

She grinned. "You know more about me than I realize."

He scratched his chin, his five o'clock shadow more like a ten o'clock one. He thought he knew her well, but not at all. "Do you believe in reincarnation?" he asked, curious.

She hesitated. "Wow. That's an unusual question. I . . . I don't *not* believe in it. It is pervasive in so many cultures, over the generations and centuries. I believe there is a presence, through life and death. And that it can shift over time. So, yeah, maybe."

He smiled. "Me, too. Maybe. Sometimes. Jesse thinks whenever a hummingbird comes right near you, it's a message from the other side."

Amanda nodded. "It's not an uncommon belief in Mexico. You see hummingbirds in a lot of Aztec art. They were sacred to Aztecs." She clearly enjoying the role of teacher. It occurred to him that she knew more about the people he had descended from than he did.

"Did Aztecs believe in reincarnation?"

She swished her wine, then took another sip. "No, I don't think so. They believed in an afterlife but not reincarnation. Let me Google it, though, because we're sliding out of my expertise fast."

She read the information on her phone, making small appreciative noises as she scrolled. "Hey," she said, looking up. "I knew there was something else about hummingbirds. The Aztecs believed if a woman died in childbirth, they became a hummingbird. Like a special designation." She looked pleased with the new information.

Did women who died when they were driving too fast with strange men become horses? He wondered if Amanda knew Flavia was pregnant when she died. He guessed not, from her tone.

"So," Amanda put down her glass and leaned forward. "If you were reincarnated, let me guess, you'd come back as a horse."

Uriel didn't like that she'd hit so close to his thoughts about Flavia/Belle. "No, actually. I wouldn't want to be a horse. I love taking care of them, but I wouldn't want to be one."

"So, what then?"

He looked out at the ranch, just barely outlined in the moonlight.

"I think I would want to come back here. As me. Take care of the horses."

"And tend the vines?"

In the darkness, he couldn't tell if she was teasing or earnest. "Yes. Tend the horses and the vines. And you? What or who would you be?"

She shivered, even though she was wrapped in a blanket, and he realized it had gotten late.

"I don't know. Maybe a bird. I'd like to fly. I don't think I would want to come back as the same person." She must have seen something in his face, and she smiled. "But maybe I do."

He felt the chill of the night air as well. Time to move inside or call it a night. He imagined them inside. Pictured her plopped on the worn-out couch where he first made love to Flavia, or on the bed where he used to watch Flavia sleep, her heavy brown hair across the pillows. Would he ever be able to be with another woman in this cabin?

"Uriel, I can't tell if you're listening to me." Amanda stared at him and he felt she was a stranger, across the table, wrapped in the blanket.

"I should probably go," Amanda said, not like she meant it. "The bugs are eating me alive out here."

This would be the natural moment to invite her inside.

"Yeah," he said. "I work early tomorrow. You too?"

She didn't answer, just helped him put the plates in the kitchen, stacked up like debris washed up in a storm. She moved close to him and placed a butterfly kiss on his cheek.

And then she grabbed him, fingers on both sides of his chin, and kissed him with intention. His heart raced, his knees weak. She tasted like wine and smoke and steak and summer. He would have reached for her, if he'd had a moment to process it.

She stepped away. "Sorry," she said abruptly. "I shouldn't have done that. But anyway . . . thank you for dinner."

Before he could decide how to react, Amanda headed to her car, her feet making crunching noises as she crossed the gravel, his blanket still around her shoulders.

Uriel went inside and stared at the bed. His imagining ended when it came to bringing Amanda, or any woman, into this room. Could he shake the memories from the blankets? Clear the spirits? Sage the mattress?

He collapsed on the couch, thinking. He had married Flavia on a whim, three months into the relationship, over a tequila-induced dare in Vegas. Flavia announced to Uriel and Chito one night that she knew Uri was not the marrying type. Determined to prove his devotion, he found a tacky chapel. They dragged drunken Chito as their witness. Flavia wore a white shift, the kind she used to throw over her bathing suit, and he joked that she had planned the whole thing.

"You don't mean to do this," Flavia had said, her voice uncertain at the last minute, scared.

"Yes, I do." And he did.

Uriel had loved being married, all nine months of it. Loved saying "my wife" when he spoke of her, loved the early morning hours, waking and finding her body next to his, her feet tangled in the sheets in an uncharacteristic vulnerability. He loved it especially when he learned she was pregnant.

He told himself the arguments were part of marriage, the mood swings hormones, the flirting with other men would stop, that she hadn't meant to lie about taking money from his wallet. That love was complicated, but you could make it work.

Uriel had focused his will on constructing the family and home he never had as a child. He'd convinced himself he was cultivating their love like a vine, and it needed a dormant, a few more seasons, to mature. He held tight to this hope, even as Flavia pushed him away. She died nine months after the wedding.

Uriel stared at the pile of dishes and instead went to bed. He slept poorly. He dreamt that Belle had bitten him again. He was back at the hospital, and he saw Amanda across the room, instead of Jim. He was eager to talk to her, but when he called to her, she wouldn't turn his way.

Chapter 10

"Drink to me only with thine eyes,
  And I will pledge with mine;
   Or leave a kiss but in the cup
   And I'll not look for wine."

—Ben Jonson, "Song. To Celia"

FOR DAYS, URIEL FOUND HIMSELF CHECKING HIS PHONE TOO often, hoping for and dreading a message from Amanda. He had not heard from her since she had slipped away, his blanket over her shoulders. He wasn't surprised, the next move should have been his.

But he hesitated.

At the vineyard, the crush permitted him to put thoughts of Amanda aside, immersed in work. Everything buzzed on the property this time of year. By seven a.m., Jesse and the cousins set out urns of coffee, plates of bread and hard-boiled eggs. Uriel made his way up and down the property. He checked on the workers, reminding the team leaders to give them breaks.

Jesse managed the tasting room for the season. Other cousins came in to help with Maya, to prepare dinners, to pour wine for tourists. Urgency pushed everything he did, from his morning shave—rushed, face nicked—to inhaling the cold chicken Jesse handed him for lunch, when he stopped at the winery.

He didn't have time to think about Amanda. Much.

He might have to accept that he was destined to live alone in this shit cabin, staring at the wreckage of his life: half-finished projects in the backyard, dirty dishes on the counter, an empty wine bottle collection, and Flavia's scarves draped over the windows.

One night, he and Jesse passed a joint back and forth while they watched a television show about "the little people of Hollywood." Jesse's pick.

"My back might actually be breaking," Jesse said. "My feet are swollen up like an old lady's. My shoulder's fucking frozen. The harvest is killing me this year." Jesse took a long hit on the joint, the smoke drifting around her head.

The smell reminded Uriel of being young and stupid, a feeling he craved tonight—stoned indifference. He wondered if he had any decent snacks in the kitchen.

"Hit the 7-Eleven?" He suddenly wanted frozen pizza bites.

Jesse shook her head. "I'm not going anywhere tonight but bed." She had come down to his cabin in her lounge pants and slippers, after a shower. He imagined she must be restless, living with folks twice her age.

"You and your dude break up?"

She'd been seeing a guy earlier in the summer, but, Uriel realized, he had not been around in some time. Jesse took a last hit on the joint. "Sort of. Not interested in talking about it." She sounded irritated. He smiled. Jesse never overshared.

"You doing the redhead again?" she retorted.

"No. Not interested in talking about it." This made them both laugh. Which was of course when Amanda called. They eyed the phone as it rang, her name blinking on the cell phone's screen.

"Dude," Jesse said. "She's like psychic. You better answer it."

Uriel took it outside, standing in the cool darkness. "Hey," he said, feeling the gentle effects of the weed.

"Hi." Her voice sounded nervous, officious. "Can you meet me for a drink downtown?"

His heart picked up, a taste of hope rising in his chest. His finger traced the splintery edge of the railing around his deck. "Sure. Where?"

"El Dorado. I'm walking in. I'll grab us a table."

He wanted to say no, not there, but she hung up. Did she have to choose that bar?

As Uriel crossed the threshold fifteen minutes later, he noticed the front window of this otherwise pristine establishment was smashed and boarded up. His stomach did a small flip as he came through the door, like he might see Flavia at the bar, chatting with a customer but winking at him. Amanda sat across the elegant room, her hair down, wrapped in a pale gray shawl and sipping a glass of white wine.

He hadn't prepared himself to see Goat, the infamous bar manager. Named for his effusive graying goatee—a stark contrast to his balding head, he had worked closely with Flavia.

Goat crossed the room, arms open wide. "Uriel! Christ, it's been so long." Uriel surrendered to a bear hug. Had he aged as much as this guy in the two years since he'd seen him?

"How the fuck are you?" Goat asked. He tipped back and forth on his cook's clogs while he talked. Uriel caught Amanda's eye. She gave him an uncertain smile.

"You doing okay?" Goat asked him.

I'd be doing better if you had stopped Flavia from getting in the car with a drunken Texan two years ago.

No. Not Goat's fault. Running interference on Flavia's impulsiveness would have been a full-time job.

"What happened to the window?" Uriel asked, pointing to the wooden board with yellow danger tape draped across it.

Goat shook his head but smiled incongruously, as if he admired the brazenness. "Drunk driver—some woman. Right into the lobby. Crazy! But no one got hurt." His smile faded and he glanced around the room. "I think about Flavia a lot, you know. Been hoping you'd stop in. Such a shame." Goat's eyes probed his. "Still at the stables and shit?"

"Yup—and shit. Listen, I'm meeting a friend." Uriel gestured towards Amanda as he stepped away.

Goat stared at Amanda a tick too long, his hand stroking the hair on his chin. "I'll bring you a drink. What do you want? On the house."

Uriel asked for a beer. He wove through the tables, acutely aware of himself as he approached Amanda. His boots sounded too loud on the floor, his hair, still damp from the shower, curled over the collar of his denim jacket, and the jacket flapped open as he walked.

Amanda gave him a light kiss and he thought about running his hands down her back, holding her close. "How are you?" she asked, taking her seat, unaware of his horny mental ramblings.

"Beat," he said, "to be honest. But glad you called."

"Is the winery full tilt?" Born and raised in the wine country, Amanda knew the madness of the season.

"Yes. Like always."

They talked about Maya's health and Amanda's lack of progress on her dissertation and the horses.

"This is better," she said, her eyes eager. "Than last time."

The edge of his mouth curled up a bit. He still appreciated her directness. "Yes. Sorry about that. The evening didn't end all that well."

One shoulder lifted. "It was okay. Our first time together in years was bound to be awkward. We never really talked about what happened. It was a long time ago, and maybe it's better to just start a new friendship and forget the past?"

"You left," Uriel interrupted. "That's what happened." The words fell out of his mouth like pebbles hitting the table, breaking the warm mood. "Sorry," he added, "for sounding so angry." Maybe the weed was making him honest.

She swallowed, waiting a beat. "I did leave. You're right. I think. I mean . . . I know at the time what I thought was that I needed to go, to do my graduate program, and try to make a life somewhere else. Not Sonoma. Not under my parent's shadow. And we weren't . . . I wasn't sure we could evolve."

Uriel folded his arms. "I don't really need to rehash it. It was a long time ago, and I'm guessing we've both been through some shit since then."

Amanda nodded. "I know. I want to be able to see you or talk to you, but I don't know if we are okay. Or whether we can shift into, I don't know—something new?"

"You mean can we evolve?"

Her smile faded. "I guess I deserved that."

Suddenly he felt irritable. What did she want from him? "This is crazy. I am glad to see you, really. I don't think I'm angry anymore about you leaving. But why are you back? I mean I know, you're here for your dad. But why with me? After all this time."

"I never stopped thinking about you, Uri."

His heart stirred, slightly. "That's a lot of time to think about someone and not reach out."

"I didn't want to hurt you again. I thought it would be wrong to call you when I was home visiting, just to leave again."

"And now?"

She waved to a waitress and asked for another glass of wine, and a second beer for Uriel. *She's stalling.*

"Now I'm here. Going through shit. And you're here. And I think about you every time I go to the stables or walk on the hill behind my house or see Chito or eat at that taco place you showed me. I don't know, just all the time."

"Think about me? How exactly?"

Her lips curved, and she held his gaze. Gorgeous emerald eyes that used to entrance him. "You know *how,* Uriel. I think about you like I did, like I always did."

There was a frantic bird trapped in his chest. "I don't know about anything serious." He lacked adequate vocabulary. "With everything that happened. I mean a date, sure—but we can't go back. It doesn't work that way."

"I know. But maybe we can go forward?"

Uriel didn't answer; his heart raced. Hadn't he expected this? Why did he feel so off guard?

"Can you tell me about Flavia? Please. It's like this huge—thing—between us. You had a wife who died. That's like all I know, Uri. Tell me the *story.*"

"Well, she tended bar here."

For a minute he could see Flavia, jet-black hair stuck up in a high pony tail, pushing past the bar backs with her generous hips, sweat beading in the cavity just above her breasts. He had met her one night when he'd come in with a bunch of guys out for a bachelor party. When the party moved on, he had stayed.

Amanda winced. "I can't believe I suggested this place. I had no idea."

Uriel shook his head. "It's all right. Probably time to face some of the ghosts. They aren't going anywhere."

Her gaze was steady, as if examining him for symptoms of grief. He told her how he drove back streets to avoid the corner where Flavia died. And avoided the place she got her hair done, the diner they had their first date, the park where she told him she was pregnant.

"Pregnant?" Amanda's posture straightened a tick. "Is that why you got married so fast?"

He saw something like relief creeping into her eyes. As if she assumed that he had only married Flavia out of some sense of propriety, not love. It irked him.

"No," he said. "We married before she got pregnant. I married her because I wanted to."

Amanda's gaze fell, and she took a large gulp of her wine. "Sorry, I didn't mean to sound like you didn't want to. I shouldn't have phrased it that way."

He examined the bubbles rising in his beer.

"Was it a big wedding?"

He thought of the three of them—himself, Flavia and Chito—in the tacky plywood chapel. Chito, even in his state of intense inebriation, kept saying it was a crap idea.

"No," he said, half smiling. "Not a big wedding. It was a last-minute kind of thing. Spontaneous, I mean. But fun. Once they recovered from their shock, my family celebrated it. Freddie had a BBQ, cooked a whole pig." He took his jean jacket off, his skin warm. "It feels like a long time ago, now. It was."

Amanda stared into the distance, as if watching his past like a movie in her mind.

"Your turn," Uriel said, wanting to shift the conversation off himself, surprised he'd told her as much as he had. "What happened to you in the last five years?"

Amanda placed a stray hair back behind her ear, as if choosing her answer with care. "A lot but also nothing. Isn't that weird?" She told him about Peru, about graduate school, about a teacher she'd been involved with—some married guy.

"No one serious?" He expected there to be one, stealing himself for the details. Better to get this over with.

"No, actually."

"This whole time?"

Her throat reddened and then her cheeks. He'd forgotten about the depth of her blushes, blooming across her skin.

"No. No one, the whole time."

He'd blundered into a painful landscape.

She bit her lip. "I-I thought I would get over you? But it was harder than I thought."

Uriel sat back, surprised. Of the various things he'd imagined she might say to him tonight, this had not occurred to him. That in five years, she'd not let him go.

"You left," he said, trying for a measured tone, wishing for more beer. "So suddenly."

"I know. I told you I was going to grad school, probably."

"You didn't even say goodbye."

"I—no, I didn't."

"No, really, Amanda. That was shitty. It was awful. I was a mess. Fucking crushed me. Why didn't you at least say goodbye?"

"I had to go. I was afraid if I stayed another day, I'd never get out. I'd be trapped."

"Trapped? That's how you felt? Because the weekend before you left, we went to San Francisco, Sake bombing with your friends. You told me you didn't care if you ever left."

"I know."

"And the day before you left, you told me you bought tickets for a summer music festival. For both of us. In August."

"I know."

The hardness grew in his voice. The anger he'd thought resolved was stored in the recesses of his mind, ready to erupt. "Do you? Do you know what it was like to find that goodbye gift on my doorstep? The only reason I knew it was from you was because my key was underneath it."

Amanda's hand shook as she reached across the table, not quite reaching his. "The tree was because you didn't like the way the sun fell in your eyes in the morning. It was to block the light next to your window. And to remember me."

He shook his head. "And that's where I planted it. I knew when I dug the hole and put it in, you would not come back. I just didn't know why."

"I had to leave right away. Something happened with my father and I flipped."

Uriel tried to contain himself. "Are you going to tell me what happened?"

Her energy shifted from him, from the conversation. "No, I don't think I am."

A coolness descended on the table. Was the conversation over, and with it the possibility of reconciliation?

"Maybe we need to let this go," Uriel said, "Stop trying to force something, if you can't even now tell me what happened. What messed things up in the first place."

Her eyes filled with tears, falling right down her cheeks. She brushed them away. "Maybe," she said. "I guess I still don't know how to talk about it."

She had tiny smears of mascara across her cheek. Part of him wanted to hold her and tell her none of it mattered. Another part wanted to shake her with frustration. "Amanda, tell me what it is you want from me. Now?"

"I thought . . . I really miss you. And we're both here. Can't we just start over? And see how it goes?"

He considered this, even as he became aware of how tired he was. Each muscle in his back and legs ached, hot red tendons and stretched sinews, holding his exhausted body together. And he was hungry, he realized. Starving.

Amanda grabbed her bag, searched for her wallet and threw a twenty on the table. "It's okay. You don't have to say anything, I can tell you think this is nuts. And it probably is. I'll go."

He nodded. Her inclination to leave when the conversation grew difficult only reinforced his fears.

Amanda stood up, grabbing her coat. "Uri, I'm sorry I keep calling you. And showing up. I know I need to pull it together. I'll stop." She didn't wait for him to answer, just strode away, crimson hair rising and falling as she crossed the room.

Uriel didn't want her to stop calling him. Not really. But his weariness won the battle, and he stayed put. The waitress asked if he needed anything.

Do I need anything? Everything. A life.

He ordered a burger, well-done, fries and a lemonade. Time to sober up. He tried not to dwell on Amanda, her probing questions and sudden tears. He did think about the smile she'd given him when he first arrived and gnawed on that while he waited for the burger, how much he still loved her smile.

"All good?" Goat asked, dropping into Amanda's abandoned chair as he placed the burger and fries on the table.

"Everything's great," Uriel said, reaching for the burger. He devoured it, trying to enjoy the meat's salty juice on his tongue and the crunch of the fries. The place had cleared out, and Goat was in no rush to leave.

Uriel noticed the bill was light—the drinks all comped. He added a hefty tip for the waitress.

Goat leaned in, as if conspiring, and mentioned that he and the waitress had a thing going. He insisted on pouring Uriel a glass of wine. "It's the new Laurel Glen Cab. I'm sorry, I know they're your competition, but—"

Uriel waved his words away. Freddie had taught him to honor the other winemakers, never begrudge them. Success in the valley bene-fited all of them. He took a sip and then another. He smiled. He could almost taste the earth in the wine, and the sun that fell on the grapes. "Okay, you're right. It's awesome."

Goat poured himself a glass. "Your friend there was a dish. She a girlfriend?"

Uriel pictured how Amanda, his feisty feminist ex-lover, would react to being called "a dish." "No. Not dating anyone. I haven't been ready."

Goat nodded, twirling a toothpick in his teeth. He shifted forward, then back, like he had something to say but was restraining himself. "I have something for you," he half whispered, serious, "that I've been meaning to give you. I held on to it for you. I don't even know if you want it. Maybe I shouldn't have."

"What?" Uriel imagined an old apron of Flavia's stuck in a drawer, or faded photos.

"I'll go get it." Goat clattered through the swinging door to the kitchen and back offices.

Uriel waited by the bar, jacket on, ready to go. It had been a strange night.

Goat returned and handed Uriel a piece of paper, yellow lined, ripped off a pad. It had the name Cat Blakely and a phone number, with an area code Uriel didn't recognize.

"Whose number is this?"

"It's . . . I know this is weird, but I've kept it, just in case. But you never came in. I thought . . . I think it might be good for you to call her. Process your stuff. Might help."

"Goat, is it like a shrink?"

"No, no. It's the Texan's wife. Her husband was the one Flavia was in the car with that night. The one who was driving, the accident . . . I just thought you two could talk?"

Uriel's earlier sense of vertigo returned, only now it was worse, his heart pushing up on his sternum, his stomach plummeting. "Why? Why would I want to talk to her?"

"She called here a few times last year with questions. Sounded like a nice lady. I thought you guys could help each other—like, put the pieces together. And then you could move on. I've been worried about you, to be honest. I know I should have called you more after the first few months. But you never called me back."

Uriel had forgotten Goat had reached out. He had only the vaguest memory of the months after Flavia died.

"Anyway, I see Chito here and there, and he tells me you're okay but not getting out or anything. So, I had this idea. Do whatever you want with it. You can toss it in the garbage right now. Whatever, I gave it to you, and I won't bring it up again. Okay?"

Uriel put the paper deep in his pants pocket and knocked his knuckles on Goat's, aiming for a nonchalance he wished he felt. "Thanks for the drinks," he said.

He loped around the square to his truck, his boots scraping the pavement. He should throw the paper away. He'd go home, get some sleep, and leave this night with all its strangeness behind. Maybe.

The truck's headlights broke the darkness as he crossed the valley. Cold air poured through the window. Despite its bitter sting, Uriel wanted the wind to clear the mud from his mind. Or maybe to rip the paper holding Cat's number from his pocket, away into the night.

Chapter 11

"Wine is sunlight, held together by water."

—Galileo

JIM PACED IN THE INNER COURTYARD, TRYING TO MUSTER THE courage to go upstairs. Not finding it, he sat down on their old stone bench. The pool, ten feet below, shimmered in the early sun. The bougainvillea Elena planted years ago bloomed profusely.

The sprawling white stucco house was not finished when they had bought it—bare walls and no landscaping. Over the years, Elena had cultivated the home like her personal garden, with color everywhere, in the flower beds and her paintings. With a path of mosaic tiles leading from the studio to the house, sea blue curtains that moved in the breeze, and a bubbling fountain in the courtyard.

How could he leave this paradise?

He had no blueprint for ending a marriage. Jim's parents stayed together for forty years, despite his mother's fiery temper and the stresses of a large family on a small income. Despite a lack of love and, Jim was pretty sure, his father's affairs. Leaving would never have been an option for either of his parents, staunch Catholics.

Jim dropped his head down, feeling sick with guilt and nerves.

Elena opened her door, looking like a bed not yet made—hair unsettled, eyes sleepy, and her robe slipping off one shoulder.

"You're up early," he blurted as she came down the steps.

Elena pulled her robe tighter. "I'm working today."

Working? His wife didn't work.

"At the art show, Jim." Mild disappointment came through her voice. "I told you about it."

"Right. The show at the museum?"

"Yes. I'm due there at ten, working all day. I have two school groups coming in." She was headed into the kitchen. "Oh good, you made coffee. Aren't you off to work?"

He had thought the conversation might take all day, so he had cleared his calendar. But it might take ten minutes. He had no idea how long it took to leave a marriage. He'd made a plan with his therapist to be available as long as Elena needed to talk. To answer every question honestly. And then to leave. Not waffle, or permit her to convince him to give it another try.

He'd known from the moment Amanda confronted him that he wanted to work things out with Victor. His life was slipping away, time moving like an avalanche picking up speed. He needed to grab happiness now.

But Elena had plans. To work, a commitment. He had nudged her to get involved with the Sonoma Valley Museum. Why should he do this today?

"Jim?" She was back, coffee in hand, looking more awake. "Are you okay?"

"Yes. I'm thinking of working from home today. No appointments in the city."

His wife gave his arm a friendly pat as she passed.

She may never do that again, touch me with a casual warmth.

"Great. Well, glad I'll be out of your hair."

"Perhaps we can have dinner?" he asked.

Elena looked puzzled. "Of course, we'll have dinner. I'll grab something on my way home. Unless you're eager to cook?" A smile played on her lips.

Oh God. She has no idea. "I . . . "

"I was only kidding. You don't need to cook. Amanda and I can come up with something."

He grimaced. "Is she back in town?" Amanda had been in Tahoe with friends. He'd wanted to talk to Elena while their daughter was away.

"She's driving down today. Not sure when. Actually, she might be having dinner out, now that I think of it."

"Why don't we go out?"

Elena's head tipped, as if considering. He noticed the wrinkles near her eyes in the harsh morning light and the gray roots. Age pushing through. "Why?" Elena sounded curious. It had been a long time since they'd gone out, the two of them.

"I don't know, just because."

Elena balanced her coffee on the banister top and crossed her arms. "Is everything all right, Jim?"

How many times in their long marriage had he heard these words? "Are you all right?" or "Everything okay?" The words could be code for "What is wrong with you now?" or "Why are you being difficult?"

He nodded.

"The treatments are going fine?"

"Yes, yes. Fine. Let's go out tonight, something different." *To talk*, he considered adding, but then she would know it was serious, and spend her day worrying. Jim watched her head back up the stairs to her studio. He hated to upset her in any way. When their stocks crashed and they lost a third of his savings, he didn't tell her. When he had pain from a twisted ankle or a migraine, he didn't show it. He liked her to be protected, safe, not stressed.

And he was about to blow up their life. For the second time.

After they lost the first baby, he had strayed. Shredded the handful of trust she had left in the world. Jim had begged her to stay with him. And despite her broken heart, she'd come back to him. He had wanted to make her happy. Had tried so hard, done so much, with this goal in mind. But he couldn't force the one thing she needed—the kind of love she wanted and deserved.

He remembered thinking, early on with Victor, am I mad? Have I actually had a break down? His grandfather was bipolar—maybe he was inheriting it?

But no, the slamming of his heart when Victor passed by, the weakness in his lungs when they said goodbye, the insomnia and giddiness, the dry mouth nervousness and painful hope—it wasn't madness, but love. The love everyone wrote songs about. Love he had never known.

An hour later, Elena patted the dogs goodbye and backed out of the garage, too fast. Perhaps he would never stand here, in the front hall, and watch his wife drive away again. Or be in this house at all. The thought picked up speed, from a penny rolling down the street to a truck going down a mountain with no brakes. His heart pounded at the myriad of repercussions he would face from one conversation. He squatted on the floor, rubbing the dog's belly, but shaking. *Breathe.*

He should pack a few of his things. He assumed she would ask him to leave right away.

He would go to a hotel, for now. He packed the clothes he wore most. Then, upon thinking about it, added more. What if he travelled over the next few weeks? And why leave a mess for Elena to sort through? He moved methodically through his drawers, putting things aside for Goodwill, placing others in boxes he'd found in the garage.

Several hours later his closet was empty, his toiletries thrown away or packed. His office was cleaned out. He threw entire bags of paper into the recycling, added more knickknacks to the Goodwill box, feeling somewhat exhilarated by the clean shelves. He should have done this years ago. A sense of determination grew as he piled the boxes and suitcases in his car. He was doing what he needed to do, what he should have done years ago. It was the best for all of them.

In the office he collected his extra chargers, checkbooks, and a few photos. In the bottom drawer he found an envelope he'd not seen in years and stared at it, irked at his own lack of discretion. Had Elena come across it? A scribbled goodbye on Marriott Hotel stationery from a lover, years before. He should have gotten rid of it. He examined the lacy hand writing. Shaking his head at his own nostalgia, he threw it away.

He lifted a paperweight made for him by Amanda, age six. Her tiny hand had been imprinted in plaster; she'd painted it gold. He traced the fingers with his own, thinking of the years when her hands were this tiny, and her bright eyes. Her smile was always devilish, as if she had a secret. Amanda was herself, unique and self-defined in every way even as a little girl.

He grabbed a pen from the bottom drawer and wrote Amanda a note, in case he didn't reach her to talk tonight. He started with *I'm sorry*, then threw it away. He tried another one, thanking her for confronting him, but it sounded like blame. He tossed it and tried another, and another.

He didn't realize he was crying at first, until the phlegm started to drip from his nose, and his tears hit his fingers, still clutching the paperweight. Christ, if he left now, he lost everything. Elena might never forgive him. Amanda would blame him for taking so long to do it. Was Victor even available? He risked spending the next twenty years, if he was lucky enough to live that long, alone in a damn condo, seeing his daughter sporadically. No wife, no lover. Would he get to see the dogs?

He could change his mind, put everything back in the rooms and feign that he had decided to clean things out a bit. No one was home. There was still time. His phone buzzed with a text message from Elena, asking if he was coming down to the Square for dinner.

Yes, he wrote back, his fingers clumsy. **I'll see you soon.**

He needed to go. Jim placed the imprint of Amanda's small hand in his coat pocket. He wiped his tears in the dogs' fur as he hugged each of them, and locked the door as he left. Before he got in his car he went back and unlocked the door, turning on the lights in the kitchen and on the porch. He didn't want his wife to come home alone to a dark house.

Chapter 12

"I tasted—careless—then –
I did not know the Wine
Came once a World—Did you?
Oh, had you told me so –
This Thirst would blister—easier—now—"

—Emily Dickinson, "One Year Ago—Jots What?"

AMANDA CAUGHT SIGHT OF HER FATHER'S BMW STREAKING through the night past her, as if surfing down the mountain, while she urged her car up. She hadn't returned his calls from earlier that evening. She'd been too focused on the conversation with Uriel, which ultimately left her feeling angry, horny, and alone. She glanced at her phone as she stepped out of the car, hoping for something from Uriel but instead found a cryptic text from her father: **I'm sorry.**

For what?

Inside, the dogs leapt up on her, a sense of desperation behind their usual enthusiastic paws upon her waist. Beaver whimpered as Amanda patted her silky ears.

"Mom?"

Her mother was huddled like a child in the corner of the living room couch, under a blanket. She squeezed Amanda's offered hand. "Amanda, this can't be happening to me."

Amanda knew instinctively what had transpired. Her stomach felt like she was on a plane as it took off, no seatbelts.

"Your father just told me he's leaving me," Elena said. Her eyes looked like a lost child. "It's been thirty years. I can't believe it."

Amanda sank down next to her mother, shock and expectation pulsing through her brain. *He actually left? Of course he left.*

Her mother told her the full story, the awful scene at a restaurant, the fact that he was in love with Victor. Amanda prayed her mother wouldn't ask her how much she had known. She kissed her mother's head. "I'll get you tea?" she asked.

"Wine," Elena answered.

Amanda forced herself to walk through Jim's bleak, modern office, now more so with the desk empty, the shelf stripped. In the bathroom garbage can, empty pill bottles lie on top of crumpled pieces of his stationery. She opened one, too curious not to, and then another. The notes were to Amanda, to Elena, and one to Jim, from someone else. Hearing her mother moving down the hall, she stuffed them like contraband into the pockets of her sweatshirt.

Glancing up, she saw a stranger in the mirror—wired, blotchy cheeks, eyes watery from holding back tears, tangled red hair falling from the tidy clip. She closed her eyes and wished herself back to earlier in the night, to Uriel's company, before their spat.

Heavy steps crossed the bedroom.

"Amanda?"

Aunt Carmen stood at the bathroom door. Her aunt was a larger, curvier version of Elena, with long unruly black hair wrapped in a scarf, and a small extra chin. Her tweezed eyebrows looked like birds taking flight, but her eyes were almost identical to Elena's—the color of tiger's eyes, curved up on the edges.

"What are you doing?"

"Nothing." Amanda's voice was defensive. She pushed the papers farther down in her pocket.

Her aunt gave her a hard hug and murmured reassurances. It occurred to Amanda that her aunt and mother had no idea that she had confronted Jim. That she was the probable catalyst to his departure.

"Your poor mom. She doesn't know what hit her," Carmen said, tightening her bright flowered scarf and sighing as Amanda followed her back down the hallway. Carmen wore slippers and sweatpants, her hips swaying.

"When did she call you?" Amanda's voice echoed in the hall, as if it was emptier without her father's presence in the family, as though even the walls knew their anchor had fallen off.

"A couple hours ago. I didn't hear the phone at first, I was in the bath. He told her at a restaurant, can you imagine? In public?"

Amanda calculated how long her mother had known. She wished her mother had reached out to her, not only to Carmen.

Elena sat up, her face streaked with old makeup. Amanda handed her a glass of red wine and poured herself one, too. "Amanda, I wish you hadn't come home to this mess." Her mother's voice was quiet, calmer now, and slightly sloppy. It was possible Carmen had given her something to calm her down.

"Dad called me a few times, but didn't leave a message."

Carmen shook her head in disgust. "Why did he call you? He wants you to come clean up his mess? What an ass."

The words cut into Amanda's heart. Defense of her father leapt to her lips, but she held it back. Futile and irrational to defend her father tonight.

"Carmen," Elena said, her voice brittle, "he's still her father."

From her tone, Amanda heard that this eternal connection dismayed her mother. Amanda was still Jim's daughter. Her mother could not exorcise him from her life completely.

"Sorry, darling," Carmen said. "I'm just pissed because he's hurting my sister." Her hand moved in the air. "And because he's a lying prick."

"Carmen!" Elena protested, but she shook her head and half smiled, too.

Was her father a lying prick? There was no denying the facts—he had lied and betrayed his wife for many years. And yet he had also stayed with her. Who was he? The most loving, loyal, and generous man she knew? A liar, a cheater, and a fake? Her head spun with the paradox.

Elena talked about her own blindness in the face of the evidence she now recognized. About the future she would have without him, about the dogs he'd insisted stay here, about the coffee pot he took, about the accounts they would need to dissolve, and whether her name was on the deed for the house.

Eventually, Amanda pled exhaustion.

Carmen waved her towards the bedroom. "I'll stay, don't worry," she whispered when Amanda said good night, passing her in the kitchen.

"She needs to sleep," Amanda said.

"We'll see. She took a Xanax, but she's not ready to sleep. It's all right, baby. I've been down this path before. Two husbands. Our own father. It will take a while, but she'll be all right."

Amanda wanted to take solace in her words, but as she said good-night to Elena, her mother's eyes looked desperate. Like Chestnut, when a snake crossed the path, the bitter sting of fear.

An hour later, Amanda awoke from a crazed dream and crawled from bed, her head banging from too much wine. Her throat was dry and her bladder too full. Coming out of the bathroom she heard her mother and Carmen's voices in the kitchen and smelled eggs cooking. She toyed with trying to eat, to help the imminent hangover. But her mother's voice was high-pitched, getting hysterical. Amanda paused and listened. The sisters had switched to speaking Spanish.

"Really, this has to be a terrible dream. He wouldn't—I mean, I can't believe this. After everything he did, I stayed with him. I stayed, when most women would—Christ, I don't know what they would have done."

"Killed him, probably." Carmen sounded buzzed.

"Yes. Killed him! You would have. Right? But I kept us together. And I don't regret that. You know I don't."

"I guess you can't afford to."

Amanda moved closer, more alert. After living in Peru, her Spanish was more fluent than ever, but could she be missing something?

Her mother's voice was more agitated. "Carmen, after I made that kind of sacrifice—forgave him for what he did. How could he do this to me?"

Amanda clung to the doorframe, trying to understand what they meant, but half afraid to know. Had he left her before? Or cheated? When?

There was a pause before her aunt answered, the sound of plates being taken from the cabinet and placed on the table. "You're asking me why a snake bit you twice, *hermanita*? That's what you want to know?"

And then she heard her mother laugh, a bitter bark with no joy in it. Amanda crawled back to bed, her thoughts spinning.

She had known this was coming, on some level, for so long, even as a girl when, fooling around on her father's laptop, she had found a photo of Victor wearing only pale blue boxer shorts. Blood had moved through her heart with a sudden pounding swoosh. Her fingers slammed the delete button, but the image stayed, floating in the recesses of her brain, in and out of murky shadows for years.

In her junior year of high school, the family spent a week in Maui, her mother determined to get Jim away from his work for a "real vacation." Early one morning, Amanda slipped outside onto the lanai, the scent of honeysuckle in the air. Her father stood on the other side of the garden, leaning on a palm tree, looking out at the ocean. She moved in close, to surprise him and say good morning.

"I love you," he said to someone on the phone. Amanda froze. The words seemed to smack her face. *I love you.* Who did he love?

While Jim swam, throwing himself into the waves, Amanda scrolled through the recent calls on his phone. Victor's name popped up again and again. Furious, she paced, longing to confront him but unable to, caught in a web of shame.

Then late one night, the summer after high school, at a pool house full of inebriated teenagers and empty Thai food containers, a girlfriend had whispered to her that she'd seen Amanda's father in San Diego the prior weekend, holding hands with another man. Amanda told her she was mistaken, she had to be. Her father was home in Sonoma all weekend. She had lied for him. For the three of them. She downed tequila shots and laughed too loudly, but she found no solace.

Finally, the summer before grad school, she decided she needed to know if it had continued. She worked in her father's office that year, long boring days, then spent her evenings with Uriel, eating up the romance like fresh chocolate. The fact that her parents disapproved made it even tastier.

One afternoon in August, her father announced that he was hopping down to LA for the night, to see a client. He did not look her in the eye as he said goodbye, and Amanda sensed he was lying. Her own furtive love had made her more sensitive to obscurity in others.

Amanda hurried out and followed her father's car when he left, through the crowded streets of the financial district to North Beach. It was Victor's neighborhood. She felt a small thrill of pursuit mixed with the salty taste of shame.

Her father parked the car and Victor appeared, as if he spent his life waiting in the shadows for Jim to arrive. They embraced on the street, like reuniting lovers, although they'd worked together that afternoon. They shared sushi in a tiny Japanese restaurant, at a table by the window. Amanda curled up in the car with a bottle of beer from the corner store, waiting, watching, and stewing.

How many times had her father pretended to be elsewhere while pursuing his secret boyfriend? Was he with Victor when she fell off the horse and was rushed to the hospital when she was twelve? Was he here when he missed opening night of her high school play? She prepared herself for the confrontation, the righteous indignation she would spew upon them, for her mother's sake. For hers. For all the lies over the years.

When the men emerged, they were laughing. Her father reached for Victor's hand and they meandered down the block, swaying slightly, close. Victor's hair was all black then, combed to the side, and his smile dipped low in his long narrow face.

Cartoonish, she thought. He's too thin, and lanky. He's not charming or funny like my father, or warm and strong like my mother. He doesn't carry his weight at the firm, or encourage the employees like my father does. He is weak, a parasite. He will destroy us.

But at that moment, her father turned to Victor, amused by something he said. His smile was wide, his eyes shining in the warm yellow bakery lights. She stared, immobilized. She had never seen him this lighthearted with her mother. *With us.*

They continued down the street, pulling closer to one another, disappearing into the thickening fog. Amanda stayed in the car, trapped, wondering if this knowledge was an apple she should have left on the tree.

She'd left California the next night, her things stuffed in a few suitcases. She didn't see Uriel. She couldn't stand to say goodbye, but she could not stay, either.

For years she kept a distance and never confronted her father. And then she did. Now she considered the aftermath of her recent confrontation with her father: her mother lost in a ball of blankets and tears. Jim driving away from them too fast. The roots of her family, usually so entangled, being ripped apart.

Chapter 13

"I pray you, do not fall in love with me, for I am falser than vows made in wine."

—William Shakespeare, *Much Ado About Nothing*

URIEL UNFOLDED THE PAPER GOAT HAD SLIPPED HIM SEVERAL times the next day. He glanced at it and slipped it back into his pocket, pushing it down deep so it didn't get lost, even as he told himself he should toss it. What would he say to this woman? Why had Goat even given it to him?

"You got some girl's number in your pocket?" Jesse asked as she lumbered by him, a case of wine in her arms. The Esperanza Winery logo was stamped across the top of the case. Maya designed it years earlier, a picture of winding vines through a heart.

"Give me that. I'll carry it."

Jesse blew a piece of damp hair from her face. "It's for the guy at the end of the bar, kind of creepy guy with the sunglasses, white hair."

"Got it."

"And you didn't answer my question. Whose phone number is it?"

"Some family, wants riding lessons for their kid."

Jesse moved back towards the register. "Yeah, I'll bet it is. That's why you've been staring at the paper all day, like it's a secret message. Is it the redhead's?" she called after him as he set off, the case in his arms.

Uriel tensed. "No." He tried to say it with a firmness that would preclude her from asking more about Amanda.

"Good."

He laughed. When Amanda had ditched him five years earlier, Jesse had been eighteen. She was outraged on Uriel's behalf. How dare anyone leave her cousin Uriel, and without an explanation? As a kid, Jesse used to come to Uriel's baseball games, drinking Coke and eating sunflower seeds with Freddie, spitting the shells in a paper bag. One afternoon, she casually offered to kill a boy from the other team, because he'd been rough as he tagged Uriel out. Uriel could never fault Jesse for not having his back.

Uriel headed back to his cabin through the descending dusk, an end of day soreness spreading across his shoulders. He cracked a beer and collapsed in the rickety Adirondack chair on the deck. Maya's old Border Collie loped over, circled Uriel's chair twice, and then took a seat next to him, as if sharing the fading view of the vineyards.

Uriel stared at his phone knowing he had already made the decision. One hand rested on the dog's matted fur as he listened to the phone ringing in Texas, a thousand miles away.

"Hello?" A woman's voice, not young, not old. "Who's this?" A white woman he would guess, maybe fifties? He pictured Susan Sarandon, for some reason.

"Uh . . . this is . . . Well, my name is Uriel Macon."

Why hadn't he planned out what to say?

"Okay. Do I know you? This is Cat Blakely. I'm sorry, I don't recognize your name." She shouldn't be apologizing. He was a stranger, about to ruffle her peace. He considered hanging up.

"I'm Uriel Macon. I got your number from a friend, the bartender at the El Dorado Hotel."

There was a silence, a beat. "What did you say your name was? U-Rina?"

He remembered taunts from the other children, all through grammar school. *Hey Urine! Hey Urinal!*

"Uriel. Sorry if this is a bad time. I can try another day."

"Well, no. I don't know. Can you explain why you're calling? Is that the El Dorado Hotel in—"

"Sonoma." He confirmed, "Sonoma, California."

Her breath caught. "What is this about, can I ask?" There was a twang in her voice, like a guitar hitting the sad note.

His throat tightened. *Shouldn't have called.* "Well, the bartender there, Goat . . . He just thought it might be good if—I don't know—we talked, I guess. He kept your number since the accident."

"I assume this has to do with Carson's . . ."

"The accident."

He heard a deep sigh.

"I'm sorry, I shouldn't have called."

"You know, I'm only now putting that whole ordeal behind me." Her voice sounded irritated, as if he was calling about an unpaid bill.

"I know. I mean, I can imagine. I won't bother you again."

"Well, hold on. Who are you? Are you that girl's brother?"

Uriel winced. Of course, why couldn't he be a brother? Why had he assumed she knew Flavia was married?

Bats dove near the watering pond, three of them shifting in and out of murky shadows.

"Flavia was my wife."

"Oh!" Another pause. "Can you wait while I get my cigarettes?" Her Texas coming through more now, *cigarettes*, the accent on the *ettes*. And then, "Listen, can I call you back? I need to wrap my brain around this. Can I call you another time, Uriel?"

Uriel was relieved to end the conversation. "Yes, of course. No pressure. You don't need to, I just—"

"I'll call you back."

She hung up and after a minute, he placed the phone in his pocket. He gave the dog a final pat then went inside and stripped down, noting that his jeans hung even looser than usual, despite all the food he ate. He'd seen pictures of his father about this age, not long before he died. He had been too thin, his face gaunt, but with the kind eyes Uriel vaguely remembered. What makes a grown man, with a wife and a son, pick up heroin after years clean? He had to know he was playing with fire.

And what made Flavia drink with someone named Carson and go for a mid-afternoon joyride with a child in her womb? His child. Too many ghosts, too many unanswered questions, but neither of them here to ask. He needed to shake himself out of this stupor and move on.

In the shower, he enjoyed the hot water pounding on his neck. The water at his feet grew pink from wine dyed into his fingers. He lathered up, the soap giving off a fresh pine smell.

He stepped out of the shower just as the phone rang. He grabbed a towel to cover himself, as if the caller could see him. He half knew it would be Cat. He heard her exhaling, and he pictured smoke blowing from painted lips somewhere in Texas.

"Sorry for the delay," she said. "I needed a minute to collect my thoughts."

"I get it."

"You actually might," she said. "That's why I called back. Most folks tell me they understand what I been through these last two years and I think that's a load of hog-shit. They have no idea what I'm going through. You're the only person in the world who might. I don't know what to tell you, though. I didn't know she was married."

"I'm surprised the police didn't tell you that."

"His son went to get him. His son from another wife. I was the third wife. Got the lucky ticket, I guess. Anyway, Carson's son knew about your wife. I just called him to check. You knew Carson was married?"

"Yes. I knew he was married, and from Texas. That they met at the bar. That's it."

"He'd flown out there to go to NASCAR, then pick up that new car. I guess he picked up your wife, too. Who knows why? Sometimes, I think, who cares? Sometimes I still miss him. It's a shitty situation."

"Yes."

"What was she like, your Flavia?" she asked. "Why'd she get together with Carson, do you think?"

Uriel's head spun. How many times had he wondered that? To get away, to pretend life was exciting for one day? "She was impulsive. She might have just thought it would be fun."

"Well, don't kill yourself over it. People have affairs for a lot of reasons. I tell you what, don't go blaming yourself. Some people have a need for something new all the time. Cars, girls . . . hell, Carson always wanted to try every new ice cream flavor, or a new kind of whiskey. Didn't matter as long as it was new."

He thought of Flavia's obsession with trying the new foods at the hotel. Grilled figs, squid ink soup, braised dandelions. Most of it sounded horrible to him.

"I don't think it was an affair. They only met that day." Uriel resented the word *affair*, this assumption that it was more than a bad ride.

"Well, he'd been seeing someone at that hotel for a couple of months. I went over his receipts after he died. Any wife would have. Carson was a sly one. He had a place in Alaska, a tax shelter on the islands. Left half his business to wife number one, even though he told me he hated her. And he'd been to Sonoma a bunch of times in the months before he died."

Uriel's heart raced. He sat on the edge of the bed, dropping his towel. His thighs tensed, as if ready to run. His dick hung between them, as if humbled by the images that raced through his mind.

"You still there?" Cat asked.

"Uh. Yes. But I need to think about this. I'd better go."

He heard the flick of a lighter and another exhalation. "I'm sorry if I'm breaking any bubbles here. I don't mean to disparage your wife. It could have been another person he was visiting. You have any kids?"

"No. I don't."

"Well, that's good at least. Not us either. Carson was quite a bit older than I am, of course."

"How old?" Uriel's voice showed his pain, he knew. "How old was he?"

"Fifty-three. Young to die, sure. But older than me by ten years. How old was your wife?"

Uriel's skin was clammy, his chest tight. He laid back on the bed, pulling the sheets over his damp body.

"You okay?" the woman asked.

"She was twenty-five." And then, his voice croaking, he added. "I'm sorry I bothered you." And he hung up.

He stood on the deck after he was dressed, drinking another beer. The moon was bright tonight. He could see the details of the winery, Freddie's place, and the pathways through vineyards. He had grown up on these paths, running through the acres in the spring, when the empty vines reached to the sun, the earth moist. During the fall's harvest, he'd follow his older cousins up and down the rows with a bucket banging at his knees. Proud of their land, even at the end of a long day.

When Flavia told him she was pregnant, he had imagined his son here. A baby riding on his back as he toured the property. A toddler's fat toes squishing grapes in a barrel, which they did for tradition. A small boy skipping across the property, carefree, off to see the horses. His son. His son would never have known a life without a father. Uriel had been so in love with that vision, and drunk with the sense of expectation, that he'd been unable to see the obvious: that the baby's mother, Flavia, drank too much, was unreliable, and often lied.

He had an urge to pitch the bottle when he finished the beer, to hurl it into the night, to scream at the sky. To shake himself hard until his dreams fell out of his ears, like tiny bits of gravel, and he could go on. Empty, but free of missing, free of hurt.

Chapter 14

"With bread and wine you can walk your road."

—Spanish Proverb

AS ELENA HOISTED A PAINTING ONTO A GALLERY WALL, WITH the help of the gallery owner, Amanda rushed in, cheeks flushed.

"Sorry. I know I'm late."

The gallery was located in Crossroads, a whimsical local gathering spot with quirky stores and gorgeous landscaped gardens. They also had a café that made the ultimate grilled cheese sandwich. Elena had offered Amanda lunch, if she helped her hang the paintings.

"Amanda can help with the rest of these," Elena said to the gallery owner, trying not to show her annoyance with Amanda. "Thank you, though."

"Are these all yours?" Amanda surveyed the various paintings leaning on the walls, next to statues and plants.

"God, no. I'm lucky if I do two a year. These are done by other local women artists. I think there's too many Sonoma landscapes. I'm glad mine are different. Where have you been?"

It seemed like an innocent enough question, but apparently not, as Amanda huffed.

"Working. I told you I promised my advisor several more chapters this week."

"Right, you did." Elena didn't want an argument. Since Jim's announcement, she'd been so fragile she felt like a strong wind could knock her down. She certainly didn't want to get on the wrong side of her daughter.

The two women worked for an hour, shifting paintings around as Elena sought the most appealing spaces, ideally under the right lights. Her mind raced as it had since Jim had left. *What now? What next? How can this be?* Her hands shook, and her mouth was always dry. Coming to hang these paintings was a good distraction, but not enough to shut down her the runaway train in her mind.

"I've never seen this one of yours," Amanda said, kneeling in front of Elena's second painting. "It's incredible."

Elena shifted, nervous about Amanda's reaction.

"Wait, is this me?"

"Yes."

In the painting, Amanda, age three, dug happily in a garden. Dirt smudged the edge of her pretty yellow dress and her forehead, that she had presumably wiped with dirty fingers.

"Is this in the Tía's garden in Columbia?"

"Yes. You were 'helping.'"

"I barely remember that trip. Tell me about it."

"It was a long time ago. You were only two or three. I'll tell you about it at lunch, if we can get these last few pieces up."

Elena watched her daughter measure the paintings and adjust the hooks, all the while remembering that first trip home with her child. She had asked Carmen to come with her that trip, to introduce Amanda to Columbia.

"Are you sure you want to take her to Santa Maria?" her sister, Carmen, the skeptic, had asked her.

"I want the family to know her."

"And when they notice she's a red-headed white baby?"

"They know she's adopted, obviously."

Carmen's reticence had irked her, giving voice to Elena's own fears. That the aunties would judge the baby as not "really" hers, or comment unfavorably on her ginger curls and her pale skin. That they would sense, somehow, the false front the adoption provided.

"They know I lost a child. They aren't going to question why I adopted."

Despite Carmen's reluctance, she had come along on the trip, enjoying her niece's first sojourn to *la familia*.

∽◯

When the women sat down to lunch, Elena told her the best parts of the trip. "We had four suitcases between us, one for Carmen, one for me, and two for your many outfits! Carmen said you were better dressed than she was."

"That's saying something," Amanda smiled. "Look at me now. Still getting dirty, like in the picture."

"The aunties called you *la muñeca. Little doll.* They cooked for you nonstop."

They made her scrambled eggs with cinnamon for breakfast and gave her warm milk and chocolate every night. They wanted her to sit still while they chatted, cups of tea growing cold on the old table, but they forgave her when she climbed down and set off to explore. In every house they went to, Amanda unearthed things. Yarn from the bottom of the couch, new oranges from the garden, pinecones from the backyard, and coins from her uncle's pocket.

"She's a detective," one Auntie said. "Or a scientist."

"A thief," her uncle said, playfully retrieving his coins while Amanda giggled and ran from him.

"She's brilliant," Elena had said.

"Why am I holding a penny?" Amanda asked now, bringing Elena out of her reverie. "In the picture you painted. Do they even have that coin there?"

Elena thought of all the ways to explain why she had painted a penny in her daughter's hand, the way the unconscious had a way of forcing itself into every work of art. The power of symbolism. The secrets she wished she could wash from her memory.

"Just something you found, I think. Didn't you say you were interviewing someone today? How did that go?"

"Yesterday. Actually, it went really well. I'm lucky this guy is visiting the Bay Area right now." Amanda loved to talk about her research in detail. "Did I tell you about Fort Ross? There's a dig planned for next summer, specifically looking for Kashaya artifacts. I may be able to work it if . . . "

She really is brilliant.

Elena could not help wonder, over the years, as she drove Amanda from Mandarin classes to piano recitals. As she framed the science fair

ribbons and listened to Amanda's senior year speech on the implica-
tions of banning abortion in a developing nation. Was any of this girl's
ambition from her? Or did it evolve from her biological parents' seeds
of brilliance?

Amanda's birth had ripped a hole in the fabric of Elena's expecta-
tions. A child offered to her, like a jewel wrapped in layers of barbed
wire. If she could unravel it, she could start her life over.

"Yes," she had said to her own surprise, when the possibility came.
"I want to be her mother. I want this child." The marriage was so empty
at that point, her voice seemed to echo in its chambers.

That visit to Columbia had been an initiation, a beginning of the
many journeys Amanda would take. Always with the spirit of curiosity.
Digging for fossils in the Mojave Desert, running her tiny fingertips
along the ridges of an oyster shell, collecting stories from strangers on
a European train, gaining knowledge in libraries and museums. And
now she studied anthropology. Part scientist. Part detective.

It thrilled Elena to have such an accomplished daughter but also
made her nervous. Elena didn't want Amanda to dig too hard, for too
long, along the shady pathways of lineage. Didn't want to have to turn
the pages back to the beginning and explain the losses that carved out
room for Amanda in this family. She didn't want to have to tell her
daughter the story she probably most wanted to hear.

Chapter 15

"O thou invisible spirit of wine, if thou hast no name to
be known by, let us call thee devil."

—William Shakespeare, *Othello*

GLORIA'S MIND RACED OVER HER PROBLEMS LIKE A CAR ON A
road full of potholes. Every time she tried to veer away from one, she
fell into another. She inhaled the briny air of the marsh, a bird sanctuary where she drank her morning coffee. Peace, Mama, she told herself.
You came here for peace, and you're stressing about money.

She liked to come here on an occasional morning before work, to
watch the wild birds picking their way through the muddy water. She
had learned their names from a pocket-sized birder's book. The herons
lifted one long leg at a time, pulling their webby feet from the mud,
head down, watching for breakfast in the reeds. Gloria loved the snowy
egrets best. Their downy white heads looked like they needed to go to
the salon for a cut and blow-dry.

She decided to ask Elena for a raise that day. It had been three years
since her last raise, she reasoned with herself. Always prompt, worked
holidays and she never broke things. Well, not many things. She
couldn't tell Elena that she needed the money to get her immigration
issue cleared up. She would say her mother's nursing home was charg-
ing more, her rent was too high, and her ex-husband was a dog. All true.

Gloria said prayers for her intentions, fingering her bracelet with all
the saints. *Lord, let Carlos do better in school. And for my mother to
recognize me the next time I go, and I need a raise. Maybe a good man?*

Miss Joy, Gloria's favorite radio host, said women needed to pray for
the husband they wanted; a good future husband. So, she did. Gloria

sure as hell wasn't praying for Diego. The Scanlons kept coming into her mind as she prayed, as if asking for attention. *La noticia de Dios*, the *whispers*. These feelings had never been indicators of good things.

At the Scanlons' house, Gloria passed the olive trees leaning over the driveway on both sides, the gates opening like magic. She chuckled. *Why have those gates if they let in a car like mine?*

The dogs rushed to her when she came in. She bent down to give them each a pat and to receive a wet lick on the cheek.

Amanda, the only one home, sat on a pillow in the living room with her eyes closed and a candle lit, a new ritual. Many small changes had popped up lately. Spiritual books on the counter, a new statue of Buddha on the back deck. Like they were turning the place into a temple. Maybe that was why their faces had floated up in her mind when Gloria prayed.

Gloria cleaned Mr. Scanlon's room first. Spotless again today. No glass by the bed, no boxers on the floor, and the closet bare. So many of his things seemed to be missing. She knew he had been ill, because she'd seen the bills on the table from the Cancer Center. She wondered for a second if he'd somehow died and she didn't know. *Don't be stupid*. But her heart raced at the thought of something happening to Mr. Scanlon, with his dancing blue eyes and deep voice.

In the kitchen, light flooded through the window, sparkling on the countertops as Gloria washed the dishes with her headphones on. She sang along with Alejandro Fernández and swayed her hips. *Hoy tengo ganas de ti.*

"*Hola Gloria, como estas?*" Amanda breezed into the kitchen, grabbing an apple from the fridge. She stopped near Gloria and gave her a quick hug.

"*Bien, gracias. Tu?*"

"*Bien.*" The apple crunched as Amanda broke into it, and Gloria's stomach spiked with hunger. She should have eaten more for breakfast. Amanda treated Gloria more like a friend than a maid, but Gloria still didn't feel she could stop her work and help herself to an apple. Some things were understood, though never said.

Amanda perched on a bench by the back door, slipping on her dusty riding boots. Lace thong undies peeked out of the top of her riding pants, and Gloria held back a giggle. Lace panties for horseback riding?

"*Hasta luego*," Amanda called as she headed out through the garage. The feeling came back, the *noticia de Dios*, like a cold wind from an open window. Gloria wished she could tell Amanda to stay home today. But Amanda would ask why, and Gloria would have nothing to say.

Despite her warm feelings for Amanda, Gloria wished the girl would stay away from Uriel. After what he'd been through, his heart didn't have the shell around it that a man needed to manage a girl like Amanda, strong-willed and too pretty for her own good.

Grabbing her cleaning supplies, Gloria headed up to Elena's art studio/bedroom. The smell of the paints hit her as she opened the door. The room had a view through the massive glass window of the hills and vineyards. Mrs. Scanlon's bed was in the second room, unmade, a sweater left on the back of the armchair, books and water glasses piled next to the bed.

Who knew why this couple stayed on opposite ends of this enormous house? Maybe having a *casa tan grande* wasn't good if it allowed people to hide from each other.

The soft scent of fabric softener filled the laundry room as she took Amanda's sheets from the dryer, shaking them. She heard the garage door open and shut.

Glad not to be caught daydreaming or on the phone on the day she asked for a raise, she folded the sheets with gusto. But Elena didn't come in right away, and Gloria moved to the living room. She placed all the family pictures in a pile on the sofa while she wiped down the tables and the piano. She liked the smell of the lemon Pledge, the shine of the wood beneath her rag. She arranged the pictures in a semicircle, so the members of the family could keep an eye on one another. She felt nervous, again, but attributed it to the impending conversation, asking for a raise.

Back in the laundry room, Gloria wondered why she hadn't seen Elena. After the car came in, did the woman slip through the house? She usually said hello and chatted with Gloria or made sure Gloria had something to eat.

Gloria heard the car running in the garage. Was Elena going back out? Or was that Amanda's car? Gloria took the last of the rags from the top shelf, listening. She hadn't seen Elena all day. Maybe she was on the phone, finishing a call? But maybe she needed help getting the groceries in?

The door out of the laundry room into the garage squeaked as Gloria opened it, the rubber lip on the bottom rubbing on the floor. The garage was so hazy, at first Gloria thought a broken pipe was spewing gasses. She slammed the door shut and ran to get Amanda.

"Amanda! Come quickly!" But Amanda had left.

Gloria turned back to the door, her heart a wild animal, scrambling. She grabbed a pink towel from the laundry pile to cover her mouth before she opened the door again. The fumes hit her, the car's poisons filling the garage. Would she die from going in there?

Coughing, she groped around for the button that opened the electric garage door. Her eyes teared with fumes and frustration.

Elena's head tilted back, as if napping in the front seat. Gloria found the button on the wall and slammed it with her hand, as if it might take brute strength to open the door, to save them both. It rose with a shudder, the gap growing wider. A sunny patch of grass appeared, then a willow tree's long arms reaching to the ground, and the stone angel statue. Clean fresh air came in, contrasting with the bitter gas.

Gloria stumbled to the shiny Lexus, cursing. *If she is dead, I'll kill her for doing this to me.* She knew it made no sense. A stab of panic pierced her chest; what if the car doors were locked? But no, thank God. She yanked the driver's door open, the bell sounding. She caught Elena as she fell towards her, then reached around her torso to turn the key. *Hurry, turn the damn car off. Stop it from killing us both.*

Elena wore her seatbelt. Like she was going somewhere but forgot to open the garage door and back out. Gloria reached over the woman and snapped the buckle, coughing. She smelled the woman's shampoo even through the fumes, as she embraced her, trying to get a grip around her waist.

Gloria yelled for help, hoping someone would hear her. Her throat burned. She prayed Amanda would come home, or Mr. Scanlon, as she pulled the woman from the car, screaming "Please! Please, help me!"

No one. The neighbors were all so far from one another. She dragged Mrs. Scanlon from the garage. She was light, insubstantial, thin and angular. Gloria thought of the blue heron she'd seen in the morning. Elena's sandal slipped off, and Gloria worried she would cut her feet on the gravel. *Is she even alive?*

Dios mío, please God let her be alive. Santa María, don't do this to me. I cannot let her die. Do not let her be dead. Please God, por favor, Señor. No, no.

Once she reached the grass, she released her burden, dropping her onto the damp ground. She reached for her phone to call 911, then remembered it was in her bag, inside. Should she run to the house? She looked for breathing, for a pulse. Not dead; her body wasn't cold. But not breathing either.

Gloria cursed at God as she bent close, opened the woman's mouth, and listened for even a small breath. *Why me? Señor, why me?*

Nothing. She placed her mouth on Elena's lips, still stained with a bit of coral lipstick. She breathed into the woman, for her, pushed her own breath into her lungs. Maybe she was breathing, a little? She tried to remember the steps. She'd learned them once, years ago, at Carlito's school. All the mothers who volunteered had to learn it. CRP? CPR? What was it called? What did she do first?

A fist under her breastbone, on her white tennis shirt with the tiny sunflowers around the bottom.

Push, Wait? Push, breathe? Push, push, breathe. Were her hands in the right place?

The woman's mouth opened a half inch. Was that a sign? Push, push, put her mouth over the *señora*'s. She forced her breath into her, wondering how this could help. Breathing for someone else? Could it matter? She pushed on her chest again, wanting to force the toxins out.

The *señora* gasped, a drop of saliva dribbling from the corner of her mouth. Gloria cried out, tears running down her face.

"Elena, wake up! Wake up. Please, wake up." She cried harder as the *señora*'s eyes fluttered, and then vomit came, spewing, brown and green, foul smelling vomit all over her tennis shirt and onto Gloria's knees. Gloria turned the *señora*'s head, a moment of clarity. *Turn her head so she does not choke.* She heard someone else gasping and moaning. It was herself. She sat back, stunned, as Elena opened her eyes, her face covered with saliva, sweat and vomit.

"Gloria?"

"Yes, Mrs. Scanlon," she managed to say through the tears, snot and fear.

Elena closed her eyes, her lids lined with an intricate map of tiny wrinkles. She opened them again. "Jesus. Oh God, Gloria. *Lo siento.*" *I'm sorry.* She turned her head away, a deep despairing sound coming from her, like a wounded animal. Her eyes filled with tears and she lifted her hand, her small delicate hand, and wiped the vomit from her chin.

"Oh, Gloria," she said. "*Pobrecita.*" *You poor thing.*

Hours later, Lourdes handed Gloria an open can of beer. "You look like shit, *prima.*"

"Thanks. I feel like shit, too." Gloria took the open can and sat down at the dilapidated picnic table outside the trailer. The night held a chill, the fall slipping away to winter. But Gloria needed fresh air, so they stayed outside.

"Is Uri coming by here tonight?" She needed to talk to Uriel.

"I told him to. After you called me. He'll be by." Lourdes opened cans of chicken broth, pouring them into a wobbly pot on her propane tabletop stove. With Lourdes, it was always like camping.

"You want help?" Gloria asked.

"Cut up those carrots. And maybe that *cebolla*, too."

Gloria hated cutting onions. She cut up the carrots, ignoring the onion for a while.

"What happened at work that makes you want to talk to Uri?" Lourdes eyed her, curious.

Gloria kept cutting, unsure what to say to Uriel. *Amanda's mother is sick. She almost died today.*

Gloria had promised Mrs. Scanlon not to tell anyone. But what if Mrs. Scanlon did it again? Then it would be Gloria's fault, for not telling anyone, or not calling 911. But if she'd called someone, she would embarrass the woman she worked for. She might lose her job. It was all shit either way.

"I don't want to talk about it yet. I should talk to Uri."

"Well, cut the onions, then," Lourdes said, polishing off her beer. She stepped into her tiny trailer and came back with three hard-boiled eggs and two more beers. She rolled the eggs on a paper plate, their fragile shells cracking. She picked off the last sticky white flakes and dropped them into the soup whole.

"You coming to the AA meeting with me tonight? See who's there? That guy Tony asked about you."

"Not tonight."

By the time Uriel climbed out of his truck, smiling as he crossed the ragged patch of grass in front of the trailer, Gloria had downed a second beer. Uriel looked handsome even when tired, his wide smile always reminding Gloria of other family members, in Mexico.

"I heard I was summoned," he said, accepting a beer from Lourdes.

"Let's talk about it after we eat." Gloria felt nervous again.

But Uriel pushed to know a few minutes later, as they slurped up Lourdes' weak soup.

"Is your girlfriend staying home with her mother tonight?" Gloria asked. She had waited outside the Scanlon's house, wishing she could see Amanda drive in, but she had not come.

Uri eyed her over his spoonful of soup. "She's not my girlfriend. I haven't talked to her in a bit. Why?"

Gloria stared at the horizon, thinking. The first stars shone through the deepening dusk. If the *señora* died, she couldn't live with that. Job or no job. Bills or no bills. But without the Scanlons, how would she manage? "Her mother tried to kill herself today."

Uriel dropped his spoon into the bowl, with a clang. "Holy shit. Are you sure?"

Gloria made a noise, a sob caught in her throat. "Of course, I'm sure! You think I'm some kind of *mentirosa*? I wouldn't make something like that up."

"Okay, okay. No one said you made it up," Lourdes said. "*Díganos.* Tell us what happened."

Uriel insisted on hearing every detail.

Lourdes said she was stupid for not calling the police, or 911. "You can't be responsible for these people. Crazy rich lady. Big house, husband making all that money, and she tries to kill herself. What's she want?"

Gloria thought of the empty closet. The cold air in the art studio. "I think she's lonely." *We're all lonely.*

Uriel looked hard at her. "So? You didn't think you should call the police?"

"She said not to. She said it was a mistake; she'd never do that again. She kept saying she was sorry and begged me not to tell her husband or daughter. She said it like—like she'd be so ashamed, she'd try again if I told anyone. She wants to forget all about it."

The three of them eyed their beers, not speaking.

"Maybe she'll be okay," Lourdes said after a minute. "Learned her lesson. You know?"

Gloria nodded, hoping she was right.

Uri took out his phone. "I'll try Amanda, to see if she's home tonight."

"Don't tell her what happened, Uri. If she knows I told—"

Uriel snapped at her. "What do you want me to say, *Tía*? She needs to be with her mother. I'll do my best."

Gloria bit her lip, thinking. She sent prayers to Santa María, Saint Francis, and Jesus. *I don't want to lose this job. Por favor. It's half my income.* "Uri," she said, the beer making her brave, "don't call her." She reached for her purse. "Let's go see them. Let me tell her myself."

Chapter 16

"What though youth gave love and roses, Age still leaves us friends and wine."

—Thomas Moore

WHEN THE DOORBELL RANG AND AMANDA RECOGNIZED URIEL'S truck in the driveway, her heart leapt. Thank God she'd showered that afternoon. She slipped the rubber band from her hair, still damp, as she approached the door, wanting her hair to be down on her shoulders. She licked her lips and opened the door, the dogs tangled around her legs.

But Uriel was not alone. Gloria stood with him, awkwardly, her arms wrapped around herself, as if clinging to the zip-up purple sweatshirt she wore over her jeans. There was something portentous about the visit, Amanda sensed.

Since her father had left two weeks earlier, Amanda had weathered her mother's emotional storms. Elena alternated between unpredictable crying jags, bursts of anger, and then occasional giddiness, as if they had survived the worst.

"I'm getting RSVP's to his birthday party! What do I say?" Elena had screamed one morning, as she brought in the mail. "Should I forward the replies to Victor?" But an hour later Elena worked on her painting, music blaring, and Amanda sensed a calm in the storm.

Her mother cycled through these emotions like a twig caught in a drain, around and around. Still, after the first week, Amanda and her mother settled into something of a rhythm. Her mother went back to tennis or walks with friends in the mornings, Amanda rode Chestnut. In the late afternoon, Amanda worked on her dissertation, writing and rewriting the same pages, while her mother took a nap. They ate dinner out, or ordered in, or shared a salad with whatever they found in the fridge, around seven. Then they binge-watched *Downton Abbey* with a box of chocolates between them.

Life had changed. Dishes piled in the sink on the days between Gloria's visits. Nothing delicious bubbled on the stove, the dogs were stir-crazy for lack of exercise, and the mail sat ignored on the table. The house felt too spacious for them. They used only a few of the rooms, and avoided the places her father's presence could be felt: his bedroom, the study, the dining room table, the Adirondack chair on the back.

It's as if he is dead, Amanda thought once. But we aren't even talking about him. If he were dead, we'd talk about him.

She knew her parents could not avoid each other forever. They needed to sort out papers and finances and the many things that connected them. Eventually, she'd see her father, have lunch with him, and try to find a path in this strange new forest.

Over time, her mother would return to her calmer self, growing basil and rosemary next to the kitchen window for her recipes, heading to San Francisco for a friend's art opening, laughing at a pun. And then, maybe, Amanda could leave again.

She had barely spoken to her father. She only wanted to know that the cancer treatment was working, that he was okay. He said he was. Amanda didn't want to know where he stayed, or whether he was having a high time of it with Victor while she cleaned up his marital mess. She'd encouraged him to tell the truth, but now felt irate about his doing so.

Still, she thought her mother was on a good trajectory, an increment better each day, until Uriel and Gloria arrived that night. The cold air gripped Amanda's bare toes on the doormat as she motioned for them to come in, but they were hesitant.

"What is it?"

"Your mother tried to kill herself today," Gloria said, her voice quieter than usual. She placed her body behind Uriel, as if Amanda might react aggressively.

"What do you mean? Kill herself? What? How . . . ?" Amanda's knees buckled, and her hands flew to her mouth, pain shooting through her heart.

"Today," Gloria's voice was clearer now, "in the garage."

Maybe Gloria had made a mistake, a strange cross-cultural misunderstanding? "My mother's fine. She's inside making dinner."

Amanda had come home to find Elena rattling through the pantry, announcing she wanted to cook "real food" tonight. Perhaps a stew.

Gloria's eyes shown with tears under the front door light and her lower lip trembled.

This makes no sense.

"My mother's fine," Amanda said again. She wanted to go back inside now, to shut the door on them. She regretted the moment of excitement seeing Uriel in her driveway. This was not a love call but a formal call, to inform her of something she couldn't possibly believe.

"Amanda, who's there?" Elena came up behind her, so quiet in her slippers that Amanda didn't get a chance to divert her.

"Oh," Elena said, when she saw them. "Oh, Gloria."

"I'm sorry, Mrs. Scanlon," Gloria said. Her voice cracked, and the tears spilled out of her eyes, wandering down her broad dark cheeks. "I was so worried."

"It's okay," Elena said, after a minute, sounding frightened and yet resigned. "I understand. Come in. *No te preocupes." Do not worry.*

Elena ushered Gloria in, her arm on Gloria's shoulder as if she were the one who had attempted to kill herself only hours before.

With her reaction, the truth sank into Amanda's bones. Her mother had done this. She had wanted to die. Had *tried* to die. When it didn't work, she'd searched the pantry for ingredients for stew. Amanda gasped, as if she couldn't breathe through the shock.

Uriel stepped forward as Amanda reached for a wall to steady herself. She grabbed onto his arm and he embraced her, holding her close for a minute. She buried her face in his chest, inhaling barbeque smoke, pine trees, grapes, and sweat: all the smells of Uriel at once. She clung to him, still in the doorway, afraid to go inside and hear exactly what had transpired that afternoon. Wanting so much for her first assumption about the visit to be true, that he had simply come to see her.

They found Gloria and Elena in the den off the kitchen, each occupying an armchair, not speaking.

"Mom?" Amanda heard her voice cracking and willed herself not to cry. "What happened today?"

Her mother lifted both of her hands. They fluttered like tired butterflies, then returned to her lap. Always graceful, even in this moment of defeat, of wordlessness. "I'm sorry," she said after a moment. "Oh, Amanda, I am so sorry. It was stupid, really stupid. I just . . . I don't even know what came over me."

"But what happened?"

Amanda wanted details, wanted the full truth. Gloria told her, as Elena stared out the window to the dark backyard.

"You left the car running? With the doors closed? So, you really—I mean, this wasn't some accident. You meant to do this?" Somehow this was the most shocking part, the chosen method. Pills could have been an accidental overdose. But this was irrefutable. Suicide.

Bile rose in Amanda's throat. She tried to run but stumbled instead, ended up on her knees, clutching a table, her stomach heaving. The vomit splayed on the mauve carpet. Uriel knelt next to her. He grabbed a towel from Gloria and wiped Amanda's face, then half-carried her to the couch.

She couldn't look into his eyes, some visceral shame coursing through her from vomiting, from the mess her family had created.

Her mother hovered behind him, tears in her eyes. "Sweetheart, I'm so sorry," Elena said again.

"My room," Amanda said, finding it hard to form words, as if drugged. "I want to be alone in my room."

As Uriel helped her to her room, Gloria was already scrubbing the vomit stains. Oh, the irony. *This poor woman probably hates us. She just tries to come to work, to clean our house, and she has to save my mother's life, break the news, clean up the vomit.*

"Gloria," Amanda said, aiming for a tone of seriousness, but afraid she sounded angry. "Thank you. For helping my mother. And for telling me. It was the right thing to do."

Gloria sat back on her haunches. Her dried tears had left tracks on her cheeks. "I'm sorry Amanda, to tell you." She stood, half lurching towards them, and squeezed Amanda in her thick arms.

Later, after crying for what seemed a long time, Amanda lay in bed, curled up around her stomach like a snail. It hurt, a ball of fear burning inside her.

Uriel came in with a cup of chamomile tea. "Your mom made this. I think she's afraid to come in here. I'm staying with her until you want to come out. I don't want to leave her alone."

The words had layers of meaning underneath them. *I don't want her to kill herself. I don't know what she'll do. She is unstable, desperate, crazy.* Amanda thought of asylums in the movies, or psychiatric wards, and wondered what it would be like to take her mother to a place like that.

"What should I do?" she asked.

Uriel sat down on the edge of her bed. "Get her some help."

Of course, that's what she would do. Find a doctor. Call her aunt. Get help. Her hand reached for his, and he squeezed it. As if they had not quarreled weeks before. As if she had a right to this kind of intimacy and support. His fingers traced the edges of her palm, over her rings, gently brushing up her fingers, as if painting them. Her panic subsided some.

"Thank you," she said.

He stared at her, and she wondered what he saw.

"I'll be out with your mom."

Amanda stayed in her room for another hour, Googling *depression, suicide,* and *local psychiatrists.* She called three of them and left messages. She texted her aunt, asking her to call. She avoided going out of her room and seeing her mother. She wanted to tell Elena how much she loved her. Express how sad it was that she had grown so desperate. To be supportive.

But mostly, as the fear ebbed away, anger crawled in. How could her mother do something so impulsive? So rash and selfish?

Amanda brushed her teeth and threw cold water on her face before she forced herself out to the foyer. Gloria had left. Uriel stood by the stove in the kitchen, spooning food onto plates. The stew abandoned, Uriel had made spaghetti. He placed the plates on the table.

We haven't eaten at the dining room table since my father left.

She went to the den and sat next to her mother on the couch.

"Amanda. I'm—"

"I know, you're sorry. I just can't believe—I mean, Mom, you could be dead. Right now. Gone."

Elena nodded, silent tears falling. New wrinkles had appeared around her mouth, and her lips turned down.

"I'll never do that again, I promise you. I knew once I came to how stupid it was."

"You need help."

"Apparently," Elena answered, as if she found the comment obvious, or trite.

Amanda wanted to correct her, to yell, *This is serious, Mom!* She wondered how much she had missed in her mother's mood changes over the last few weeks, whether the hysterical pitch to her voice when she joked about Victor was actually some kind of manic break. Whether her mother had tried before, had been harboring this plan all along.

"Look at me, Mom."

Elena raised her eyes, dark, inscrutable, wiped clean of makeup from the crying.

"Do you promise not to do this again? Swear to God? Never again. This has to be the lowest point, the bottom, the thing that makes you turn around."

Elena took in a breath, her sternum rising above collar of her pale yellow T-shirt. "I promise."

"We'll go see a doctor tomorrow."

Elena nodded. "All right."

"Are you okay for tonight?" *Can I keep you safe?*

Elena wiped her cheek with the back of her hand. "Yes, I'm okay."

They rose, as if they had agreed without saying, to go to the table and eat dinner.

Uriel poured them three glasses of water, but Amanda found a bottle of wine. They ate the simple food—pasta with vegetables and drank the wine, a dry white that tasted watery against the pasta. They searched for topics to talk about that carried no charge.

After dinner, Amanda tucked her mother in on the couch under an afghan. She wasn't ready to let her go to her bedroom alone. She didn't meet her mother's eyes as Elena apologized again; just handed her the TV remote.

"We can figure things out tomorrow, Mom."

"Sweetheart, I promise you, I will be okay. But please don't tell anyone else. I'll get help. Don't call Carmen. She'll rush over and there's no need . . . and please, don't call your dad." Amanda tensed as her mother reached up with surprising quickness, her small hand wrapped around her wrist. "*Mija*, please. I . . . I can't stand to involve him. He'll want to come in, save the day—he'll blame himself. God, please let's not make this worse. I'm asking you to be—discreet."

Amanda almost snapped that the maid already knew, so how discreet was that, but held her tongue. She shook her mother's hand from her wrist, promising nothing. "I'm going to say goodnight to Uriel."

She followed Uriel out to the front porch. "My dad left two weeks ago," she explained. "The night I saw you. When I came home, he was gone. It's been hard. I guess too much for her to take."

"I wish you had called."

Amanda shook her head. "To whine about my parents splitting up? It's so juvenile—to be floored by that. I'm twenty-seven, for God's sake. But it has been harder than I expected. And my mom—well, you see. I thought she was getting better. Hah. Seems ridiculous now."

Uriel sat down on the front steps next to her, close, his breath forming small clouds. She wondered why she wasn't colder in just a sweater. Wine and fear?

"Did she expect this—his leaving? Did you?"

Amanda thought of the layers of secrets that had kept her at a distance. Not just from her family, but from home—from Sonoma, from her life here, from Uriel and old friends. "My dad's in love with someone else."

Uriel looked unsurprised. As if when a man leaves his wife, he's bound to have someone else he's going to.

"He's in love with Victor, his old business partner."

Uriel's eyes widened, and Amanda felt some satisfaction in surprising him. "See, my family is crazy, too."

Uriel put his hand to his chest in mock pain. "Are you saying my family is crazy?"

She laughed. "Sorry. No. Just mine."

"Did you know?" His voice grew more serious. "Or ever . . . suspect? I mean, I don't know your dad well. But—it feels out of character to me. He's so . . . "

"Straight?"

Uriel shook his head. "I don't mean that. More like—a guy who wouldn't do something to hurt his family. He seems so devoted."

"Yes," Amanda said with some bitterness. "I know. He's like the perfect guy. Great Dad, awesome person. He's fun but works super hard, does well. Blah blah . . . yeah. I knew."

"You did? For how long?"

She told him about the night she'd foolishly played spy, following her father while he spent the evening with his lover. How she came home and, unable to sleep or face anyone, had packed her bags to head east.

"That's why you left?"

"Pretty much. I mean, all summer, my anxiety was growing. I realized how easy it would have been for me to stay, to forget grad school and settle down as a horsey girl in Sonoma. I thought I would never really get out from my parents' shadow. But then when I saw him—I don't know. Everything I knew flipped upside down. It's kind of horrifying how much of your identity is your parents. Who they are or who you think they are. I couldn't make sense of it."

She was talking too much, revealing everything. Her own story sounded awkward and strange. But it was such a relief. She should have told Uriel. Why had she run away? She should have confronted her father then, not five years later. Things could not have been worse for her mother than they were now, it seemed.

Uriel reached for her hand, and she felt a physical tension, like a tightening rope. She'd wanted him back for so long, wanted whatever she could take—friendship, sex, or love. Amanda wanted to memorize the lines on his face when he was thinking, to watch the flicker of passion when he rode horses, to feel the heat coming off him at the end of the day. She squeezed her arms close to her sides, to keep from grabbing him and begging him to take her back. Her mother's actions had left her vulnerable.

"Will you be all right tonight?" Uriel asked, as if sensing her growing anxiety.

"I think so. I'll make her sleep with me. And find a doctor in the morning."

"Can you call me tomorrow to let me know how you're doing? Or should I call you?"

"Yes." She could cry again. Instead she kissed him before the tears could start. Kissed him hungrily, reaching for him and pulling him towards her. Wine, garlic, the taste of his mouth, of saliva and memories and longing. He responded, wrapping his arms around her. She switched to his face, peppering it with small kisses, crying as she ran her hands through his hair, holding back sobs as he lifted her into the truck and let her kiss him again and again.

"I was so happy to see your truck at first." Her voice sounded edgy, and she felt grateful for the darkness. "I thought you were here because you wanted to see me." She wiped her nose, swallowed tears, and buried her face in his collar bone. "I thought," she said, sounding frustrated with herself, "that you came to court me. To woo me back. But instead you needed to tell me about my mother, and now I'm attacking you."

He brushed her hair away from her eyes and made her sit up and look at him, deep into his eyes. He reached out and traced the outlines of her face, touching her brows, her lips, and her damp cheeks. "I do want you, and to woo you."

She laughed and rested her head on him for another delicious minute, aware she'd left her mother alone for too long, that she needed to go inside.

"Woo me tomorrow?"

"I will. I'll call. Just hang in there. She'll be all right, I think."

Amanda untangled herself from his limbs and climbed down from the truck. She waved goodbye, and tried to hold his kisses and promises close, to guard against the fear. She'd recently experienced this feeling for the first time, when her father called to say he had cancer, and now it returned, tenfold. The fear of losing someone she loved, a recognition of their fragility.

But now the fear had sunk down, a knife plunging deeper. She could have lost her mother in the worst way possible. And it would have been preventable, if Amanda had been paying closer attention. Even Uriel's attentions couldn't soften it. She could have lost her mother today, to have failed in the worst way.

Chapter 17

"Give me women, wine, and snuff
Until I cry out 'hold, enough!'
You may do so sans objection
Till the day of resurrection;
For, bless my beard, then aye shall be
My beloved Trinity."

—John Keats, "Women, Wine, and Snuff"

URIEL AND CAT BLAKELY OF AUSTIN, TEXAS, HAD DEVELOPED A surprising habit of talking every day or two. He liked the cadence of her words, her easy empathy, and her even drawl.

They both wanted to know more about the other's experience. But they would also compare the weather, wine, and raising horses in Texas versus California. One day she asked him about the way wine was made, and he asked her if you really ran into armadillos on the road there. Eventually, they always returned to the topic that connected them: the details of their shared loss. But at that point, Uriel often chose to wrap up the call.

"Did you have to use her death certificate to get out of your wife's cell phone contract?"

"Yes. It was awful, fighting with Verizon about proving her damn death."

"Those people are creeps, aren't they? The worst. I kept saying to the girl, just Google it, it's in the goddamn paper. He died in a car crash. No, I had to send them an actual death certificate. Did you have to fight with the banks, too?"

"No. Flavia didn't really have any money."

"Well, that's too bad. Did you get any life insurance?"

"No. We didn't have any."

"Course not. You're just kids. Who buys life insurance that young? Oh, Uriel."

He heard her moving around, water splashing in the background, and pictured her next to a fountain.

Saturday morning had come at last. Uriel stretched out on his couch with a half-finished egg sandwich perched on his stomach and coffee cooling by his side.

She went on, "You ready to talk about them? How well they knew each other and all?"

Them. Flavia and Carson. The death mates.

"No. I doubt there's much more to say. We aren't even sure they met before that day."

"They did."

Uriel sat up, the sandwich sliding. "How do you know?"

"I told you, he'd been going to Sonoma for a few months, looking at properties, and cars. Always acquiring something."

"That doesn't mean he and Flavia were together."

"I asked about the cell phone thing for a reason. I still have all his information. His contacts, texts, emails. That stuff never really goes away. Also, I knew from the credit card he'd been buying things. A pair of ladies boots—Nine West, size eight—too big for me. A dozen roses sent to the hotel in Sonoma before he arrived. And then some jewelry. Just shit he could have gotten any of his girls, I guess."

"I didn't notice any new jewelry." Uriel rubbed his palms down his sweat pants. He didn't want to hear that Flavia knew this guy before that day. In his mind, she'd made an impulsive choice, not months of lies. But something nagged at him.

Did Flavia get new boots before she died? Would he remember?

He moved to the closet as Cat kept talking, digging past his jackets and old shoes. Jesse had taken most of Flavia's things, but a few items remained. A pair of slippers, sweatpants, a leather jacket. No boots.

Cat sounded ready to let it go. "Well, anyway, let's just say he was courting someone."

Uriel sat on the floor, feeling a shred of guilt over the search. "She didn't have new boots or jewelry. He must have been seeing someone else."

"And she got in the car with him because?"

"A dumb mistake. That's all. It's not like we had the perfect marriage. I told you, the relationship was up and down. But she loved me, and we were having a baby." He hadn't told her that before.

"You were? When was the baby due?"

"January." The lump in his throat grew. Over the last few months, the ache he used to feel when he thought of Flavia had dissipated. It returned when he thought of the baby.

"Wasn't she drunk, too? That day? Why would she be drinking if she was pregnant?"

Cat Blakely would make a good detective, he thought, suddenly weary of her calls. She prodded, making more of things than they needed to.

"I think it was just a really bad day."

He hung up a few minutes later, relieved, but sorry for being short with her.

He glanced at the phone to make sure he hadn't missed a call from Amanda. He hadn't seen her since the night of her mother's suicide attempt. She'd been immersed in doctors' appointments and pharmacy visits, making meals and constructing some sort of "schedule" for her mom. She had called him the last three nights, exhausted and not very talkative. He wanted to see her but did not go.

The night he'd been there with Gloria he had a feeling of crisis-driven camaraderie, an unexpected invitation to be part of the family. Making spaghetti and bringing her mom tea felt good. When he came home, still feeling Amanda's kisses, hope coursed through him. He couldn't sleep. His mind returned to the idea of being Amanda's lover over and over, like a thirsty animal to the drinking hole.

But by morning he switched, worried it was a mirage. Doubts had circled him that day. Could he really get involved with a woman who might fly away again without warning?

On the phone, in the evenings, her voice seemed cooler and distant. The familiar feeling of detachment had returned, the intimacy ebbed away in the daylight.

"Mom's going to see the psychiatrist three times a week right now, plus medications."

As he listened to Amanda's attempt to save her mother, her frantic comparisons of Lexapro and Wellbutrin, her debate over yoga versus aerobic exercise, he felt himself detach. There was no room for him in these plans, no role. This wasn't his family. He and Amanda were probably friends with blurry lines at best; and wooing her, as he'd jokingly promised to do, felt inappropriate in the face of her growing responsibilities.

Besides, exhaustion had taken over his mind. Things hadn't slowed down at the winery or the stables. His aunt was having a poor week. Her limbs were betraying her and her pain increased, which meant someone always had to be at the house. He was needed here, and being needed was like a drug for him. It settled him, motivated him, and made it easy to avoid any distractions.

He shook off his Saturday morning malaise and threw a pot of water on for more coffee to get his brain pumped up for the day. Out the kitchen window, he saw two wild turkeys make their way out of a knoll of bay trees behind the vineyard. They roamed freely in Sonoma but didn't usually come so close to the winery, as the dogs chased them off. The sun was coming through the morning fog, light filling the vineyard. Uriel decided to get a nice long ride in today.

A knock on the door surprised him. *Amanda?*

Gloria stood on his doorstep. Dressed in jeans and a Beyoncé T-shirt, she carried a vacuum and a mop.

"*Tía!* What's up?" He smelled a waft of hairspray as he gave her a hug.

"I'm here to clean the house."

She had not been here in years, since Lourdes remained unwelcome. Not that Gloria wasn't welcome. Freddie had a soft spot for Gloria. Maybe Freddie had hired Gloria?

"Up the hill, you mean? At Freddie's place?"

"No. Your place. Your mother said she's sure it's a mess. No one's cleaned it since Flavia died, right?"

Uriel shook his head, annoyed at Lourdes flapping her lips. "Not true. I clean it up once in a while."

"Well, I came to help you clean it up some more."

They stood in the doorway. "Come on in. But I'm not going to let you clean my house, Gloria. Do you want a cup of coffee?"

"Your mom would do it, but she's not allowed over here, I guess?"

"Freddie's not a fan of my mother."

Gloria shrugged. "Lourdes is not for everybody." She dropped her things in the living room and scanned the room as if analyzing what needed to be done

"Did my mother put you up to this? Why does she want my house clean?"

Gloria, adamant, headed towards the kitchen. "It was my idea." She caught her breath when she discovered the dishes piled on every surface.

"It's the crush," Uriel felt a need to explain himself. "I work long hours right now."

Gloria looked at him. "It's fine, Uri. I just wanted to thank you for helping me last week. I didn't get fired, and I'm glad that Amanda knows what happened. I don't know what I would have done without you that night." She surveyed the kitchen. "If Amanda came over here, she might never go out with you again."

She turned the water on in the sink, and started to search the counter. "You have any dish soap?"

The pile of dishes towered a foot high. Maybe he did need some help? "No. I ran out of soap. That's why the dishes aren't done."

"A month ago?"

He smiled. "Not that long. I can run up and borrow some from Maya."

"Go. I'll start in the living room."

When he returned with the soap, Gloria was vacuuming the rug, which was long overdue. His vacuum died a year ago, and he never replaced it. He scraped dried food from the dishes into the overflowing garbage, thinking about what the house must look like to Gloria. Like a teenaged boy lived here. Five boys, maybe. He needed to do better.

"You want all these things?" Gloria held up two sweaters and a women's coat.

"Are you cleaning out the bedroom closet?"

She nodded. "I was looking for a place to put the vacuum. I'll leave it here. It's an old one."

"You don't need to do all this, *Tía*. The other night was no big deal. I was glad to be there for Amanda."

"You and Lourdes are all the family Carlos and I have here, Uriel. Lourdes is more like a sister than a cousin. Let me help you out."

He found it painful that she relied on Lourdes as family.

"You want these clothes, still?" Gloria asked. She held up a worn leather coat, a caramel color. He had liked it on Flavia. She wore it the day they went to the ob-gyn for her sonogram. Afterwards they talked about baby names. Later that night they fought. She wanted to have a beer, and he'd refused her.

"No, let's clean it out. Do you want any of these things?"

Gloria considered it. "No, they won't fit me. Flavia was taller than me." He didn't point out that everyone was taller than her.

"Give them to Goodwill then."

As his aunt collected the clothes and stuffed them in a bag, he observed his own inner emotional compass. No anguish. Some anger? Mostly empty, as if he had dreamed about a marriage to Flavia and was just waking up.

Gloria attacked the next closet, sorting out Flavia's clothes, folding his, making a pile of sheets, one of towels. He marveled that she had established order in such a short time. He went back to washing dishes. He liked having someone else in the house while he worked. He opened the window, breathing in the fall air.

"Uriel," Gloria called from the other room. "I'll take that coffee now."

He brought it to her in a freshly washed mug, black. "Milk's gone," he said. "Sorry. You want me to run up to Maya's?"

Gloria laughed. "Is Maya like your 7-Eleven? Poor lady! No, I can drink black. You got sugar?"

"I put in two spoons."

"Good. Hand me those shirts, and we'll hang them on this side."

Uriel helped her reach things higher in the closet. He smiled when they both reached for something—her head came to his chin—she couldn't possibly reach things up top.

"Are you laughing at me, Uriel?"

"No, I'm in awe of your skills. It's like a new closet."

He asked about Carlos, whom he hadn't seen since Labor Day when they had gone to the beach together.

"He's all about skateboarding this week. He looks like a man to me now. So tall. He's kind of a pig like you. Maybe it's genetic."

Two more hours passed before she was done. The kitchen tidy, floor washed, the dining room table gleaming from her polishing. Uriel promised he'd put the sheets back on the bed when they came out of the dryer; she didn't need to wait around. "I'm not completely helpless, Gloria."

She raised her hands as if pointing to evidence of the contrary.

"Can I pay you?"

"Shut up, Uriel." She bundled up her supplies and dropped the empty cup in the sink. "Wash that—don't leave dishes in the sink or they pile fast."

They stood in the kitchen, Uriel feeling embarrassed and grateful at once. "I owe you one."

"You should have Amanda over now and show her your beautiful house. Look at that view."

He thought of the last time Amanda came, the awkward conversation, the abrupt goodnight. "Maybe. We aren't—I'm not sure what's happening there. We're from different worlds."

"I know. I thought it was a bad idea for you to date her." She put one hand on her chest. A bracelet with saint medals dangled from her wrist. "But then, the other night, I changed my mind. You're a good friend for her. She needs you right now."

"I don't know if she could be satisfied, in the long run, with someone—like me."

Gloria's eyes scanned the horizon. "I know what you mean. But maybe she could. Maybe you should bring her to meet your mom. Find out how she does."

Uriel shuddered at the idea of bringing a girl home to his mother. "Lourdes?"

Gloria's eyes grew more excited about the idea. "Yeah. I mean, then you would know for sure. You can see what Lourdes thinks of her. I know she's met Amanda, but she hasn't really talked to her. Lourdes' good at figuring out people, you know. She knew Diego was a rat the first time she met him. Anyway, Amanda should know your mother, and your . . . life as a kid. If that doesn't work, then don't keep dating her. Listen Uriel, you made one mistake with Flavia. Sorry, but it's true. This time, let Lourdes weigh in. And let Amanda see who you are. See if it fits."

Uriel couldn't argue with her logic. He had rushed into things with Flavia, and it had been a poor match.

Gloria placed a hand on his shoulder, giving him a final bit of advice before she left. "But listen, Papa, you're not getting any younger. So get going already. If not Amanda, someone else. Don't spend your life with just horses."

Chapter 18

> "There is not the hundredth part of the wine consumed in this kingdom that there ought to be. Our foggy climate wants help."
>
> —Jane Austen, *Northanger Abbey*

"I KEEP ASKING MYSELF, WHAT WAS I THINKING? HOW COULD I have done something so drastic?" Elena's hands were tucked in her sweater pockets and still she had a chill.

"And what does your self say back?" the doctor asked Elena.

Amanda had found Dr. Love—that really was his name—the day after Elena's suicide attempt. An older man who rotated brown jackets and faded sweater vests, his calm demeanor reassured Elena.

"Nothing clear. I barely remember the week leading up to my . . . accident. I just had this anxiety, all the time. I would wake up and be shaking."

"You were very scared."

"And angry. I kept thinking of the lies he had told. Wondering what else I didn't know. Hating myself for being naïve. And the feelings kept growing, getting so intense I couldn't stand to be in my body."

"That is the 'flooding' we talked about."

"Right."

Dr. Love made her feel almost normal, and fixable. He told her, in a calm and warm voice, that the medicine would help soon.

The first meeting, Dr. Love had given Elena two choices: hospitalization, or strict adherence to the doctor's plan. The plan included herbs and vitamins that she tasted in the back of her mouth all day, medications that made her sleepy, meditation, yoga classes, individual therapy two or three times a week, and volunteering.

What is worse? The side effects from the medications, talking about her life to a stranger, or volunteering in a nursing home?

The tight schedule kept Elena going from activity to activity. She had started to cherish the one hour alone between therapy and yoga class.

"This is insane," Elena said when she first reviewed the schedule that Amanda had typed up neatly.

"No, Mom. Sitting in a car while it fills up with carbon monoxide is insane. This is what you do instead."

Amanda always had a way of putting things, like a chainsaw, cutting right to the core of matters.

"How did your meditation and yoga class go this week?" Dr. Love asked her, reviewing his notes.

"I don't think I'm a very good Buddhist. I hate sitting still. And yoga hurts my shoulders."

"You could try an alternative exercise."

"Maybe I'll go back to tennis." Elena could feel the racket in her hand, reaching high and connecting with the ball with a satisfying thwack.

"We both agreed you needed to change your routines," he pointed out. "And the cast of people you interact with."

True. The women at the club made her cringe. The forced look of concern about Jim's departure, hushed voices, and flawless faces. She could swat them with her racquet.

Dr. Love stared at her. The light from a side window reflected off his glasses. "You said Amanda asked you to go riding? Horse riding can be therapeutic."

"Horseback riding reminds me of Jim." Early on, Jim had helped her up onto a small Bay, then rode with her on the dunes near Santa Cruz. He knew she would be safe there—a fall would be onto pillows of white sand.

"In fact, we went horseback riding the day he proposed."

"Tell me about that."

They had come up to Sonoma for the weekend, just the two of them, escaping the city.

"He had it all planned out. Horses from a local stable, a picnic in his backpack." She laughed, dryly. "He said we would live in Sonoma some day, ride horses, and drink wine. I was swept away by his romantic gestures."

"Jim sounds very dramatic."

She agreed. Riding would be too tricky, like she could slip right off the horse into the abyss of her past. "I'll try yoga again."

Dr. Love moved on to other topics, recording her optimism on a scale of one to ten, her mood, and her sleep pattern. He showed her the chart, with its promising subtle upswing. "What do you *want* most, Elena?" Dr. Love asked as the session wound down.

Elena's mind went back to the morning after the attempt. She had found Amanda crying. When Elena tried to comfort her, Amanda screamed, "How could you do this? You would have just *left* me?"

Elena couldn't explain to her daughter that in her muddled brain, she didn't really want to die. She had just wanted the nightmare to end.

"I want Amanda to forgive me," she said. "For things to be like before."

"Before?"

"Before Jim told me, or before the cancer . . . just before." Before he announced he fell in love with a man; before he packed his things in suitcases and boxes and left.

"Things can't go back to before, Elena. What do you want now?"

Elena wanted to give him an answer. But the question loomed, vague and unwieldy.

"One thing," he clarified. "Tell me one thing you want, off the top of your head. Don't think too hard—even something small."

"Hot chocolate," she blurted. She felt silly, but she had been craving it for days.

"Okay, good," Dr. Love responded, smiling. "That one's easy. Go get some."

After leaving Dr. Love's office, Elena strolled through the Sonoma Square, trying to enjoy the moment. It centered the town, with two playgrounds, city hall, and a small crowded duck pond. Shops and restaurants lined all four sides. The Portuguese pastries at the Basque

Café were legendary. She sipped the thick hot chocolate with tiny marshmallows floating on top. The best depression antidote so far.

Carmen texted to say she had to skip coffee as they had planned, a homeowner was making her life difficult.

No problem, Elena texted back.

Finally, a few minutes alone.

Amanda had agreed not to tell Carmen what had happened, as long as Elena stuck to Dr. Love's plan.

Her sister, a font of encouraging advice since Jim's departure, would not understand Elena's despair. Carmen had always managed her own adulterous husbands without going over the deep end. Even as a teen, in the face of their own father's adultery and mistreatment, Carmen had stayed strong.

On an impulse, Elena stopped at the Mission, the buildings and church built in the early 1800's, on the corner of the square. Amanda had volunteered here one summer, bringing home historical anecdotes each evening about the local Indians that had been forced to build and work at the Mission. When Elena brought her lunch one day, Amanda had showed her around. Elena remembered many of the details, because they came from her daughter's mouth. She learned that the first vineyard in Sonoma had been planted there at the Mission, under General Vallejo.

"He later stole the vines he planted," Amanda explained, "when he lost the battle. He re-planted them in his own vineyard. Really, this is where it all began. If he hadn't been a viticulturist and planted his vines here . . . well, who knows?"

Elena went directly to the chapel, after paying her three-dollar entrance fee. Its solid thick walls and colorful Spanish style altar made her think of her family's church in Columbia. At one end of the long narrow room, Elena stopped and enjoyed the authentic wooden statue of Mary, looking very Spanish with a red mantilla over her head. Although Elena was no longer religious, she prayed. She believed there was some type of being in the heavens who listened.

"I'm sorry," Elena said to whomever was listening above—Mary, God, the angels and the saints. "I'll keep trying. I won't give up. Help me not give up, ever again."

She rested on a bench outside by a dried fountain. Memories of Columbia, as detailed as the stone tiles on the ground, filled her mind.

The memories had stayed buried for years. When she met Jim, his solidity had made her believe her painful past remained just that—a past. That her family's dysfunction was cultural or geographic—a pattern she could escape. Her life in Sonoma was so drastically different from Columbia, it was as if she had shifted not just countries or hemispheres, but universes.

Elena's mother, all the aunties agreed, had chosen poorly when she married Elena's father. Her mother had to work long hours at menial jobs, but they never had quite enough. Their tiny house had no screens on the windows and was missing a front step, her neighborhood prone to late night shots in the darkness.

Her father shifted in and out of their lives, less predictable then the weather. When he lived with them, he ate the largest piece of fish, left the bathroom a terrible smell, and insisted the windows be open at night for the breeze, despite the mosquitos that bit the girls. He never stayed more than a few months. Then he would go out for a drink and disappear.

One day, a girl at school with a pug nose and a hairy upper lip told Elena that her father had moved into the girl's house. "He is my father now, not yours," the girl said smugly.

Elena's blood boiled with humiliation. Her hand lifted almost on its own accord and slapped the girl's face. When the girl started to wail, Carmen appeared beside them and clamped her hand over the girl's mouth.

"Shut up," Carmen said, her voice a harsh whisper. "You can keep our father with his shitty farts." Carmen dragged Elena away in a firm grip. Elena remained stunned by her own reaction. She could still feel the girl's soft cheek where she had slapped it.

Within a few weeks, their father returned.

Her parents continued their on-and-off drama for years. He would show up, they would drink and fight. The girls would hear their mother crying, and his voice murmuring, then the two of them screwing in the living room, too loud. Carmen would pull the covers over them, cocooned from their parents' squeals. Elena hated her father more each time he convinced their mother to forgive him.

Finally, one day, Elena's mother changed the locks. Her father pounded on the front door, cursing at them, while the girls and their mother watched the TV in the only bedroom. Elena's mother's hands shook as she drank a warm beer.

"Do not open that door," her mother said to them, her jaw set in a new way. So they didn't. It wasn't long before he came back. A few weeks later, their mother was dead.

Elena wished she had asked her mother what finally made her change the locks. Most of all, she wished that the locks had held.

Chapter 19

"Wine enters through the mouth,
Love, the eyes.
I raise the glass to my mouth,
I look at you,
I sigh."

—William Butler Yeats, "A Drinking Song"

CHESTNUT GRAZED IN THE PASTURE WHEN AMANDA ARRIVED, morning sun shining on her deep brown coat. She chased a younger mare playfully and Amanda watched from the fence with delight, gratitude, and something like longing coursing through her. This animal had meant so much to her, every summer home from college, especially the year after college.

The mare came to the fence before Amanda called her, crossing the tall grasses with light, graceful steps, mane lifting in the wind. Amanda ran her hand over her warm, damp neck. The horse's wide eyes sparkled, stones shining under water.

"Let's ride, sweetness."

Amanda's confidence soared once mounted on a horse, her hair swept up under her helmet, her back arched. She leaned forward as Chestnut cantered down the path. It hadn't rained enough, the California drought made obvious by the empty reservoirs and acres of dry, dead grass. Sweat pooled at the base of Amanda's back, her jeans growing damp. She wiped a bug off her cheek.

The hills on both sides of the path had grown brown from lack of water. She wondered, as they passed a vineyard, how the grapes would fare. She let Chestnut rest at a stream, reduced to a small trickle. In the winter when her hands were cold she dreaded grooming her, but today they would both enjoy it, the cool water from the hose a welcome reprieve.

She checked her phone by habit, surprised to see a text from Uriel: **Long shot, but can you come on over for dinner, about 7?**

Amanda leapt back on the horse, thinking about whether her mother would be all right alone for the evening. Maybe she could subtly ask Carmen to come over? She would figure it out.

The first stars twinkled above soft low clouds over the valley when Amanda knocked on Uriel's door. She waited on his rough doorstep, next to his muddy boots. She could hear music playing in the house and, after a minute, let herself inside. A tantalizing mixture of fragrances hit her—something rich and delicious in the oven, crisp fall air through the open back door, and something else. The smell of a clean house? A waxy lemon scent.

The coffee table in the living room shone, no plates or cups piled on it. A vacuum had made clean lines across the rug, and the books in the corner were stacked neatly. A vase on a wooden table by the side window held fresh flowers.

"Uriel?"

Uriel leaned on the railing of the back deck, the kitchen lights shining on him in the gathering dusk. His head tipped as he talked on the phone. Her heart took an extra beat, his proximity like a drug that sped her up. He waved and hung up as she stepped outside.

"Hey," he said, moving closer. His hair looked trimmed, and he wore a teal button-up shirt—new, not frayed like most of his shirts—a crisp linen. Had she ever seen him dressed this way before?

Amanda wished she'd taken more time to get ready herself. She'd run out the door in jeans and a loose blouse as soon as Carmen arrived. She crossed her arms against the night's chill. "I let myself in—I don't think you heard me knocking." Standing three feet away from Uriel, but not touching him, was like being next to a pool she couldn't drink from after days in the desert.

He leaned in and kissed her cheek, his face smooth and shaven. "Sorry, I was on the phone."

She wanted him to kiss her on the mouth, not the cheek, to grab her and hold her as he had the other night. But the awkwardness had returned between them. As if their late-night confessions in the truck hadn't happened.

"Who were you talking to?" she asked, and then wondered if that was prying.

Uriel half smiled but didn't meet her eyes. "A friend. Come on in."

Amanda wondered if the friend was a woman. "I'm sorry I'm a little late." She followed him through the kitchen door, the screen squeaking on its hinges.

He glanced at the clock as they entered the kitchen. Eight o'clock, an hour later then they'd planned.

"I didn't realize how late I was. I'm really sorry, Uri. It's hard to get out the door right now. I waited for Carmen."

His voice held a cool note. "I thought you weren't coming."

The words startled her. "Why?"

He took two wine glasses from the shelf, his eyes on the wine as he poured. "I don't know—just not used to you being late. You're usually on time. Or maybe you do run late, and I forgot. But—I thought maybe you changed your mind."

She shook her head, feeling flustered. "I had to wait for my aunt. I don't want to leave my mom alone yet."

He nodded. "That makes sense."

"But I should have called." She wanted warmth, not wariness. Shit, she'd blown this. In the midst of the drama with her mother, thoughts of Uriel kept her going. That he seemed interested in her again. That he answered her calls, even late at night, fatigue in his voice. That she could be in his arms again soon. "Uriel, I wouldn't change my mind. About dinner. Or us. I was so glad you invited me."

His shoulders fell. "It was a long hour. I didn't know what to expect."

"I guess I don't have a great track record."

The enormity of what it would take to earn back his trust settled on her like a heavy wet blanket. She took a long drink of the wine. Red, earthy, something delicious as usual. She reached up and touched his hair. "I like the haircut."

His smiled. "Overdue."

She felt a shift in the air between them, and a drop of hope bubbled up. "Something smells amazing. Which is good, because I'm really hungry."

"Mole. Maya's recipe."

"Wow, you've been busy. Cooking and cleaning."

He rocked on his heels, then shrugged, as if confessing. "Jesse made the mole dish earlier for the house. I stole some and put it in the oven. She told me to pretend I made it, but I'm a terrible liar."

Amanda grinned. "I couldn't cook that either. And the cleaning?"

His smile grew wider, even as his eyes looked embarrassed. "I had some help this morning. That's why I asked you over, to enjoy the clean house before I destroy it again."

She laughed and pointed at the Esperanza wine bottle on the table, open. "Well, did you make the wine yourself at least?"

"Sure. Just don't tell Freddie I'm taking the credit."

He reached out and pulled her in for a kiss, a real one this time, slow and smooth. She ran her hands over his back, her fingers grabbing the pressed shirt. The kiss went on for so long, she thought she might faint, but she wouldn't break away. She dropped her purse onto the floor. They stumbled to the wall, as if they needed to brace themselves from the longing that flooded through them.

"Sorry again about being late," she whispered.

"Sorry I freaked out," he answered. He led her through the tiny hall, her hip bumping boxes stacked in the corner, into the bedroom. A worn quilt covered his bed, which filled most of the small room. A wide window gave the room a touch of spaciousness. Amanda remembered waking up here in the mornings, sunlight flooding the valley. She'd imagined being back here so many times. Standing here now, she had a sense of dreaming. She'd convinced herself for years she could not go back, that Uriel was the treasure she'd lost, unrecoverable.

He pulled her onto the bed, and she kicked off her boots. They lay facing one another for a moment. Dimly lit from the hall light, his dark eyes were hidden in the shadows.

"I missed you," she said, her voice husky, holding back tears. Emotions welled up inside her like a river.

"Don't cry," he said and kissed her again, holding her closer. "Let's make a pact not to cry tonight."

She agreed. They peeled off one another's clothes, urgently as if afraid the moment would pass, that one of them would change their minds. He kissed her neck, her chest, each breast. She heard herself gasp, her body moving, pulling him towards her. Once naked, they played, slipping and tumbling like otters in the ocean. He floated above her, and then she climbed onto him, slipping him inside her, leaning over to suck on his lip, hungrily, as he thrust. Go deeper, she wanted to say, go so far in you cannot leave. Stay in me.

But he gasped and shuddered, too soon.

"Sorry," he said sheepishly. "It's been a while."

The words were a subtle reminder of what he had been going through—being widowed, alone. She didn't want to think about that, about anything in their past. She touched the bruise on his arm around the horse bite. He'd told her about Belle's fierce bite, but she hadn't really seen the purple and blue marks on his upper arm.

"That horse is a bitch," she said.

He gave her an elusive smile. "She has her moments. The owner, Noah, has started taking lessons. So maybe he's going to take her back. But he's a terrible rider, so far."

"Are you upset? That Belle might leave?" She knew he loved that horse and cared for it obsessively. Everyone at the stables could see that.

He didn't quite meet her eyes. "We'll see. Do you want to eat?"

"Can we have sex again first?"

He laughed. "I forgot about this. How insatiable you can be. Yes, definitely."

She grinned. "I'm not insatiable. That was two minutes."

He hushed her with a finger on her lips. He kissed her toes, nibbling on her pinky toe in a way that made her giggle. God, she'd missed this side of him, this playfulness that came out only here, in bed, naked. Like a child, discovering a new world, he moved up her body, touching, kissing, licking, teasing. His fingers played near her clitoris lightly, like a soft melody on a piano, making her wild with wanting. By the time he entered her again, it was her turn to cry out. She came hard, her body rocking, a throaty burst of praise bubbling up from her. "Yes, yes. Uriel, oh my God."

He traced her body lightly with his fingers while she recovered, examining her closely.

"Okay, I know this scar," he touched the half-moon on her chin, "is from falling off Chestnut as a kid. How about this?" He pointed to a scar across her knee.

"Skied right into a post at the bottom of the mountain, in Vermont. About three years ago."

"Ouch. Glad I missed that one. And these?" She had two large bruises, one on her shin and one on her thigh.

"I fell down the steps from my mom's studio. Yesterday? No, a couple days ago. My brilliant idea to move her stuff downstairs and get her settled in my dad's room. Take back her space. I slipped, with all the boxes in my hands."

"I could have helped you move that stuff."

"I wasn't going to take you away from work this time of the year. And I thought I had it."

"Hard fall?"

She remembered the pounding in her chest when she'd missed a step, the slow-motion tumble. When she'd finally settled at the bottom, she'd burst into tears. Cursing, for the first time, her father.

Her mother had brought her an ice pack and soothed her as Amanda railed against her "fucking selfish father." For a few minutes, the roles had been reversed, mother caring for daughter. Order restored, briefly.

"That was a crappy day. It's been only crappy days this week."

"Not today." He leaned down and kissed her stomach lightly, and she moaned in pleasure, but stopped him.

"Let's eat. We need nourishment!"

"Not yet."

His hands massaged her thighs and inched upwards, his mouth on her belly. She let herself succumb to the giddy feelings still sprouting her body. Instead of feeling like she had desire, it was as if desire had her. As if the sex had an energy of its own and wouldn't let them go until their bodies were joined.

Afterwards, they lay spent, his leg tossed over hers, the bedclothes thrown to the floor, stains on the fresh sheets.

"We needed to do that about a month ago," she said. Then, sitting up, breasts slick with sweat, "And I'm ravenous."

"Good thing I cooked," he murmured, sounding tired.

"Good thing you have a cousin who cooks for you."

Amanda stepped into the shower, running the water quickly over her body, wanting the sweat and juices off. She looked up and saw him standing in the doorway, smiling.

"You look pretty happy with yourself," she said.

"Three times! At my age? I should be."

"You're twenty-nine, Uriel. Not exactly an old man."

"Thirty at the end of the month."

She knew that. Remembered celebrating his birthday one Halloween, years ago. She took a towel from the stack, folded like a scalloped shell. It looked familiar.

"Hey. Did Gloria fold this? Wait, did she clean your house?"

He threw up his hands, looking embarrassed, as he stepped into the steamy shower. "She insisted! As a favor. I guess my mother convinced her I needed domestic assistance."

"You did need it. I recognize the way she folds the towels. Like little fans."

The water sprayed on muscles of his shoulders, running over his ass. He took his head out of the spray. "It's weird that my mother's cousin cleans your house."

She thought about the stark differences in their lives splayed out in this statement. "It's weird that she cleans yours, too," she said finally.

Uriel appeared satisfied with this answer, for now, and she went to find one of his T-shirts to wear with her underwear. She wanted to stand in his kitchen in his clothes, eating the food he'd placed in the oven. She couldn't stay and leave her mother alone overnight, but for a few minutes she could pretend to be at home here.

In the kitchen, she looked for plates and silverware, refilling her wine glass. His phone lay on the counter, a new text message notification across the screen. She glanced, knowing she shouldn't. A name she didn't recognize. Cat Blakely.

Cat? Amanda tried to think of someone named Cat, Catherine, Cathy. Someone Uriel had mentioned. A cousin? He had a lot of cousins, but Cat Blakely didn't sound like part of his extended Mexican family.

She listened for the shower, still running, then slid the bar on the phone down, so she could see the beginning of the message.

Sorry we couldn't finish talking tonight. Call me tomorrow and we . . .

We *what*? Christ, it took all her strength not to open the message further. But he would know if she did that, by seeing the opened message. And this was rude. She had no right. She knew this, and yet she hit the call button to see his recent calls. Scanned the last few days, seeing Cat Blakely's name twice.

She had a flashback to the day she looked at her father's calls and first learned of his liaison with Victor. Christ, she would do this now, with every man?

She wanted to trust Uriel. She did trust him, didn't she? She'd planned this. As the miles had shrunk, on that plane home from Peru, she planned to see Uriel again. To earn back his love. To open her heart to the man who had never betrayed her.

So why pry? And why was she afraid to ask him, as he came through the door, a towel wrapped around his waist, smiling. *So, who is this Cat person?*

She couldn't handle the wrong answer.

"You look pale," he said, kissing her forehead. "We played for too long! Let's get you something to eat."

She sunk into the chair, telling herself to hold onto the hope she'd had a few minutes before. She squashed the urge to run away and hide. She marveled at her own vulnerability, and his. The way the heart could come out of its shell again and again—it was madness, wasn't it?

She ate the mole and a butter lettuce salad. Ripped pieces off a warm loaf of bread, and sipped her wine. She let each flavor roll on her tongue, and told herself to stay, just stay, and let him feed her.

Chapter 20

"Great wine requires a mad man to grow the vine,
a wise man to watch over it, a lucid poet to make it,
and a lover to drink it."

—Salvador Dali

GLORIA WONDERED IF GOD HAD A REASON FOR MAKING TEEN
boys so difficult. To help the parents force them out of the nest? Or
to keep the girls from falling for them too early? Carlos, her smelly
man-child who ate through her money faster than she could make it,
was betraying her.

Out of the blue, last week, Diego and his new girlfriend had invited
Carlos on a vacation. Gloria had hovered by the door to listen to Carlos on the phone.

"Sure," Carlos had said, his voice eager.

Sure. Like his father was a good guy who deserved this warm reception on the phone. Diego offered to take him to Tahoe on a ski trip,
after skipping child support payments for months. Worst of all, Carlito
was leaving her alone for the holidays. But he wanted his presents
before he left.

"There are no presents," Gloria told him.

A blue papier maché cross hung on the wall, Carlos had made it
when he was four or five, at church, painting it carefully with his small
hands. She looked away from it, determined not to feel guilty.

"*No hay regalos, si no estás aquí.*" There are no presents if you aren't
here.

He ran his hand through his thick hair and continued as if he hadn't
heard her. "*Call of Duty* has a new game called *Ghost.* In case you want
to do Christmas when I get back."

Ghost. Good name. Her ghost of a son, going off with his ghost of a father. Anger stung her eyes as if she had touched a jalapeño. Why had Diego decided to invite Carlos for the holidays? To prove he was a family man to the new *puta*?

Diego had sent her a text message after he spoke to Carlos. Carlos needed some ski clothes before they went, so would she meet him at The Big Outdoors store on Saturday?

With whose money? If Diego tried to get Gloria to pay for the clothes, or anything for this damn trip, she'd bludgeon him with his ski pole.

On Saturday, Gloria and Carlos pulled into the mall parking lot ten minutes early. Carlos rocked to the music on his iPod, ears plugged. She quickly applied her favorite lipstick, a warm pink.

"Ma, you don't have to come in." Carlos reached for the door handle.

She glanced down at her athletic pants and tired winter coat. Dressed for work, on her way to clean the house of a gay guy with a Chihuahua. She liked the owner, but that dog bit her ankles every time. The dog could wait.

"I'll come in for a minute."

"Ma?" Carlos said reluctantly, his baggy jeans falling halfway down his ass, "why are you coming inside?"

It would be easier to drive away after the dismal scene at La Ronda, the last time she saw Diego. But if she didn't go inside, her ex would think she was hiding from him. She wouldn't hide. She had made a decision in the early morning hours, drinking coffee and watching the sky lighten. She would insist Diego help her with the immigration papers. He could divorce her next year, once her green card came through.

Shoulders back, Gloria yanked open the snowflake painted door. Imagine Diego pretending to be a skier! He hated the cold and had never strapped anything athletic to his feet.

"Hey guys!" Diego grinned as he crossed the store, a ski hat balanced on the top of his head, reminding Gloria of the Chihuahua.

Carlos' face lit up for a minute before he regained his cool, adolescent mug. Diego gave him a quick hug with a slap on the back, and Gloria a peck on her cheek. The stubble on his cheeks rubbed her face.

"Morning, Gloria."

"Diego."

"Carlos, you ever try snowboarding before?"

When would he have done that? Do you think we have money for snowboarding?

"Nah," Carlos said, as if trying to sound casual. "But it's like skateboarding, I think. So I can probably learn it fast."

"Yeah sure. My first time, too. Sheila's dad works in a hotel there, getting us a deal. Should be great." Diego grinned at Gloria. "A white Christmas!"

"Isn't that for white people?"

Diego's eyebrows lifted, but he laughed. "If you need to get going, we're fine," he said. "I'll drop Carlos home after."

"She's going to work," Carlos offered.

Gloria's mind told her to go and get out of the way while Diego acted like a father for a change. But she stayed. The momentary feeling of being a family, the three of them together, touched a longing inside her. She stood next to an enormous stuffed bear—it loomed over her with menacing lifelike paws—as Carlos tried on ski jackets, zipping them up to his nose. She glanced at the price tags. *Dios mío*, had Diego made some money? Was he doing something illegal? It wouldn't be the first time.

"Diego?" A woman's voice floated across the store. "Hi! Is that Carlos?"

Time stopped as Gloria examined the girl crossing the store, Diego's new friend. The most remarkable thing about her was how *unremarkable* she was. Gloria had predicted some hot young girl, probably Mexican, skinny with bouncing breasts, flashy car keys, and colored hair.

Instead, a plump, dark-haired, acne-faced white girl with a neon pink jacket and slipper-like fuzzy boots reached for Diego to give him a kiss.

"Hey, babe." Diego's voice rose up. "You're early."

Diego glanced at Gloria, his brows raised. Gloria in turn looked at her son—what would he think of this Sheila person?

Carlos noted the situation and then zipped up another jacket, black with a North Face label on the chest.

"Too tight," Sheila said, before even being introduced. "I used to sell ski jackets in Tahoe. You want to go up a size. I'm Sheila," she added, holding out her hand to Carlos, who took it.

"Carlos."

"Nice to meet you." Sheila released her long hair from a ponytail, grabbed at it nervously, and wrapped it back up in the rubber band. She looked young enough to be Carlos' older sister, or his babysitter.

Carlos extended his arm and touched his mother's shoulder. "This is my mom, Gloria."

Gloria could have kissed him for making that statement: *This is my mom.*

Sheila clearly hadn't noticed Gloria behind the enormous bear. "Oh . . . hi! So great to meet you! Diego has told me all about you guys."

Sheila looked at Gloria's hand as she shook it. Clearly Diego hadn't told her about his ex-wife's missing finger. She continued chatting after a beat. "But anyway, it's so great he's coming up to Tahoe for Christmas. Aren't you excited?" She looked at Carlos like a hungry puppy.

"Um . . . yeah. Totally."

"Awesome." Sheila had that young, white way of talking, as if everything was exciting. Exciting!

Gloria and her best friend in high school had coined these girls "the mermaids." They swam around the sea, flapping their tails, unaware of the rest of the fish. It wasn't how the girls looked exactly, but the expectation that whatever they did or said was interesting to others. Too loud in restaurants, laughing obnoxiously at movies, gossiping at the mall. Swimming in their self-absorption. Diego was dating a mermaid.

Sheila's cheeks grew pink. "Carlos is such a big boy! The picture Diego showed me—well, he looked younger."

"What picture?" Carlos demanded.

Diego shrugged. "An old one on my phone." He pointed at a rack of ski pants near the dressing rooms. "You need pants, too. To go with the jacket."

The guys wandered off and Gloria found herself wedged between the huge bear and Sheila, eyes perky. Up close, she was even less attractive, her pores large, her lips chapped. She did have a talent for intricate eye makeup.

"How old are you?" Gloria asked, unable to stop herself.

Sheila's eyes clouded briefly. "I . . . I'm a lot younger than Diego. I know. I mean, I'm twenty-four. But we're really compatible. *Super* compatible. It works out! I mean, age isn't that important to me."

Did Sheila know Diego was older than he looked? Forty-three this month.

"We've been dating since I was in college, but we didn't want to make it official or serious or anything, until I graduated."

Gloria nodded. A college girl.

Sheila shifted from one leg to the other, as if she couldn't stand still. "I graduated in June. And we got our place in July."

Gloria calculated. Diego had dropped off some child support—about a tenth of what he owed—on the Fourth of July. He had been flirtatious as usual and vague about his plans. No indication that he was living with someone new.

It didn't matter. Gloria shouldn't care. "I need to get going to work."

Sheila looked relieved. "Oh, okay. Well, it's good we met, right? And we'll take really good care of Carlos and everything."

Sweat pooled under Gloria's sweater. Diego had probably had ten girlfriends over the years, maybe twenty, but she'd never met one.

"Thanks," Gloria found herself saying, as if possessed by another person, a polite one, who didn't mind her son being away on Christmas. A cheerful woman who didn't have an expired green card and a deadbeat ex. "Thanks for taking him skiing."

"Oh sure, no worries. My dad wants to meet Diego." Sheila's face grew red when she mentioned her father. "I mean, I think it will be fine. It's just sort of awkward. My dad's pretty intense, you know? But Diego can manage him. Totally."

Gloria glanced around for Carlos, wanting to say goodbye, but saw no sign of him.

Sheila followed her gaze. "I think they went to try things on, maybe."

Gloria edged towards the front door, while her brain spun with conflicting thoughts. This silly young girl was making a mistake, trusting Diego. Gloria felt for her. But she also impeded Diego from coming to the damn INS office.

Gloria could easily give the girl enough information about Diego to make her run away. Instead, she was letting Diego and this *chiquita* take her son for Christmas. "Tell Diego to call me later, okay? About the child support he owes me?"

Sheila looked uncertain, biting one of her chapped lips. "Uh . . . okay?"

"I know he's busy," Gloria said, giving Sheila a wink, "and probably just forgot. But he's a few months behind. Well, actually he hasn't paid since July."

Sheila's eyes flapped wide open, like painted butterfly wings.

"Anyway, really nice to meet you." Gloria gave Sheila a peppy we're-all-family-now kind of smile and strode out the door. She'd shaken a tree. It could drop some money, like leaves, or send out a platoon of angry bees. A shiver ran up her spine. She just might dropkick that Chihuahua if he bit her today.

Chapter 21

"Wine is bottled poetry."

—Robert Louis Stevenson

"Mrs. Scanlon? Hold up!"

Elena turned to see the volunteer coordinator of the hospital, a heavyset woman who wore too much perfume, heading her way. Elena had made countless origami cranes and flowers with the residents during her three-hour shift and was eager to go.

"Mrs. Scanlon, thanks for your help today." Mandy smiled, eagerly.

"Oh, I'm not sure I helped that much," Elena said.

Mandy went on, "I was wondering if, well—we have a lot going on this weekend and are short-staffed. Any chance you could come in Sunday?"

"Sunday? I don't know. I'm on this crazy schedule. I mean, my schedule is quite full."

Mandy glanced at her clipboard and sighed. "Okay. You really make a difference in the art room. And we're doing this, I don't know, crafts bonanza thing. You know—for the holidays."

The holidays. A pebble rolled through her stomach. Elena and Amanda had scraped through Thanksgiving surrounded by a bunch of Carmen's wild girlfriends at her home. Both of them were missing Jim and the holidays of the past, but neither said so.

"I'm sorry," Elena said, irritated by Mandy's reminder of the holidays. "Maybe another time. If I knew earlier—"

"Sure, sure."

Elena exited quickly, the November day cold and gray, which suited her mood. Give her rain storms, gray skies, and reasons to hide in her house.

Today was Wednesday. She pulled her wrinkled schedule from her handbag, although she knew already what it said for today: therapy, check. Volunteer, check. Yoga at five, then dinner with Amanda. She drove to the yoga studio, grabbing a parking spot right out front. A sign displayed a woman doing an impossible back bend with the word Zen painted on her abdomen.

Elena stared at the studio moodily. To hell with yoga; she wanted a nap and a cup of tea. She drove home, parking in the driveway. She hadn't parked in the garage since her "accident." Elena had a flash in her mind of Gloria screaming, bent over her, crying for help. Gloria had not looked her in the eye since that day.

Elena stepped out of her car to see two deer staring down at her from the hill across the street, as if saying hello. She nodded to them. "*Hola, amigos.* Are you here to eat my flowers?"

One of the deer tipped her head, as if considering it.

Elena loved it here. Despite all that happened, she didn't want to give up her home or leave the valley. But once she was in the house, alone, staring at the empty spaces where Jim's things used to be, she wondered if she should have gone to yoga. She ran her hand over a dusty, empty shelf where Jim's signed baseballs had lived. She needed to find something to fill the empty spaces.

The cold had crept into the house. Elena cranked up the heat, finding herself shivering. She knew she needed to eat something but nothing appealed. But she wanted something—wine, sweets, anything to fill the emptiness inside and out.

Maybe a bath? That's what Carmen would do. She would run a hot bath, light candles and put on nice music. Elena couldn't picture her sister standing in the middle of the living room, cold and lost, missing a man.

In the bathroom, she rummaged through the drawers looking for bubbles or bath salts. She found an old razor of Jim's, his stubble in it. Elena lifted it to her nose and smelled a hint of his favorite shaving cream. She had bought him some for Christmas every year, for his stocking. Would they still exchange gifts this year? Even a token?

She closed her eyes, thinking of Christmas with only herself and Amanda at the table. Even worse, would her daughter spend part of it with Jim? Her heart raced at the thought of the impending lonely moments. The room spun, as if she was drunk with anxiety.

The razor went in easier than expected, one sharp dash across her forearm, bubbles of blood forming on the perpendicular lines, like angry red tire tracks. Her right hand shook, as she absorbed the damage she had done to her left arm. As the pain hit, she threw the razor in the garbage, shocked and ashamed of her own impulsiveness.

Christ, were the medications not working? Where was the promised sanity?

A sob erupted from deep inside, and she slid to the floor, letting the tears flow. She missed Jim. She missed talking to him at the end of the day, even about mundane things. She missed hearing his car as it purred up the driveway, and watching him kneel and nuzzle the dogs. She missed knowing he was in the house, even across the house. They had stopped being lovers, but she really thought they were friends. The blood, seeping through the towel, seemed like evidence of the pain she didn't quite know how to show.

Holding a towel on her arm, Elena ran up the stairs to the art studio, her sanctuary. She dropped the bloody towel in the garbage, covering it up well, determined Amanda would not see it. The pulsing cut focused her, strangely. She felt calmer as she washed the wound with soap, opened three band aids and placed them carefully, sealing the cut completely. *Cover this up.*

She curled up in her bed, telling herself everything would be okay. *None of this is really happening.* She had learned this skill as a young girl, when things were rough. When she heard her father's bellows, her mother's cries, the sound of a fist in the wall, or the thud of her mother as she fell.

It's not really happening.

Elena took a book off her night stand and tried to read. Distraction had worked many times before. But as she read, desperate thoughts floated by. *I have to stop. I can't be unstable like this. God, please let me feel better.*

It took enormous energy to stay sane in this world. She needed to talk to Dr. Love about that feeling. How did other people do it? Stay sane while their lives slipped away like old water funneling down the drain? Her mother had not managed. But Carmen had. Elena needed to be more like her sister.

She woke to the phone ringing. Not her cell, the house phone. She pulled herself out of a deep slumber, confused. "Hello?"

"Mom?"

Elena glanced around for a clock. "Hi, Amanda."

"Are you okay, Mom?" Amanda's voice was high, panicky.

"Yes, I'm fine, honey. I took a little nap, I guess."

"You didn't go to yoga. I went to meet you at the studio, but I couldn't find you. And you aren't answering your cell. I've been calling you for fifteen minutes." Amanda's voice sounded like she was trying her best not to cry. "My car is getting fixed today, remember? It's not ready. I couldn't get home and you wouldn't answer. Oh God, Mom, are you sure you're fine?"

Guilt welled inside the chambers of her heart. "Yes, yes. I'm fine. I'm sorry—didn't mean to worry you. I didn't feel like going to yoga today."

"But you're supposed to go anyway, remember? Dr. Love said that's when you most need to go. Did you take something? Is that why you're asleep?"

Take something? Pills.

"Oh God, no, Amanda, I'm just tired from volunteering. Do you want to go out to dinner? I can pick you up."

She heard Amanda take a deep breath. Knew the face she was making, the way her eyes grew narrow when deciding something. "No. I mean, yes to dinner, but you don't have to pick me up. Uriel can drive me. Actually, never mind, pick me up." Elena rarely heard her daughter rattled. "Christ, Mom, I was freaking out."

Elena wanted to tell Amanda she was overreacting. But her daughter had every right to be like this. "I'll get you at the stables. Be there in fifteen, okay?"

"Thanks."

Elena gathered her courage to face Amanda's disappointment as she drove. Past the vineyards, vines looking like huddled figures in the dark, past the diner with the flashing coffee cup, across a bridge and up onto a ridge where the stables sat. The stables, her daughter's second home.

Amanda gave her a hug, like they had not seen each other in weeks. She smelled of cold air, horses, and sweat.

"Good afternoon riding?"

Amanda held onto her a moment too long, and then finally released. "Yes, it was actually. Before."

"I'm sorry." All she could offer lately were apologies. *I'm sorry, I'm sorry, I'm sorry.*

Amanda answered her, as she often did. "I know."

The car grew warmer with the two of them in it, making their way to town. At a stop light, Amanda reached across the car and touched her mother's cheek, briefly. As if to make sure she was real.

Chapter 22

"If we sip the wine, we find dreams coming upon us out
of the imminent night."

—D.H. Lawrence

THE PHARMACIST WENT OVER THE MEDICATIONS WITH AMANDA
as she placed them in the bag. An antidepressant, a sleeping pill, birth
control, and antibiotics. The antibiotics were for a sinus infection
Amanda had been weathering for months. The birth control was a
day late. And the rest were for Elena. Amanda was tempted to say the
psychiatric meds were not hers, but that was obvious from the names
on the bottles. Besides, why would the pharmacy tech care? It seemed
like the pills were working for Elena, at least.

Meds in hand, she met her mother at a Thai place they had recently
discovered, tucked in a strip mall. Amanda ordered a Thai iced tea and
downed her antibiotics before broaching the dreaded subject with her
mother.

"Mom, have you thought about Christmas?"

"I don't want to think about the holidays, Amanda. Let's just let them
slip by this year. Or, I don't know—maybe we can check with Carmen
to see if she wants to come over?"

Amanda imagined the three of them around the table, alone, the
forced cheer. "Uriel has invited us to his house. His uncle's house.
We're both welcome. It's a great family—it could be fun. Do something new?"

Elena's eye dropped to her wine glass, filled with a Chardonnay.
"I don't know. That feels soon."

Amanda took a minute, dipping a fried dumpling in a sweet sauce.
The flavors of cucumber, shrimp, and honey burst in her mouth. She

had to bring Uriel to this place. "Too soon for what? To meet Uriel's family?"

"Too soon for me to meet anyone's family. I just don't feel like myself, *mija*. Anyway, what would his family think about us?"

Amanda released a breath. "That you're getting a divorce, Mom." She felt a surge of frustration. Her parents' tendency to hide things made Amanda want to scream. "Mom, you really didn't know? Before Dad told you?"

Her mother's eyes narrowed, a new crease between her brows deepening. "About Victor?"

"Yes, about Victor."

Elena shook her head, firm. "No." She looked up, puzzled. "Did you know?"

Amanda's throat tightened, as if her body wanted to keep the answer inside. "Yes, I knew." She exhaled and went on before she lost her nerve. "I confronted him, and I think it's why he finally left. So it's kind of my fault. I'm sorry. I didn't . . . I thought it was better to stop having all these secrets. Obviously, things hit the fan. I guess I didn't think it would go this badly."

Elena put down her fork and stared at her, clearly surprised. "I wish you had told me."

Amanda nodded. "So do I." She tried to read her mother's face, the subtle emotional cues in the wrinkles of her forehead, the frown on her lips. Angry? Sad? Maybe she shouldn't have admitted this.

"How? How did you know?"

"I . . . The first thing was seeing calls on his phone, years ago. When we were in Hawaii."

The waitress refilled their water glasses, and both women stopped talking, a sense of hurt in the air.

"He called Victor all the time. He was his business partner. How did you know it was more than that?"

"I saw them, in the city . . . " Amanda told her mother the full story, the various clues, seeing them together as they walked hand in hand. When she finished, she played with her food, while Elena sat back, staring into the darkness. Amanda had no idea what she was thinking. Clearly, reading her mother was a skill she had not perfected.

"Mom? You still with me?"

"Of course I am."

"Remember when you took me to see Tierradentro?" Amanda tried to break through Elena's fog. "The summer I graduated high school?"

Elena looked at her strangely. Maybe she was trying to decide if she was angry or not? "Yes. I think you decided to be an anthropologist there."

The summer Amanda was eighteen, the two of them had travelled around Columbia. Elena had never seen most of the country before, knew only her hometown. Tierradentro was an archaeological site, a series of deep, elaborate underground tombs. They'd followed rough dirt roads with their guide, bumping along in an old Jeep, then walking into the cool, dark caves. No one knew who had created them, and Amanda remembered feeling if she took a wrong turn she might never find her way out.

"I already knew I would study archeology. Always. Anyway, that's what you feel like sometimes, Mom—like you have all these deep places I don't even know about."

Elena waved her hand, as if Amanda was being silly. "I'm not that hard to figure out, Amanda. It was your father who had the secret life."

"I would never have imagined you would get this messed up by Dad. I mean, you both had such distinct lives. I never thought you'd get this depressed. About *anything*. Not so depressed that you'd would do what you did."

Elena's lips pursed together, and she reached for her wine glass. "It was a stupid, foolish moment. It's more complicated than Dad. I've struggled with moods since I was a girl."

"I know. Carmen told me. But she also said you're strong. She said to ask you about the ashes."

"What?" Elena's eyes lifted.

"About your mother's ashes, or something?"

Elena shook her head. "God, sometimes Carmen frustrates me. She doesn't have to drag up all these old—"

"I don't know anything about your childhood, Mom! All I know is that you were pretty poor, and your mom she died when you were like sixteen."

"Fifteen."

"Okay, fifteen. It was an accident, right?"

Elena played with her teaspoon in an empty cup of tea. "I hardly remember, it was so long ago. And I'm not sure it's the best thing to talk about the past right now."

Amanda didn't know if it was either, but Carmen had said Elena was stronger than she recognized, that she just needed to reclaim the person she used to be. "What *do* you remember?"

Elena waved to the waitress, "Can I have another glass of wine, please?"

"I'll take one, too," Amanda said, abandoning her plan not to drink with the antibiotics.

Elena looked directly into her eyes. "You really want to know about this? It's not a happy story, Amanda."

"I know."

"My teen years were like a terrible movie. My father was not good to us. I've told you that. Not a good husband to my mother."

The aunties had made that much clear to Amanda. They spit when they heard his name.

"He was living with another woman, taking care of her children before us . . . Finally, my mother had enough, and she changed the locks."

Amanda held her breath as she listened to the story of her mother's life in Columbia, of the losses she'd kept so well hidden.

Two weeks after her mother changed the locks, Elena's father had come back, pounding on the door when his key didn't work. He demanded they open the door. When they didn't, he broke the back door off, the cheap wood splintering like cardboard. Elena remembered hiding near the table as he came into the kitchen. Her father's voice bellowed like a crazed, wounded animal as he hurled insults at them, and whatever objects he could grab. A vase full of wilted flowers, the coffee pot, a Virgin Mary candle, a full can of coffee.

"The can of coffee broke the window." The color of Elena's cheeks darkened as she recalled it, as if she'd like to go back and stand up to her father. "Glass crashed down on me in a hundred shards. One piece cut my shoulder." She pulled her sweater to the side and showed Amanda the small, rough scar. "There was a lot of blood. A neighbor came when he heard the noise, and someone called the police. I was so relieved. You know, I thought my father might kill us."

Amanda's dinner sat too heavy in her stomach. Maybe she should not have insisted on knowing this story.

"After the police came, my father took off for a few weeks. But my mother got quieter. She kept the lights on all night, and she put cans near the doorway, to hear him if he came. He didn't come back, but still, she was vigilant. She would pace by the window and pray to the Virgin. We were supposed to cross the street if he ever talked to us."

Amanda thought of Elena's rituals the week after Jim left. Pacing, locking doors. Maybe the illness was genetic.

"And then one day at school, Carmen came running to me. Her face was . . . white. I had never seen her so upset. I knew it was about Momma. That she was dead."

"How? Did your father do it?"

"She was hit by a car. The driver said he never saw her, that she came out of nowhere, stepping in front of him. My aunts think she was pushed by my father. It may have been an accident or suicide. I always thought my father killed her one way or another."

"Did you see your father after that?"

"Rarely. A few times—he wanted us to live with him." Elena barked out a bitter laugh. "My aunts had taken over. One of them stayed with us at the house, the others visited often. And then he announced he was moving back in."

Amanda slammed down her wine glass. "He moved in with you and Carmen?"

Elena shook her head, as if baffled even now by his audacity. "He said it was his house—technically he owned it. My mother had paid for most of it with her shitty jobs, working non-stop—but they were still married when she died. He showed up with his new girlfriend. He said, 'You can still stay here if you want, both of you. But Dulce and I are moving in, too.'"

Amanda shuddered. *Dulce.* The girlfriend's name meant *sweet.*

"My aunts raged. Carmen wanted to let out rats under the beds, or put snakes in the closet. I was numb. I remember I took every picture in the house of my mother. I packed all my things. But I didn't feel. It was as if someone had put a blanket over me." She stopped, then added, as if realizing it for the first time, "I was depressed."

"Of course you were. What a nightmare." Amanda wished she'd left it alone, and was annoyed with Carmen. She finished her wine, not sure what to say. "What was it about the ashes?"

Elena's looked like her mind was racing over the memories, like they were books on a shelf and she was running her fingers over the spines. "There was a fire."

"Where?"

"At my house. The house my father took over. My mother's house, really. He was living there with his woman, her children. Anyway, the fire destroyed the house. It was totally gone."

"Did your father get hurt?"

She shook her head. "No one was home. I don't remember if it happened at night, or day. Just that our old neighbor came and told us the house had burned down. I couldn't believe it."

"You must have been devastated. Your childhood home?"

"It wasn't ours anymore. Carmen thinks our uncles set the fire, as revenge." She drank a gulp of wine. "We went over the next day, Carmen and I. It was strange. These random parts of the house had survived. Part of a wall, the sink. It was a tiny house, and I think it went up fast. An inspector was there. He said it was arson. It's vague, like a movie."

"The ashes?"

Elena ran her hands through her hair. "That part—I never think about it. But Carmen does. We had this silly purple plastic radio we took everywhere. Carmen put it on the ground, playing, while we poked around in the ashes, looking for anything familiar. Seeing the house— gone—should have made us sad. But it didn't. There was something kind of freeing about it. With my mother gone, I didn't want my father in her home. Our home.

"Anyway, we started being silly. Making up stories about how the fire started. Talking about that mean girl at school, how maybe she had died in the fire. It sounds terrible, but we were angry teenagers."

Elena smiled. "Carmen kept saying maybe Mom came back and started it, to get him back. This song came on the radio. It was always on then." She glanced around, then sang the words quietly to Amanda. "Baby, baby, where did our love go?"

"The Supremes."

"Yes. Carmen and I loved it. And so she turned up the volume." Elena looked as if she was picturing it all again.

"I started to dance. At first, on the dirt area that was our backyard, but then I moved into where the house had been. I danced in it. And the soot and ashes kept coming up—all over my legs, and on my uniform. Even my hair was gray with ashes. And yet, I kept dancing." She shook her head, lost in the memory.

"And Carmen?"

"Carmen watched me, as if I was someone she didn't know. But I think she was proud of me, too."

Amanda pictured Carmen as the observer.

"And now," Elena went on, "when I complain too much, or get too down, she reminds me. *You are the girl that danced in the ashes.* As if that shows something."

"It does." Amanda said. "You lost your mother, your home. Your father turned you out. A lot of people would be defeated by that."

"Maybe it's easier to be brave when you're young. This time, when I thought I was losing everything again, I didn't feel brave."

Amanda moved to her mother, unable to have a table between them. She put her lips on the top of her mother's head and whispered the words she'd been wanting to say for weeks. That she was sorry she stirred up this mess. That she loved her.

"You are brave, Mom. You forgot that for a minute is all. And you didn't lose everything. You didn't lose me."

Chapter 23

"When a man drinks wine at dinner, he begins to be better pleased with himself."

—Plato

"DAD? I GOT YOUR MESSAGE. WE CAN HAVE DINNER IF YOU WANT." Amanda didn't sound excited, but willing. "But can you come up to Sonoma? I can meet you downtown about seven-thirty."

Anxiety propelled Jim up the highway, driving too fast. He made it from San Francisco to downtown Sonoma in an hour, fifteen minutes faster than usual.

As he drove, Jim tried to prepare himself for yet another difficult conversation. He thought of the snow globes he used to bring back for his daughter from his trips when she was a child. Amanda would watch wistfully as he shook the miniature worlds, and the white flakes fell. Jim was about to take her world and shake it, just like that, pieces floating everywhere.

Telling Amanda the circumstances of her birth had not occurred to Jim, initially. His therapist had planted the seed. Over the last few months, ping-ponging between manic excitement about his reunion with Victor and guilt about his family, the therapist had managed to dig into Jim's protected secrets, areas of his mind shrouded with denial. In one horrifying session, Jim had told her everything.

When she stated that Jim needed to tell Amanda the truth, he balked. She didn't relent.

"You're in your sixties. You have cancer. No one is immortal, Jim. You need to tell your daughter everything. She deserves to know."

The words rang true to him. "She has no idea."

The therapist had scooted up in her chair to make her point. "You said that about coming out, Jim. And it turned out Amanda knew all along. Be reasonable. You came out to your wife and daughter. How much harder can this be?"

By the time he got to the restaurant, an Italian place they both loved, he was sweating despite it being a cool December evening. Christmas lights glittered, strung across the square, around the huge pine trees near City Hall, and across the side alleys. In every window, elves, angels and Santas posed with shiny baubles or expensive jewelry. Elena always loved the square during the holidays. Would she be able to enjoy it this year?

"Hey, Dad." Amanda stood outside Della Santina's, an enormous Santa sleigh next to her. A navy blue wool coat set off her red hair. Jim squeezed her tight when he hugged her.

"Do you want to walk for a few minutes before dinner?" she asked. "There's a wait. I put us on the list."

He agreed, although he was tired and hungry. They strolled up the street lined with gracious older homes with wide porches. Each one was well appointed—caroling light-up angels, Christmas trees in wine barrels, a trio of metal deer.

"Has Mom got the lights up?" It hit him that Elena might not be able to string the lights without him. Maybe he should offer to help?

"God, no." Amanda looked at him with some annoyance. "She's not exactly festive right now."

"Right. Sorry." He had a sinking feeling about their evening, that he was going to make a series of blunders like this, false assumptions that life in Sonoma had gone on normally. He wished, as he had so many times over the years, that he could be two people. One could be the man the family needed him to be. The man, his therapist had pointed out, that he had pretended to be. The other could live with Victor and openly love him.

"Is there anything I can do?" The words embarrassed him as he said them, so feeble in the light of his absconding.

"No. I mean . . . Let's not do this okay? Life is rough at home. You can't help. That's all there is to say about it."

He blew out a breath into the cold dark air. "How is she?"

Amanda pushed her hands deep into her coat pockets. Her hair was in a braid over her shoulder; and it rose and fell as she walked, that purposeful stride she'd had since she was a child.

"Dad, I can't talk about Mom with you, without feeling like I'm betraying her. I didn't tell her about our plans for dinner. She's away with Carmen. Let's talk about other things."

As they meandered back to the restaurant, he asked her about the dogs, a seemingly safe topic.

"Honestly? They miss you. It's been hard for them, too. We don't get them out for many runs. Beaver mopes a lot."

He knew he deserved her frustration, but it was not an ideal state for giving her his news. Maybe he was being hasty in telling her the truth?

Once they entered the restaurant, he relaxed. He ordered easily, from years of practice. A bottle of Chianti was brought over right away.

They shared a Caesar salad, dipped bread in olive oil brimming with garlic, and had two bowls of seafood stew. The garlic opened his sinuses and the Chianti warmed him to his toes. He told her this was better than any place in San Francisco.

"I want to come down to the city soon. I feel claustrophobic up here."

"We'd love to have you."

Her eyebrows raised. "We? Are you like . . . living with him? Victor?"

Shit. "Only kind of."

"You don't have to hide it, Dad. I'm just surprised. It's fast."

"No, I'm not hiding it. We're together. He's in the process of moving to California. Half the time he's still in New York. But yes, when he's here, he's with me."

"In your hotel room?"

"I rented a condo."

"Wow. You didn't tell me."

"You haven't been that easy to reach, Amanda. I try . . . "

She nodded, wiping her mouth with the cloth napkin. "Okay. Fair enough. I haven't wanted to know what you're up to. I'm too pissed off."

The stew tasted salty, and he pushed it away. "Obviously, you're angry I left. I understand. Although, I thought you encouraged me to go."

"I did. But I didn't think you'd, I don't know . . . go so quickly. And completely."

"That part is your mother's decision. I'd be thrilled to be more involved, to help with things. She doesn't want me around. For now, at least."

Amanda refilled her wine glass, a few drops dripping on the table cloth. The wine spot spread, bleeding into the fabric. "You're right that she doesn't want you around. I guess it's too hard. I'm glad you came clean, I think. But I can still be pissed, Dad."

"Yes."

"This went on for half my life. That's a bizarrely long time to lie to us, Dad."

"Yes."

Amanda's skin flushed when she was tired or emotional, her chest and neck growing pink. It reminded him of his mother, when her temper flared. He remembered shaking as a child, begging her to stop yelling. To say that she didn't mean all those horrible things she had said.

His mother would come to his room eventually, sometimes late at night, asking forgiveness for her Irish temper. "I got my Irish up, is all."

His heart would melt and he'd curl up in her arms, relieved to be loved again. But during the hours he waited for her, he ached inside. The brothers all suffered her tough days, but Jimmy was her favorite and therefore took it the hardest. He'd never learned how to weather the anger of someone he loved. Never been able to face their disappointment. He'd chosen to lie rather than confront, to avoid rather than reveal. He took a deep breath and readied himself to tell Amanda the rest of the truth.

"Did you ever love her?" Amanda asked abruptly. She sat with both elbows on the table, alert.

"Of course I did. I still love your mother."

"But not like that. Not like you love Victor."

His chest tightened. "No. I don't feel the same way. I didn't know, honestly, that I had never really been in love until I met Victor."

"And then you realized you didn't love Mom?"

He tried to find the right words. "Not in the same way. The kind of love I had, I have, for Victor, was . . . compelling."

This was strange to talk about with his daughter. But he wanted her to know that real love existed. That she should never settle for less. "When I fell in love, it hit me that we use that phrase for a reason. You *fall* into this state. This kind of love isn't rational. You stop trying to fight it after awhile. But it's incredible, so you don't mind that it's taken over."

Amanda stared at him like she was meeting a stranger, her eyes examining his, with caution.

"I sound a little crazy?"

She shook her head. "No. I know that feeling. And you're right. It's totally irrational." She smiled reluctantly. "I guess I've never heard you be so poetic."

"Is that how you feel with Uriel?"

She examined her cuticles before answering. "It was. When I met him after college, I felt that way. It was the most amazing, wonderful thing in my entire life."

"And now?"

She played with the stem of her glass. "I . . . I don't know. Leaving him was a huge mistake. I'm glad to have a second chance. But we're both kind of—holding back parts of ourselves. Maybe we're afraid to fall in love again." Her eyes moistened.

"Afraid why?"

"Because we both know I might fuck it up again."

Jim didn't remember what had happened, why her relationship with Uriel ended. At the time, he had assumed Uriel was one in a string of boyfriends. Not *the one*. "Didn't you break up when you left for graduate school?"

"No." Amanda gave a slow shake of her head. "We broke up because I left, very abruptly."

He had the feeling of a vague *déjà vu*. Uriel had come to the house once, asking for her. Jim remembered the shock registering in Uriel's eyes when he heard Amanda had left. "Why did you leave?"

Amanda blew out her cheeks. "I saw you and Victor together. I followed you from work one night and spied on you."

Jim's stomach hardened, as if he had just taken a punch.

"I freaked out. I realized everything I knew about my family was a lie."

He ran his hand through his hair, trying to decide how to react. It was shocking, somehow, that she had spied on him. But also, he wished she hadn't seen him in that light. Sneaking around.

"I'm sorry," he finally said. "I had no idea you knew, and that it had such an impact on you."

"I left the next day, Dad. Didn't you notice it was sudden?"

Jim thought about it. "Yes. But you said you'd decided to take your car back east. It didn't seem that out of character for you to take off a month early."

Tears slid down her cheeks, and he wished he could wipe all her sadness away.

"I waited for months for you to call me and say, 'What's up, Amanda? Why the sudden departure? You didn't say goodbye . . . ' I was all ready to have it out with you."

He winced. "What did I say instead?"

"Nothing. You sent me a Lehigh sweatshirt. You made funny jokes on the phone when I called the house, about why I took the world's oldest car across the country. Said you would have bought me a new one. You acted . . . kind and generous, and funny. And still you."

Amanda gave him a begrudging smile. "At some point, I decided not to tell you I knew. But I couldn't face you either. And I never explained to Uriel why I left. And so . . . I just moved on. Buried myself in school. Tried not to think about you too much. I wanted to put it behind me."

Jim wished he could go back and unravel even one of the mistakes he had made. He pulled his credit card from his wallet and put it on top of the check, ready to go home. To pour a Scotch and lie on the bed and wait for Victor. He knew when Victor laid his head on the pillow next to him, it would all be worth it.

He forced himself to face his daughter. "Can you explain all that to Uriel?"

"I'm trying."

His affair with Victor had robbed them in so many ways. He had told himself he was providing all he could for his wife and daughter a family, a home, a lifestyle, security. He'd been a fool.

Amanda gave him a long hug goodbye, her narrow shoulders crumpling, her head resting on his lapel. "I'm glad you came up," she said.

"Me too." He couldn't tell her what he had come to discuss. Amanda didn't need more ugly truths. She needed to get out from the shadow of his past, not wallow in it.

He would tell his therapist this one was staying in the vault.

Chapter 24

"The discovery of a good wine is increasingly better for mankind than the discovery of a new star."

—Leonardo Da Vinci

GLORIA SPENT CHRISTMAS MORNING PAINTING HER TOENAILS red and watching *White Christmas* on TV, trying not to think about Diego and his new girl dancing in the snow with Carlos. She pulled on her reindeer sweater and mittens. She stuck them in her pocket and headed off to see her mother, even though her mother might not know it was Christmas. Her cousin Lourdes always worked holidays at the nursing home, because they paid double, so at least Gloria could say hello to her.

A fake tree covered with origami birds and blinking red lights welcomed Gloria in the front hall. The smell of overdone turkey and grease permeated like old smoke. She said *Feliz Navidad* to the janitor who responded with a blessing on her new year. A heavy cross swayed around his neck, and she thought of her father's unfortunate obsession with evangelizing in public places.

Her mother's cheek crinkled like dry paper when she kissed it. A present sent by her brother rested on a dresser, unopened. *"Feliz Navidad, Mami."*

"It's terrible they make you work on Christmas," her mother said. She'd assumed Gloria was one of the nurses before. She slipped Gloria a wrinkled five-dollar bill. "A little tip for you."

"No, it's me. Your *hija*. I don't work here, remember?" Confusion stirred in her mother's dark eyes, and Gloria changed her stance. *"Sí, Mamá*. It sucks to work on Christmas." Gloria smoothed her mother's lipstick, which the older woman put on every few minutes without looking in a mirror, often appearing clown-like.

Her mother was excited for today's episode of *Days of Our Lives* in Spanish. Once it started, Gloria put on her jacket. "Thanks for the tip," Gloria said to her mother, waving the five- dollar bill.

"Buy yourself a drink, Miss."

In the hallway, Lourdes came towards her, pushing a wheelchair a little fast. The patient's head wobbled like a chicken's.

"Carlos really go to Tahoe?" Lourdes asked her, once they'd said hello. "That's shit. Well at least you get a break from him. You're always telling me what a pain in the ass he is."

The one day a year Gloria didn't need a break from Carlos was Christmas.

"Is Uriel coming over later?"

"Nah. I told him I'm working. He's with Freddie and all them anyway. Pretty sure I'm not invited."

The old man in the wheelchair stared at the two of them. Gloria offered him a small smile, feeling badly for him. He looked back at her, expressionless.

"He don't know nothing that goes on." Lourdes nodded toward the resident in the chair. "He's in a coma, sort of. But his body still works." She turned to him and bent down. "Right, George? You're still trucking, huh?"

When he didn't respond, she turned back to Gloria. "Well, what are you going to do today then?"

"I don't know. They should have a place for mothers whose sons aren't home for Christmas."

"They do. It's called a bar."

Gloria laughed.

"No, seriously, I'll be at Plaza Tequila after work, around four. They have five-dollar peppermint margaritas all night tonight. You should come out."

The knot of loneliness in Gloria's stomach loosened. Would it be fun to go to a bar on Christmas? She remembered dressing up as a girl, going to church with her whole family, eating tamales afterwards. *That* was Christmas.

Lourdes gave her a wave and headed down the hall, humming jingle bells. "See you later, *prima.*"

Gloria headed to the lobby. A black man leaning on his walker gave her a candy cane on her way out. "Thank you," she said to him, meaning it.

"Gloria!"

Gloria was amazed to see Mrs. Scanlon out front, a basket in her arms.

"*Feliz Navidad!*"

"*Feliz Navidad.*" Gloria answered. Then curiosity got the better of her. "What are you doing here?"

"I volunteer here now. I'm just bringing in some treats, and I'm supposed to work in the rec room for a few hours."

"Oh, that's very nice, Mrs. Scanlon." Gloria wondered if she was sad without her husband on Christmas. She wished she could invite Elena to come to the bar with her and Lourdes, but that would be too strange. A line they did not cross. "Will you be with Amanda later?"

"Yes, I am going with her to see Uriel's Uncle and Aunt, actually."

"Oh, good. They are very nice."

They said goodbye, and Gloria was surprised when Mrs. Scanlon reached out and kissed her cheek. "Have a good Christmas, Gloria."

"Thank you again," Gloria called out. She had been given a hefty Christmas bonus. It would help with the immigration lawyer.

Gloria drove down Highway 12 towards home, thinking about the Scanlons. She ignored a call on her phone from Carlos. She'd call him later; she needed to get in the right frame of mind. At the last minute, she turned the car into the parking lot of Plaza Tequila, the tires hitting a pothole. Her mother had said to buy herself a drink, so she would.

Gloria was well into her second peppermint margarita when Santa sat down next to her. He took a stool for himself and then a second one for his enormous bulging red bag, presumably filled with toys. He was a large man without any apparent need for Santa belly padding. He yanked his fake beard off, the elastic snapping past his ear. He had olive skin with a small pimple near his chin, and a significant nose.

"Aren't you supposed to have delivered those by now?" Gloria waved her drink at the bulging bag. "It's like three o'clock on Christmas Day."

"Got one more stop," he said, shrugging under his red jacket. "Some church does their party at five on Christmas. They want me to show up and hand out crucifixes."

"Those are all crucifixes?"

He reached into the bag and held out a plastic Jesus stretched on a three-inch cross. Jesus' hands sported splashes of blood on the palms. "They light up," Santa added, reaching under the bottom of the toy and pressing a button. Jesus' chest lit up with a pink heart, rosy blood oozing from the sides.

"Wow. They're giving these things to little kids? It looks more like a Halloween toy than a Christmas one."

Santa nodded. "I think it's weird, too. But I get fifty bucks to pass them out with a *Ho Ho Ho*. This is my last stop—I did ten all together."

"You made five hundred dollars today being Santa?" Gloria didn't hide her envy. She should get herself a damn Santa suit next year.

"Yeah." He grinned, showing nice white teeth. "Can I buy you a drink?"

The alcohol made her feel bold, and the bitterness of missing Carlos twisted in her heart like a kite caught on a branch. She couldn't quite dislodge it. She held up her glass. "Why not? You're Santa, after all. And I didn't get much else this Christmas. I'd better switch to beer though. This pink stuff is too sweet."

When the beers came they clinked their bottles. "Merry Christmas," Santa said.

"Merry Christmas."

Santa told her about going to a few churches in the morning, and then a nursing home and two children's wards at the hospital. "Those are tough," he said, running his hand through his hair. As he did so, white paint came off on his hands, and he revealed a jet-black mane.

Gloria examined him with interest. His girth was more solid than fat, and his hazel eyes looked right at her when he spoke. She liked that. "The hospitals are hard?"

"Sick kids. I always feel bad for them. I work in a hospital and I should be used to it, but I'm not. They're trying to be excited for Santa, but they feel like shit. And most hospitals have it all set—like I hand out to specific kids, you know? A Polly Pony for Alison, cause that's what she asked for. Then she goes nuts because she's so happy. That rocks. But some places—man they just give me a pile of wrapped toys and say hand them out. So some eight-year-old boy gets a makeup kit. And he's looking at me, like—*Really, Santa? You thought I wanted makeup?* Now instead of being a sick kid in the hospital on Christmas, he's also a kid who knows Santa's a crock of shit. I mean, really. If they aren't gonna buy them what they want, they should give them all crayons or something." He sat back, releasing a deep sigh. "Sorry, that was pissing me off today."

"Sounds awful." Fifty dollars didn't sound like enough to deal with that shit.

"You got kids?"

For a moment she thought of saying no. No kids. But instead she pulled out her phone to show him a picture of Carlos. There was a text message from Carlos waiting.

Merry Christmas Ma.

And then another one: **Can you call me?**

She avoided it, not ready to hear about the fun time he was having. She pulled up a picture of Carlos standing in front of Spring Lake in Santa Rosa. They'd gone swimming on one of those intense hot days, and his black hair was wet and glistening in the sun. More importantly, he was smiling, reminiscent of the child she'd known. A joyful kindergartner who carried a Harry Potter wand and wore a cape every day.

"This is my boy, long time ago. He turned fifteen a couple of months ago. He's in Tahoe with his dad."

"That's not cool. You should be together on Christmas."

Her throat tightened, and she nodded.

"Good lookin' kid. He play sports or anything?"

"He plays stupid video games."

Santa laughed.

"And he skateboards. I need to call him back, actually."

"Yeah. I should get a move on, really."

She didn't want him to leave yet. "Stay. I'll only be a minute. You didn't finish your beer."

"All right," he said again, agreeably.

Gloria stepped outside to call her son, the cold air biting at her fingers as she pushed the buttons on her ancient cell phone.

"Ma?"

"Merry Christmas, *mijo.*"

"Hey Ma, Merry Christmas. Dad says Merry Christmas, too."

"Okay." She didn't have anything to say to his dad. "How's Tahoe?"

"It's awesome. There's like a ton of snow, and Dad got me a snowboard. It's kind of hard but I'm getting better at it. Sheila is teaching me."

Gloria flinched. "You sound like you're having a great time." She tried to keep the anger out of her voice, but she sounded petulant anyway.

There was a momentary pause before he answered. "Yeah. It's cool. What about you, Ma, what are you doing?"

What do you mean what am I doing? Nothing. My brother's across the country. My friends are with their families. My mother doesn't know who I am. Didn't you think of that before you left me here?

"I went to see Grandma. Now I'm having a drink with a friend."

"Oh, that sounds good. Well, I have to go soon. I think we're going to eat dinner at the hotel."

Where was her ex coming up with this money? She had to get on him about the support payments. He should help with the damn lawyer bill.

"Okay, *mijo.* I think we're going out to dinner, too. Me and my friend." The lie rolled off her tongue. She didn't want Carlos worrying about her. She didn't want to be the lonely pathetic ex-wife to his dad.

Gloria looked through the window and saw her "friend" had finished his beer. His red jacket was stretched around his wide back. A seam looked like it was about to burst, a rip already started by the shoulder. She imagined Mrs. Claus would have that darned in a minute.

"I should go soon, *mijo.* He's waiting for me."

"Okay. But, um, Mom? I wanted you to think about something. I don't know if you . . . Well, it's that Dad is moving up here. He found a job here in the hotel. That's part of his surprise. That and the snowboard."

A chill came over her, like a draft under the door; her ex was up to something.

"So, anyway," Carlos went on, "he might want me to come up here with him."

The cold air pressed into her lungs as she listened, her heart starting to race. "Like, once in a while?"

"No, I think, um, to live. For the rest of high school. He says the schools are really good. And I can work at the hotel on weekends. Or snowboard. He's going to have a two-bedroom place. I know I've been driving you kind of crazy. But, I don't know. What do you think?"

Santa glanced out the window at her. Gloria waved, trying to decide how to react. Her stomach sloshed with too much alcohol and melancholia. She thought for a minute about her apartment, empty, the small fake Christmas tree in the corner. It was all she'd had the energy for this year.

"I don't know, Carlos. Sounds good, I guess. If you want." She heard the pain in her voice, despite her attempt to hide it.

He didn't respond immediately, and then, "Yeah. I don't know. I mean, I don't have any friends up here. I'd miss them."

Anger flared through her, jumping from her belly to the tip of her tongue before she could stop herself. "Your friends? You're going to miss them? Nice, Carlos. That's nice. You won't miss me?"

"Mom, I didn't mean it like that."

"No, that's fine. Say Merry Christmas to your father. And good luck. Tell him I said good luck being your parent. Too bad he missed like ten years." She hung up before she could hear him answer, tears stinging her eyes, the cold hurting her fingers.

She took a deep breath, already regretting her outburst. Son of bitch, that kid got to her. But she didn't want to fight with him on Christmas. His damn father offered him a Disney life in the mountains, not even discussing it with her.

"Hey, you okay?" Santa had stepped outside and stood next to her, taking up a considerable part of the side walk.

"I'm good. Sorry. You know—kids."

"You coming back in?"

"Yeah, yeah. But I'm not going to drink anymore. I need to eat something, I think."

She ordered a burger and fries and after thinking about it, he joined her.

"Funny Christmas dinner," he said, "but I've had worse." He went on to tell her about a Christmas he spent as a child in a homeless shelter, and another one, as a young man, on a boat off of China.

"I was a longshoreman for a while," he said. "Then I decided I needed to spend more time on land. The thing about spending your life on the ships. It's not solid, you know?"

She couldn't tell if he meant to make a joke, but she laughed anyway. "I guess it wouldn't be."

"What happened with your kid, on the phone?"

She glanced away. The restaurant was filling up with other folks too lonely or lazy to cook on Christmas.

"If you don't mind me asking."

She didn't really. It was better to talk about it. Gloria relayed the conversation.

"Well, a boy can get a lot from time with his father. I mean, I never had one so maybe that's bullshit. But that's what folks say."

"His father won't last ten minutes as a parent. He doesn't have the patience. And he's too weak. Diego always walks away when things are hard."

"Well, there you go. Tell your son he can go if he really wants to, so you're not the bad guy. Your ex will send him back soon enough."

"Maybe." She glanced at her phone but there was no message or call from Carlos. "Hey, it's four-thirty. Didn't you say you have to be at that church at five?"

He slid off the stool and reached for his beard. "Shit, yeah. I better go. It's across the valley." He dropped a twenty and ten on the table. "That should cover everything, I think."

"You don't have to do that."

"No, it's all right. Merry Christmas. My name's Danny by the way. We never said."

True. "I'm Gloria."

"Huh. Like the song, right?"

"'G-L-O-R-I-A'? The Van Morrison one?" She was so sick of people singing that song when they met her.

"No. I meant the Christmas one. *Glooooooooria . . . in ex hell-ish day-o*? Something like that. Anyway, it's cool to meet a Gloria on Christmas." He shook her hand. "Well, Gloria, I hope to see you again."

She didn't want him to leave, but it was pathetic to say so. Christian children waited for Santa and their crosses. "Me too."

"You come here a lot?"

"No. Not really."

"Well, I do. So, look for me if you come in." He strode across the bar, his red hat in hand, his bag of crucifixes over his shoulder.

Gloria finished her burger and both of their fries. She signaled for the bill from the waitress, just as Lourdes came through the door. Their eyes met and Lourdes winked, taking off her coat. She'd changed out of her uniform and wore a red sweater that was too tight for a woman her age, but looked great anyway.

"Hey girl, you took my advice on the peppermint things?"

"Yeah, I had a few. Then a burger. I was getting ready to go."

"What? Where you going? It's early. Come over to the bar with me and buy me a drink. It's Christmas, and I just finished watching that damn *It's a Wonderful Life* movie with your mother. Again."

Guilt tugged at Gloria's chest; she should have stayed longer. "She loves that movie."

"I know. They all do. I hate that shit. That weird Clarence Angel and all the people giving money to the bank. What is that? Fucking banks probably made that movie!" Lourdes grabbed the stool recently vacated by Santa Claus and ordered two more drinks.

"Make it a Chardonnay," Gloria told the bartender. No more peppermint for her. Lourdes had friends at the bar—two middle-aged guys and a woman, with the puffy faces of dedicated drinkers.

Lourdes led a lively conversation about the best and worst Christmas movies. "I liked the *Home Alone* ones," she said, "but Uriel always hated them. Freaked him out the way the parents kept leaving that kid behind."

"With you as his mother, can you blame him for being worried?" a red headed guy said.

Lourdes waved him off. "Fuck off, Tommy. I never left my kid." After a minute she added, "Okay, a couple times. But I didn't get far before I realized he was missing." She finished off her martini and popped the candy cane in her mouth.

Carlos called Gloria again around six. The cold air slapped her cheeks as she stepped outside to answer. The sky was dark. She hated how early the horizon disappeared in the winter.

"Hey, Ma. Sorry about before."

"Yeah, me too." She really was sorry. Why fight on Christmas? "What are you guys up to tonight?"

"Nothing much. They're asleep. I'm watching a movie."

"In the room?"

"I'm down in the lobby. They wanted—you know. Some time alone to take a nap. So I came down here."

Her stomach clenched, as she pictured him alone in a hotel lobby. So that his father could get it on with his girlfriend.

"It's fine. I have money for snacks and stuff. I had a burger."

"Me too."

The two of them had burgers for Christmas dinner, in separate places. She flashed on Christmas years earlier, her mother well, Diego present. They had passed around baby Carlos, eating tamales and drinking rum.

"We're gonna come home New Year's Day. I think Sheila has to work or something."

That was two days earlier than she'd expected them. Trouble in paradise? "Oh. Okay. Good. You know, Carlos, you can go live up there for a while with him if you want. I understand. If you need time with him or whatever."

There was a pause before he answered. "You sure?" His voice sounded young and vulnerable. He was at that age when he could sound like he was twenty or twelve in the same conversation.

She thought of Santa's advice and forced the pain from her voice. "Yeah. I mean it's probably not forever, right?"

Chapter 25

"From wine what sudden friendship springs!"

—John Gay

ELENA TRIED TO KEEP HER MIND IN A ZEN PLACE DURING HER yoga class, while the man in front of her managed to distract her from her "yoga breathing." His glasses kept slipping down his nose as he tried to jackknife his body into a clumsy downward dog, and when his shirt rose up to reveal the vertebrae of his spine, she thought of dinosaur bones.

Did she recognize him from somewhere?

After class, he stood near her, gulping from his water bottle, as she rolled her mat. He had long and narrow feet with a small tuft of hair on his big toe.

"First class?" she asked him.

"Second. Is it that obvious I'm new?" He grimaced, his lower lip pulling down. It could have been creepy but instead was comical. "We met at the stables last month, right?" He stuck out his hand. "I'm Noah."

That was why he was familiar. "Yes," she answered, "I think so."

It had been an unusually warm winter day, and Elena, feeling restless, had gotten out of the car and wandered around the stables while waiting for Amanda.

Noah was slipping off a horse, finished with a lesson from Uriel. There was straw stuck to Noah's boots, and he offered a youthful smile, although he looked about her age. She remembered his skin was smooth and supple when they shook hands.

Today Noah wore sweat pants, not those silly men's yoga tights, and a plain black T-shirt that clung to him, sweaty. She was probably a mess herself. She tucked her hair behind her ear.

"I'm Elena," she said as she stood up. Meeting new people was on the list of things Dr. Love had spelled out for her to do—part of "scaffolding a new life."

"Nice to see you again." His smile was mischievous, a deep dimple in his chin. "Do you recognize me from anywhere else? Other than the stables?" He sounded as if they shared a joke.

Her mind raced over possibilities—a friend of Jim's? An old boyfriend of Carmen's? "No, I'm sorry."

"Oh, well, never mind." He looked away, as if looking for someone else to talk to, or a yoga prop to hide behind.

"Did we meet . . . another time?" She was too curious to let it go.

He shrugged. "Not really. It was a silly thing to say." He gathered up his mat and started towards the door. He turned back to her after a moment. "It's nothing really. I happened to notice that on Saturdays mornings we both—well, I think our therapists are in the same suite? So, we're both there—in the waiting room. Saturday at ten-thirty, right?"

She squirmed, feeling like a child who wanted to hide behind her mother's skirt.

He bit his lower lip. "Sorry—probably broke all kind of boundaries even bringing it up." He had large fleshy lips that she found strangely appealing. Kissable?

"No problem," she managed to say. Her unwieldy mat slipped from her sweaty fingers. She bent down to re-roll it, and when she looked up, he was gone. She tried to picture Noah across the muted waiting room at the psychiatrist's office. If he observed her every Saturday morning could he tell she'd lost her sanity, at least briefly?

Outside, a moist, piney smell drifted in from the trees surrounding the studio. The contrast from the yoga room made her stop and breathe, deeply. *Think calm thoughts*, she reminded herself. Her meditation teacher's words. *This is the only moment that exists.* She shouldn't let a small encounter with an odd man rob her of her yoga calm.

A zippy black car pulled up next to her, her own reflection bouncing off the windows. Noah was behind the wheel and he lowered the window. He looked more compact in the car.

"Do you want to grab a cup of coffee?" His eyes were pools of uncertainty.

She glanced at her watch. Five p.m. More like cocktail hour than coffee time, in her mind. But it had been a long time since a man asked her to coffee. She glanced at her naked ring finger and wondered if Noah would notice the wrinkles on the back of her hands.

"Sure. A quick one, why not?"

In the parking lot of Peet's Coffee Shop, she dabbed on lipstick before heading in, but no amount of makeup would conceal that she was fifty-five, wearing no foundation, and had just worked out.

Maybe he wanted to talk about yoga?

Noah insisted on paying for her Zen Green tea. She squeezed a packet of honey into the steaming cup, licking the excess off her fingers. His gaze seemed quite focused on her, and she nervously touched her brow for sweat. Dry, but had she just gotten honey in her eyebrow?

"Do you do yoga often?" He moved his chair closer to the table.

"Uh, no. Well, only when it's prescribed by my psychiatrist." She might as well joke about it.

He sputtered, a gulp of coffee caught in his throat, then smiled. "I'm doing yoga on my therapist's recommendation as well." His lips turned up. "What a coincidence."

"I wonder if the yoga teachers give our doctors a referral fee?"

His smile widened. "The psychiatrists are making plenty without it." Then he added, "Maybe the shrinks should give a percentage to the people who send us to therapy in the first place." When he smiled, his eyes crinkled, like the folds of origami paper.

"Hm. That would be my ex."

He nodded. "In my case as well. Wouldn't that be great, if we could bill our ex-spouses?"

She thought for minute about that, trying her tea. "Would we have to pay for their therapy though?"

"I'm not paying for hers," he said, with finality.

After a beat she nodded in agreement. "I'm not paying for his, either."

"I never expected to be single," he said, seemingly perplexed. "At this stage of the game. Even after taking the right steps, life can go awry."

She was struck with his words, his ability to express her own feelings. "It's not fair, is it?"

"Exactly," he said. And then, after a minute, "Would you like to have dinner with me?"

She was startled. "Now?"

"Or later?" His eyes twinkled as if he might be kidding.

"I'm supposed to have dinner with my daughter," she said, feeling torn about turning him down.

"Yeah, it's last minute. Sorry." He looked away, fingers lightly drumming the table. The sweat on his shirt had left a ring around his collar, and she thought vaguely of scrubbing it out.

"Maybe another time?" he asked.

"Yes." She wondered if she should offer another specific time. Was that his role or hers? She really had no idea how relationships worked anymore.

"So, your daughter lives nearby?"

"I can cancel with her for tonight," Elena blurted out. "She'll probably be relieved."

His eyes brightened. "You sure?"

"Yes." She tried to muster confidence in her voice. "Yes, I am."

They parted in the parking lot with a plan to meet in an hour. Her head spun. She was so used to saying no, the word *yes* made her tingle. She said no to her tennis friends who wondered why she'd disappeared. No to going horseback riding with Amanda, to extra yoga, to spending time with Uriel's family. No to a drink with Carmen's friends. No, no.

Saying yes to fun things betrayed her angry, lonely, miserable self. And she'd grown attached to that self. But here she was, driving home with the music playing, thinking about what to wear tonight. Her cell phone rang as she turned onto the long road up the mountain.

"Hey, babe!" Carmen's voice was high, ebullient. She had probably closed on a house. Real estate was Carmen's drug of choice. "I've been trying to track you down. Did you get my email? I haven't heard back from you on the Costa Rica thing."

"I never sit in front of my computer anymore. Sorry. I'll read it later tonight?"

"For now, I have us booked for the salsa classes and doing the jungle zip line. You're in the air for a half mile at a time. Doesn't that sound awesome?"

Did it? Elena tried to picture herself flying through the sky, her legs dangling. "Can I take a look and get back to you?"

"Seriously sister, let's do this. You need a life."

"I have a life."

"Since fuckhead left, all I've heard about is yoga and eating dinners with Amanda."

Elena took the turn onto her street too hard and the tires skidded. "I should go. I'm driving."

"Are you meeting Amanda for dinner?"

"No." After a minute, she added defensively, "In fact, I have a date tonight."

"A date?" Carmen's voice rose an octave. "Who?" she asked. "And wait, what are you going to wear?"

"No idea. Nothing fancy. Just a guy from yoga. I'll call you tomorrow about the salsa thing."

"Seriously? Tell me his name at least!"

Elena said goodbye again, smiling as she hung up. It was nice to surprise Carmen for once. Stepping into the house, she texted Amanda and told her she was having dinner with Carmen. She couldn't tell Amanda she was going on a date. With a stranger.

Upstairs, Elena paced naked in her bedroom, half aware of her body in the side mirror. *Delgado*, her mother would call her. *Skinny*, and not in a complimentary way. She looked more like an underfed street dog than a sexy woman. She threw clothes on the bed, trying to choose.

A purple poncho, jeans and boots? No, dressing too young would come off as desperate. The white dress with gold pumps was elegant but too formal. Her black pants slipped off her hips since the divorce, a size too large.

She hopped into the shower, hoping it would soothe her angst. The water hit her neck and chest, her clavicle holding a drop like a spoon. She rinsed her breasts with lavender soap, trying to imagine Noah seeing them, touching them. They seemed smaller, droopier, and older than she'd ever seen them, the nipples pointing towards the floor as if in resignation.

God, she needed to cancel this dinner, get out of the shower and call him. She couldn't possibly be naked in front of another man, ever again. And dating was a prelude to sex, eventually. Wasn't it?

But when she picked up her phone, she saw Noah had texted the name of the restaurant and **See you at eight** with a winking emoji. She couldn't cancel on him now. The man went to a therapist, for God's sake. Her rejection could put him over the edge.

One meal together would be fine. After all, his head, while large for his neck, was nicely shaped under his thick hair. She'd have trouble drawing him if she tried, because his features lent themselves to caricature, not portrait. Yet all the parts combined with his carefully strung together words and quick smile made him endearing, even handsome.

Elena chose a long black skirt with a gray sweater and gray suede boots, aiming for mature and unpretentious. She borrowed a red scarf she noticed slung over the back of Amanda's door. She felt a little giddy as she tied it.

The restaurant was in Kenwood, twenty minutes north, in an adobe inn. Lanterns shone on the thick white walls, and a fountain bubbled in the center of the courtyard. In the tiny crowded bar, Noah leaned on the wall, sipping a glass of water. The music was something jazzy from another time period, and she wished for a minute she'd worn something splashier.

Noah looked handsome in a heather blue jacket. She caught her breath. How had she managed to be on a date? He greeted her with a quick kiss on the cheek. "Thanks for coming," he said. He sounded genuinely grateful, and she wondered what he would otherwise have done this evening.

Once seated, she tried to be comfortable with eye contact. How soon could she order a drink?

"I stumbled on this restaurant last week. I'm only in Sonoma on the weekends, so I'm still exploring," Noah explained. "I work in the city during the week."

He had a complete life elsewhere, in San Francisco. She thought of Jim's secret life with Victor all those years.

"What kind of work do you do?"

"I'm a neurologist." He played with a spoon. A tight nervousness radiating through him. "At UCSF."

She flashed on the cancer center where Jim had gotten his diagnosis and treatments. Everything had smelled like salad dressing, the walls painted a depressing, pale yellow. A neurologist. Maybe his brain was larger than other people's, hence his large head. "It sounds serious."

He smiled. "It can be. Shall I order wine?"

"Yes, please." Wine would help. She really did like his smile.

He handed her the wine list. "Your choice."

She chose an Alborino by Imagery. She didn't know wine that well, but she had gone there to picnic and play bocce once with Carmen, and the wine had tasted lovely. She wanted to taste the memory.

He ordered a robust paella for both of them.

"This is superb," she almost purred, the paella was so good. "I wonder if I could make it at home."

"Do you cook much?" he asked.

She thought of her empty refrigerator. "I used to. And I'm starting to again. My daughter gave me a cookbook for Christmas, actually."

Noah seemed fascinated with the mundane details of her life. Which yoga class did she like? Had she seen the movie playing at the square? Had she read the new memoir about the man who survived all those years as a POW?

By the time the waiter cleared the dinner plates, the bottle of wine was gone.

"I'm not ready to call it a night." Noah said, as he drained the last drop in his glass.

"Dessert?" she suggested.

"Definitely," he answered. He ordered them both a glass of dessert wine and a flourless chocolate torte to share. "With extra raspberries, please."

She excused herself to go to the women's room. Hoping she didn't look tipsy as she crossed the room, she glanced at her phone. Carmen had sent a text as well, a photo of a beach hut with a monkey perched in front.

What do you think? Carmen's text said, **Can I book it?**

She'd call Carmen in the morning and tell her to go for it. Costa Rica! Why not? Elena hummed along with the music as she strolled back through the restaurant. Blue Bayou. Could she be enjoying herself? When she returned, the dessert was on the table, with a glass of wine for each of them.

"Have you dated much since your divorce?" Noah asked, out of the blue.

"I'm not even divorced yet. So, no." She tried not to sound defensive. "You?"

"A few disastrous forays into the world of relationships. I wouldn't call it dating."

"Tell me more about this."

He shifted in his chair. "Oh, I don't think so."

"No, really. I need to know what it's like out there. Share your research tips with a fellow divorce survivor."

Noah snorted, laughing into his port. She noticed a splash of light jumping from his watch to the glass of white wine, like a firefly.

"What's so funny?"

"Well, as it turns out," he said, not quite meeting her eyes. "It was a research partner who I had a thing with. A young woman at work, who I can only imagine had a daddy complex. Or she was truly passionate about neuron pathway structures. Anyway, major mistake."

Elena took a small bite of the torte, trying to ignore the way her heart had raced at the words "young woman."

"So, was it fun, being with a younger woman? Kind of a midlife dream, right?" Her voice didn't hold the lighthearted humor she'd hoped to portray.

Noah placed his wine on the table, reached his hand across the table and touched the edge of her hand. "I don't know how that came up. I was trying to find out if you're seeing anyone. But no, it wasn't much fun. It was unprofessional, messy. It forced me into therapy." He stopped and took a breath. "Sorry. I'm still figuring myself out. Tonight has been great." His eager eyes stared at her from behind his glasses. "For me."

"Yes, this is fun," she admitted, a smile slipping out unbidden. She took her hand away and helped herself to a large bite of the torte and a sip of the dessert wine.

"Was your husband unfaithful?" he asked. "You sound hurt. Was there another woman?"

"Nope," Elena said, a bitter laugh slipping out. "There was no other woman." She felt his curious gaze on her face, and went on. "I knew things were not right. But I carried on, so to speak. And in the end, he left anyway."

Noah's eyebrow lifted.

"He's with a man." She said it fast, as if the words would hurt less if she said them quickly. "A nice man, I thought. Victor. He came to dinner many times over the years."

Noah assimilated this information, his lower lip frowning, as if disturbed in some way. "That's terrible."

"Yes. I didn't see it coming. Oh, and my husband had cancer when he told me. Maybe still does, but I don't ask. And my daughter knew about the affair, it turns out. It's been tough."

Noah groaned. "It sounds awful!"

It was enough encouragement for Elena to go on, spilling it out, enjoying the release. "He told me one night, after dinner. In a restaurant."

Noah kept his eyes trained on her, listening. She warmed to the experience of being listened to, and speaking the truth. She told him about the last few months.

"When it gets close to dinner time, I start thinking about what to cook, and then it hits me—I could cook nothing. I could skip meals. That's what put *me* into therapy. Grocery shopping! I was standing in line with the eggs and a few mushrooms, and suddenly it crashed in on me. I couldn't believe it. I was that woman, cooking eggs for dinner, alone."

Elena didn't speak the rest of the story out loud. How she came home from the store and parked in the garage, unable to face another day. "Would you like to go?" she asked, looking up. She needed to hide. She was not ready for company.

He shook his head. "Only if you do. I'm sorry you're going through all that."

She looked away, embarrassed by his empathy. "This is all new to me." She nibbled her lip, determined not to cry. "And I think I'm wiped out. I didn't realize how late it was."

Noah nodded. "You're right. Proving my point. We must be having fun if the night went so fast. Right?"

"Right," Elena said. But her heart had been laid open. She needed to rewrap the wounds. "I just get tired. I think it's the meds that shrink has me taking."

He tilted his head, interested. "What are you taking?"

"Lexapro. Fifteen milligrams."

"Geez," he said, "I'm only on ten. You must be crazier than I am."

The words floated in the air between them. Crazy. Crazier. She saw the garage again, the line of daylight at the bottom of the door, the gloom inside. Remembered thinking, as she fell asleep, that it she should have chosen somewhere beautiful for her last moments, not the garage. She had wished she'd jumped off a high, beautiful mountain.

You're crazier than I am.

"I should get home," she said.

He must have felt the shift in their energy. "Stupid joke, sorry. It's been a great night. For what it's worth, I think you're quite sane."

Chapter 26

"Give me wine to wash me clean of the weather-stains
of cares."

—Ralph Waldo Emerson

URIEL COULDN'T BELIEVE HE WAS BRINGING A GIRL TO MEET HIS
mother.

"Did I tell you about the first girl I brought home?"

Amanda was riding in the passenger seat of his truck, trying to finish her makeup while they bounced over the rough roads. "I'm not the first girl you're bringing to meet Lourdes?"

"I was in kindergarten. Jenny, I think. It was okay at first. Lourdes made us snacks, and we ran around in the backyard, you know, like normal kids."

"Then?"

"The girl's dad comes to pick her up. Maybe five o'clock. And then after a few beers, he and my mom tell us we are having a 'sleep over.' So, of course, Jenny and I are like, 'Yeah! Sleepover!'"

"It doesn't sound that bad. Mildly inappropriate."

"Sure, until his wife shows up at like midnight, calling my mom all sorts of things and dragging Jenny out of there."

"Eek."

"Yeah. Got a few more of those stories."

"Now I'm getting nervous."

Uriel thought about the black girl with tiny braids woven in intricate designs he'd fallen for in sixth grade. She came over on a Friday afternoon to watch movies on the fold-out couch, a bag of popcorn between them. He watched her toss in kernel after kernel, never missing, and thought this might be love.

Then Lourdes had stumbled in and yelled, "Who is this *puta* in my bed?" The girl had fled, crying.

"Never mind, it will be fine."

Gloria's suggestion that he introduce Amanda to his mother had sounded far-fetched. But that very night, after the hours of lovemaking, Amanda had asked him why she'd never met Lourdes.

"It's like you're hiding me or something. Or are you hiding her?"

"Ha," Uriel answered. "Both."

But tonight, they were heading out the door when his mother called, asking for "a little help with the rent." It was New Year's Eve, the rent due in the morning. Hadn't he already given her a check earlier in the month?

Amanda brushed on mascara, looking in the truck's rearview mirror as Uriel turned into the trailer park. "Why don't we invite your mother to go with us to dinner?"

"Oh no, don't do that," Uriel said.

"Do what?"

"Suggest we do things with her. Or try to be really nice to her. She doesn't appreciate nice. Trust me on this."

The wreath he'd bought Lourdes had fallen off the door. It laid on its side in the dirt and dead stalks stuck out of dry dirt in her flower pots. Everything looked shabbier with Amanda as his witness. Lourdes' version of holiday lights, a light up Virgin Mary, teetered on the top of the picnic table.

The trailer door opened, and a streak of gray shot by. "God damn it, Bilbo! Get the fuck back here!" Lourdes stood on the front porch, hands on her hips. Her hair was bundled in a high messy bun, and a faded Sonoma State sweatshirt fell over her jeans. "Uriel, get that cat."

The cat was halfway across the street and running hard, clearly escaping.

"Since when do you have a cat? I was here yesterday, and you didn't have a cat."

Lourdes hurried past them, the scent of beer wafting behind her. The wayward cat scampered under the trailer across the street. "Bilbo! Come on, dude!"

"Do you have cat food?" Amanda spoke up. "Cats come out sometimes if you open a can of food where they can hear it."

Lourdes stared at Amanda, as if trying to place her.

"Mom, this is—"

"I know. We met one time at the supermarket."

"Hi." Amanda put her hand out. "Amanda. It's nice to see you again. I'm sorry your cat got out."

Lourdes gave her hand a quick shake. "It's not my cat. The cat lives over there. I'm just watching it for the weekend."

"Why?" Uriel asked.

"Because the guy's away. In Vegas. And the cat doesn't like staying alone, I guess."

Uriel tried to imagine his mother being neighborly enough to watch someone's cat. "Is he paying you?"

Lourdes shrugged. "He said he'll get me a bottle of something good."

Ah. Pet-sitting for alcohol.

Amanda examined his mother. Uriel wondered what she saw. The lines around her eyes were deeply etched and her skin patchy from long days in the sun, but she didn't look her fifty-one years. Trim, with bright eyes, an appealing smile.

"I'll put this in the trailer," Uriel said, pulling the envelope from his pocket.

"All right, thanks." Lourdes continued to call for Bilbo. "Hey Uriel, bring me a can of cat food. The bag's on the bench in there."

Inside, the usual smells hit him: beer, cigarettes, the acidic tint of cleaning products and sweetness of the old fruit in a chipped bowl. He dropped the rent check on the counter and grabbed the cat food.

"And bring us a couple beers from the fridge," Lourdes yelled.

He tried to ignore his instinctive reaction to her bossy tone. Uriel grabbed two cheap beers quickly, nervous about leaving Amanda outside with his mother. The beers weren't very cold. "Ma," he said, as he stepped outside. "Your fridge isn't cold enough."

"Yeah," she shrugged. "It's broken. The landlord said he'll bring me a better one once I pay up on the rent."

He squinted at her. "You should be paid up on the rent. That check's for January."

Lourdes didn't answer, more or less confirming she'd spent last month's rent money on booze.

He handed each woman an opened beer, then stepped back inside and grabbed the check off the counter. He would deliver it to the landlord himself, tomorrow. When he stepped outside, Lourdes was babbling at Amanda about something. He opened the cat food and called to Bilbo, who was cowering under the other trailer.

"I know you from somewhere," Lourdes said to Amanda, before taking a hefty gulp of her beer. "Not just at the supermarket that time. Now that you're close up, you remind me of someone. Maybe I knew you as a kid? Where'd you go to school? Sonoma High?"

Amanda put her beer down on the picnic table and came over to help Uriel. "I went to Sonoma Academy."

Lourdes' eyebrows lifted, and Uriel knew she was thinking about spoiled rich kids. Lourdes shook her head. "No, wouldn't be from there. I don't know. You seem familiar."

"Here you go," Amanda said, as the cat came creeping out from under the trailer. She placed the can closer to him. Bilbo approached the food and began to eat.

"Grab him," Lourdes said.

"Not yet," Amanda answered, kneeling down. "Better to get him to trust me." She used a low voice, talking quietly to Bilbo, whose tail began to wave slowly as he ate. It reminded Uriel of Amanda's patience with horses. Her ability to calm a horse was one of the first things that drew him to her. Once he finished the can, Bilbo leaned on Amanda's legs, and she scooped him up.

"You're good with cats, huh?" Lourdes lit a cigarette, taking a deep drag.

"All animals," Uriel answered for Amanda, trying to resist his urge to brag to his mother about his girlfriend. She can shoot a gun too, he wanted to add. *I taught her how, but she's a natural. And she knows how to fix a flat tire in the rain.*

They sat at the picnic table, despite the chilly evening, the trailer too small.

"Do you feel you've met me before?" Lourdes asked Amanda, eyeing her closely. She added, "I like that hair of yours. It's pretty darn red."

Amanda's fair cheeks blushed. "I don't think I knew you before. But you feel familiar because Uriel looks like you."

"You think so?" Lourdes examined Uriel, as if she didn't see him daily.

"Sort of," Amanda said. "You guys have the same shaped eyes."

"Huh. Maybe I know your mom, and you look like her?"

"I don't think so," Uriel said.

"Anyway," Amanda added, "I'm adopted. I don't look like my mom. So it's not that. Maybe you've seen pictures of me? At Uriel's? Or at the stables?"

"Nope," Lourdes shook her head. "I never go around there. Uriel's uncle doesn't like me."

"Oh." Amanda looked away, looking like she was trying not to smile.

"Well, we should go," Uriel interjected. "We're having dinner with Chito downtown." It was a lie. They weren't meeting Chito. He hoped Amanda knew enough to go along with it.

Lourdes shrugged. "Give me the cat, then."

Amanda passed Bilbo to Lourdes, the cat complaining about the transition. "It was really nice to meet you. I was thinking maybe you recognize me from yoga classes? I go to a couple different places. I teach sometimes."

"Yoga?" Lourdes grimaced as if that was a good joke. "No. I don't go to yoga. It's more like, you're familiar. Maybe you kids went to the same youth group or something."

"I doubt that," Uriel said. He guided Amanda towards the truck, ready to go.

"Coming by for breakfast?" Lourdes asked her son.

"Not tomorrow, Ma."

"All right then, see you." Lourdes shook a cigarette from her pack as he started the car. He saw the smoke curling around the head of the cat before he swung out of the driveway and down the block.

"Well," he said, annoyed that both Gloria and Amanda had suggested such as crap idea. "Now you've met Lourdes."

Amanda gave him a forced smile then looked away. "She's fine. I mean, I get why she annoys you, but it was fine."

"Cool. Glad it's over with."

"It was weird though—right? How determined she was that she knew me?"

He shook his head. "Lourdes is weird about stuff like that. Thinks she's psychic or something. Some family gift. Gloria thinks she has it, too."

Amanda glanced back, looking hesitant. "Maybe Gloria does have it. She saved my mother when she got a feeling she should go in the garage. Gloria doesn't usually go in there."

"Well, she heard the car running."

"Still. It would have been easy to ignore it. To think someone was coming or going." Amanda's voice grew quieter. "And my mother would be gone."

"You can't let yourself think about what ifs. Trust me, I did that for months after Flavia died, and it never helped."

"I try not to."

"I felt like I knew you, when I met you." Uriel had observed Amanda for weeks, coming and going, before he gained the nerve to talk to her.

She smiled. "I remember you said that at the time. Probably from the stables, before we actually met."

"Maybe I have the family juju. I could tell we were *meant* to meet."

"You might have the family gift for bullshit, too."

He laughed, relieved.

"Shit, Uriel. We forgot to leave these." She held up a basket of wrapped treats from Jesse and Maya. "You told Maya you'd give them to your mom, to take to her work."

Frustrated with himself, Uriel swung the car around and headed back to his mother's place. He jogged up to the trailer, eager to drop the basket and go. He knocked quickly.

"Yeah?" Lourdes called out. She had changed into a black sweater and had her hair down. She sat in the breakfast nook, doing her makeup in a small mirror. "Just getting ready to go out. What's up?"

"I forgot to give you these. For the old folks at the nursing home."

She glanced up. "More of Maya's cookies? Put them on the table. People think I'm an angel, baking those cookies. They love them." She pulled on a boot. "And what happened to the rent check?"

"It's for rent, right? So I'll drop it off with the landlord."

Lourdes sat up, a vertical line deepening between her brows. "I told you I'm short this month."

"And I can help you with the rent, Ma. But I don't want you to drink it away."

"Uriel. Don't pull this shit on me. I got it figured out. I need some cash now, but I'll get paid Friday. I can pay the rent up on the third with no penalty. Don't treat me like a damn kid."

Uriel hesitated near the door. He didn't want drama with Amanda waiting in the car. Instead of the check, he laid three twenties on the counter. "Don't spend it all in one place," he said, an expression he'd picked up from Freddie. "I'll drop the check off with the landlord."

Lourdes grabbed the bills and offered a begrudging, "Thanks." His mother pulled on her second boot, shiny and black. Not the ones she usually wore around the trailer park.

Something about them rattled a bell in the recesses of his brain. "Nice boots."

"Thanks. You bought them."

Uriel didn't remember that. "When?"

"I don't know. You gave them to me after Flavia died. They were brand new, still in the box. I figured you bought them for her at some point."

Uriel's heart raced. "I don't think so."

"I mean, you didn't *give* them to me, exactly. You said I could go through the closet and take some stuff. Me and Jesse. I don't know what else I brought home—a couple jackets and paperback books? Freddie got his nose out of joint about it."

After Flavia had died, Lourdes visited more often, almost like a normal mom. Freddie wouldn't tell her not to come on his property the week Uriel's wife died. But it hadn't lasted.

"Can I see one of the boots?"

"You want me to take off my boot?"

Uriel glanced out the window where Amanda waited in the truck. "Yeah, real quick. I want to see what kind it is."

Lourdes narrowed her eyes but pulled off a boot and tossed it to him. The boot was scuffed, the leather stretched and molded to his mother's foot. But the inside label was still clear: Nine West. On the bottom, he recognized Flavia's size.

He thought of Cat Blakely's voice on the phone. *You'd know if she got these boots. Nine West. Expensive. You would have seen them.*

That's why they'd stayed in a box. To wear them would have been too obvious. Cat said her husband purchased the boots in August. Months before Flavia died. How long had the affair gone on? Had she known the Texan before she married Uriel?

The intricacies of her betrayal broke through his mind. The months of duplicity, keeping him in the dark. The lies. Was it even Uriel's baby

she had carried? He felt like he was standing at the ocean's shore, looking down for the first time during low tide and seeing the muck and
shit that was his life. That *had been* his life.

"Can I get my boot back?"

Uriel came back to the present. His mother grabbed the boot and
put it on. "Why don't y'all drop me at Gloria's? That way I don't have
to drive."

He looked outside. In the truck, the overhead light shone on
Amanda as she applied lipstick. Her cheeks looked flushed, her breath
making tiny designs on the window.

Lourdes sprayed herself with the same powdery body scent she'd
used since he was a kid. She headed to the truck, looking purposeful.
Off to the bars.

Uriel crossed the trailer's mangy yard behind her, trying to return
to the present and a better mood. Difficult to do, while he followed the
footprints of his dead wife's boots across the muddy yard.

Chapter 27

"Bring water, bring wine, boy! Bring flowering garlands to me! Yes, bring them, so that I may try a bout with love."

—Anacreon, Fragment 27

LOURDES CALLED GLORIA IN THE MORNING ON DECEMBER 31. "You coming out again, *prima*? We had fun at Christmas."

Usually Gloria and Carlos ordered Chinese, make brownies and watched the ball drop on TV. Being alone seemed too pathetic. So, although the last night out had left her with a morning headache, Gloria mentally picked out her clothes before she hung up.

She squeezed herself into a pair of gold pants she hadn't worn in years and straightened her frazzled hair into a smooth sheet. Her mind flitted to Diego only once as she applied her mascara. Time to move on for real. *Diego is long gone.*

They met in the parking lot, Lourdes looking her up and down like she was a stranger. "*Chica*, you look sexy," her cousin said as they traversed the parking lot, frigid air slipping under Gloria's sweater.

"Thanks, Lourdes. You too."

A tired Cadillac missing a headlight floated by her like a bloated shark and sank into a nearby spot. Danny, AKA the "Santa" she'd met on Christmas, stepped out of the car, like a bear climbing out of a hole.

Gloria's heart jumped as he lumbered over. His stomach fell over the edge of his blue jeans, but his broad shoulders were appealing. His hair was combed straight back, making his forehead appear higher.

"Hey," he said as if they'd planned on meeting there. "Happy New Year." His voice was smooth, like a voice on television that sold cars or life insurance.

He held the door for them. *It feels like we came together*, Gloria thought, surprised how much the idea appealed to her. Floating Champagne bottle balloons dangled from the ceiling. "How were the Christian kids you delivered the crosses to?" Gloria asked.

He smiled. "Pretty excited about the light-up crucifixes, actually."

"Jesus, they must keep those kids in a bubble. My son would never have been excited about that."

Lourdes winked at Gloria as she headed off with a couple other regulars. Danny steered Gloria through the crowd, his large hand resting lightly on her arm. Gloria felt naked walking in front of him in her too-tight gold pants. Why hadn't she worn jeans? They sat at a booth again, as if they'd already established a routine. A waitress appeared, offering them a menu with one hand as she wiped the table with the other.

"I've already eaten," Gloria said.

"Me too. I'll take a mojito," he told the waitress. "You should try it," he said to Gloria. "It's like mint candy with a real kick."

Gloria ordered a glass of Champagne, and asked Danny if he wanted to order a dessert.

"Ha," Danny smacked his belly under the red shirt, "that's all I need. My wife tells me I'm getting too fat."

Wife. A shaft of disappointment slid from her throat to her belly. After a minute, she swallowed and was able to speak without, she hoped, showing her surprise. "I'll take the lava cheesecake," she said, pointing at the photo of the oozing sugary mess. "With two forks."

She wanted to say, *What are you doing here alone on New Year's if you have a wife?* But instead she answered his many questions. *Where was she from? What kind of movies did she like? Had she been to Disneyland?*

She tried not to enjoy his warm eyes on her too much. *He's married.* But was he really? *Where's the wife tonight?*

When the cheesecake came, she plunged in, the cream melting in her mouth, sweet sticky caramel on her lips. "It's delicious," she said.

Danny took an enormous bite. "Incredible. And probably low-fat." They both laughed, and he waved for more drinks.

After two glasses of Champagne, Lourdes came by and dragged her onto the tiny dance floor. A few minutes later Gloria accepted a shot from Lourdes' friend, while her cousin danced to the Macarena.

Lourdes kicked it up on the dance floor with a pair of shiny boots. "Lourdes was dancing to that when we were teens," Gloria said to the guy, realizing her voice sounded husky.

Gloria joined her, giggling. Danny leaned on the bar behind them, enjoying their performance.

Gloria didn't argue when Danny offered to drive her home hours later; she didn't think she could drive. But in the car, she wondered if she was too trusting. She didn't even know this man. Did she want him to know where she lived?

"I should take my car," Gloria protested. "Or I won't have it in the morning."

"I can pick you up in the morning and run you back, no problem." Danny pulled out onto the highway, heading towards her end of town.

He is not a psycho, and he won't hit on you. If he did, she would say no. *Just say goodbye in the parking lot and thank him for the ride.*

Danny escorted her to her door and kissed her once, lightly, on the lips. And then he kissed her again, for real. As they stumbled inside, pushing Carlos' shoes out of the way, she willed herself to send Danny home.

But the touch of his hand on the small of her back made her pelvis arch towards him. He smelled like sugar, rum and aftershave. It had been too long since she'd been near a nice-smelling man. She wanted the kisses, to have her clothes tugged off, to feel the wetness between her legs, and her nipples to wake up.

Gloria wanted sex. That's what she had wanted for Christmas, and he was Santa. He was just delivering her gift a week late.

She clamped her lips on his mouth like she wanted to eat him up. His hands clutched at her waist, then found their way under her coat and slippery tank top. Kisses everywhere, and his hands sinking under her layers and peeling them free.

Gloria led him to the bedroom, trying not to think about what a mess the apartment was. She kicked Carlos' video console out of the way and knocked the clean laundry off the bed.

They sank down, the mattress groaning beneath them as they groped and rolled amongst the unmade sheets. She lay back, grateful for the dim lighting to hide her stretch marks, then helped him pull off his jeans. For a minute he stood above her in boxers, his winter jacket still on. She giggled.

He sighed. "I know I'm not in shape—"

"Sorry, it's the jacket and boxers."

"Which one should I take off?" He winked and yanked off his jacket. He buried his face into her breasts, nuzzling them like baby bunnies.

She thought again of his wife and had a spasm of guilt and jealousy. "Hey, Danny?"

He looked up from her breasts, his face red and hot. "Yes, Gloria?"

"I don't mean to ruin the moment, but . . . Did you say you have a wife?"

His brows raised a tad and he shifted his eyes back to her breasts, as if they might help him answer the question. "Yeah. I might have mentioned her."

"So, you are married?"

"Yeah . . . yeah. I'm married. But—"

"But?"

"But it's complicated."

She sat up to look into his eyes. "Complicated—so you don't spend holidays together?"

"Nah. I go sometimes on visiting day. But not very often."

Visiting day? Gloria thought of her mother in the nursing home. Maybe he had a lunatic wife in an asylum? Like that book she read in high school, with the deranged wife in the attic.

"She's—staying somewhere? Away?"

He grunted. "Oh yeah. She's away. Couple more years at least."

"Oh." Jail. For some reason she only thought of men as going to jail. She wondered what the woman had done. Probably, she shouldn't ask. "I don't know if this is okay then, or not."

"It is for me. As long as it is for you. But if you want me to go home, I can. I mean, I'd understand. But I'd rather not."

A wife in jail wasn't really married, was it? Gloria examined his wide forehead and soft gray eyes, looking for signs of deception. In her alcohol haze, she saw instead a half-dressed man in her bed, eager to eat up her lumpy body like another slice of cheesecake. She rolled over and climbed on top of him. A woman could suffocate under this guy. On top, she felt like she was riding a float in the Macy's parade.

In the morning, Gloria found him playing her son's video game, shooting bad guys and drinking a cup of coffee in a chipped mug, still in his boxers. She considered him for a minute, thinking about the fact that he was still there. Her hangover made each thought take twice as long to process. She pulled her robe tighter around her faded night gown.

Danny's sonorous voice sounded louder in the small room. "Hope you don't mind, I made coffee."

"Mind? No. I'm glad." Gloria poured herself a huge cup. Maybe the coffee would help the headache leaning on her temple like a car horn. "Hey, I need to go to the store soon, get my kid a present. He gets home late tonight."

"You decided to get him something, huh?"

"Yeah. I guess I'll get him that game he wants. Mummy or something."

Danny paused his game. "*Ghost*. He asked for the new *Call of Duty*, right?"

"Right."

"It's called *Ghost*. I'll go with you if you want, make sure you get the right one for this system."

Gloria could probably figure it out without his help, but she didn't really want to. "Okay. That'd be good, thanks. I need a ride to my car at least."

"Come sit down with me for a minute, first." Danny resumed his game.

"Okay."

He reached out an enormous arm and pulled her in, still shooting terrorists on the screen with one hand, like a cuddly, overweight sniper. Gloria leaned into him. "Your kid comes back today?"

"Yeah." She placed her feet on the table. She needed a pedicure. Things she didn't think about until a man slept over.

"You think he'll move up with his dad?" Danny asked. "To Tahoe?"

"I took your advice and told him it was up to him."

He smiled, still staring at the screen. "Good. But let him know you want him to stay here, really."

She paused to think about it. "I did. And he said he'd probably just stay here. Like I should be grateful, instead of him."

Danny squeezed her arm. "You guys will be all right."

"I guess."

"I can tell you're a good mom."

Gloria shrugged. Maybe. In a few minutes, she'd get up and make them eggs. Then they could go buy Carlos his game. For now, she let her head rest on this man's enormous shoulder.

Chapter 28

"Age and glasses of wine should never be counted."

—Italian Proverb

ELENA RESTED IN HER FINAL ASANA, HER MUSCLES MELTING into the cool wood floor, rain pattering on the roof of the yoga studio. When she opened her eyes, Noah squatted next to her, the faint scent of sweat rising from under his shirt.

The Saturday after their date, Elena saw Noah in the therapy office but managed to avoid a long conversation. The date had left her feeling vulnerable, and she resisted repeating it.

The next week Elena noticed Noah across the yoga room chatting with someone, and she managed to slip out quickly after class. She kept her text messages pleasant but short when he reached out. But there was no avoiding him now.

"Hi," Noah said. A small, bashful grin broke through his face. "How are you?"

"Good," she had to admit. In her sleepy, yogic mood.

"When can I see you again? Tonight?"

Her guard was down. "Okay."

Elena arrived at the square early and wandered around, enjoying the unusually warm winter evening, the sky brushed a deep pink as the sun slid down in the sky. Lights hung from the oak trees, creating a magical feeling in the dusk. Noah waited for her near the duck pond, his hands in the pockets of a woolen jacket. She was relieved to see his casual dress, as if they had both decided to take it less seriously.

One of the ducks waddled right past him, close to his feet, and they laughed at its boldness. "Don't these guys go south in the winter?" Noah asked, looking up.

"I don't think so. They always seem to be here." The chubby mallard glided into the water, ripples following him.

"I thought maybe Portuguese food?" Noah tipped his head towards the far side of the square.

"La Salette?"

He nodded. The place was one of Jim's favorites, but Elena couldn't avoid everywhere she and Jim used to go. She needed to find a way to reclaim the territory of her life, one block at a time.

Once seated at a window table, the scent of garlic and seafood wafting from the kitchen across the tiny restaurant, Elena ordered caldo verde, sea bass, and the Portuguese macaroni and cheese. She was excited to be back in this small haven of savory delights.

Over dinner, she asked Noah about his divorce.

He waved his hand in the air. "Ugh. A typical story, but to me it felt shocking. My wife went to parents' weekend at our daughter's college last fall. She called me from Boston at the end of the weekend and ended the marriage. She met some handsome alumnus at the volunteer booth."

Elena caught her breath. "Just like that?"

"We'd drifted for years. But I don't know if I would have ended it. So, I went from having a wife and daughter in the house to only myself. I am now a single man with two houses. Two cars. And a horse. Mostly things my ex-wife bought over the years. It's strange. I need to downsize and sell the houses, all that. In the meantime, I visit her horse and drive her fancy car."

Elena laughed. "You do drive a fancy car. Tell me about the horse."

Noah told her about this lovely Bay named Belle. "I'm trying to learn to ride from Uriel. But really, I don't think I'm teachable. Uriel's a great teacher, but the horse is a handful." He lifted his shirt and showed Elena his latest bruise, which looked like a flower tattooed on his side.

"Ouch!"

"Yes. Uriel turned his back and I fell right off her." They both laughed. "Is your daughter still dating him?"

Elena hesitated, a little surprised he knew about it. "Yes." The relationship still made her uncomfortable, for reasons she didn't understand.

"It's an interesting family," Noah said. "Uriel's great of course, but Maya and Freddie are, too. I've been a customer for years, but recently I've had dinner there a few times."

"I haven't gotten to know them well. Although we were invited for Christmas. I went for dessert. And they are clearly very nice."

"Oh no, only dessert? Then you missed Freddie's cooking. Did you see that garden?"

A surge of irrational jealousy flew up in her mind as he talked about the Macons. Amanda had found a new family, a nicely stitched together one.

But, her new voice told her, *you don't need to compete with them.* She'd try harder, she decided, to get to know Uriel.

Noah told her anecdotes about his therapist, and she told him about her debacles at the nursing home. "I served one guy regular coffee instead of decaf and set off his pacemaker. I thought he might die."

"Ha, I doubt he'd die from it." He took her hand as she rolled her eyes. "Trust me, I'm a doctor."

By the time the check came, Elena found she'd laughed so much her makeup had wiped off. Later, exiting onto the lit-up alley, they heard someone singing the song, "Georgia." The voice was deep and gravely, Louis Armstrong-esque.

"Where is that coming from?" Elena asked, puzzled.

"Down here," Noah pointed. "It's called the Speak Easy, a tiny jazz place that popped up recently. We could have a night cap?"

The bar, tucked in the alley corner, right off the square but well hidden, was filled. A crowd drank local wines from water glasses and squeezed together, swaying with the live music.

Elena had never seen the bar. How many hidden delights did she pass right by? The music filled her like a long cool drink. A man belted out the song while a handful of brass musicians and a keyboard backed him up. Noah gave her a glass of Cabernet and they stood in back.

Two songs later Elena was dancing. Her long skirt floated around her ankles as she moved her hips gently to the rhythm. A woman sang about "The Girl from Ipanema" in a velvety, soft voice. Christ, was she having fun again?

Noah insisted on taking her home in a cab. As the car bumped up the long hill to her home, he reached over and took her hand. Elena let him hold it for a minute, amazed at the way her body lit up, electricity shooting through her. She pulled away. This was too much. *Wasn't it?*

When the cab stopped outside her house, Elena hopped out. The driveway was dark. She'd forgotten to leave the outside lights on, and Amanda was out.

"Walk you to the door?"

On the front step, she tried to say thank you without seeming eager. Noah embraced her, his hand placed on her back while his lips met hers in a long, gripping kiss. His mouth tasted like the wine, as his rough cheek rubbed hers. Elena almost disentangled herself in surprise. She was used to Jim's carefully polished skin, his dismissive pecks.

And yet, her heart leapt. She had an urge grab him and drag him into the house, another urge to send him away.

Noah said goodnight, as if the kiss had not happened.

Shaking, Elena turned her key in the lock and stepped inside. She flipped on the lights, waved, and shut the door. She collapsed on a chair, stunned. Her first true, deep, passionate kiss in years. She moved to the kitchen and drank a tall glass of water, staring out the window at the dark night.

Her phone buzzed with a text. **Still outside in the cab. At the risk of being too forward, can I come in?**

What was it about this man that made her think of the word *yes* instead of *no*? Elena pressed the button that opened the front gate and unlocked the door.

When he came in, she went to him and he kissed her again, this time more slowly, but still a kiss that said, *I want you.*

A current flashed through her body. She lifted herself up to meet his lips. Her hands grasped his arms, finding them ropey and muscular under the jacket. She pictured him upside down, in yoga class. "Follow me," she managed to say, her voice a hoarse whisper.

Elena led him through the foyer and across the courtyard to her art studio, the only place that felt truly free of Jim. The room where she had existed as more than a wife or mother.

Their bodies seemed to fall up the flight of stairs, defying gravity. The allure of sex lifted them up the steps as they tangled and laughed. Her hands grabbed his back as he pressed into the bannister at the top of the steps. His face moved down, kissing her neck, her chest, the edge of her breasts.

The wine had carried her far enough away not to think about the wrinkles he might be encountering, or sun damage, or sag. They fell through the door to the studio, giggling. Elena fumbled for the lights and then thought better of it, switching them off and guiding him towards the bedroom.

"Wait," Noah said. "I want to see your place."

"Not now," she answered, holding firmly to his hand, then yelping as her shin hit the edge of the coffee table.

"Lights?"

"No," she whispered although no one could hear them. They fell to her bed, tossing the many throw pillows out of the way. The mattress melted around them, comforting and welcoming.

"Oh my God, this bed is heavenly," he said.

She placed a finger on his lips. "If we are going to do this, you need to stop talking. If we stop, I don't think I can start again."

"I will definitely stop talking then." Noah grinned down at her and she really saw him, more than she had before. His chin with a hint of shadow, his nose large but strong, his serious brow and warm, lively eyes. Saw that he wanted her. She touched his wiry, curly, hair as he kissed her again.

The wine had her brain spinning. When she reached down she found him hard, pushing through his trousers. Good God, how long had it been since she knew the urgency of a man being hard for her?

Elena pulled her sweater over her head and moaned as his fingers traced the outline of her breasts. She struggled with his belt, until he took over, slipping off his pants. His skin was damp with sweat.

"God, you're lovely," she heard Noah say as he ran a hand up her thigh.

Elena caught her breath, thinking she may have heard footsteps. She sat up fast, knocking into his face. Had she imagined it?

"Mom?" Amanda's voice sounded too close.

Elena shot up. The bedroom door flew open and lights flooded the room.

Amanda stood in the doorway, her hair glowing from the light behind her, a ruby halo above her. Her eyes were wide as shock rippled across her forehead. "Mom!"

Elena tried to discern the look in her daughter's wild eyes. Fear? Disgust? "Amanda?"

Noah tried to get his pants back up while Elena groped around for something to cover her chest.

Carmen stepped into the room from behind Amanda. "Christ, you really did have a date! Oh my God! Sorry."

"Mom, who is this?" Amanda, in a coat and boots, moved further into the room, rather than backing away, as Elena would have hoped. "Why did you tell me you were with Carmen tonight? I thought you—I thought something might be wrong. You didn't answer your phone, I couldn't find you. You scared us both!"

Noah turned away from the women and rearranged his clothes. Elena wondered if the erection would flee in the face of several generations of her family. She tried to get her sweater back on and found it backwards, and sweaty. She had a sudden surge of frustration. Anger replaced embarrassment. "Carmen, I told you I had a date!"

"I know. I'm sorry! Amanda called looking for you. And when she told me you were going out with me tonight . . . we thought maybe you had made up the date. So you could be alone. Which I know shouldn't be a big deal. But Amanda worried all night."

Amanda interrupted. "I didn't know why you would lie unless . . . something was wrong."

She thought I was trying to kill myself again. Christ. Elena deserved this. She'd given Amanda reason to worry. Then lied.

Noah sat on the edge of the bed, his hair a mess, his eyes watery, looking like a dog cornered by three cats. His face said, *Help.*

Frustrated, Elena rose from the bed, in her underwear, and put her hands on her hips. She needed to end this mess before Noah got wind of her recent mental state. She waved at her daughter and sister. "Can you just wait downstairs?"

Obediently, they turned abruptly and left.

"Who is he?" Elena heard Amanda ask, as they went back down the stairs.

"Maybe the yoga guy?" Carmen answered.

Elena turned to Noah. "I'm really sorry."

"Yeah. Well. That was a first."

"Me too." She sat back on the bed. She wanted to get under the covers and hide for a very long time. "I'm really sorry," Elena said again. What else to say? "I'll kill them later."

Noah smiled briefly at that. "Really, I shouldn't have rushed to be with you so soon. I had such a good time tonight. I haven't enjoyed myself like that in a long time. But I think I should go."

"Yes," she sighed. "I guess you should go."

"Only, I don't have a car."

"Oh, that's right." They stared at each other, as if baffled by their mutual impulsiveness. "I'll borrow Amanda's," Elena said. "I think I am sobered up by embarrassment."

They made their way out to the driveway a few minutes later. The night air was chastening. They walked to opposite sides of the car. A deer stood at the edge of the driveway, staring, antlers shining in the moonlight.

"Holy shit," Noah half laughed. "He scared me."

"He keeps watch. He's here most nights."

"Well, between him and your daughter, you're well-guarded up here."

She nodded, starting the car, letting the engine warm up and watching the buck spring away into the fields.

"Like sentries to the castle." Noah added, poetically.

Like sentries to the castle. But he had gotten in.

Chapter 29

"It is the wine that leads me on, the wild wine that sets
the wisest man to sing at the top of his lungs, laugh like
a fool—it drives the man to dancing . . . it even tempts
him to blurt out stories better never told."

—Homer

"I'M OPENING SOME WINE," CARMEN SAID, COMING INTO THE
kitchen with a bottle of red and two glasses. In a long colorful dress
and flat-soled, suede boots, she looked shamanic, like she could dance
around a fire.

"I found it in your dad's wine cellar. I can't believe he hasn't come
back to claim that collection. Holy cow, he has some nice reds. A Zinfandel sound good?" Carmen uncorked the bottle with a blasé expertise and poured two glasses. "God, this is yummy." She examined the
label. "Do you know this winery? Bump?"

"It's on the square." Amanda marveled that Carmen was unfazed.
"They know Dad."

"Everyone knows your dad," Carmen declared. "We never ate dinner!
I'm starving. Tracking down your wayward mother was hard work."

Amanda grunted at the word wayward, her stomach still in knots.
She had stumbled in on her mother and some random man after
spending the evening in sheer fear, unable to locate her. Her throat
tightened each time she thought of the Golden Gate Bridge, or an
empty bottle of pills.

Amanda rummaged in the fridge and found a half a piece of brie,
olives, and shrunken cherry tomatoes. Nothing very appealing. She
added some grapes from the fruit bowl. By the time she had created

their small meal, Carmen's glass was empty. Amanda took a long sip of her own, as if wanting to catch up. Her mind jumped to the image of her mother and that man.

"I almost threw up when we stumbled in there."

Carmen shared a hearty laugh as she refilled her glass. "*Mija*, that was something. I never thought that would happen so fast." Her face sobered when she took in Amanda's discomfort.

"*Lo siento*," *I'm sorry.* "I know she's your mother and we all think, you know, parents shouldn't have sex."

Amanda nibbled an olive. "Clearly, my father is having sex. With a man. So I'm not sure why this is freaking me out so much. Just, you know, *seeing* it."

Carmen licked wine from her lush lips. Carmen made Amanda think of the word *ample.* Ample breasts, words, touch. Ample ideas and energy. Appetites. Her aunt touched the glass with long nails, making a clinking sound like a brittle memory. "You'll get over the shock. We should be celebrating. Your mom is moving on."

The crackers tasted stale. Amanda threw them away and grabbed an apple. Nothing tasted quite right. "She's still vulnerable. It's only been a few months since my dad left."

Carmen counted on her fingers. "Four, five? I think. That's long enough to mope around."

After days of threatening clouds, the skies opened and rain hit the windows. Amanda stared, transfixed by the sudden downpour.

Of course, her aunt didn't understand why it was much too soon to risk "moving on." Carmen, who blazed through life like comet, had no idea that Elena had curled up in the car and tried to die. "She isn't ready."

"Well, none of us are at first, *mija*. But you just got to get back out there." Carmen stopped and looked at her. "You're upset."

"No, I'm fine." Amanda finished her glass of wine, refilled it, topped off Carmen's and checked her phone. Close to midnight. "Do you think she'll be back soon?"

"Not to worry. She'll be back soon. Not sure I want to go anywhere though if I keep drinking. Especially with the rain. I may stay the night."

"That's fine," Amanda said.

"I know it is," Carmen answered.

Amanda glanced at her aunt, irritated. "I mean, of course it is."

Carmen waved her hand apologetically. "Sorry, I don't mean to be bitchy." She pronounced *bitchy* like *beachy*, with her subtle accent, and Amanda smiled in spite of herself.

Her aunt squeezed her hand. "I think we're both protective of your mama in our own ways. You want her to heal, I want her to move on. It's the same thing. We love her." Carmen's breath was sweet and winey. "Let's try a new subject. Tell me about your Mexican friend."

Amanda sighed. "He's more than a friend."

"I hear he's a cowboy." Carmen leered, and it made Amanda laugh.

"Kind of. He manages the stables. And helps his uncle with the winery." She heard her own voice pick up as she talked about the way Uriel made people feel at ease, his skill with the horses, his sense of responsibility for others. The troubles he had. *I should slow down. I sound like a school girl in love.* But she kept going. "He's really smart. I mean I think, in different circumstances, he would be the one getting a PhD."

Her aunt bit into the last piece of apple, smeared with brie. "What kind of circumstances?"

"He had a tough childhood. I met his mother this week. She's intense."

Carmen's brows raised, interested. "Intense how?"

"She kept acting like she knew me from somewhere. Like she recognized me or something." The front door opened and shut. Amanda glanced at her phone. Twelve forty-five a.m.

"Hi." Elena stepped into the kitchen. Her hair and jacket wet, she brought in the scent of the night. Wet asphalt and wind.

"Hello, love bird!" Carmen giggled at her own joke and Elena flushed.

Elena leaned on the counter and crossed her arms nervously, perched like a bird on a wire. "Sorry about the confusion. I should have told you about the date."

"Yes, in the future, no keeping such hot secrets, *hermanita.* We were just talking about Amanda's paramour. He sounds like a keeper."

Elena took off her jacket, shaking the rain from her hair. "I don't know him well, but he is very nice."

Nice. Was there a more damning word in the English language? "*Porque no le gustas?*" Amanda switched languages on purpose.

Sometimes switching to Spanish made her mother answer more quickly, more honestly.

"I do like him—of course I do. I appreciated his presence when—you needed him." Elena edited, making sure not to mention the night he helped most.

Carmen threw her arms back in a stretch. "Amanda just told me she met his mother."

Elena came sat down on the bench of the breakfast nook. "Yes, I didn't hear much about it. You said she was odd?"

Amanda had a surge of irrational defensiveness on Lourdes' part. "Not odd. Just unusual. She had this idea she knew me. And she wouldn't let it go."

"Knew you how?"

"I don't know. She thought she recognized me. I mean it's a small town but . . . Uriel and I didn't cross paths until after college. I never even realized the trailer park existed until Uri took me to meet her."

Carmen's glass on the table came down a little too hard, the noise jarring. "What do you mean? What trailer park?"

Amanda flushed. Her aunt sold multi-million-dollar homes for a living. Even if she came from nothing in Columbia, Carmen could be judgmental. Amanda went on, trying not to sound strident. "Uriel's mom lives in a trailer park in West Sonoma. It's like a small house."

Carmen's spine straightened, and her brows rose as she looked meaningfully at Elena.

Anger flashed through Amanda like her finger had touched a socket. Who did they think they were to judge Uriel, with their fractured, messy lives? Her mother and aunt who drank too much wine, had cheating husbands and a past that neither liked to talk about. "God! Why are you such fucking snobs?"

Both women stared at her and Elena's mouth dropped open. The family resemblance appeared in their reaction—their eyes, the color of dark polished onyx, widened, and a wrinkle furrowed between their brows.

Words erupted from Amanda, like a lava flow of frustration. "I know what you two are like. You think trailer park means bad or cheap. But

Uriel is good. He is better than the stupid jerks I knew in high school, better than Dad and his shitty lies. And you judge him because he comes from a trailer park?"

Amanda started to cry. Goddamn it. Too much wine. She didn't want to cry, but they both kept looking at her. "Hell with you guys, then." She stood, sobs erupting. She wanted to be far away, alone, even as her aunt brought a hand to her shoulder and pushed her back down.

Elena shook her head. "Amanda, calm down. I don't judge him! You're putting words into my mouth."

"I don't think so. You haven't invited him over."

"I haven't exactly been entertaining, but I'd like to."

Blood rushed to Amanda's cheeks. "You were entertaining tonight, it turns out. I never have Uriel over and you bring home some random guy! I invited you to meet his mother with me and you about choked on your food."

"Stop." Carmen spoke with authority. Then she turned to Elena. "You know, this is weird."

Elena shook her head. "What? It's nothing."

"You didn't tell me he was from the trailer park." Carmen did not take her eyes from Elena.

"Is that really the problem?" Amanda wiped tears off her cheeks.

Carmen leaned across the table to her sister. "She has to know. It's enough already. Think about it."

"Carmen, I swear to God." Elena's voice rose, sounding on the verge of being irate.

Amanda's frustration ebbed into confusion, as her mother recoiled from Carmen's words, shaking her head frantically.

"Shut up, Carmen." Elena said, completely out of character.

Carmen grabbed her sister's hand and leaned forward. "Elena, get serious. Who are you protecting?"

Elena rose, bumping the table. The wine glasses teetered. "When I tell you no, I mean it, Carmen. Stop!"

"What's going on?" Amanda was baffled by the change in conversation. She looked at her mother, who turned away. "Mom? What is she talking about?"

Elena's voice grew as hard as stone. "Nothing."

"Think about this, Elena." Carmen said. She no longer sounded buzzed from the wine, or as strident. Her voice had become calm, and Amanda knew they were wading into something important. Carmen continued, "You know this is wrong."

"Mom?" Amanda heard herself pleading. "What is it?"

A murky despondency filled Elena's eyes, as if surrendering to something. "We're all tired tonight. It's late."

"Mom." Amanda switched to the language of her mother's heart. *"Por favor, Mami. Dime."* Please, tell me.

"Your aunt is overreacting. And it's not for me to tell." Elena stood and crossed the kitchen. "Not yours either, Carmen. Amanda, you can speak with your father anytime you want about his past. It's not mine anymore. I'm going to bed."

Elena dimmed the lights in the kitchen as she passed through the awning, leaving Amanda and Carmen sitting in semi-darkness, like actors on a stage as the lights went down.

Amanda retreated to her room. The rain hammered on the roof, and the dogs insisted on being on her bed. She moved methodically, connecting her devices to their chargers, brushing her teeth, locking the front door. Finally, she sat down on her bed and re-read the note she'd found in her father's trash, months ago. Amanda looked at the loopy, young handwriting. The note, on Marriott stationary, said goodbye to Jim, in simple, poignant words. Signed by someone named Penny, undated.

In the dark, Amanda let her fatigue settle with her like a fragile friend. So tired. Of her family obligations, of picking at their secrets, of discovering things about their past, tiny parcels, handed out sparingly. She didn't want to do this any longer. To be here caring for her mother. Not able to focus on her work. To live on the top of a mountain, in a houseful of memories but with no future plans. Amanda needed to leave soon. But then . . . Uriel. If she left quickly, as she was longing to do, she knew the door to his heart would close harder than before. She would lose him.

She picked up a Mexican wooden statue that Maya had given to her on Christmas. It looked like a wooden hand, delicately painted with Mexican symbols. Amanda had been touched to receive it. She traced the five fingers. A variety of saint medals were hammered on to the fingertips, and in the center was a medal Guadalupe. Amanda had taken to placing it next to her bed, hoping the tiny saints would watch over her as she slept.

She missed Uriel, and after a minute she put the statue down and called him. "I'm sorry it's so late."

"It's okay." He sounded sleepy. "What's going on?"

She filled him in on her long night and Carmen's cryptic comments. "Can you ask your mom if she remembers why she thinks I am familiar?"

"I forgot to tell you, she figured it out. You remind her of some pre-school teacher I had. She found a class picture with the lady. No big deal."

"Did you see the picture? Of the teacher?"

"Yeah, she looks like you I guess. But my mom's a freak about remembering things like that. Don't stress about this."

Amanda wished he could be lying next to her. "Can I see it?"

"Sure, I'll grab it. She has all my school pictures in a box. You'd think she was a decent parent or something."

The wine loosened her tongue. "I miss you," Amanda said, tucking her feet under the dogs at the foot of her bed.

"Come see me tomorrow."

"I will. I'm coming to ride Chestnut in the morning."

They said goodnight, and she fell asleep quickly, exhausted from worry and wine. She dreamt about Carmen. Her aunt whispered to her through a screened window, but Amanda couldn't quite hear. "What?" she asked. "What did you say?"

Amanda woke up sweaty and confused, wondering what Carmen had said, what she had missed.

Chapter 30

"He who does not risk, does not drink Champagne."

—Russian Proverb

"WHY DON'T YOU COME TO MY PLACE THIS WEEKEND?" DANNY suggested to Gloria on a Wednesday afternoon. His hand rested on her waist as he nuzzled her in the front seat of his ancient Cadillac, which smelled vaguely of tacos. Parked down the street from her apartment, she could see the blue screen of the TV through the window, and knew Carlos was home.

"You don't have to work?"

"I'm off Sunday. You could come for the afternoon, if you don't want to leave Carlos all day."

Carlos would love being left alone all day, but she didn't trust him.

They had squeezed in dates. Coffee in the afternoons, or if she managed to stay up until eleven when he left work, they shared a pizza and a pitcher of beer, at a bar with a jukebox. They both loved Santana and Elton John, they discovered. He didn't come over if Carlos was home or might be coming home, which was most of the time.

Danny's hands unbuttoned her blouse and lifted one of her breasts from her stretched lace bra. Gloria might have enjoyed his hunger for her body, if she could move her legs. Sex in a car? She wasn't twenty-two anymore.

"Danny, I think my leg is falling asleep. It's tingling."

"You sure that isn't me?"

She extricated herself. "I should go in. It's getting late."

"Sunday?"

She readjusted her bra.

Danny's voice became hesitant. "Or . . . do you not want to? Is something wrong?"

Gloria sighed. "You said you live at your wife's house."

Danny's eye twitched. "She's not exactly my wife. I mean she's inside for another four years . . ."

"But it's her house?"

He nodded. "Yeah. I guess that's weird. I've just been kind of taking care of it for her. I mean, she knows I want a divorce—I told you that."

Gloria crossed her arms, deciding what to say to him.

"She owned it before we met. And it's rent free, so I stayed."

Gloria looked out the window, where cars of people pulled in and out of the gas station. Was she being unreasonable? Danny's wife, a nurse, was in jail for a second DUI and stealing drugs from the hospital. He said he had wanted to end their marriage before the arrest. A drama-addict, he called her.

Why being married matter more to her now than on that first night? she wondered. But it reminded her of Diego, always being at someone else's place.

"I don't want to, you know—be in her bed or her room. And if I come over, that's what we'll do. But it's not right."

Danny's chin stiffened. She felt a chill, but she had to say this. "Really, if you're still with your wife—I don't know if this is going to work out, Danny."

Danny turned quickly towards her. "Whoa! This went from me asking you to come over to you breaking up with me?"

Gloria's heart raced. She didn't want to ruin things, but her gut told her to speak up now, not in a year. "I don't want to be someone's other woman. I already had a cheating husband. And it seems like maybe you're comfortable being married . . . I don't want to get hurt again." She reached for the door handle and pushed the heavy door open. "I like you, Danny. But I want it to be right."

He ran his hand through his hair, and stared straight ahead. Gloria expected him to stop her or say something to make her stay, but he didn't. She opened the car door, stepped out and walked towards her apartment, a knot growing in her stomach with each step.

She heard Danny's car pull away from the curb and drive the other way, and she bit her lip to keep from crying. Diego would have followed her and changed her mind. But Danny wasn't Diego. *A good thing?* Danny was supposed to be a one-night stand, she reminded herself. A married guy is always heartbreak. Even one whose wife is in jail.

Gloria didn't hear from him the next day or the next. By that Friday, she realized it was over, that he had disappeared like one of the men Lourdes cycled through. Gloria talked to her cousin late at night on the phone. "He seemed better than this. I thought he cared."

"Just because you only date like one guy a year," Lourdes said, sounding buzzed but peppy, "doesn't mean you're going to get the good ones. A lot of fish in the sea, though, Mama. You want to go out tomorrow? See what else you can catch?"

"No. Maybe? I'll see. I got other things to think about anyway."

"More problems with Dickio?" Lourdes loved her nickname for Diego.

"Something like that."

Diego still refused to help with her green card. He had come over a week ago and handed her two hundred dollars, about a tenth of what he owed her.

"Why now?" she asked him.

"You got Carlos on my ass about the support now. Thanks for that."

Gloria held back a smile. She'd had no idea Carlos had joined her cause.

Diego shook his head, annoyed. "But Gloria, I can't go into INS and say we're still married or anything. You have to figure that out another way. I could get into too much trouble."

She held her breath, counting. Yelling at Diego wouldn't help. She needed some leverage, but she didn't know what.

Diego had flopped down on her couch, like he still lived there. He plopped a plastic clothing bag next to him. "Where's Carlos? I have something for him."

"He's at a friend's. What do you have, more ski clothes?" Diego shook his head and pulled an iPad out of the bag. "It's from Sheila. It's used but works good. She thinks it will help him with his homework."

"She's giving him an iPad? He's doing fine in school." Gloria came and looked at it. "But he'll want it."

"Sheila said he needs it for math. You know she's been tutoring him?"

"What?"

"Yeah. She's been meeting him by the school on Thursdays, helping him with algebra. She says there's a program on here he can use. Says his basic skills aren't good enough."

Jealousy bubbled up, mixed with defensiveness. Why hadn't Carlos told her about Sheila? And Carlos' math was solid, wasn't it? Gloria didn't know. She never understood his math homework. She excelled at history, loved quizzing him on that, but not math.

"I don't know why he didn't tell me Sheila's helping him." Gloria sat down, deflated.

Diego raised his hands to the air. "He probably thinks you wouldn't like it."

Gloria imagined, as she often did, what her mother would have said, before she lost her memory. She handled everyone—from the grouchy minister to the rich people she cleaned for—with tact. Polite, but always firm. She would not turn away free help for her grandson.

"I'll tell Carlos it's fine to take her help."

"Good."

"And tell her thank you for the iPad."

Diego's eyes narrowed skeptically as he stood. "Okay, will do."

Gloria watched Diego cross the street to his car, his shoulders looking more resigned than usual. Diego hadn't meant to be responsible for anyone. He must be tired.

Gloria spent Saturday night alone, wondering if Danny would call her or if she should call him. She was glad when Carlos texted and asked if he could invite a friend over.

The boys devoured a bowl of popcorn, then played video games, laughing at the ways they could chase one another on the screen. Gloria hovered in the kitchen, smiling. It was worth it to be here, not out with Danny. *Right?*

But maybe Danny would join the kids. He'd beat them at the game, grab some popcorn, and laugh with them. Had she acted too quickly? She didn't see a way back. If Danny wanted her, he wouldn't have driven away.

The following Tuesday, Valentine's Day, Gloria bought Carlos a chocolate heart, knowing she would eat most of it herself. She stopped for a Little Caesar's pizza, Carlos' favorite, the smell of garlic filling her car. When she came through her front door, balancing the pizza and her keys, she found Carlos examining a vase of flowers on the kitchen table.

"A delivery truck brought them," Carlos said, looking impressed. "A couple of minutes ago."

Lush, long-stemmed red roses filled a tall vase. A card on the top read *Love, Santa*. Her cheeks grew hot.

Carlos grabbed the pizza then nodded to the card, one eyebrow raised. "Santa?"

Her heart swam in her chest. She wondered if Carlos sensed her excitement. "It's a friend. It's only a joke."

Carlos shrugged and opened the refrigerator, grabbing a Coke. His body had grown so much his presence filled the kitchen. "There's something written on the back of the card," he said, his back to her.

She pulled off the card and flipped it over. There was only an address: 214 Spain Street, 32A.

Carlos grabbed it from her hand before she could stop him.

"Carlos!"

"Is that your friend's address?" he asked.

Gloria's mind raced. That address was in Sonoma. She'd never been to Danny's house, but he didn't live near this address.

"No . . . I don't think so."

"Mom, is this like a booty call?"

She reached up to slap him, lightly, half joking and half wanting him to know he was going too far. He dodged her hand, starting to laugh, a slice of pizza dripping on the counter. "Don't mess with me, Mom. I'm a black-belt."

"In what? Black-belt in bullshit."

"You got a boyfriend, Ma? I never heard of this guy. Santa!"

"It's not a boyfriend."

He grinned as he put an entire slice of pizza in his mouth at once. "Remember Mr. Swanson?"

She groaned. Her son's balding, second grade teacher had sent home cheerful notes home to Gloria and offered to have her and Carlos over for dinner. Finally, Carlos had apparently cleared it up, telling his teacher, "My mom just isn't attracted to you, Mr. Swanson."

Gloria had to avoid eye contact with Mr. Swanson the rest of the year. Carlos grinned, thinking about it. Pizza grease dribbled from his mouth.

"Carlos, that looks disgusting."

He kept eating, pulling a new piece off before he finished the first. "I'm going out in awhile," he added. "Celio's little sister is having a Valentine's party, and his mom said she'd pay us to help watch the kids."

Gloria thought about the chance to call Danny and thank him in private. "Homework?"

"Done."

He probably hadn't touched it. On the other hand, it would be nice to have him busy, making a little money. Celio's sister was only ten; the party would be innocent enough.

"Home by ten," Gloria said, hoping to sound authoritative, as she went to her bedroom and kicked off her shoes.

"Sure."

Before Carlos left, he stuck his head into her bedroom and caught her holding the card that came with the flowers. "You going to that address?"

Gloria squeezed her eyes shut, thinking. "None of your business."

"What's Santa's real name? I didn't know you had a boyfriend."

"I told you he's not my boyfriend." *He's kind of married.* "But his name is Danny."

Carlos leaned on the door frame, his skateboard dangling in his hand. "Well if you *are* going to his place, could you drop me at Celio's so I don't have to skate over there in the dark?"

Should she go? Maybe this place was a bar? Or a restaurant? Gloria had been up at six-thirty that morning, cleaning a house by eight. She wore her scruffy sweats and no makeup. "Give me a few minutes."

"Deal."

Gloria tried not to notice the wrinkles around her eyes as she applied eyeliner, or the scuffs on her shoes. She put on one of her nice dresses, a black one that made her look thinner, she thought, but hugged her perhaps too tightly. Should she fix the chips in her nail polish? She glanced at the clock, debating.

What did he mean, writing an address on the card? If this was a booty call . . . well, she'd probably still go.

"Whoa." Carlos admired her as she came into the living room. "You like this guy, huh?"

"Shut up, Carlito. Let's go." The roses made the apartment smell like summer. Gloria took a deep breath before stepping outside.

She dropped off Carlos, then ran into the drug store. She bought Danny one of the last boxes of chocolates, an extra-large heart sized box. Gloria made her way to the address, checking the numbers as she drove slowly up a small road, her car dropping in and out of potholes. A mixture of large family homes with children's toys out front, older condos, and apartment buildings lined the street.

Danny must be taking care of someone's house again, she surmised, slightly annoyed. He dog-sat occasionally. She'd made it clear that she didn't want to be caught screwing around in a stranger's place.

Gloria turned into a complex of town houses, all painted shades of blue. The sign saying 214 was lit by a street lamp. She drove cautiously. She passed by rows of identical attached houses, two stories, shingled, a bay window on the bottom. Her pulse fluttered when she recognized Danny's car.

She took a minute to reapply lipstick and breathe before she rang the bell. Danny opened the door, looking fresh in a maroon button-down shirt.

"You're wearing red again. You must be Santa."

His lips parted into a wide smile. "I guess I like red." He waved her inside. "Come on in!"

She moved into an empty living room, feeling timid. A lone futon lie in a corner. A few pictures leaned against the wall. "Wow, it's . . . "

"Empty, I know," Danny said. "I just got the keys today. My lease starts tomorrow, but I convinced the guy to give me the keys a day early." He winked at her. "He knows I have a date for Valentine's Day."

Shyness descended on her, like shifting light. "Thank you for the flowers."

Danny leaned in to kiss her. The kiss beckoned her to move closer, intimate and inviting. It was different in a warm, lit room, not sneaking in the car or hurrying before Carlos caught them.

"This is really your place?" Gloria asked, when their lips parted.

"You bet. You wanted me to have my own place, right?"

She flushed. Had he gotten an entire house because she told him to? What would he expect now? She wasn't ready to move in with him or something extreme like that. "I . . . I didn't mean you had to."

"I know. But I couldn't defend myself, the other day. What was I doing getting involved with you if I lived in my wife's house? I mean, other ladies hadn't minded, but I like that about you. You did mind."

To cover her blush, Gloria ambled into the tiny kitchen. An old calendar hung on the wall but not much else, not even a table. The bedroom contained only a pile of boxes in the corner.

No bed to relax on right now. But never mind, they would have time for that eventually. Images of long nights here slipped over her like a new, elegant dress. She saw Danny grilling on the outside barbeque, pictured herself sipping wine on a nice chair in the corner.

"What do you think?" Danny asked, behind her.

"It's really nice," she said.

In the kitchen, he held a bottle of Champagne and two plastic cups. "I thought we could celebrate the new place?" His eyes brightened in the dusty light. Sweat beaded on his forehead. He acted nervous. As if she might refuse him after he had gone to this trouble.

"I just remembered. I have chocolate for you in the car!"

He grinned when she brought the box in. He took off the bright ribbon and draped it on her like a necklace, then kissed her again. The sound of the Champagne as it popped made her gasp as the bubbles overflowed, and she laughed as he filled her cup. Taken aback by how easily life could surprise her, and the sweetness she had found.

Chapter 31

"Without bread and wine, love goes hungry."

—Latin Proverb

ON A SATURDAY AFTERNOON, JIM YANKED OPEN THE DOOR OF A bustling café on the San Francisco Bay, his stomach a pulsating knot. Amanda waited for him outside at a table overlooking the bay. Jim knew this place well, knew that the table would wobble on the deck, and the beer would be local. Amanda's hair shone in the sun like glistening water. Or like a piece of redwood, he thought, shellacked and polished. As her mother's hair had, years ago.

Amanda didn't rise. He kissed her cheek anyway, wishing he could embrace her and beg for forgiveness. She was in an old Obama T-shirt and faded jeans, with dark circles under her eyes.

"Dad?" she said, her voice hoarse, "I need you to explain."

Amanda had called the night before, crying and saying she needed to see him. She wanted the truth "about my adoption." She didn't want to talk on the phone.

Jim feared that Amanda knew the worst. He wanted to call Elena to ask why she'd told Amanda. Elena had never wanted Amanda to know the truth. Why now? Did she tell her out of spite, in anger?

Jim couldn't bring himself to call his ex-wife, so he had spent the night pacing, imagining the ways he might explain things without alienating Amanda. He knew he would fail. Some secrets defied explanation and he specialized in them.

Jim accepted a menu from the waitress and ordered them two beers and fried potato skins.

"I need to know about Penny," Amanda said, as soon as the waitress left. "I think she was my mother. I mean, I'm pretty sure. I have a picture of her and I'm like a frigging clone."

Jim ran his hands through his hair, completely unclear on how to proceed. "How did you—"

"Carmen basically told me there was some mystery to do with the trailer park. And Uriel's mom is psychic or something and couldn't stop talking about how she knew me before. Anyway, Uriel's mom remembered who I look like. Penny was a teacher at his daycare. His mom still had the class picture and she couldn't get over the resemblance. When I saw it, neither could I. And, of course, I might not have put any of it together, if I hadn't found a note from Penny."

"A note?" Jim's mind was spinning.

"The day you left. I took it from the garbage."

Jim could barely remember the day he cleaned out his office, the day he left his wife. His anxiety that day had produced a type of amnesia.

"I knew she must have meant a lot to you, because it looked old."

Jim's heart pounded. Was it possible Penny had worked in the daycare Uriel attended? Penny worked at the community center when he met her. She *had* lived in the trailer park.

"Carmen told me that my birth mother lived in the trailer park. That's why she was so weird about Uriel being from there. Tell me Dad, if Penny is my mother, who's my father?"

Jim felt his blood pressure rising, his chest tight. A part of him wanted to run away, simply get up and leave.

"Just say it, Dad. It's you, isn't it? I'm your daughter. Your actual biological daughter. But you never told me. You chose to raise me as if I was *adopted*."

He blew out a deep breath, his heart about to burst out of his shirt. Christ, he couldn't stand to lose the last of his daughter's trust.

"How did this fucking happen, Dad?"

He hated that language from his sweet girl. He hated that he'd hurt her, the betrayal in her eyes. "Yes . . . I'm your father." Jim stumbled, trying to imagine where to start. "You're my daughter."

The look she gave him made his stomach clench. Had he really thought this would never come out? Shame flooded through him when he remembered the day he discovered he was a father, and not with his wife. He had put that memory away, too.

"But, Amanda, you're our daughter. Elena's and mine. Both of ours. Equally. Don't let this change anything."

"I think it changes everything, Dad. Too late."

Her emerald eyes bored into him. The color of his own mother's eyes. For the first time, he could acknowledge the things that marked her as his biological daughter, a genetic member of the Scanlon clan. The loss of this, all these years, was another piece in the list of his regrets.

Amanda clenched her hands, as if she would like to punch him. "Christ. So, what, you cheated on Mom and she chose to raise the baby? Is that about it?"

Jim stared at the table, tears burning. "Please, Amanda, don't judge your mother in this. She did what she thought was right. I was grateful to her. You have an amazing mother."

"She lied to me my whole life. Both of you did. Do you not get that?" Amanda perched on the edge of her chair, and for a moment he thought she might rise, literally levitating in anger.

"I need to know the details. I have that right. I had that right all along. Telling a different story doesn't make it true."

The words slapped him from his denial, as if he was plunged into the cold water under the dock. *Telling a different story doesn't make it true.* He felt naked as her eyes rested on his.

"What happened?"

He shook his head, momentarily mute.

"Tell me who Penny is. How you knew her. When. All of it."

Jim inhaled, hoping for courage and composure. He used a napkin to wipe the sweat off his forehead. "What do you want to know?"

"What the hell do you think I want to know? Everything. Start at the beginning and tell me all of it."

Jim nodded, his mind trying to find the beginning, where to start. How to explain his lapse in judgment, the way he had strayed too far, a weak time in his life. "I met Penny," he said, finally, "at a fundraiser in town." He glanced at his daughter briefly, her chin set, arms crossed. "Do you want this kind of detail?"

"Yes, everything."

Christ. "It . . . We were raising money for the community center, kids programs. In Agua Caliente, down the road. At the last minute, your mother—Elena—didn't come. We had grown estranged at that point and didn't spend much time together."

"Why?"

"It was after we lost our first baby. Months later. Things fell apart between us." Jim took a drink from his beer, steeling himself. He sat up, trying to pull strength from deep inside, to go on. His father used to chide him for trying to wade into the cold water at the lake. He needed to plunge in, fearlessly.

Eventually, he told her the rest. That Penny worked at the fundraiser, taking coats, handing out bid numbers, running for more ice. Jim noticed her. Not in the way of a man thinking about picking up a woman. He had been married five years at that point and had never come close to cheating, despite the widening gap between them.

"We lost the baby in the spring, and it literally sucked the life out of the marriage."

Amanda looked away, and he saw her considering this.

"Elena travelled for most of the summer. Down to Columbia. She was angry at me, even though it didn't make sense. I just worked, trying to get through it."

"Did you try to get her help?" Amanda asked. "Maybe she was depressed."

"Yes. I tried that. Offered to go with her. Or to adopt. Everything. She was . . . hard to get through to. Really, like a different person."

Amanda absorbed this, as if it perhaps struck a familiar chord.

"So, I went to this thing alone." Jim remembered the wine being good but the food uninspired. Huge bouquets of fall leaves and pumpkins decorated the rickety tables of the community center. Not a fancy place, but checks were being written, which made him feel like at least he was still part of something good. His spirits lifted after a few glassed of Pinot Noir.

Penny caught his attention as she bustled by, strands of her copper hair falling loosely on her shoulders. She moved through the room with fluidity, a quickness of step. Jim was surprised when he overheard that she lived in the area. With her confidence among the wealthy winery owners, he'd assumed she was one of the donor's daughters, or a young professional.

"Penny?" his friend, Lou, had said. "She works down at the center as a teacher's aid or something. Nice kid. The director likes her. Tonight, she's just earning a few extra bucks."

When Penny handed Jim his coat at the end of the night, he impulsively handed her a card. "I'm Jim Scanlon," he said.

Penny's green eyes brightened as they talked. He could tell she cut her own hair, her bangs slightly off on one side, and she had a tattoo, a lizard, peeking out of her sleeve. She was rough around the edges when he got closer. "I see you're a hard worker. Call me if you are looking for a job. Sometimes we need extra help at my office. Clerical or whatever."

Penny took the card, wiping sweat off her brow with the back of her hand. Jim noticed. People who hustled attracted Jim, like an evolutionary turn on.

"Thanks," she said, her sharp eyes taking him in quickly from head to toe. She wasn't as young as he'd first thought either. Twenty-nine, thirty? Not a "nice kid," as Lou had said, but a woman.

As Jim headed to his car, he wondered if he would hear from her, and if he could justify hiring a new clerk. But as he drove home, he decided he needed to try harder with Elena. He put the conversation with Penny, his own impulsivity, behind him. He came in eager to tell Elena about the night, about the wonderful work the center did. But a note on the table said that she had a headache—would he mind sleeping in the guest room, to avoid waking her?

"So, she came to work for you?" Amanda rested her chin on her hand, looking skeptical. Angry. And uncannily like Penny.

Jolted back. Jim feared he had said too much in his meanderings.

"Yes. She came to work for me for a few months. Maybe six. Then she moved on. She was over-qualified for the job really, just a stepping stone."

"You're leaving out the point, Dad. Me?"

Jim wondered if the deck moved underneath them from the water, or if it was vertigo from anxiety. He never thought he'd have to tell his daughter this story. The last few months he'd been revealing himself too often, like a striptease, pulling off his disguises one by one. A sick and vulnerable man hid beneath the layers.

"Go on." Amanda's voice sounded cool and determined.

"I barely saw her when she first started to work at the office. You know how I am there, always traveling, distracted. Then, I don't know exactly when . . . " A lie. He knew the season, the month, maybe even the day. Close to Thanksgiving. "I offered her a ride back from the city to Sonoma. It seemed pointless for her to take the bus when I was driving up there. She accepted, I drove her home. And . . . " He held up his hand.

"And that was it? You drove her home and did it?"

"Christ! No." He sat back. The rawness of the words set his teeth on edge.

"It . . . it led to more rides. It became a habit, a few nights a week, if I was in town. I'd give her a ride home . . . Over time, I looked forward to it, to seeing her. Just having someone to talk to, you know, at the end of the day."

"Could have been Mom."

Jim nodded, forcing himself to hold back the retort that "Mom" was in Columbia or off with her sister Carmen or a tennis clinic in Palo Alto. He went on, choosing his words carefully. Brushstrokes, to paint the picture, to show that it was more than "doing it."

Thinking about Penny, his heart warmed, and he felt carried back. He cared for Penny. He liked the way she put her head back and laughed, her throat pulsing, when he told her a story. Liked to hear about her life, about the hard luck that had led her to bad places, and the resiliency that led her out. Plucky, that's what he thought when he remembered Penny. Long gone from her parents in . . . was it Pennsylvania? Ohio? She'd drifted west. Following some guy, taking low- paying jobs, always getting the next one, because she worked hard.

He remembered one morning, in the car, heading south to work. They shared an enormous cinnamon bun that she balanced on her knee. She ripped off pieces and handed them to him, while telling Jim about her various jobs.

"Let's see." Penny tipped her head and counted them on her long pretty fingers, after licking off the sticky sugar. "I was a nursemaid to a sleazy old man who tried to grope me. I threatened to tie him up if he grabbed me again. Then I worked in a farmer's market fish truck—God, I always smelled like salmon. Then waitressing in Seattle, down near the wharf. I worked on a berry farm one summer in Oregon. And then the daycare, when you met me. And now this job. Clerk. And carpool buddy." She'd turned to Jim, her lips in a teasing half smile. Carpool buddy.

"And friend," he answered. Because that was what she had become. A good friend.

But it frustrated him. By February, he waited too expectantly to see her at the end of the day. He avoided travel so they could carpool more. The weekends began to drag without her.

Finally, on a Friday night with Elena away again, he cleared his throat as they crossed the Golden Gate Bridge and asked whether she wanted to stop for a drink.

"Sure," she had said. "Why not?"

That's really all it took.

Amanda made a sound, something between a gasp and a grunt, a guttural expression of her dismay, and Jim returned. This story had taken on a surreal, dreamy quality over the years of living in his mind only, but he saw pain in Amanda's face. He waved to the waitress for the check.

"I want to hear the rest," Amanda said.

"Okay." He rubbed his face. "But let's walk?"

His daughter strode ahead of him out of the crowded café, looking purposeful. The same way that Penny had once walked away from him, a long time ago.

Chapter 32

"I have dreamed in my life, dreams that have stayed with me ever after, and changed my ideas; they have gone through and through me, like wine through water, and altered the color of my mind."

—Emily Bronte

URIEL WAS SLEEPING SO DEEPLY, HE BARELY HEARD THE KNOCK-ing. When he stumbled to his door well past midnight, he found Amanda standing in the pouring rain, crying.

"What is it?" He pulled her inside. "Babe, you're soaked. What's going on? I thought you went to see your Dad."

"I did." She wore a soaking wet sweatshirt and jeans. She wrapped her arms around him, drove her head into his shoulder and shuddered.

"Tell me what's wrong?"

Amanda's body was slippery in his arms, insubstantial, as if she was dissolving with the rain. He brought her into the bedroom and peeled her things from her—the soaked sweatshirt, muddy sneakers, damp jeans clinging as he took them off. He gave her a dry Esperanza T-shirt. When she eyed it without moving, he pulled her wet shirt over her head and put the clean one on. "Get under the covers. If you aren't going to tell me what's wrong, at least let me warm you up."

She lay down, calmer, but tears still trickled. He held her until they both fell asleep, Amanda's fingers wrapped around his wrist.

When Uriel awoke later he found her naked, her fingers trailing the edge of his shoulder blade. His erection was immediate, his body ready before his mind. She climbed on top of him, where she rocked gently at first, and then faster. She leaned back and he admired her breasts outlined in the early morning light, her thick hair falling behind her as she arched. He came, unable to wait for her.

Later, he woke again to find her gone from the bed, a damp impression on the pillow. He wondered how much she had slept.

In the living room, Amanda curled up on the saggy couch under his bathrobe and staring out the window. Her freckles stood out against her pale skin, in the dim light of the early foggy morning.

He grabbed sweats from a pile on the chair. "Are you okay?"

She shook her head, lightly. "I have ridiculous shit to tell you, but first, I have to know something."

His gut clenched, as if he might be in trouble. "Okay?"

"I know this is jealous girlfriend behavior, but I looked at your phone a long time ago."

His couldn't imagine what she could have seen that would upset her. He didn't think he had anything to hide.

"And based on how absurd my life just got, I have to know where we stand. Are you seeing anyone else?"

His head snapped up. "What?"

"Or maybe just when we first got back together? I mean, that's fair. I need to know because I can't take one more lie in my life."

Wide awake now, anger flushed through Uriel's mind. "You show up in the middle of the night, won't tell me what's wrong. Then get up in morning and ask me if I'm cheating on you? What the fuck, Amanda?"

She moved across the room, her back to him. The T-shirt she wore reached to her knees, and her hair hung like a wet veil. Uriel had a vision of a nun, cloistered.

"I know I sound nuts. But who's Cat?"

"Cat?"

"The name on your phone, Uriel! You were talking to her. She's in your contacts . . . and I've seen it pop up other times."

He felt himself lift on his feet, a habit he had from arguments with Lourdes growing up. A longing to run when angry. "She could be someone I teach lessons to, or a friend or a winery client. Do you expect to know about every person I talk to?"

"Why aren't you answering me?"

"Do I have to? Can you just trust me?" He didn't want to tell her the whole weird story, didn't want to hash out the details of Flavia's betrayals. But mostly, he didn't want to be questioned.

"I'm low on trust right now. For anyone."

Uriel ran his hands over his face, trying to find patience. "Did I do something?"

"No." Amanda sat on the edge of the couch, pulling her knees under the T-shirt. "No, you didn't. I recently found out something that left me feeling—raw. Or sick. Nauseous. I've been nauseous for days. So, can you humor me and explain who Cat is?"

He exhaled, resigned. "She's the woman who was married to the guy that Flavia had an affair with. The one in the accident. I don't know why we talk to each other but we do, sometimes. On the phone. I've never met her, but it's helped."

"Flavia was having an affair?"

"Apparently."

Amanda hit her head with her hands. "Christ, I'm sorry. I didn't know that. Everyone lies. It's so fucking pervasive."

Uriel tried to follow. "You're talking about who, now?"

Her voice was high, a little hysterical. "My father is my father."

"Like you're trying to accept what he did to your mom?" *A cheater.*

Amanda blew out a horse-like snort of frustration. "No, I mean he is my father. Really. Like I am not adopted. Or, I don't know. I'm half-adopted. He's my *father.*"

Her meaning penetrated slowly, like liquid moving through a sponge. "What? How? Are you sure?"

"Believe me, I didn't believe it at first. It took that picture of Penny to know that she was my mother."

Uriel felt two steps behind. "The school teacher?"

"Well, you have to admit, I look just like her."

He sank down on the couch next to her, beginning to follow the strand. Lourdes' odd memory had led to this incredible truth. "Wow. My preschool teacher was your mother? That's bizarre. And she had a child with your Dad. This is nuts."

Amanda rested her head on her knee, exhaustion sketching deep lines in her forehead. "Yes and no. I always assumed my birth mother came from So-Cal because I was born down there. But she lived here for a while. And it's a small town."

"What did he say?"

She shrugged and told him the story. "When he found out she had a baby, he knew he would do anything to keep me. They'd already lost a child."

"And your mom accepted that?"

"My mom . . . must be nuts. She decided to stay with him and *be a family.* I know how it sounds, but now that I know more about her awful life, it makes sense. My dad was the best thing that ever happened to her. Also, she had been depressed and they weren't really together when he and Penny . . . Anyway, they decided it would be like a normal adoption. Elena didn't want me to grow up feeling like the bastard child. Which is ironic, because doesn't everyone who's adopted feel like a bastard child?"

Uriel didn't know how it felt to be adopted. He knew life as the fatherless child of a drunk. Not adopted.

"They decided not to tell me about Penny. And then they fucking stuck to it. I'm twenty-seven years old, and they never told me. My father could be dying, but he would go to the grave before he told me the truth. I'm angry. I feel sick inside. I sat outside in the rain before I knocked on your door last night, because I thought I might puke. I can't believe they tricked me."

He debated trying to hug her. "It doesn't sound like your mom meant to trick you."

Amanda's eyes flared wider. "She didn't mean to, but she did. And all this time, I kept asking them, 'Do you know anything else about my birth parents? Anything?' And they told me nothing."

Uriel felt her sadness rising off her, like mist. "It's remarkable that your mom stayed all these years."

Amanda pulled on the end of a long strand of hair anxiously. "I know. I guess she really loved him. And she said she wanted a baby and a family, even if it was a painful way to begin. And she always told me that once she met me," Amanda grabbed a tissue, her eyes filling again, "she knew I was her daughter. She loved me instantly."

"She really does love you. That's obvious."

"I know. That's part of what sucks."

"And your other mother, the . . ." Uriel searched for the best wording. "Your birth mother?"

Amanda started to pace. "I guess she didn't want me, so she figured at least I had my dad." Her voice cracked, and he took her in his arms, trying to squeeze out her pain.

"Do you know anything about her?"

"She still lived in California, as of about ten years ago, according to my dad. I have an address."

He grabbed her a tissue. "Nearby?"

"No. Santa Barbara." Amanda pulled away and looked at him. "I think I need to meet her."

"Hm." Uriel thought of all the ways this woman could hurt her.

"Yeah. I know it's soon, but I knew the minute I heard the truth that I would meet her. I've been waiting for this my whole life, in a way." Amanda paused. Her voice grew cool. "And then after that, Uriel, I want to go away."

The words made his heart sink, like a stone thrown into a pool. Uriel had known this would happen. That she would leave again. But not now, not so soon. He took a seat. Some part of him began to give up, already disengaging.

Amanda grabbed his arm. "Uriel, listen."

"It's okay. I knew you wouldn't stay. You don't have to explain."

"Uriel, wait. I came here to ask you something." Her green eyes stayed steady on his face, and he felt her breath on his cheek. "Will you go with me?"

"What?"

"Will you come? I need to get away. Maybe for only a while but maybe for longer. I'm going to go back to Peru, to finish the dissertation. Then I don't know—maybe look for a job? Or teach English somewhere? I need to get away from them."

Uriel shook his head, frustrated. "Didn't you do that already?"

"Yes, but this time I'm not leaving you. I'm asking you to come with me."

He wanted Amanda to go home. He would make a cup of coffee and start his day and forget about her. But he also wanted her to stay with him all day. Forever. "I'm not like you, Amanda. I have a job and my uncle needs me. I take care of a lot of things here. And I don't have a father who bankrolls me. I can't."

Amanda shook her head, a strand of hair stuck to her cheek. "Uriel, we can figure it out. I don't want to go without you. And babe, think about it—maybe we both could use a fresh start?"

The rain started again, drumming against the roof. He knew the leak in the kitchen would require a bucket put under it, and that his uncle would expect him to get up to the stables soon, to make sure the horses weren't upset by the storm.

"I can't leave that easily." He wanted to add: I am a grown-up. I have responsibilities. The desire to strike out at her impulsiveness coursed through him. "I don't do time off. The last time I went away was to Vegas, years ago."

"Exactly."

"No." Uriel got up and crossed the room, needing to move. "I married Flavia on that trip. Probably the worst decision I've ever made." Relief came to him, as he spoke those words. He could acknowledge now that the marriage was ill-fated, unhealthy. That he'd been grieving a fantasy, not Flavia. Amanda had given him that.

She reached out her hand. "This would be a better trip."

Uriel imagined traveling in South America with Amanda. He'd always wanted to ride a Paso horse up the hills. Could his uncle manage without him? "What about my Aunt Maya? I can't leave Freddie right now. And what about your dad? Is he done with treatment?"

Amanda moved to the window, looking out at the rain. "I think Maya would want you to go. You never do anything for yourself, Uriel, and she loves you. And my father . . . He's okay. And he has Victor to be there."

"And your mom?"

Amanda's voice grew hard. "Elena needs to live her own life for a while, and for me to go live mine. I can't take care of her forever."

Uriel wanted to hold her but held back. "Don't be too mad at your mother. She's taken good care of you."

"Yeah, but I don't get her. I don't even know her, in a way."

"Well, running away isn't going to help you get to know her."

Her eyes flared. "Touché. I'm not running away though. I'm just moving on." Amanda started towards the bedroom. "I wish you'd come, Uriel."

"But you're going, either way?"

Amanda had turned away, but Uriel knew the answer from the firm stance of her shoulders.

Chapter 33

"Language is wine upon the lips."

—Virginia Woolf

JIM HAD AGREED TO GO TO SONOMA TO PICK UP THEIR DOGS, albeit reluctantly. Apparently, both Amanda and Elena were going to be away for a few days, and Elena didn't want to board the dogs. But she also didn't want Jim at her home, so, after some emailing, they agreed he would pick the dogs up from Uriel, at the stables.

Jim's hands were clammy as he drove, anxiety seeming to drive blood through his heart at a faster pace than usual. He had felt ill with anxiety since Amanda confronted him. He wasn't sure if she would ever forgive him, whether he had any right to ask for forgiveness.

Victor was somewhat disgusted with him as well, once he came to know the full story. "Really, Jim?" he'd asked, incredulously. "You didn't think she'd find out? This is Amanda. She found out about us years ago. And didn't you think she deserved to know?"

"Of course, she did—I see that now." Jim tried to explain the way things developed over time into a joint belief system he hadn't dared dismantle.

Victor's face had grown pale. "Occasionally I see the carapace of self-deception you've lived under, Jim, and it shocks me." He'd been distant and cool ever since.

They would get through it, Jim assured himself. He could weather Elena's silence, Amanda's fury and Victor's disappointment simultaneously. It just caused his chest to be tight and his stomach in knots.

As he turned onto Highway 12, his heart lifted at the beauty around him. Cows wandered peacefully in the field to his left. The mustard flowers were in full bloom, creating what looked like rivers of yellow cascading down the hills, between the vines. And the vines themselves were a deep, lush green. Good God, he missed Sonoma. Maybe he could spend some time here soon? If Elena's ire died down?

Jim turned up the long drive to Esperanza, bordered with high conifers, his tires splashing in a few puddles left from recent storms. There was no sign of the rain today. Pure, warm sunshine and the scent of honeysuckle on the breeze surrounded him as he got out of his car.

Within a minute, Beaver was pounding across the parking lot towards him, with Lady right behind. He braced himself for the onslaught of wet paws and frantic licking. He heard himself laugh with joy for the first time in days. Maybe the dogs would be the perfect antidote. The only creatures in his life that would still see him as worthy of their unbridled affection.

"Hey, Jim." Uriel came from the stables, a damp T-shirt covering his broad shoulders and a scruffy cowboy hat on his head. His eyes were cool, but his voice was cordial. "Amanda said you'd be up closer to four. You're early."

Jim tried to keep the dogs down, despite their eagerness. He wondered what the pups had thought. Did dogs wonder about you, when you disappeared?

"I was excited to see the dogs. And thought I'd beat traffic up."

"Right. Well . . . I have their leashes and things in the office."

Uriel walked away, his back clearly tense. He was on the list of people who thought Jim an ass, apparently. In the office, Uriel handed over two leashes, a large bag of dog food and water bowls.

Jim attempted to carry it all and corral the dogs, but Uriel took the food bag back. "I'll walk you out."

"Do you mind if I see Chestnut?" Jim asked, impulsively. If he couldn't see his family, he could at least see the animals.

Uriel's step slowed slightly but he nodded. "Of course. He's your horse."

"Oh, he's clearly Amanda's horse."

Uriel smiled. "True."

They dropped their load in Jim's trunk, then walked to Chestnut's stall, Jim feeling Uriel's feelings thaw as they chatted about the wet weather and the growing season. Chestnut whinnied as they approached. Jim let himself in and ran his hand over the horse's muscular back.

"He looks great," Jim said.

"Amanda's been keeping him well exercised." Uriel reached for his phone and pulled up several pictures of Amanda and Chestnut, jumping. "He looks younger than he did a year ago, before she got home."

"Well, that's one good thing," Jim said. *In this otherwise shit year.*

"Yes," Uriel answered. "There's been some good things."

Jim decided to take a risk and ask. "You two are . . . ?"

"Unclear."

Jim nodded awkwardly, wishing he hadn't asked.

"She wants to leave again," Uriel said. A pool of pain welled in his eyes.

Shit.

"She's just angry at me," Jim offered.

Uriel nodded, his warmth dissipating. "Yes. Anyway, I have to go close up the winery."

"Well, thanks for keeping the dogs for us today."

"Of course."

"Is Amanda . . . away for long?"

"No. She's—I'm not sure, actually. She had some research to do." Uriel was halfway across the stables when he called back to Jim. "Do you want to come down to the tasting room for a glass of wine?"

Surprised, Jim quickly agreed. "I'd love to." I'll leave the dogs up here?"

"They come in all the time," Uriel said. He whistled and both dogs followed him, as well as a mangy mutt that seemed to live at the stables.

A drop of optimism bubbled up as Jim followed Uriel down the hill to the tasting room. Vineyards surrounded him, his dogs still loved him, and his daughter's boyfriend was giving him a chance. Maybe Uriel could encourage Amanda to forgive her parents for being human.

The tasting room was quiet, just a few customers at the counter. Uriel waved him over to a table and poured them both a hefty taste of a red blend.

"It's sixty percent Cabernet Sauvignon, thirty-seven percent Zinfandel and three percent Petit Verdot."

The wine seemed to open on Jim's tongue, tasting earthy, like dark fruit and fall leaves. "It's wonderful," he said, meaning it.

"It won the *San Francisco Chronicle*'s silver award a few years ago," Uriel said with pride.

Jim enjoyed seeing him in this role, as part of the wine-making family. They chatted about the winery, Jim learning more about the history. Jim realized he had been pulling for Uriel in his mind, ever since Amanda talked about loving him.

"I think Amanda will stick around this time," Jim said. "Once she gets over the latest . . . upset."

"That's a big thing to get over," Uriel said. Clearly, he knew everything. Jim's optimism withered. They didn't talk about it more.

Uriel insisted Jim take the rest of the bottle of wine home with him when he rose to leave. Jim bought several more, "as gifts for clients." When they parted, Jim didn't quite meet Uriel's eye. His affair, almost thirty years ago, might be the reason Uriel lost the chance to be with Amanda. No, the affair created Amanda. It was Jim's lack of honesty that led to the current situation.

"I should have told her," Jim blurted out.

"Yes," Uriel said. "You should have."

On the way home, the dogs panting happily in the back seat, Jim felt like he saw apparitions of Penny on every corner, heard her voice on the car radio. He had agreed to try to locate her, for Amanda, but found himself unable to take the first steps. It had been years since he'd let himself remember the months they spent together.

He pictured her on that first night together, when they'd stopped impulsively for "one drink." Penny wore a purple dress and with her red hair and green eyes, she looked like a queen. Jim had let himself imagine, briefly, being more to each other. Penny knew the deals he worked on, the staff he promoted, the staff he let go. She knew his travel schedule, his need to clinch the deal with a new client, and what he ate for lunch that day.

Wasn't that more than he had with Elena?

They ended up in a nearby hotel. He would never bring her to his house, and she clearly didn't want him in her trailer. When he lifted the purple dress above her head, she grabbed him and pulled him to her. She was stronger, more muscular, than any woman he'd known, and it aroused him. Then she became delicate and vulnerable in another minute, placing tiny kisses down his chest, and he melted.

He hesitated before entering her, thinking for a minute of the many reasons not to do so. He was probably plunging into an enormous mistake. He could lose his marriage, ruin his work relationships, and hurt his wife deeply. He wasn't even wearing a condom. What was he doing?

But he succumbed, her hands tight on his ass, her wine-tinged breath on his cheek. She squealed as he entered her, as if in surprise, and despite himself, he came. It was over too quickly. He had wanted so much more than this.

Despite their agreement to not repeat the transgression, they got together again months later, on Valentine's Day. Elena had gone on a girls' trip with her sister. Penny had no one special to share the night with. Why, they justified, should either of them spend Valentine's Day alone?

He took his time that night, gently removing her layers, refusing to kiss her until he had massaged her toes, stroked her back, and murmured the things he had wanted to say to her for months. Finally, she grabbed him, and he'd let her straddle him, feeling like a much younger man. The echoes of grief from his lost child finally dissipated, his anger at Elena for pushing him away softened, and his heart broke wide open as he came.

Later, he had reviewed the details of that night meticulously. He had brought a condom, but she said it was not needed, she was on the pill. He remembered her reassurance of this. In the morning, she announced it needed to stop there. He was married. He had agreed, reluctantly.

But in mid-March, Penny's birthday came, and he couldn't stand not to be with her. When he offered to buy her dinner, she showed up a short black dress he'd not seen before, and a new bobbed haircut. He gave her an emerald bracelet for her birthday, to match her eyes. He remembered holding her hand to his lips after she put the bracelet on, and inhaling the scent of her. He knew it was a mistake, but not how to stop himself. Elena was back in Sonoma, and his conscience poked at him even in the fog of gin and tonics and a bottle of Pinot Noir.

"I shouldn't be here," he said, finally. But when he saw the pain spark in her eyes he regretted it. "I'm sorry. I don't mean to . . . it's my problem, not yours."

She placed a strand of hair carefully behind her. "No, Jim, I'd say it's my problem, too. But let's have one more dinner? We can both go home after that."

He agreed, raising his glass. "Yes, let's have a birthday dinner. Here's to thirty-one."

"Actually, I am only turning twenty-eight," she said, with a shrug. "I lied. I wanted you to think I was older that first time I came to your office. I knew even then that I wanted you. But now I don't have to pretend. I'm twenty-eight today."

Jim's stomach sunk at the idea that he'd been sleeping with a twenty-seven-year-old. He tried not to show it, ordering a series of courses and dessert, lingering at the table.

Over dinner, he told her he that he cared for her, that her friendship meant the world to him at a particularly difficult time in his life. He told her that she was smart, and funny, and he loved her strong, if wrong, political opinions, and the way she never let life's crappy luck stop her. Her resiliency attracted him. By the time he told her all this, he had talked himself back into staying the night at the hotel with her. When he woke up the next morning, she was gone. Jim lifted the note she had left him with shaking hands.

Jim, I won't be there on Monday, it would be too hard to be near you, but not with you. And don't feel bad—it was fun for both of us. But don't look for me, I need to move on before I get stuck on you. I like your resiliency too, Jim. Thank you for my birthday. I'll miss you so much. Love, Penny.

He didn't hear from her again for nine months.

Chapter 34

"Wine is the drink of the gods, milk the drink of babes,
tea the drink of women, and water the drink of beasts."

—John Stuart Blackie

ELENA CALLED DR. LOVE FOR AN EXTRA SESSION. HER ANXIETY
had risen so high she couldn't sleep. The trust Elena had earned back
since the suicide attempt had dissipated from Amanda's eyes after
she heard about Penny, like a puff of smoke in the face of gale winds.
Amanda wasn't speaking to either parent at the moment. She mostly
stayed over at Uriel's, licking her wounds.

Elena moved the tissue box off Dr. Love's desk as she came in, and
put it on the table in front of her. "I really miscalculated. I thought she
would be upset with Jim, more than me. I thought she would see that
I sacrificed, to be her mother . . . but it was the only way."

"Amanda may be too hurt to hear much right now."

"I just want to know that she'll forgive me, eventually. That I haven't
ruined things . . . *Irrever?*—what is that word?" She could feel it on the
tip of her tongue. "The word that means something can't be fixed?"

Dr. Love eyes narrowed. "Irrevocably?"

"Yes, that's it." Sometimes English words still eluded her when her
mind jumped around like a kite in the wind. Even Spanish words
sounded wrong. Under heavy stress, she felt like a woman with no
language, rather than two.

"Mother and daughter relationships are always complicated. Right?"

Dr. Love hesitated. "Right . . . although I will say this is an extreme
circumstance."

"It is?"

He leaned closer, as if trying to soften his words. "Lying to children about their origins is always a mistake, in the long run."

His clarity made her feel foolish, that she and Jim had been so wrong. Dr. Love was usually supportive.

"I know it was a mistake. That's obvious now. But at the time—what could I do? Raise my daughter knowing she was the product of her father's affair? Or do you think I should have told her when she became an adult?" Elena pulled on an already torn cuticle.

Dr. Love's voice was firm. "You probably should have told her before now. But as you said, it's easy to recognize after the fact. I'm not trying to make you feel worse, Elena. But you and Jim need to accept how painful this is for her. That's the only way you'll all heal."

"I did say I was sorry, over and over, to her. She was so angry she wouldn't listen."

"Try again. And make sure you clarify that you realize you made a mistake to lie to her."

Elena wished they had a better for word for lying, when you had no choice. When all you intended to do was create a safe life for a child. Not to mislead her. "I didn't think about this part—about her being an adult and having questions. She was a just a baby with no mother."

"When did you find out Jim had a child?"

Elena thought back to that time, and a shiver ran through her. Ironically, she had lost her trust for her husband and gained a child the same day.

"I came home with groceries one day and found Jim in the house, in the middle of the day. I remember it being this gorgeous fall day. I had bought pumpkins for the porch. Jim and I were letting go of the past, finally—losing the baby, separating. Jim had brought up adoption a few times, but I was so hurt after our son died, I couldn't talk about it. But on the day we found out, I planned to call him, and to tell him the land next door was for sale, that he could finally have his vineyard. He'd been eyeing it for months. I wanted to show we could move on. Together."

"You didn't know about the affair?"

"No, but I suspected. In a way, I didn't care what he had done. I'd been removed. But we were back on track. I started to think our lives would be all right. Not an ideal place, but stable, together. Then that day, I found him standing in the kitchen. I knew it was something serious. His face looked gray—like ashes. He kept saying he was sorry, but I had to hear him out. To try to give him another chance. Amanda was a few days old."

"He didn't tell you before that? About the pregnancy?"

"No. He didn't know himself. He hadn't seen Penny the whole pregnancy. I don't think we would have known about Amanda, except the social workers insisted Penny tell them Jim's name. She was putting the baby up for adoption." Elena felt the old anger flaring, at this stranger. "She didn't plan to tell him."

Dr. Love frowned. Elena couldn't quite read the look in his eyes. Amazement that she had been weak? Judgment on Jim? "What happened then?" he asked.

"Jim had to leave right away, to drive to the hospital in LA. He was frantic that Penny would place the baby with someone before he could arrive, or might leave with the baby. Even through the shock, I was struck with his determination to get that baby. With or without me, Jim would bring his baby home. I locked myself in the bathroom until he left. Then, when I heard his car leaving, I wanted to run after him. But I didn't. I decided to leave. I didn't see how to stay with him. I packed some things, called Carmen and told her I needed her help."

Elena stopped, seeing it again. Carmen came in minutes. She looked up divorce lawyers in the phone book, then called Jim and cursed at him.

"And then?" Dr. Love's eyes had softened.

"He called me from the hospital, begging me to stay long enough to hear him out. 'You can leave, Elena. But please, not yet. Let me get home. Let's talk. What do you have to lose by listening to me? If our marriage is over, you'll wish later we at least talked.'"

"And so I waited. I remember standing in the baby's room, the one we called the baby's room, even though our son had never come home. Thinking, there is going to be a baby here after all. And it isn't mine."

Elena barely realized she was crying now, until the tears multiplied. She wiped her face with the back of her hand, then grabbed more tissues.

"Jim came home a few days later, walking into the foyer with the car seat in his hand. Amanda was so tiny. Even for a baby, she looked tiny. And of course I held her, while Jim warmed a bottle. I couldn't not hold the baby. It wasn't her fault that Penny had abandoned her, or that her father cheated on me. She was an infant."

She offered a soft laugh. "She had intense eyes. Even though they hadn't turned green yet, they shone, and followed everything. I knew she would be strong. And I thought she would have to be, without a mother. Then I remember thinking Jim would marry someone else in a few years, who would be the baby's mother. He wouldn't stay alone for long."

She stopped for a moment, lost in memory.

"Jim kept asking me not to leave yet, to consider being a family. And I yelled at him, calling him names . . . Then the baby woke up. I heard her crying, and she sounded lonely. I brought her a bottle. I couldn't help myself. I started to question my plan. Why would I let someone else have this? This rocking chair I chose. This house I helped design, this man who was a good provider. This healthy baby I could probably never have otherwise. But still, it seemed wrong, to let Jim win. For him to be a cheater and still have a family. I went back and forth for days."

In the end, she had stayed for Amanda. Elena loved her tiny fingers, her sweet breath. The way her petite legs stretched when she woke, and the way she stared. Amanda possessed an intense wisdom, even as a baby.

"I stayed because I wanted to be that baby's mother more than anything else. I still do." She wiped another tear away and sat back, relieved. She rarely talked about any of it, this secret-riddled past.

"Did you tell her that?" he asked.

Elena pulled her sweater around her, tightly. "I don't know. I tried."

"Try again. Tell her like you told me. How much you wanted to be her mother. Can you do that?"

"Yes," Elena said. "Of course. Do you think what we did, Jim and I—I know you said we should have told her. But is it forgivable?"

"Almost anything is forgivable, when it is done for the right reasons."

Elena took that as her hope, as she stopped to buy a bouquet of sunflowers, Amanda's favorite, and as she drove up the bumpy road to the stables. She thought about the mistakes one makes, out of love, and prayed her daughter's heart had not grown too hard.

Chapter 35

"Boys should abstain from all use of wine until their
eighteenth year, for it is wrong to add fire to fire."

—Plato

THE DAY THE POLICE CALLED GLORIA'S CELL PHONE, IT WAS
raining so hard her Toyota could barely grip the road, slipping on the
mud and leaves as she made her way down the hill towards town. Her
heart ran faster than the car, galloping like a wild horse, as if it would
arrive at the station ahead of the rest of her body.

She would grab Carlos and slap him when she saw him. How could
he do this to her? Or maybe she would grab him and hold him. Her
baby, locked in a cell. Dios mío.

Would the police ask for her ID? Could they know her papers were
expired? She had the right to be here. But not to work. God, Carlos, don't
say your mother is at work. Would they be harder on him because of his
dark skin? She'd heard of boys being thrown to the ground when the police
arrested them or cracking their heads on the rim of the car. Mexican boys.

At a red light, Gloria called Lourdes. Lourdes had been to jail before.
She would know what to say or do. But she didn't pick up. Gloria left
a message, as a car honked for her to go.

Gloria cried as she drove. Carlos, mí Carlos. Should she call Diego?
He was his father. He had not seen Carlos lately, back to his old ways.
He avoided her calls, texting back one-word answers. She had told him
she needed some money. Carlos needed new sneakers and they cost a
fortune, and the rent loomed at the end of the month. Child support
is supposed to help with that, she reminded him.

Diego picked up Carlos after school as a surprise, taking him to
Sonoma Old School, Carlos favorite skate store. Carlos strode into the

apartment an hour later in a new pair of Vans. A pair of sneakers, but no rent money. What kind of father was Diego? The kind that came to the police station when his son got caught doing something with pills at his school?

The principal had talked fast on the phone, saying Carlos admitted to being the source of the pill distribution. Distribution? Where would Carlos get pills?

Outside the station, she stopped under the awning in front of the door to answer her phone. She began to cry as she told Lourdes what was happening.

"He's in a jail? You sure? Carlos is too young. He must be in juvie."

Gloria gulped. "I don't know. I've got to go inside and find out, but Lourdes, I'm scared. If he gets arrested for drugs . . ."

"Did you call the lawyer?"

"What lawyer?" Gloria feet were cold in soaking wet shoes, the rain torrential.

"The immigration one. She can help you, I bet. What's her name?"

"Maria Salvatore. But I don't think she would help with this. And she's busy."

"She's still a lawyer. Go inside and find out what's going on. I'll call you when I get off work."

Gloria wanted to ask her cousin to leave work, to come over and help her, but she couldn't. She needed to shoulder this responsibility.

Inside, the station was not busy or clean like CSI, not frightening like in prison movies. It looked like a dentist office.

"Help you?" An older black woman with short hair and a tired face stood behind the desk. She repeated the question in Spanish as well.

"I'm looking for my son," Gloria said. "The school said he was here." Her stomach churned with the tuna fish and chips she'd had for lunch. She gave the woman her name, then sat on a wobbly plastic chair.

"The arresting officer is back over at the school, so you need to wait. He wants to talk to you."

Each word tightened the muscles of her neck more. Arresting. He wants to speak to you. She rubbed the small nub where her finger used to be, as if missing the piece of herself long gone in Mexico.

Her phone rang. The cop pointed to a sign on the wall that said no cell phones. "Sorry," she said, and went outside.

"Gloria?" Uriel sounded worried. "Lourdes told me Carlos is in trouble."

She tried to tell him what was happening. Her throat tightened, and she began to cry.

Uriel interrupted her as she apologized. "It's okay. I'll come down. And Gloria, call a lawyer."

Her hands shook as she dialed Salvatore's phone number. The lawyer didn't answer. She never picked up. Gloria took a deep breath and left a message, relieved she could do it in Spanish. Somehow it sounded less frightening in her native tongue. *My son got in some trouble at school. I don't know if you could help me.*

An Asian cop and Uriel came in at the same time twenty minutes later, both dripping. Uriel gave Gloria's hand a squeeze, his hand cold and damp. "You all right?" Uriel asked her. His wore dirty jeans, his hair stuck under a knit cap, probably coming right from the stables.

Before she could answer, the Asian cop came over, peeling off his jacket. His wet shoes left marks on the linoleum. "Mrs. Ramirez?"

"Yes." Gloria tried to speak clearly, although she shook. *Don't act guilty,* she told herself. *You don't know if Carlos did anything.*

Uriel stood next to her protectively. The cop glanced at him.

"You the dad?" he asked.

"I'm his uncle."

Gloria was glad Uriel didn't try to explain their relationship. The son of her first cousin would sound like nothing to this cop. But they were family.

"Okay, I'm Officer Lu. Come on back."

They followed him to his small office, crowded with three desks. Another cop talked on the phone in Spanish, saying for someone to call him later, not at work. Officer Lu offered a chair to Gloria and dragged another over for Uriel.

A good sign, she hoped, that the cop cared to get them a chair. Maybe it showed he thought that Carlos hadn't done anything too bad. Could it all be a mistake?

"Why don't we start with the basics? Can I get your current address?"

Gloria took a deep breath and answered his questions. Their address, Carlos' birth date, his grade at school. The man typed as she talked, slowly, and it made her want to scream. Tell me where my son is! Give me back my Carlos!

"I don't have any record on Carlos," the office said, tapping his computer a few times. "Does that mean this is his first interaction with the justice system?"

Gloria wasn't sure she understood the question.

"Yes," Uriel answered for her. "He's never been in trouble."

"Well, that's good. That will help."

"What did he do?" Gloria couldn't stand it anymore.

The officer looked surprised. "I thought the school explained. Carlos sold pills to kids on campus."

"Crap," Uriel muttered. "Are you sure? Carlos is a good kid. He doesn't even smoke weed. I can't see him selling pills."

Gloria wondered if Uriel knew this for sure or just needed to defend his cousin.

"We're sure. He had the bottle of pills in his backpack. Sold some to a freshman who took it and then got scared, so she told the school nurse."

Gloria's grasped her hands together so tightly her fingertips grew pale. She looked at the dirty floor, rocking as a wave of shame swept over her. Her son sold pills to a freshman girl.

"Where did he say he got them?" Uriel asked. Thank God Uriel was doing the talking. She couldn't speak. Selling pills? He could have killed someone. Here she had thought she had a psychic ability. She didn't even sense the trouble her own son might be up to!

"He won't say where he got them. But we're trying to contact the person it is prescribed to."

Gloria looked up, confused. "There is a name on the bottle?" she asked.

Lu's gaze pierced her, like a laser into her mind. "Yes. The kids usually steal the pills and then sell them on campus. Grab them out of someone's purse or break into their house."

Gloria shook her head, tears falling down her cheeks. "No," she managed to get out. "Carlos is no thief."

At that moment, the door opened, the officer at the front desk coming in with someone right behind her. "Sorry, boss, your phone ringer off again?"

Maria Salvatore came pushing past her into the office, a long rain-coat over her shoulder, her short choppy hair and cheeks damp with rain. Gloria had never been so happy to see someone.

"Officer? I'm Maria Salvatore. The Ramirez family's counsel. You're holding a minor here? Why isn't he at juvenile hall? Is he in a protective cell at least?"

Officer Lu sat back, sighing, and crossed his arms. "He's in his own cell."

"And has he been questioned without an adult present?"

Lu shook his head. "No, Ma'am. Of course not. I questioned him with his principal in the room. So, why don't we get Carlos to join this party?" He stood up, clearly irritated. "I need two of you to wait out in the hall, it's too small in the interview room for everyone."

Gloria looked at her lawyer and knew Carlos needed her more than his mother. "We'll wait in the hall," she said. And then she switched into Spanish. "Thank you so much for coming."

"Happened to be in the neighborhood," Ms. Salvatore answered. "And your cousin Lourdes kept calling me until I picked up."

Gloria watched the woman's broad shoulders follow the cop down the hall, sending up a prayer of thanks to Guadalupe for lawyers and cousins. Uriel insisted on getting her a cup of coffee, though she could hardly drink it, staring at the dark, muddy color. Uriel paced.

Half an hour later, Salvatore came out to speak to Gloria. "I think we'll get him out of here today, as long as he agrees to youth court. It's a good program. It will be okay. No record, if he does what they tell him."

Gloria's lungs opened, and she realized she hadn't had a deep breath in hours. He was coming home. Thank you, God, Santa María, Jesus and all the angels. Gracias, gracias.

Salvatore went on. "Cop has a couple questions for you, though. If you aren't sure of anything, don't answer it."

In a small room that did look like the TV shows, Carlos sat at a table, biting on his nails. He reached for her as she pulled the chair to the table, his eyes filled with tears. "Mom, I'm really sorry."

She shook her head. Not now, Carlos.

Officer Lu explained about youth court. "Did you know Carlos was carrying illicit substances?"

"No, of course not."

"And do you know how he came to get them?"

Gloria shook her head, adamantly.

"Does Carlos take amphetamines himself?"

"What?"

"Or any medication—for ADD, or focus?"

"No. He doesn't take anything." Her brain couldn't absorb the word amphetamine.

"Do you know Sheila Hanley?"

Gloria shook her head, but started to wonder. Sheila. What was Diego's girl's last name? Hanley? She glanced at Carlos, who stared at the table. He moved his head, just slightly. No. Gloria thought of the stupid girl in the ski wear store, her bouncy eyes. And then Carlos' cryptic mentions about her after the Christmas trip. "She's nice," he had said. "Just kind of weird."

Gloria didn't know whether it would be better or worse to admit the pills belonged to Carlos' father's young girlfriend. Would they report them all to Child Protective Services?

The cop and Salvatore examined Gloria. "No," she said, trying to keep her voice strong. "I don't know her."

"Well, I'll be contacting her to find out how Carlos might have come across her medication. If she's reported a theft, there will be further charges."

Should she tell them now? Was it better or worse that Carlos might have taken them from someone they knew?

The cop went on. "I'll call you tomorrow with instructions. If he doesn't follow their instructions to the T, pay his fine, and do community service, he'll be back here." He turned to Carlos. "This is for first time offenders only. Don't mess this chance up."

"I won't," Carlos said, serious. To Gloria, he sounded scared and sincere. But maybe she didn't know her son so well.

She texted Diego: **I need to talk to you.**

Maria Salvatore came outside with them, standing in the vestibule so they didn't get soaked while Uriel ran for the car. Gloria thanked her again for coming. "You can send me the bill," she added.

Salvatore nodded. "Any progress on the other thing? Your husband ready to help you out?"

Gloria shook her head. She didn't want to talk about it in front of Carlos.

The lawyer didn't take the hint. "Tell him he has two choices. He can pay you the back child support and get a divorce, clean. Or he can show up and get your green card renewed. But if he doesn't want to help you with the green card, tell him we're coming after him for the support. Every penny."

"He says he doesn't want to lie."

"Great, he doesn't need to. He needs to say you're married, and that you need to work. Both are true."

She had a point. Lawyers made things clearer sometimes, Gloria realized. That's why they cost so much.

"Stay out of trouble," Salvatore said to Carlos, turning to him, before she opened the door. "Your mom can't afford this." She strode down the rainy street, like a soldier to the next battle.

Uriel drove them home, the three of them shoved into the front of his truck like pigs in a small pen, Carlos in the middle.

Gloria cried, unable to hold it in. When they got to their apartment, Uriel turned the car off and announced he was coming in. Gloria felt Carlos stiffen beside her. Good, he needed to be afraid. To have a man in the house he respected. If she saw Diego right now, she'd spit on him, furious.

"Where did you get the pills?" Uriel asked, as soon as they were inside.

"From Sheila," Gloria answered for him. "Diego's girlfriend. Her name is still on the bottle."

Uriel's voice broke out like a tiger's roar. "She gave them to you?"

Carlos stood near the wall, arms crossed, hands under his arm pits. "She didn't mean to get me in trouble. She gave them to me to help with math."

"You need drugs to do math?" Uriel paced in the living room as Gloria collapsed on the couch.

"They're for studying. She has them because she has ADD. A lot of kids take them."

"And you decided to sell them?" Uriel's voice was razor sharp.

"I . . . I don't know. It was stupid. I don't like them, so I wasn't gonna use them. And some kids wanted them. They sell for like twenty bucks each. I only did it a couple times."

"You sold them to a freshman," Gloria said, hearing the disgust in her voice. "A girl."

"I didn't sell it to her! She asked me for one and she didn't have any money, so I gave her one. Cause she's doing really bad on the tests. But she like, freaked out."

"She could have died, Carlos."

"Mom, you don't die from one ADD pill."

Uriel's eyes narrowed and his shoulders tensed, like carved wood.

"Unless you do, Carlos. Unless you have an allergy or you're on some other medicine or have a heart problem."

"But she didn't."

"You don't know that. It was fucking stupid, Carlos! Tell me you get that." Uriel voice echoed in the apartment, reverberating on the thin walls. "Tell me, Carlos."

Carlos pressed himself into the wall. "It was stupid, I know."

"No, the whole thing. Really fucking stupid."

Carlos looked at Gloria, as if expecting her to intervene, to stop Uriel from yelling at him. She wondered if she should. But she didn't.

"Carlos, tell me you're never doing anything this stupid again." Uriel's anger filled him up, making him appear taller and wider.

Carlos dropped his head, surrendering. "It was really fucking stupid and I won't do it again."

"Good." Uriel sat down hard on a kitchen chair, the wood creaking. Gloria pictured it shattering underneath his anger.

Carlos turned away, crying. It's okay, Gloria told herself, let him cry. "Are you going to tell Dad?" he asked, glancing at her.

"We have to, Carlos. I texted him already to come over."

Carlos shook his head, adamantly. "Mom, he's going to flip."

"Sheila's name is on the pills, Carlos. They're going to call her."

"What did the lawyer mean?" Carlos asked. "About Dad?"

She thought about saying nothing, but he'd heard too much. Uriel, who had been getting the car and missed the conversation, eyed her curiously. She explained all of it—the issues with her green card, Diego wanting to get a divorce, the lawyer's plan.

Carlos took it in. "Dad's a dick," he said, finally. He left the room, bumping the chairs as he strode by as if the kitchen was too small to contain this emotion. Gloria heard his Xbox firing up in the living room and decided she'd tell him later he would need to forfeit that privilege. He had to have a consequence. But later.

"You should have told me about the immigration shit, Gloria."

Gloria examined Uriel's profile, the clean lines of brow, nose, hard cheeks. He looked like his father, as much as she remembered him. "It's my problem, Uriel."

"We can help you."

"You did help. Your mom helped. She found me that lawyer. But there's nothing I can do if Diego won't come with me. Like I said, the lawyer thinks I should file for support. I've never done it—not legally. He doesn't have that much."

"Because he doesn't work much," Uriel said, dismissively.

"He's a lazy dog. I knew it when I married him."

Uriel shook his head. "Doesn't matter. Diego has a son. He needs to be a father. It's not a job you quit."

Gloria smiled at his righteousness. She wished she'd chosen a man more like him. Diego loved Carlos, as much as he could. Like a five-year-old loves a puppy, until the dog nips.

"Tell him what the lawyer said. He backs you up or you sue for support."

"It won't work. He acts like he doesn't owe me anything."

"Add the part about the pills," Uriel went on. "If he doesn't back you up, you're going to tell the cops Sheila gave Carlos the pills. They weren't stolen. She gave a minor a bottle of pills. She'll be the one in court. Tell him Carlos can't be around that idiot Sheila, either. Diego writes his first check today or sets a date for the green card. Give him the lawyer's card."

Uriel placed Salvatore's card on the table. "She gave it to me in case I needed to reach her." He grabbed a pen and wrote on the back.

Gloria glanced at it. For Diego, from Uriel.

"Tell him I wanted him to have her card. To call her and get this shit going. Otherwise, he'll recognize her name when she serves him child support papers."

Gloria's lips curved as she took the card. She glanced at her cell and saw a missed call from Diego. And another from Danny, who she should have met after work. She'd forgotten. She'd have to make her apologies and see him later. She would talk to Diego first, try out Uriel's strong reasoning.

She lifted her phone and texted Diego to come to the apartment: It's important.

Diego would never be the father she'd wanted for Carlos, but he could do this for her. Strangely, Carlos' trouble had only made it clearer to her that she had no co-parent. It was her job to be here. In this country. On the job. She needed a green card. She needed to stand up to Diego to do her most important job: being Carlos' mother.

"Okay," Gloria said to Uriel, feeling she'd woken up from a messy dream with new clarity. "I'll tell him today."

Chapter 36

"Thou hast shown thy people hard things: Thou hast
made us to drink the wine of astonishment."

—Psalms 60:3

AMANDA BREATHED IN SALTY OCEAN AIR, MAKING HER WAY
down a long rough pier. She spotted the pale blue boat Penny had
described to her. *La Vida Loca* was written in the side in slanting
script. *The crazy life.* Algae clung to the bow.

"Amanda?"

A woman stepped deftly from the boat's deck to the pier. Her leather
sandals planted firmly on the dock. A wave rolled under them, the
water sloshing around the posts beneath them. Amanda imagined losing her balance and falling into the arms of this stranger, her mother.

"I'm Penny." Penny's long fingers, held out to shake Amanda's hand,
looking eerily familiar, with freckles amassed on the backs of them.
She wore a white ball cap and sunglasses, so Amanda didn't have to
look into her eyes yet.

"I thought so. I'm Amanda." The strangeness of the moment made
the air heavy and Amanda's tongue thick. She had the feeling of being
upside down on an amusement park ride. Fear, giddiness, blood running hot to both cheeks. "You live here, on the boat?"

"I do. Come on board." Penny turned to lead Amanda onto the boat
and then stopped and stood still. "Should I give you a hug? Or is that
too weird?"

"I don't know." Amanda didn't know what she wanted. To be touched
or not, to hear everything or run away. The boat bobbed, the railing lifting. She wanted firm ground beneath her. "Can we take a walk

instead of going on the boat?" Amanda gestured towards the beach. The sun had burned through the morning fog, and the pathway from the marina to town looked less claustrophobic than a boat.

"Sure. Let me get my things."

The offer of a hug dissipated, and Amanda wondered if she had hurt her feelings. Her mother. No, she had a mother. Her biological mother—but she didn't like that phrase.

"Let's head up the beach?"

She'd taken her sunglasses off. Penny's eyes were also green, although a darker shade, and she had a deep line between them, as if she worried too much. Amanda looked into her eyes, saw the reflection of herself, as if she was looking in a mirror, but at the same time felt an otherness. Penny was a stranger, as well as her mother, and the paradox sent a chill down Amanda's spine. Her hand lifted, and Penny took it, grasping her fingers tightly.

"It's good to meet you," Penny said.

As they strolled, Amanda observed Penny through side glances: the long legs, dark red hair, and awkward elbows jutting out. Penny's feet came down flat and heavy, and her shoulders curved a bit under her T-shirt, like a bird whose wings haven't opened up. A snapshot of her future self. *Eerie.*

"We sure do look a lot alike." Penny said, as if she had been looking into the reverse mirror.

A line of birds flew near the water's edge, skimming the surface, bright sun flashing. Amanda had a fleeting thought that she would love to live by the beach. Like her mother? "Where are you from?" Amanda asked. "Before California, I mean."

"Pennsylvania mostly, then I travelled some around the country before— well, before I had you. Settled down after that. Been here twenty-seven years. If you can call it settled. We sail about six months a year."

"We?"

"Me and Gio. He's my boyfriend. More like my husband, but we never bothered. Been sailing together for twenty years. Maybe you'll meet him later. He's great."

"Okay." Amanda didn't think she cared to meet Gio. But maybe she did? Her certitude about tracking Penny down had dissipated when she woke this morning in a roadside motel. She had stared in the mirror, her eyes looking frightened, and wondered aloud why she had been so sure she needed to do this.

"What if she's mean?" she asked her reflection. "Or stupid? What if she's an alcoholic like Lourdes, or mentally ill? Do you really want to know?" They had had one awkward conversation on the phone earlier in the week. After a few minutes of silence, Penny had agreed to meet her, somewhat cautiously.

"You probably have a lot of questions," Penny said now.

"I do. But I don't know where to start."

"Well, I can understand that."

"Why?" Amanda blurted out. "I guess that's my main question. Why did you give me up?"

Penny straightened and looked away, straight into the sun, squinting. "Uh, okay. I guess I should have expected that one . . . I struggled with that myself for a long time. The best answer I have is because I knew I wouldn't be good at it. Being a mother. I had a shitty one myself and wasn't ready and—I don't know. I didn't want to be a parent. I couldn't imagine giving up the rest of my life already. I was mad at your dad for not wanting me. Sad about being alone. Nothing felt settled—I didn't have a job, a partner. Nothing solid to hold onto back then."

"My father would have helped you. If you wanted to keep me, he would have supported you."

Penny nodded slowly. "That's probably true. And I would have been the girl who slept with a married man and got him to support her forever." She glanced over at Amanda, who could feel herself reddening.

"You're about the age I was when I got pregnant. Would you be willing to do that? To let someone take care of you forever, who wasn't your husband or anything? I couldn't face myself. I felt guilty enough about the whole thing."

"About being pregnant?"

"About being with your dad. It was the only time I ever made that mistake—a married guy. It's not like I thought your dad would leave his wife. I don't know *what* I was thinking. I fell in love, I guess. Probably sounds foolish to you, but really that's what happened. One day we're driving to work, like buddies, no problem. The next, it was like I couldn't stand to be away from him. Always thinking about him. I even followed him home once. I became sick, in a way. I tried to stay away from him, but I couldn't do it."

Amanda stared at the water as it lapped at the shore, thinking about the way the feelings for Uriel had taken over, time and again, a force beyond her control.

They turned off the beach and onto a main street with cafés, kids on skateboards, and shops with baskets of beach toys out front. A young girl and her brother chose plastic buckets.

"Did you think about raising me . . . together? With my dad?"

"He never knew I was pregnant until much later. We'd broken it off months before. I left town and tried to not think about him. It's my way—if I get hurt, I leave."

Amanda's heart quickened. Could running away as a coping method be genetic? Brackish air filled her lungs as she took a deep breath.

"I'd already left my abusive mother, so I knew how to break away. But leaving Jim hurt. The first few months were kind of a mess. Didn't have a job, so I had to stay at my brother's place, down here. That's how I ended up in Santa Barbara. He crewed on a couple boats here. I had started to move on, not thinking about your dad so much, when I realized I was pregnant. I knew if I talked to him, the feelings would come back."

"Did you think about getting an abortion?"

"No. Well, yes." Penny gestured to a bench to sit. At first Amanda thought there was a man on the bench, then she realized it was a statue, a man made of cast iron perched on the bench. Powerfully lifelike.

After a minute Amanda joined Penny on the bench, finding it strange to be between her long-lost mother and a steel statue that resembled her father.

"I didn't want to have another abortion. I'd had one as a teenager."

"Me too," Amanda said, impulsively. "I hated it."

Penny gave her a sad smile. "So did I. Two abortions was too much. For me. And I—I actually liked the idea of doing something positive with my life. Creating something. But at the same time, I was pretty sure I couldn't raise a child."

"Why didn't you tell my father earlier?"

Penny's mouth turned down, as if she was thinking. Her brow, freckled with sunspots, lifted. "I tried to tell him once. My brother drove me up to Sonoma, to your house—like seven hours in the car. I had to keep stopping to pee, and my nerves were shot. I knew your dad would guess it was his baby, once he saw me. I wanted to do it in person. I don't know what I thought would happen."

"What did happen?"

"I waited outside your house. I saw Jim's car in the driveway, but I wanted to make sure your mom was out. We waited for like an hour, with no sign of your mom or your dad. Then a woman came out and left. My brother insisted I go ring the bell and tell Jim. God, I was so damn scared when I rang that bell. But your mom answered the door. I guess the woman who left was a friend. Your dad was away. I don't think your mom had any idea who I was. I pretended I was going to a party and was lost. I felt really, really shitty and dumb. She was super nice to me, which made it worse. She wanted to call around to see which neighbor it was. I couldn't believe how pretty she was. I didn't understand why your dad had ever been with me, with such a nice, beautiful wife.

"I made my brother take me back down to Santa Barbara. I cried half the trip. I don't think I felt so cheap in my life as that day. I knew I couldn't tell your dad, and ruin that woman's whole life just because I screwed up."

Amanda imagined the scene, her mother having no idea Penny was Jim's lover, on the front step. She'd had a similar thought when she first saw Penny. Nothing special—why would my dad cheat on my mother for her? But she knew life wasn't that simple or clear. Elena could be distant and cool, and her father needed someone in his sphere at all times. Someone to admire him, and someone for him to take care of.

"What did you think you would do when I was born?"

"I talked to a couple adoption agencies. Didn't sign anything. Afraid I would regret it. But my brother was getting ready to leave on a major sailing trip. I had to stay at some random apartment the agency set up. It was tough. I knew I just had to get through the last few months of the pregnancy, have you safely, and then I could go away. It helped me through, thinking about sailing away."

Penny glanced at Amanda apologetically. "I tried to do everything right to make you healthy. I never drank. I went to the doctor. Took lots of vitamins." She half smiled. "I even sang to you a lot. I tried to send you lots of love without getting too attached."

Her eyes grew watery, and for the first time Amanda felt the sorrow in the story. "I wanted you to have the life I didn't have. A normal one. A good childhood, with two parents, and a house. I don't know. Maybe it was wrong, but at the time, I thought I was doing right by you."

Amanda remembered her mother taking her to Columbia every year, the soft sand at the beach, the taste of coconut cookies. Thought of how her aunties fussed over her. Of growing up in Sonoma, surrounded with beauty. Of riding Chestnut on beautiful days. She could not in fact imagine a different life. Or, in most ways, a better one.

"It was right. If you didn't want to be a mother, it was definitely the right thing to do."

Penny stared hard at a fountain in an adjacent courtyard. "It's not that I didn't want to be a mother. I didn't want to do it *badly*. And I would have. I was a kid, in some ways. I mean, the same age you are now, but you seem mature, compared to me then."

Amanda didn't feel particularly mature. But she knew she'd never give up a baby. "So, when did you decide to give me to my father?"

"Oh, I didn't really. Near the ninth month, the adoption agency kept asking me about the baby's father. The social worker said we had to tell him, to be legal. I broke down and told them Jim's name after you were born. So that he could sign the papers.

"He called me, right away. I thought he would be angry, you know, for not telling him. Or for being pregnant at all. But he kept saying, 'Are you okay? I'm so sorry I wasn't there. Oh Penny, you poor thing, on your own. But you're okay? And the baby is healthy. Thank God.'

"It hadn't occurred to me, but he told me later you could have had that same genetic thing that made his first baby die. That was a trip, thinking about the risks. I don't know if I would have kept the pregnancy, if I'd realized the risk." Penny reached over and touched Amanda's arm. "But here you are. Look pretty darn healthy. I'm glad I didn't know to worry."

Amanda's mere existence suddenly felt fragile. She stood up, looking back towards the beach, and Penny rose as well. "Can I see you another time? In case I have more questions."

"Sure. Anytime. Well, I still sail a lot. We're taking a boat down to Cabo for someone next week. But when I'm here, we can talk. I'd like that."

They started to walk back towards the boat. Amanda said, "You like to travel."

"Mostly, I never learned how to stay in one place. Born with wanderlust, Gio says. Thinks it's my red hair. You sail?"

Amanda shook her head. "I do yoga. And I ride horses."

"Well, you probably get that from your grandmother. The horse part. That's the Navajo in you."

Amanda stopped. "Navajo?"

"Yeah, your grandmother was about a quarter. I'm an eighth. So, you're . . . a sixteenth? I think? My dad met my mom in New Mexico when he was traveling. Anyway, yeah, she loved horses. She used to take us to this place in the hills to ride once in a while. I'm more of a sailor . . . But that's good it got carried on to you."

"Is she alive? Your mother?"

Penny's forehead wrinkled. "Honestly? I don't know. We think so, my brother and I, because we haven't heard otherwise. She's difficult, though."

The anthropologist in Amanda jumped for joy. Navajo. She just might have to expand her field research for her dissertation.

Penny watched Amanda type into her phone the scant details Penny could provide about her family history. "I know it must have hurt, not knowing your background. And I'm sorry they didn't tell you more. But I'm not sorry they raised you, Amanda. You turned out pretty well. I don't think you'd be getting your PhD if you'd stayed with me."

Amanda's throat closed as a lump lifted its way from her heart. She wanted to say it didn't matter if she hadn't gotten a PhD or had a fancy house. She should have been with her natural mother. Except she couldn't for a minute think of Elena as anything but her real mother.

This woman, Penny, was a nice person. She could see that. And getting her family history would be priceless. But when she left here she'd find a quiet place to call Elena.

Amanda had carried the results of a pregnancy test in her purse for two days, and she knew it was time to tell someone. She vacillated between fear, excitement, and curiosity—would Uriel dance a jig or shut down on her? Did she wanted to raise this baby on the road? Or in a cabin in Sonoma?

One thing she knew for sure. Her mother, Elena, was the person she wanted to share her news with first.

Chapter 37

"In water one sees one's own face; but in wine, one beholds the heart of another."

—French proverb

WHEN ELENA CALLED JIM AT WORK ONE SPRING MORNING, HE fumbled for words. It took a minute for him to acclimate to her voice on the phone. It had been months since they'd spoken, after so many years of daily contact.

She suggested they get together to talk.

"Yes," he said, before she finished her sentence. He longed to pull down the painful wall between them. "Of course. Do you want me to come up?"

"No," she answered, right away. "I'm in the city today. Let's meet downtown."

He felt caught off guard by her presence in the city, thinking of San Francisco as his territory and Sonoma as hers.

He called Victor, who had gone to meet with clients in San Jose. "I don't know what to say to her. I don't know where to start."

"See what she wants to talk about. Maybe she's ready to sign the papers and walk away. Or maybe she's just being friendly."

"Or maybe she wants to tell me again what an asshole I am."

"Possibly, yes."

They hung up and two minutes later the phone rang again. Victor's voice was tight, even abrupt. "Jim, I want to say one thing, and don't overreact or get defensive with me."

Jim immediately felt defensive. "Okay."

"Tell her the truth, Jim. Whether she wants to talk about the weather, or Amanda, or your money—just promise me, no lies. Don't tell her what she wants to hear, unless it's the truth."

Shame blossomed inside his gut. "Right. It wasn't out of self-protection that I lied, you know. It was because I loved her. And you and Amanda. I was trying to protect everyone."

"I know. I do. But it's over now."

After the call Jim closed the blinds to the main office and shut his door, a clear message to the staff that he did not want to be disturbed. He fell into his chair, his heart sinking inside of him. The man he loved more than life itself had enough forgiveness in his heart to call Jim and remind him to be honest.

He left early, determined to be receptive to whatever Elena needed to say. Halfway there he realized he'd left his coat in the office, and that his phone and wallet were in the jacket. He'd been so distracted lately, he kept losing things. So unlike himself. He dug in his pocket and found two twenties. Enough to get them coffee or lunch. Not worth going back for his wallet.

But what if she tried to call him? If she had changed her mind or was running late? He kept walking, curiosity and a sliver of hope propelling him forward. He rounded the corner to their meeting spot in front of the Museum of Modern Art. Elena stood outside in a pale green dress. Her thick black hair was cut shorter, and she wore an intricate wire and stone necklace—no diamond studs anymore. She wore less makeup than he remembered, looking like she'd thrown on her frock and headed out with very little fuss.

Both guilt and longing rose up inside of him, like a wave, and for a horrible moment he thought he might start to cry again. Elena turned, and a flash of surprise arose in her eyes. As if neither one knew how they came to this moment, here on this busy sidewalk, not a mile from where they had first met thirty years before. He pictured her young, dancing salsa in the shadowy club that first night.

"You look great," he said, honestly. The young and relaxed girl he had once known had re-emerged, with wiser, and a shade sadder, eyes.

"Thank you." She did not return the compliment. Jim wondered if he should kiss her cheek, but she held a plastic cup in front of her as a barricade.

Elena said, "I thought we could take a walk in the park? I've been sitting all day. I'm here for a class."

"Sure." He had assumed they would have lunch, his stomach growling a bit, but he was in no position to bargain. "I'm glad you called," he said, following her down the block to the crosswalk. When she pushed the button on the light, he saw she her hand shaking.

"I thought it was time," she said, "for Amanda's sake."

They crossed the street with a crowd—tourists, a homeless man, young people in skimpy clothes. The tide of city life carrying them into the park, Yerba Buena Gardens.

"Remember when you did this project?" Elena asked, staring at the manicured lawn, the MLK fountain grown gritty over the years, the modern buildings.

Jim had been involved on the finance end during the planning phase, a young associate, trying to gain traction in the Bay Area. He had brought Elena to the closing dinner. He'd been proud to have her on his arm, his lovely Columbian jewel.

"I'm so sorry," he blurted out, overwhelmed. "About everything. I don't know what else to say to you. It's all I can come up with."

"I didn't call for an apology, Jim. Although you owe me a hundred. But it's done, and saying you're sorry will never erase the lies."

"I know."

"I trusted you, because of who you are. In many ways, you are so good. Even after Penny, I trusted you. Madness, I see now."

He watched her drink her iced tea and wished he had one. Wished he could walk away, get some lunch, go back to work and pretend she'd never called. Acid pooled in his stomach. His heart, when faced with his own duplicity, seemed to stop for a minute.

"Why did you call?" He sounded abrupt, he realized. "I'm glad you did," he added. "But I wasn't sure why."

Elena kept walking. He wished she would stop. Wished they could take a seat, order a bite, and make this a reunion. A forgiving, warm moment.

"I think for Amanda's sake, I'm ready to file or get the papers done, whatever. I know the lawyers have a settlement in mind. I wasn't ready to think about it at first. You moved so fast."

"I thought it would be better to do it quickly. Actually, for your sake."

"That made it harder. I couldn't catch my breath. More awful news came every day. You wanted to sell my stocks in the company. You wanted to sell the house. You wanted Amanda to get your stocks. You wanted Victor in your will. Every day it's something else Jim, like a hurricane."

"I . . . I'm trying to protect everyone. I have cancer, Elena. I didn't know if I had time to wait, to clear things up."

"And do you? Have more time?"

"I think so, yes. They think I'll be cancer-free, eventually."

Elena stopped by a bench, absorbing. "Amanda doesn't tell me about it. And I don't ask."

Jim opened and closed his tight hands. "I don't blame you. And right now, Amanda isn't speaking to me."

She nodded. "She's furious at both of us."

"My fault," he said. Elena didn't correct him. "I'm very tired," he added, looking around, feeling confused. Fatigue overwhelmed him.

She eyed him, curiously. "You're tired?"

"Do you mind if we sit down?"

He saw the change in her face, from anger to concern. The old Elena emerging from the new, detached one. "Of course."

They took the empty end of the bench, sharing it with a nanny who read a book while her charge slept. They both stared at the baby.

Elena said, "I don't want to sell the house."

Jim examined her face, the way her mouth slipped down at the edges when she wasn't smiling. The sunspot on her left cheek that she usually covered with makeup. "I know you don't, but I don't know how realistic it is for you to keep it. You'll have to decide. It's your choice. It will be part of your half of the settlement."

"*Settlement* is a funny word. As if it is all settled, like a problem sorted out."

"But it's not?"

She shrugged. "You got what you wanted—Victor. I am getting over it. Amanda is hurting. Things still hurt. They might always hurt. But I don't want to fight with you. I called because we need to find a way to support Amanda."

"I'm ready to do anything. You know that."

She didn't point out the ways he had already failed his daughter. His own conscience listed his sins in the back of his mind, like bullet points on a whiteboard.

"I wish we'd told her," Elena said. "It was absurd not to."

"Yes. Hindsight."

"I never really know what you mean when you say that. *Hindsight.*"

"It means it is easy to look back and know things we did wrong, hard to see it when it is in front of you."

Elena bit her lip. "I have a lot of hindsight lately."

"You don't have anything to regret, Elena. You were wonderful to me and to her. Don't blame yourself for my idiocy."

"I don't," she said, easily. "I did at first. I tried to kill myself two weeks after you left."

"What did you say?" Jim couldn't quite believe what he'd heard. But he knew. His mind reeled. Acid climbed up his chest. "No!"

Elena turned and looked at him, eyes narrowed. "Yes. I'm sorry to tell you so bluntly. I decided you should know, so there would be one less secret for Amanda to carry around. The poor girl has told no one at my request and taken care of me for months."

Jim didn't try to stop the tears this time. He cradled his head in his hands. "It's my fault. All of this mess is my fucking fault."

"Yes and no." Elena's voice and demeanor stayed calm as her eyes scanned his face, like a stranger. "I don't blame anyone but myself for giving up. I'll never forgive myself for that. But I'm better now. I got help. A lot of help. All winter. I'll never do something like that again. Never do anything to hurt Amanda. The guilt has been horrible."

"I know that feeling."

She eyed him and then, after a minute lifted her hand and squeezed his arm. "I guess we have that in common."

Jim brushed away his tears, embarrassed. The sun beamed too bright across the grass. He had to squint to look ahead. "What can I do?"

"Nothing. I'm fine. In fact, I am well. Happy enough, or I will be once Amanda and I get back to normal." She stood up. "Send me the papers again, and I'll sign this time. If the lawyer thinks they're fair."

"They'll be fair." Jim didn't want her to leave yet. "Can I walk you somewhere?" he asked.

"No. I'm meeting a friend," she said. "Take care, Jim." Elena waved and walked away, cool and determined.

His eyes followed her as she left the park, not looking back. He felt inconsequential, and foolish for feeling so. Self-disgusted and hopeless. His work was cut out for him, for years. He needed to earn his daughter's forgiveness, to create ease with his lover, to come out to his brothers, his clients, and his world. To find a way to create a picture with the pieces he'd broken. Maybe even earn the forgiveness and friendship of his wife.

Just thinking about it exhausted him. He did not get up. Elena had left her ice tea, still half full. He drank from it, thinking of the hundred drinks they must have shared over the years, of the way marriage was about shared glasses, beds, toilets, mornings.

And then wasn't. The marriage had ended long ago, when they'd stopped sharing drinks, the same bed, early morning thoughts, late night love-making.

Jim felt nauseous, and so tired. He tried to stand, to get going, but the world was tilted, on edge. Pain shot through him, and he thought, *I deserve this.* His heart was breaking and the bile in his throat finally rose. He vomited on the pavement, bent over, and saw the pavement rise to meet him. The world fell away from him, far away. For the first time in sixty-two years, Jim Scanlon let it all go. And the crushing pain around his heart released him into a welcome darkness.

When he woke up, they kept asking him who to call. "A wife? A family member? You've had a heart attack, sir, but you're stabilized. Can you tell us anyone to call?"

Elena, he thought for a moment. Hadn't she been there when it happened? He couldn't quite remember the day. Or her number. "My phone?"

"You didn't have a phone when we brought you in sir."

Where was his phone? He'd been at Yerba Buena. He remembered now. And yes, he'd forgotten his phone.

A male nurse stood by his side, dark skin, and warm eyes. Jim wanted the man to reach out and hold him. Calm him. "I'm Luis. Can you tell me your name?"

"Jim." His voice sounded rough, and old. "Jim Scanlon."

"Okay, Jim. Who can I call for you?"

"Amanda?"

"Who's Amanda, sir? Do you know her number?"

Jim wanted Amanda to come, to be here. But she was far away, he remembered. And barely speaking to him. He wouldn't burden her again.

"Sir, it's okay, we'll reach someone. It's normal to be confused right now."

He realized his tears wet his cheeks, his collar wet.

"The doctor's coming right back in."

Victor. He should call Victor. Would they let a lover in? He closed his eyes and tried to go back to the dark place he'd been, to the peace of being far away, of not being Jim.

"Sir, I'm going to keep you awake. You hit your head when you fell, so we are going to stay awake for now."

Jim's bed rose, like magic, forcing him to sit up, to be present, as someone flicked the IV in his arm, and someone else put an oxygen tube near his nose.

He remembered now, the meeting with Elena. What she told him. His shock. Jim could see her walking away, her purse loosely over her shoulder, her shoulders back, head high. He had wanted to call out to her as she left, tell her something was wrong, that he didn't feel right. But it wasn't her job to care anymore.

"Sir, what can I do to help?" Luis took a warm washcloth and wiped Jim's face. *Wiping my tears away.*

"415-772-5700." Jim said. "That's my office number. Can you please call them?"

Luis jotted down the number. "I'll do it right now. No family you want me to call?"

"Ask for Victor. Tell him I'm here." He put his head back, holding back more tears, and waited for his lover to come.

Chapter 38

"Wine is sure proof that God loves us and wants us to be happy."

—Benjamin Franklin

MAY 2016

Belle was leaving the stables. A year earlier, Uriel would have been devastated. Now, he thought it was for the best. She had been more and more agitated, as if she sensed his attention ebbing away. She needed an owner who could train her and spend adequate time with her, not Noah Rosen. Poor guy still couldn't ride.

Uriel was about to get out of his truck and go into the stables when Cat Blakely's name flashed on his phone. He hadn't heard from her in some time and assumed their relationship would fade away.

"Cat? How are you?"

He heard her dry voice, which had reminded him of an old movie star. "I'm doing fine, Uriel." She had learned to say his name correctly. "How are you?"

"I'm doing fine as well. Heading to the stables. One of the horses is leaving today."

"Well, is the horse coming to Texas? Maybe you can come for a visit."

He smiled at the idea of riding up to see her, the woman behind the voice on the phone. "Not this one. What's going on?" He tensed, slightly. If she was going to tell him something else about Flavia and her husband, he didn't want to know.

"I'm calling to tell you something. I don't know why you'd care really, but I figured I'd share the news. From one survivor to another."

"Okay?" A hawk hovered in the wide, bright sky.

"I'm getting married again next week."

He pictured Cat Blakely in a wedding dress and cowboy boots. "Well good for you, Cat. I think that's great."

"I'm nervous this time. I figured you would understand that."

He grabbed his jacket from the back of his truck and headed towards the stables. "Actually, I really do. But go for it. Most marriages don't end the way ours did."

"How about you?" she asked. "You moving on?"

He thought of the postcards from Amanda piled neatly by his bed. She sent them every few days, with jokes and tidbits of life in Peru. He Googled the places she was visiting in the evenings, looking at the photos, reading blogs. But he hadn't bought a ticket, or told Freddie he needed time off. And his emails to Amanda, when he reread them, still came off as cryptic and non-committal.

"You said you're dating someone, right?" Cat went on.

He stopped near the pasture fence. This stranger from Texas managed to get him to talk about things his own family skirted. He squinted in the sun. "I was seeing someone. She's . . . away, for now."

"She coming back?"

"Maybe." He looked at Belle, who leaned over the window of her paddock, eager for his attention. "Probably only if I go get her."

"Well then, get going."

Uriel looked around the stables. The hay was low, and the office looked closed up when it should have opened for the day ten minutes ago. Carlos, who had begun spending Saturdays working at the stables, was just arriving. "There's a lot to do here," he said. "It's not that easy to get away."

"Sometimes it's easier than you think."

Uriel turned her words over in his mind as he prepared Belle's paperwork. *Sometimes it's easier than you think.* Two hours later, a shiny new horse trailer arrived for Belle. She'd been exercised, washed, brushed, and fed. Uriel had a binder of paperwork on her, and a new saddle thrown in by Noah as part of the deal.

Noah stood awkwardly to the side while the horse handler signed for Belle. Uriel escorted the horse into the trailer, talking to her throughout. Guilt rode up under his ribs: she was going in this easy because she trusted him.

Uriel ran his hand over her large flank one more time, whispering to her. "You saved my life, Belle. You're a good horse. You're the best horse I ever knew. Be good now."

He couldn't watch the trailer drive away, his gut a hard knot. Noah hovered near the office when he came back in.

"You're all set." Uriel said. "Paperwork's all there. Make sure the stable fees don't show up on your bill next month. Should stop at the end of the month."

Noah stood awkwardly, his hands thrust deep in his pockets. "Okay then," he said, offering a smile. "Great. Thank you so much, Uriel." He hesitated, as if he had something else to say.

Jesse barged in, apologized, and grabbed the ringing phone. "Esperanza Stables," she barked. Noah looked startled. Uriel had gotten used to Noah's funny mannerisms, his somewhat cartoonish smile.

"You're done with riding lessons, I assume?" Uriel asked him.

"Yes. Very much." Noah threw his hands in the air, as if the mere thought of riding made him lose his balance again. "But it was fun to try. So, have you heard much from Amanda?"

Uriel nodded. "Are you still seeing her mom?"

Noah's long face widened with a smile. "Whenever I can. But I don't want to misrepresent it—I would say she categorizes us as friends. But she's a good friend."

"That's great. Say hello for me."

Noah nodded. He didn't seem to be leaving, and Uriel carried a lengthy to-do list for the day. "I heard you might go meet Amanda?" Noah said. "Down in Peru? Travel a bit?"

Uriel glanced at Jesse, who was eyeing him skeptically. "I haven't really figured it out. Not sure I can get away."

"Oh." Noah looked thoroughly disappointed, as if he had planned to go along. "Well, I had something for you. In case. I'll bring it in anyway. You never know."

In a minute, he was back, carrying an enormous framed duffel bag. "It's the best backpack I could find. This will hold six weeks' worth of clothes, but only weighs five pounds. Aluminum frame. Rainproof. Anyway, I really wanted to get you something as a thank you for helping me with the horse deal. It's probably stupid, if you're not going to meet Amanda. Elena said you were . . . Well, actually, to be honest, I emailed Amanda and asked her what she thought you might need."

"And she told you I needed a backpack?"

Noah nodded, his smile growing. "I think she wants you to go down there."

Uriel lifted the pack. It was surprisingly light, the tags still on it. He could probably get cash for it, if he returned it. Or he could go home and pack. He said thank you and Noah left, slipping into his shiny sports car.

"Why don't you go see Amanda?" Jesse asked him later.

A calm had finally descended on the stables, the day winding down as they headed to the winery to check in with Freddie. Uriel's hand swept the vista: the vineyard, the stables, Maya and Freddie's house on the hill.

"I can't just take off."

Jesse poked his shoulder. "It's not forever, Uriel. We'll survive without you for a little while."

"Will you?"

"Better than watching you mope around like a sad dog."

"Bullshit, I've been fine."

Jesse ticked off words on her fingers. "Depressed, isolating, grouchy."

"Cheerful, actually. I think I've been cheerful."

As they entered the tasting room, she announced to Freddie that Uriel was taking a trip, to Peru. "Check it out, he even has a new backpack. He's going to visit his rich girlfriend."

Before Uriel could explain to Freddie that he wasn't leaving, Freddie had lined up three glasses on the counter.

"Thank goodness," he said. "Maya said I was going to have to fire you if you didn't take a vacation soon." Freddie opened a bottle of one of his better cabs. "To your journey," he said. "And Amanda."

"To Belle," Jesse said. "A biting bitch she was. But a good horse, in her way."

Uriel's eyes clouded when he thought of Belle, miles away. "To the winemaker," he said. "This is a beautiful glass of wine."

The three of them stayed until the wine was gone and they had toasted the family, the wine, and the horses.

Later that night, tipsy from wine and anticipation, Uriel brushed his hair before he hit the Facetime button on his phone. Amanda had insisted he upgrade to an iPhone so they could see each other when they talked, but he rarely used the feature. He didn't like the way his nose filled the screen, and how she was so close to him, but still untouchable.

"Uri?" Amanda's face broke through the gray screen. She was rubbing sleepy eyes.

"Shoot, is it later there?"

"No, well yeah, but it's fine. What's up? You never Facetime me."

"I wanted to show you something." He angled the phone towards the backpack where he had propped it, next to his passport that he'd gotten a few weeks earlier, just in case.

"Holy shit, is that a backpack?"

"Top of the line, thanks to Noah."

"Does this mean you're coming? I'll kill you if you're messing with me."

Her face looked puffy, probably from sleep, and her hair was matted with sweat. All of which made him miss her more.

"I'm not messing with you. But I don't have a ticket yet."

"Yes!" She covered her mouth, lowering her voice. "I shouldn't yell. I'll wake my landlady."

"You have a landlady?"

"*We* have a landlady. Don't worry. I told her you would come eventually."

He laid back on the bed and propped the phone up with a pillow, pretending she lie next to him. "You were pretty confident, huh? I didn't even know I was coming."

"I couldn't really face you *not* coming, so I kept telling myself you would. And now you are."

"I'll work on a ticket tomorrow."

She sat up, looking like she wanted to jump into the phone.

"Can we visit some Peruvian horses?" he asked.

"Definitely. I think I have maybe a month left here. Sound good?"

"Sure. Sounds awesome. I can barely afford that. But I didn't know you had decided to come home in a month."

She looked into the camera, then glanced away. "Me either. But you're coming means I can come home. It's complicated. We have a lot to talk about. But we'll have plenty of time. Call me tomorrow when you get your ticket."

He paced the cabin after they hung up, trying to sort through clothes, but stuck on *a lot to talk about.* Had she met someone else down there? Had a fling? He wasn't going to put himself through all that again. No lies, no secrecy. Flavia had cured him forever of trust placed too easily. Finally he texted Amanda, telling her he couldn't sleep. He needed to know what she meant by more to tell.

Hold on. I'll send a picture.

The picture came back a few minutes later. He sat in the dark, staring at it, unsure. He turned it one way, and then another, making sure. A long white plastic stick. A pregnancy test. Two lines across the center. He knew what it meant. Before he could respond, another picture came in. The first sexy picture she'd ever sent him. She stood sideways in the mirror, topless. The tips of her small breasts lifted up like flowers to the light, and her white belly, usually so flat, had a soft lump pushing out over her panties.

He went outside to breathe before he answered, taking long gulps of the cool night air. He smelled the grapes just budding, the earth releasing the last of the winter's moist blanket. He remembered his vision of a child running through the vineyards, of a baby's toes jumping on fat grapes.

He thought about the way stories had beginnings that come from endings, long ribbons that unfurl in the least expected ways. The way his new life was growing in a faraway place but would be planted here, on his family's land. He lifted his phone, texting through his tears.

I'll be there as fast as I can.

Denouement

"Now may God give you of the dew of heaven, And of the fatness of the earth, And an abundance of grain and new wine."

—Genesis 27:28

THE PHOTOGRAPH HAD TEARS ON THE CORNERS FROM YEARS OF being stuck in a box, but Amanda picked out a blue wooden frame that covered the edges. She chose a spot on the wall in the bedroom, near the changing table, and across from where they planned to put the crib. She had hung several pictures of both of them as children: Uriel at a rodeo, about age seven. Amanda in Columbia, holding Elena's hand.

This one felt like the key in the lock, the last piece of a puzzle.

The class picture of Sonoma Head Start Preschool showed twenty-two small children in front of the duck pond, most of them squinting from the sun. Amanda's finger traced the outline of four-year-old Uriel's face, the round cheeks. He stood with his shoulders back, even then, although without a smile. He stared at the camera, as if daring the photographer. *Here I am.*

"Was your father alive then?" She didn't know what prompted her to ask, something about his countenance.

"He died that year, in late September. I don't know when the picture was taken."

They turned it over. *November 1985.*

"He'd been gone about a month then. No wonder I was so serious."

Amanda rested her hand on her increasingly large belly. It pulled the sinews in her back like rubber bands, about to snap. She examined the woman in the photo to the side of the group, her red hair in a low pony tail, wearing a sweater and tight jeans. She didn't look like a typical teacher. She offered the camera a warm smile.

"Penny met my father that month."

Uriel shook his head, still struck by the coincidence. But not. He picked up his hammer. "You sure you want this one on the wall?"

Amanda was sure. It was the beginning of their shared history, oddly. Uriel standing just feet away from her birth mother, looking solemnly into his future. Waiting for her.

Acknowledgements

BRINGING THIS BOOK TO THE WORLD HAS INDEED BEEN A LONG labor. First written as set of short stories it took a series of friends, readers, editors and mentors to understand I had a novel on my hands, and then do the hard work of birthing it. WiDo Publishing, especially Karen Gowen, embraced this story and has given me the support and platform to publish *The Vines We Planted*. I have long needed to free these characters who reside in my mind like old friends, and share the incredible, beautiful, world of Sonoma.

For many years I met frequently in the welcoming home of Willie Gordon, and was inspired by Clive Matson, Jade Raybin, Nate Lindsay, Gina Kutchins, and of course Willie himself. All of them read entire drafts of this novel. I additionally received inspiration, guidance, camaraderie and a solid support group at *Squaw Valley Community of Writers*. *Santa Barbara Writers Conference* graciously gave me free entrance to their conference which boosted my determination, learning and love of late-night writers. *Algonkian* (especially Paula Munier and our group of mystery men) taught me what elements bring a story to life. *The Redwood Writers Branch of the California Writers Club* has been exceptionally supportive. *Path to Publishing*, at Book Passages, put me in touch with the lovely Molly Giles, who read an early draft and encouraged me to go on. Cristina Pippa and Samantha Bohrman, editors with a heart, helped turn an enormous overwritten monster creature into an animal I could tame and train.

In terms of research, I relied heavily for historical details on Lynn Downey's helpful book, *A Short History of Sonoma*. There are many wineries that offered a place to "research my setting," a few favorites being Rancho Maria, Bump, Benziger, Roche, and Laurel Glen. The Robledo's family history was a true inspiration for the Macon family.

An artist needs a tribe. I've been blessed with a large and talented one. My children, nephews and nieces show up in my work as characters, editors, listeners and cheerleaders. They knew as young children not to bother Mom when she was writing . . . and she was often writing. I am so grateful for the room they've made in our lives for this endeavor, and for the wonderful friends and partners they've brought into our tribe. It takes a village to raise a novel, and I have one.

My friends, local and far, old and new, read my work, give me honest feedback and share my published writing with the world. They post, tweet, comment, blog and show up. There is a special group of women all named Leslie in my life, who had my back every step of the way while I wrote the novel (and my entire life). Big love to all mis amigos.

My parents raised me to be a writer. Both educators, I was reading by four, writing poetry by five. There's no greater gift than the one they gave me: to be my true self. My siblings and I honed the art of storytelling around the kitchen table. My family provided a bottomless well of material and love. Although some of have moved on, we will always be connected.

A writer needs a tribe, but also a partner. Thank you, Harry, for twenty-six years of red marks on the paper, chuckling in the other room as you read one of my stories, never flinching at the time or money it took, never doubting I should write, even when I faltered, and for loving me. Writers need love. You helped me plant the seeds for this novel. Enjoy the harvest.

Love flows from this writer's heart to you all.

About the Author

JOANELL SERRA, MFT LIVES with her growing children, husband and dogs in the lovely Sonoma Valley. After years of publishing short stories, essays and plays, *The Vines We Planted* is her debut novel. She can be found polishing her second novel at a coffee shop, sipping a perfect Cabernet in a Sonoma winery or at her website: www.JoanellSerraAuthor.com.

CPSIA information can be obtained
at www.ICGtesting.com
Printed in the USA
FSHW04n2228030418
46303FS